Kelven's Riddle Book Five
The Stronghold of Evil

D1714557

Cover Art: Lance Ruben Smith

ISBN-10: 1502859467
ISBN-13: 978 - 1502859464

This book is dedicated to those men and women of the United States that willingly don the uniform of America's Armed Forces, and go into the dark and dangerous corners of the world, risking everything that the rest of us might remain free and secure in the homeland.

This book is also dedicated to my brothers and my sisters, both of blood and by marriage, and to my children, both of blood and by marriage, and to my nieces and nephews, and to my closest friends. All of these fine people – and they know who they are – will find their very best attributes exhibited by the characters that live among these pages.

Finally, this book is dedicated to her.
My wife.
My life's companion.
My treasure.
My love.
Karen.

He comes from the west
And arises in the east.
Tall and strong, fierce as a storm upon the plain.
He ascends the height to put his hand among the stars
And wield the Sword of Heaven.
Master of wolves, Friend of horses;
He is a prince of men and a Walking Flame.
He enters the stronghold of evil,
To bring down the mighty,
And return peace.

Kelven's Riddle

1.

Manon, the grim Lord of the World, stood in the opening high in his tower and gazed to the southeast across the earth where he'd sent the Laish to kill the woman, the mate of the upstart heir of Joktan who had brazenly declared himself the enemy of a god. But those great beasts had gone into the south many days ago, in the dark hours before dawn. It was now nearly two weeks later, mid-day, and the sun was high, pinned to the apex of the sky.

There was only silence from the southeast.

There had been screams of fear and pain in the hour that the sun rose in the east on that morning that the dragons had killed and burned and destroyed up and down the length of that far-off valley. Manon, privy to the thoughts of his indentured servants, had been satisfied that all had gone as planned. The woman was dead, and the anger of the dragons soon to be satiated upon the pitiable souls that dwelled there.

But then, within an hour of each other, the dragons' minds had abruptly gone silent. With each, before the silence, there had been a momentary howl of anguish.

Had they been slain?

Had the Brethren involved themselves, or sought help from the Astra?

Manon doubted the involvement of the Brethren. In ancient times, when Aberanezagoth opened the secret door and unleashed them upon the world, the combined strength of the gods had been insufficient to slay the fearsome beasts. Even the mighty Astra had to settle for containment. There were two of them that traveled with the man, Aram, it was true, and he possessed a mysterious and powerful sword. Still, Manon did not think it possible that such a combination could have destroyed the Laish.

What, then? Had they attempted to fool their master? Had they somehow cut him off from their thoughts and sought to escape his control? No, it could not be that, for if it were, they would no doubt have gone for their child, imprisoned in cavernous mouth of the Deep Darkness. Manon had opened the eyes of his second self in that dim and distant place, and in none of the days since he'd sent them southward had there been rumor of the dragons.

He would continue to be vigilant for treachery, but as the sun passed through mid-day yet again, for the thirteenth time since he'd commissioned them to slay the woman, he had not seen or heard any sign of them. It was apparent that there had been no act of betrayal. Something entirely different – and unexplained – had occurred.

The eagles and hawks of all the earth had allied with the man, Aram, and had driven the grim lord's spies from the skies above that valley and the countryside round about, effectively blinding him. His earthbound servants, serpents and the like, were too limited in their movement to aid him without the help of winged creatures, and wolves had proven notoriously untrustworthy. As a consequence, it had grown increasingly difficult for Manon to acquire dependable intelligence from the southern regions of the world.

What had happened to the Laish, therefore, was unknown.

There remained another possibility, of course. Perhaps, as before, the Astra had summoned aid from their own kind and had once again managed containment of the giant beasts. If so, well enough. Manon had no further use for them anyway.

He began to turn away, but then his eye caught a flash in the sky, far off to the southeast.

An instant after the first, there was another flare of light from that distant horizon.

And then more. Fire flashed again and again, illuminating that horizon and the sky above it.

Manon focused his attention there.

Another flash, and then another, as if lightning blazed on a clear day, but arising from the earth rather than striking from the sky.

Abruptly, he understood, and he smiled to himself. The Laish, then, as he hoped and believed, had been successful in killing the woman of Aram. The flashes of distant fire came from the man's sword as it reflected the heat and light from the sun as had been described to him by those of his servants who'd witnessed the phenomenon.

Manon closed his eyes and sent the tendrils of his mind out, out, and over the horizon, feeling for potency from the one who wielded the flashing sword. The distance was great, almost too great even for a mind as powerful as his had become. Further and further he reached out, feeling ever further southward, across valleys and rivers, over mountains and high hills. The distance grew ever greater and his senses dissipated with the miles; but, then.....

Ah.....there it was.

Fury.

Fury, and pain, and – *loss*. There was no further doubt. The dragons had slain Aram's woman, and he was sending a challenge into the north in the only way he could.

Manon opened his eyes and watched the lightning flash and flare above the distant horizon.

Good, he thought, *very good. Now you will come to me, and then everything will change.*

Satisfied at last that – whatever had become of the Laish – that which he desired was accomplished, he turned away, into the interior of the tower, sweeping the door shut with a slight motion of his hand. Sending a thought down through the tower, he summoned that child who was now his First.

"Hargur – come to me."

"Yes, master."

The grim lord waited in the center of the vast round room until Hargur appeared in the doorway. The great beast hesitated and stood still, uncertain, his bulk filling the opening.

"Come, my son."

Hargur approached diffidently until he stood with downcast eyes but a few meters from his master. Manon studied the immense lasher that had been his Second until the death of Vulgur – and now was his First. The god had come to understand that, in the creation of life, only the primary aim of that process was controllable. The final product always bore the result of a measure of chance. As a consequence, his First Children displayed sometimes surprising differences of personality.

Vulgur had been implicitly faithful and ever diligent in carrying out the Great Father's instructions, never thinking for himself beyond the bounds of that which the god allowed. This particular child, however, had often shown a streak of independence. Though this unusual trait of Hargur's had never once devolved into insubordination, nonetheless, he had demonstrated a willingness to alter Manon's instructions in the field. These alterations were always of a tactical nature that never actually subverted the grim lord's desires, but that nonetheless showed this child thought for himself beyond his Great Father's commands.

"Look at me, my son," Manon said to him.

Hargur looked up, meeting the obsidian gaze of his master.

"You have recalled all the wagons that are used for bringing human women to this tower – as I instructed?"

"Yes, Great Father," Hargur replied. "There are but two of our trains that have not yet returned. The vultures say that they are in Bracken, three days away."

"And the harvest wagons have begun to move south?"

"Yes, Great Father."

Manon fixed him with his baleful gaze. "You will alter the transport wagons and then you will send them back into the south to aid in bringing the balance of the harvest to this tower."

Hargur blinked his flat black eyes. "The balance, master?

"Yes – all of it, from all across the plains, from the valleys to the east, and from Bracken. And gather all my First Children here, in Morkendril."

"Yes, Great father." Hargur dared to keep his gaze fixed upon the face of his master. "What of the slaves? Winter comes. What will they eat?"

And there it was again, the Great Father thought – this particular child's penchant for thinking on his own, wondering about his master's instructions, of their reasons and purposes, something Vulgur had never done.

Regretting once again Vulgur's death, Manon nonetheless suppressed irritation. Then, after a moment's consideration, Manon decided to explain his decision to his newly-appointed Eldest.

"The man that is our enemy will bring an army to this tower in the spring. I know him, my child – he will have pity on the people of the plains when he finds them in distress. He will no doubt give them of his own supplies, and anything that weakens him assures that you and your troops will defeat him when he stands before you."

Hargur lowered his eyes and spoke hesitantly. "But if the slaves starve before spring, master – how will he be weakened?"

"They will not starve, my son. Many have secret stores they have laid aside – and you may leave them their oxen to eat, if you do not require them for transport of the harvest. Also, grasses and roots abound in those lands." Manon made a dismissive gesture. "Let them scavenge what they can; they will not all die. Enough will survive to distract our enemy."

Silence fell while Manon studied Hargur but the huge lasher kept his eyes respectfully upon the floor and said nothing further.

"Go, my son," the god said finally. "Do as I instruct."

"Yes, Great Father."

2.

Kelven stared in disbelief at the shimmering outline of his ancient friend.

"He slew them? You are certain of this?"

"I was there," Joktan replied, "and I saw it. I witnessed him destroy them both."

"There are two Astra that travel with him," Kelven persisted, his tone saturated with doubt. "Are you certain it was not they that slew the beasts?"

Joktan shook his hooded head. "They aided him, but it amounted to little. It was the Sword he wields that brought down the dragons."

"How did he come upon them?" Kelven demanded. "Did he hunt them – or did the enemy send them to attack him?"

"Neither, my lord," Joktan answered. "They were sent into his valley while he was away, in Elam. Apparently they were meant to kill the woman, Ka'en." He went silent for a moment and gazed down into the spring. "By chance, he returned in time to prevent her death. He battled the dragons and slew them for her – to protect her. He came back into the valley just before they found her. Still, before they were slain, they killed many and destroyed much." The ancient king lifted his eyes and turned to face the god. "I told you, my lord, did I not, that his love for this woman would be the salvation of our cause?"

"You did say this," Kelven admitted, but then added a word of caution. "Of course, he has not yet defeated Manon." He continued to stare with an unqualified expression of astonishment upon his handsome face. Deep inside his eyes, molten gold churned and seethed. "Aram slew them both – with the Sword – *he slew them both*." It was both a question; and an utterance of amazement.

"He did." Joktan's reply was firm, as was the nodding of his hooded head. "I witnessed it."

The god turned away and gazed at the distant walls of vertical stone that surrounded his valley. "Remarkable," he stated quietly, and then again, "Remarkable. This, I did not foresee." After another long silence, he shook his head in wonder. *"Who is this man?"*

Joktan watched Kelven for a moment and then looked away as well. His head came up slightly.

"He is my son," he replied.

3.

Aram paced nervously back and forth outside the door to the bedroom, stopping every other step to cock his head near the wood and listen. Once in a while, there would be the sound of low voices from the room beyond, and an occasional low moan from Ka'en. Mostly, there was only silence.

True to her vow, Ka'en was giving birth to their first child in Regamun Mediar, the city of Aram's fathers.

Aram had wanted to stay with her throughout, but she told him in firm tones to wait outside with Eoarl.

"Dunna will take good care of me," she promised, gritting her teeth against yet another contraction.

"I will, you may depend on it," Dunna assured him, as her jet-black eyes sparkled. "This is woman's work, and your lady is strong. She will be just fine."

Dunna became a surrogate mother to Ka'en almost upon their first meeting in the previous winter, and that bond had only strengthened when the older woman from Lamont had come east to care for her son, Muray, injured in the Battle of Bloody Stream. After Muray recovered to the point of insisting that he would accept no further mothering and would return to the fortress to rejoin his men, even if he must lean upon the aid of a staff, Dunna and her husband Eoarl had come north into the valley to be with Ka'en.

The expected day had arrived shortly thereafter. Reluctantly, Aram agreed to remain outside while Dunna and Cala attended to Ka'en as she gave birth.

Ka'en's pains had started just before sunrise and – to his great concern – had continued throughout the morning and into the afternoon. After he'd been hustled out of the bedroom, Aram had nothing to do but pace and worry, back and forth, even as Eoarl, his friend and Dunna's husband, encouraged him to go out into the sunshine, or to sit and enjoy a smoke with the older man.

"Dunnie will take good care of your mistress, lad," he said, forgoing the use of Aram's title in the familiarity of the moment. "These things always take a while; you'll have to be patient. The child will come when it's ready. Come, sit, have something to eat and drink."

For a while, now and again, Aram would comply with this suggestion and try to remain calm and distract himself with talking with the older man, whose company he normally enjoyed. But as the day wore on he would find himself once again pacing and listening at the door. Eventually, the day faded away. In the valley outside the city, evening deepened toward night. With the passing away of the day, Aram grew ever more concerned as the only sound from beyond the door continued to be an occasional low moan of pain from his wife.

Then, after a period of prolonged quiet, during which Aram seriously considered ignoring Ka'en's stricture and charging into the room, she let out a sharper sound of agony. Aram froze and glanced over at Eoarl. The older man had fallen asleep and was dozing before the fire. Pivoting, he reached for the door, but at that moment another sound came from the room beyond.

It was the cry of a child.

He burst into the room to find Dunna turning toward him with a small bundle in her arms, wrapped in a blanket, while Cala sat near Ka'en and bathed her forehead with a cool cloth.

Dunna's dark eyes shone.

"You have a daughter, my lord," she said.

Aram reached her in two strides, taking the bundle from her arms and looking down upon the tiny human with pink skin, tufts of golden hair, and brilliant blue eyes. After a long moment of gazing upon this small marvel, he looked over at Ka'en. She smiled tiredly up at him.

The sight of her, flushed with fatigue, her skin moist with exertion, sent a shiver of fear through him.

"Are you alright?"

She nodded weakly. "I am fine, my love." But her soft voice was quieter than usual.

He frowned. "Are you certain?"

15

"Yes, yes." She smiled weakly. "Just very tired. What do you think of your daughter?"

He returned his gaze to the tiny wonder in his arms. "What is her name?"

At this, Ka'en went quiet.

"What would you like her name to be?" She asked after a moment.

Watching the tiny fingers entwine around his thumb, Aram shook his head. "It is not mine to say. We already discussed this, remember? I thought you would give her one – your mother's."

"What was your sister's name?" Ka'en asked softly.

Frowning, Aram looked over at her. "Maelee."

She thought for a moment with her eyes closed and then smiled and nodded. "I like it."

Aram's frown deepened as he watched her. "What do you mean? For her name?"

"Yes – I mean that we will name her after your sister, and call her Maelee."

"Not Margra'eth, for your mother – as we decided?"

Ka'en shook her head. "Her name is Maelee."

Aram watched his wife for a long moment and then nodded and gazed down into the two tiny, sky-blue eyes. "Hello, Maelee – I am your father."

The child watched him with wide eyes and then made an odd, small sound.

"She's hungry, I think," said Dunna.

Ka'en held out her arms. "May I have her, my love? Let's see if she will eat."

Aram handed down the precious bundle and then sat on the side of the bed as Ka'en held the child to her breast. In but moments, the tiny girl was suckling contentedly. Ka'en smiled up into Aram's eyes.

"Are you pleased?"

Aram didn't trust himself to speak. He nodded silently and returned her smile. After the distress and pain of the last few weeks, the miracle of his child's birth lightened his heart in ways that could not be measured.

Behind him, the door moved on its hinges.

"Ah – it's a wee lass, is it?"

16

Aram turned to see Eoarl standing with Dunna near the door. Eoarl inclined his head to Aram. "Congratulations, my lord, on the birth of your daughter."

"Thank you, my friend."

"Yes, it is a great thing – and a great day." The older man smiled broadly. "Well, then, my Dunnie and me will leave the little family alone for a while."

"I'll go, too, mistress," Cala told Ka'en. "Just call for me if you have any need."

After they'd gone, Aram turned back to Ka'en. Noting again the lines of fatigue around her eyes, he asked her once more, "Are you sure you are alright?"

"*Yes*," she assured him. "Although I am very tired, and sleepy. After she eats, I think Mae and I will get some rest."

He nodded. "I'll stay until you're both asleep," he replied. Leaning down, he kissed her on her forehead.

When they slept, he stayed for an hour, watching the gentle rise and fall of the breast of the woman that meant more to him than life, and the tiny fair-haired likeness of her that lay asleep in her arms. For the first time in many days, the world receded beyond the horizons of his life and took its troubles with it. He smiled happily upon his sleeping wife and child; then he stretched out in his chair, closed his eyes, and rested.

Later, when the small, hungry cries of her child woke her, Ka'en was surprised to find her husband asleep in his chair.

Though his heavy, slow breathing affirmed that his sleep was deep and sound, his face nonetheless wore a smile.

Unseen by her husband, she returned that smile.

And she wondered if it might be that beneath those lids, above that smile, the hard, frightening green ice deep in his eyes had finally melted away.

And she was made strangely glad by that hopeful thought.

For another week after the birth of his daughter, Aram stayed in the valley, resisting the demands of destiny for the sake of his heart.

Every day, after the sun climbed high enough in the sky to make the world below sufficiently warm, he held his daughter in his arms while he and Ka'en strolled back and forth along the southern end of the great porch. As the days passed, Ka'en recovered her

17

strength. Aram was at last able to let go of his worry over her, and instead simply enjoyed the novelty of being a father. Cree often came down and sat on Aram's shoulder as he walked.

"That is a fine child," the hawk reiterated more than once. "A fine child. Beautiful – like her mother."

During those pleasant days, Aram had his first taste of what life might be like if the world was made free of the overhanging malice of Manon, and to a lesser extent, that of the likes of Rahm Imrid. Deliberately, he put thoughts of his enemies away and enjoyed each day to its fullest.

Then one morning he awoke to find a rime of frost lining the blades of grass in the low spots near the city, and he knew that the thing which he intended to do before winter could be put off no longer.

After lunch, when Ka'en had fed Maelee and they were sitting together in the sunlight on the veranda of their house, Aram turned to his wife.

"I must go away for a few days," he told her abruptly, but as gently as he could. "It cannot be avoided. But I will be gone no more than fourteen or fifteen days, and then I will return and we will have a quiet winter."

He watched her after he finished speaking but she kept silent, with her gaze turned away from him and out over the valley.

"Ka'en?"

Finally, she drew in a deep breath, let it out slowly, and looked at him. A soft, sad smile touched her mouth.

"I knew," she said.

He frowned. "What is it that you knew?"

"That you would be going away."

His frown deepened. "How did you know?"

"Because I know *you*, my love." She reached out her hand and entwined her fingers in his. "And I know when something besides me is on your mind." She squeezed his hand and looked away. "Something has changed in you because of – because of all this; I can feel it – and see it."

He stiffened at the tenor of her words. "I have not changed at all toward you, Ka'en. I love you – more each day."

18

"I did not mean to suggest it," she answered and shook her head, still looking away. "I know you love me, and I love you. But you *are* different and it frightens me."

Hearing the distress in her voice, knowing why it was there, and what had caused it, Aram felt the deep, pent-up fury that had smoldered inside him since the day of the dragons begin to surge. With an effort, he fought it back and lowered his voice in an attempt to keep that fierce anger from coloring his tone as he replied. "Manon sent his beasts to kill you, Ka'en. He intended to take you from me – to use my grief against me to manipulate me for his own purposes." He drew in a calming breath and glanced over at the wolf lying asleep in the sun. "If it had not been for Gorfang, they – and he – would have succeeded."

After a moment, he went on, "And there is another thing..."

She turned her head and looked at him. "What other thing?"

"You were right in coming here," he told her. "And I was wrong to try to prevent it. The dragons came for you, Ka'en – there is no other explanation. Manon meant to harm me in a way that would destroy me, drive me mad and cause me to behave rashly, granting him ultimate victory." Aram looked away, toward the southeast. "If you had remained in Derosa, the dragons would have found you easily, and would have burned that town to the ground, killing everyone, just as they did with River's Bend."

He continued to look away from her and his voice broke. "It is only because you were able to get under the mountain that you survived. I thank the Maker that you were here, in the city – and not still in Derosa."

She let the silence lengthen out for a few moments and held tightly to his hand as he looked toward the southern end of the valley. "Where are you going?" She asked then.

"Elam," he said simply.

Her eyes flew wide. "Elam – *again*? Why?"

He felt his gaze harden involuntarily as he moved his head to look back toward the western reaches of the southern horizon. "To remove an impediment."

Ka'en felt her heart skip and catch. "You're going back to war?"

"No."

19

She watched him, holding tightly to his hand, and staring at the thick black hair on the back of his head as he gazed toward the southwest. She tried to gauge his mood through his posture and in the flesh of his fingers but saw – and felt – only determination. "What are you going to do, my love?"

"As I said – I am going to remove an impediment."

Her quiet voice softened until he barely heard her.

"An impediment to *what*?"

He turned and looked at her. The green ice deep in his eyes that had appeared on the day he slew the dragons but had been absent since the birth of Maelee was there once more. And it was as hard and cold as ever.

"My path to Manon," he replied.

She watched him with widened eyes for a long moment and then she closed her eyes and put her head against his shoulder. She asked no further question, for she feared the answer.

He stroked her hair gently for a time and then he stirred himself. "I will leave on the morrow," he said. "Today, however, I need to find Borlus."

She lifted her head, leaned back, and stared. "Borlus? Why?"

He smiled at her. "I need his advice on something."

She sat up straighter. "Can Mae and I go with you? I would love to see Borlus and Hilla. I haven't seen them since – that day."

Regretfully, he shook his head. "Borlus' advice will undoubtedly send me further on into the hills. And I must travel light and fast." He thought for a moment. "I won't be long in Elam. When I return, if it is still warm enough, we will take Mae and go see them together."

She watched him for another moment and then agreed. "I will hold you to that, my love."

He nodded and stood. "I need to find Thaniel and go, then. I will be back before supper."

4.

Borlus was overjoyed to see Aram come up the small valley where he and his family made their home. As Aram dismounted from Thaniel's back, the bear rumbled up gladly.

"Welcome, master, welcome! The hawks tell us that you are now a father."

Aram smiled a greeting. "Hello, old friend. "Yes – Mistress Ka'en and I have a daughter." He winced as he said it, but Borlus, whose own daughter had been lost in the battle for the city, seemed not to take notice.

"I am very glad for you, Lord Aram."

"Thank you for that, my friend," Aram responded, and he inclined his head respectfully to Borlus' mate, Hilla, who had come up to sit behind her husband. "If you and Hilla are agreeable, I will bring my family to visit in two weeks or so, before the winter – before you sleep."

"We would be honored, master."

Aram glanced toward the grotto where the bears lived and then looked around the narrow valley, frowning. "Where is your son, my namesake – where is Aram?"

Borlus sat back on his haunches and his small eyes gleamed. "He has gone north, into the hills, to find a mate."

Aram's smile returned. "I remember when his father went northward into those same hills for the same reason. May he be as fortunate in his search as you were in yours, my friend."

The bear was watching Aram closely. "I see that you have come for a purpose, master. How may I assist you?"

"You are as perceptive as ever, old friend," Aram laughed. Then he grew serious. "Where is a cave, or another deep place, where I might get under the earth? I need to send a message to Lord Ferros, if possible."

Borlus tiny eyes widened. "I sometimes forget that I am friends with him who talks with gods." He turned and looked toward his own home. "You are welcome to use our dwelling, master. I know that you met him there once before."

Aram shook his head. "No, it was not Ferros, but his servant, Bendan. It is Bendan that I wish to meet with again." He looked up the valley at the opening to the bears' grotto and then, after a moment, shook his head again. "It is true that I met him there once before, but on that occasion I informed him that I was in that place to visit a friend. He will know that it is your home, and might not respond to my presence there." He looked back at Borlus. "No, my friend; I need to find a place where he will interpret my action as a need for his assistance."

Borlus thought for a moment, and then he rose and pivoted to face west. "At the end of this valley, where this stream arises from the earth below the mountain, there is a small cave. I once considered it for a home, but as I said, it is small." He lifted his head and studied Aram. "It is not tall, master, but I believe that you may be able to stand in the center, just inside the opening. But will Lord Ferros' servant require more room?"

"I think not," Aram replied. "I am not certain, but I do not think that rock is an impediment to his kind." He looked beyond the bear, up the valley. "This small cave is next to the mountain?"

"Yes, master, at its base. When you reach the place where this stream arises from the earth, look up and to your right. It is there at the base of the mountain."

"I will go and find it." Aram reached out and touched Borlus on his shoulder. "Thank you, my friend. I will bring Ka'en and Maelee to see you in a few days' time."

"Maelee – that is your daughter's name?"

Aram nodded. "It was the name of my sister."

The bear was silent for a moment. "She it was that the evil one took from you."

"Yes." Aram frowned at him. "How did you know?"

"Leorg the wolf told me."

Aram considered. "He must have known it from Durlrang."

"I am sorry for the loss of your friend, master," Borlus said.

Aram hesitated as he rose to move away toward Thaniel. He looked away from Borlus, down the valley, and then looked back at him. "We all lost much – too much – and I am sorry for us all. Farewell, my friend. Ka'en, Mae, and I will come before winter."

"Farewell, master."

The cave pierced the slope of the mountain several yards above the spring that fed the stream, atop a grassy hill that ended at the base of the rock. Leaving Thaniel in the meadow among the lush grass by the place where the spring of the valley stream bubbled up from the earth, Aram climbed the slope to the opening and stepped inside. Though small, it was perhaps not as cramped as Borlus remembered.

He found a place where the ceiling of the chamber allowed him to stand fully upright and turned his back upon the bright day outside. As he peered into the darkness of the depths where the cave narrowed down to nothing, waiting for his eyes to adjust to the dimness, he wondered if Ferros would remember his promise and honor it once again.

He needn't have doubted.

Within moments, the shadowed interior brightened with a faint reddish glow. A moment later, Bendan appeared.

The servant of Ferros bowed to Aram and surprised him with the use of his title. "You have come under the earth, Lord Aram. Are you in need of my master's aid?"

Aram inclined his head in respectful response. "I am in need of information which I believe your master, Lord Ferros, might be able to provide, sir. Greetings, Bendan," he said then. "Thank you for coming. I did not know if Lord Ferros would remember me."

"Lord Ferros remembers all, and always keeps his word," Bendan replied. "I am here at his command. What is your need?"

"I wish to know if there are more dragons loose in the world other than the two that I slew in my valley. I need to know this for the security of those I love."

Bendan's response to this was to stiffen and stare at him, his gray-orange eyes seeming to glow in the darkness. "You *slew – dragons?*"

"I slew them," Aram affirmed, surprised by Bendan's response. "There were two. The grim lord sent them to burn and kill in my valley. I need to know from Lord Ferros if there are more that threaten the world. Will you ask him – or do you yourself know the answer to this?"

Bendan, his eyes still round with astonishment, held up his hand. "Please wait here, my lord, if you will."

The servant of Ferros disappeared on the instant.

As he waited for him to reappear, Aram kept his back to the sunlit opening of the cave and thought about his immediate plans. If Ferros could verify there were no more dragons abroad in the world, he would feel more comfortable with leaving Ka'en in the valley as he went to see about his business with Elam. Padrik had sent almost a hundred of his wolves into the hills north of Aram's valley in order to strengthen Leorg's diminished numbers and the hawks between the valley and the far north remained on constant alert. Ka'en would be as safe in the valley as she could be anywhere – so long as there were no more of those alien monsters to threaten her.

The red glow strengthened once more.

But it was not Bendan this time.

Aram was astonished to see the smooth head and face and the fiery eyes of Lord Ferros himself appear inside the small cavern.

Quickly, respectfully, he bowed. "Lord Ferros! I did not mean to trouble you –"

Ferros impatiently waved Aram's protestations away. The god gazed at him with burning eyes. "I am told that you slew the dragons that my brother loosed upon the world. Is this true?"

Aram nodded cautiously. "It is true, my lord." He lifted one hand to indicate the Sword upon his back. "Though I must confess that it was the power of this weapon that doomed them," he said.

Ferros' glowing eyes glanced briefly at the Sword. "Yes, there is sufficient power in that weapon to wreak havoc down into the very foundations of the world – as I learned when you so callously and deliberately pierced a mountain with it. But *you wield it*, Aram. That weapon can do nothing on its own. So – in truth, you slew them, if indeed they have perished." He leaned forward. "They are dead? Their carcasses lie upon the earth? I require proof."

"They are dead, my lord," Aram contended. "I swear it. You may look upon their carcasses, if you like. The bodies burned after their deaths, and only their bones remain." He moved his hand, indicating the outside. "I will gladly show you, my lord."

24

"There is no need for that." Ferros leaned closer, his fiery, fearsome eyes coming close to Aram's. "I will know the truth by your answer to one question. The bones of these beasts – *how do they appear?* Describe them."

"They appear as if they are made of burnished metal – steel perhaps, or another metal unknown to me," Aram replied, mystified by the question. "I do not think it is steel, but whatever it is, it is similar in appearance."

The god watched him for a moment longer and then leaned back and nodded slowly. "I see that you speak the truth; they are slain." Ferros straightened and smiled coldly. "No, it is not steel. You are right in that assertion. The substance of their bones is not found on this world."

He studied Aram for some time in silence. "The Astra – they aided you?"

"Yes, my lord."

"But it was not their strength that slew the dragons?" The god persisted.

"No, my lord," Aram answered. "Their aid, as always, was invaluable. But as I stated, it was the Sword that destroyed the beasts."

Ferros' eyes slid briefly upward once more and then came back to rest on Aram's face. "And you wish to know if there are more of their kind that threaten the world."

"I do," Aram replied. "I need to know it, my lord, for the sake of my family and others that are dear to me. Pray, tell me – were they all, or are there more?"

"There are three mated pairs of those creatures that yet exist on this world," Ferros stated. "They are imprisoned in the earth, in chambers that lie far below the mountain of the Deep Darkness." He held up one gray hand. "You need not fear, Aram. Manon will not get past my guard again. He will release no others of their kind upon the earth. You may trust my word on this."

Aram nodded slowly, relief flooding through him. "I do trust you, my lord, and I thank you." Then he hesitated as he thought of the egg in the cavern far to the east. "There is one other of their kind yet alive above the earth."

"Yes, there is another," Ferros agreed. "The child inside the mouth of the Pit."

"What do I do about that one, my lord?" Aram asked.

Ferros' hard eyes narrowed. "*You*?" Then he laughed quietly. "You have grown confident in your strength, have you not?"

Aram frowned in response, as he chafed in acknowledgement of the rebuke. "I mean no impertinence, my lord – but something must be done about that one, does it not? If it hatches –"

Ferros held up his hand, cutting him off. "Believe me when I say that I watch the child more closely than does my brother. When it breaks out of the egg, my servants will spring a trap I have laid, causing Manon to destroy his 'other' – thereby destroying the young dragon as well." He went silent for a moment, gazing with his molten eyes past Aram and out into the brightness beyond, and then he continued with something akin to regret dampening his words. "Though the child is innocent in all this, nonetheless it must be slain."

Aram waited until the god looked at him. "I will leave the matter in your hands," he said and bowed his head. "Thank you, my lord." Then he looked up. "I did not mean to trouble you, Lord Ferros. I thought that your servant, Bendan, would suffice to answer my questions."

The flame in Ferros eyes subsided somewhat and the god smiled thinly. "I care little about what occurs upon the skin of this world, as you know. I confess, however, that I have often been troubled by the actions of my brother in releasing the Laish. When Bendan told me of your claim to have slain them, I came to discover the truth of the matter. It pleases me to know that they are slain – for as powerful as Manon has become, he would not contain those creatures were they to rebel against him."

With that, Ferros stepped back and turned to go but then hesitated and looked closely at Aram. "I remember the age of kings," he stated. "I remember it well. I admit that in those years my labor seemed expedient – in ways that have not been true since that time." The flame in the depths of his eyes flared and brightened. "If you mean to return the earth to such a configuration as existed then, you will need to depose my brother, and Manon will not go easily."

"I know this, my lord," Aram stated quietly. "That is my intention, nonetheless."

"And how will you do it?" Ferros demanded, and his gaze flicked upward to the Sword. "With that?"

"It was forged for that purpose," Aram admitted.

"And who was it that forged such a weapon?"

"I am told that it was forged by him who is named Humber," Aram replied.

Ferros considered this, and then slowly shook his head. "Lord Humber is good and strong," he said. "He is the Eldest Brother of all my kind. But he did not make a weapon that can slay a dragon. No – it is the construct of One higher – I am certain of it." He studied Aram for a moment longer. "Tell me, how do you intend to employ that weapon when you stand in the presence of Manon? – if, indeed, you ever do so."

"I will pierce him with it," Aram answered. "I have witnessed its power. If it can destroy the earth, it can bring down a god."

Ferros' smile came back, haughty, thin, imperious, and cold, and the flame in his eyes flared again. "So, you wish to be more than a dragon slayer – *you wish to be a god slayer as well.*"

Aram flinched and bowed his head at the ferocity of the god's tone and demeanor. "I care not what I am called or how I am named, my lord. I wish for no such appellation." Looking up, he dared to meet Ferros' gaze squarely, though with cautious respect. "Manon's oppression of my people must end, and I mean to end it. I mean to make the world free of his malice."

The proud, cold smile slowly faded. Ferros' gray features became smooth, emotionless. The red-gold flame in his eyes flared once more and then faded to a simmering glow. He gazed at Aram in silence for a long, tense moment; then, "Hear this, now," the god stated quietly. "I will aid you in any way that I am able."

Aram stared back at him, astonished, and could not speak.

The god of the Underearth's eyes went once more to the Sword, where they rested for a moment, and then he turned to go. "You should think on that weapon, Aram," he stated. A reddish mist appeared in the gloom and he stepped into it. "It was forged by the Maker Himself. I suspect that it has a purpose far and beyond that which you imagine."

Then he was gone.

Aram gazed after him, wondering at the meaning of his parting words, but could not decipher it. After a moment, he turned and left the cave, coming back out into the bright sunshine.

Thaniel saw him reappear and came up. The horse stopped in front of him and watched him in silence, waiting.

Aram did not greet him at once, but gazed out over the valley, still thinking on Ferros' enigmatic last words. After a long silence, in which Thaniel shifted his great bulk in increasing impatience, Aram looked over at him. "There are no more dragons," he said. "Lord Ferros himself declared it so. The world will not again be threatened by their kind."

Thaniel's impatience abruptly dissipated; the horse stared. "You saw Ferros?" He swung his great head and looked up the slope at the opening to the cave. "He is in that cavern?"

Aram laughed shortly. "No, my friend; he is not there now. But he came there – out of his deep realm, in answer to my need, as he promised."

"Ferros kept his promise?" Thaniel stated this in amazement. He continued to gaze up the slope at the mouth of the cave and then he swung his head back. "And there are no more dragons?"

"There are no more."

"That is good." The horse looked again at the dark opening of the cavern up the slope, and then he turned to allow Aram to mount up. "So – we are free to see to our own affairs."

Aram put his foot into the stirrup and swung up into the saddle. "We are," was his simple reply.

The next morning, Aram took leave of his family and he and Thaniel went across the rivers and over the crest of the green hills where they camped by the familiar spring. The following dawn, they continued down onto the plains and turned southwest toward the fortress, arriving before midday. Aram immediately found Wamlak and sent him and Braska hurrying toward Derosa to fetch Findaen and Prince Marcus.

5.

By the time Marcus made his way into the fortress from Derosa where he'd been visiting with Thom, Kay, and Mallet and his wife, the sun sat on the western horizon, and evening had fallen. Lamps were lit along the stairs leading up to the war room. Lord Aram was already there, engaged in quiet consultation with Edwar, Boman, Andar, Matibar, and Findaen. Marcus stepped inside and waited until Aram saw him and beckoned him forward.

He moved close and inclined his head. "You wanted to see me, my lord?"

Aram nodded and tapped his finger on a crudely drawn map positioned on the table in front of him. "Where in Elam may Rahm Imrid be found at this time of year?"

Though surprised by the question, and especially by the suggestive tenor in which it was rendered, Marcus nonetheless answered readily. "In Farenaire, at the palace."

Aram looked down and tapped the map again. "Show me."

Rendered abruptly cautious by Aram's demeanor but made curious by his interest in Elam, Marcus studied the tall lord as he moved closer to the indicated parchment. The king seemed cold and distant; harder and more determined than was usual even for him. It was as everyone said; a change had occurred in him since the killing of the dragons.

Looking down, Marcus examined the map which, while crudely drawn, was nonetheless fairly accurate in its placement of cities, towns, and roads across Elam. He placed his finger on a point in the southwest quadrant of the great green land, at the edge of the Iron Mountains. "Here – this is Farenaire."

Aram was watching him. "And Rahm is there at this time of year?"

"Yes, of course," Marcus affirmed, "at the council of which I told you. The heads of the Great Houses always meet twice a year, for several weeks, once in Spring and once again in Autumn. They will have begun their Autumnal conference within the last few days."

For some reason Marcus couldn't immediately fathom, this information seemed to please Aram. The king let his eyes move slowly down over the map from north to southwest, to the point indicated by Marcus, and then he nodded to himself. Placing his finger on a line that ran down the length of the land and looking up, he met Marcus' eyes. "This main road – it goes near to the palace?"

Marcus nodded in affirmation and then put his own finger on the map where another line intersected the first. "Farenaire is no more than twenty miles west of this junction."

"And these towns in between the gates and the south – they are substantial?"

"Some, though not all," Marcus replied, and he indicated a point on the map. "Only Calom Malpas is of any great size, and it is a substantial city."

"Is it gated?" Aram asked.

"It is, my lord."

Aram studied the map for a moment longer and then looked at Marcus. "You are fully armored these days?"

"Yes, my lord."

"And your mount – Phagan?"

Marcus felt a thrill run through him for which he could as yet identify no cause. "Phagan has a breastplate and head-gear only," he replied.

Aram turned to Findaen. "Go to Derosa with the prince. Find Arthrus – see that Prince Marcus' mount is fully armored by the second morning from today. Tell him to lay everything else aside." He looked back at Marcus. "Go with him," he instructed the young prince. "Make certain that you are fully armored as well. Where is Thom Sota?"

"He is on leave in Derosa – with his wife."

Aram nodded. "Bring him, and be certain that he and his mount are fully armored as well."

Marcus glanced around at the men assembled there before bringing his gaze back to Aram. "May I ask what this is about, my lord?"

"We leave for Elam on the morning after tomorrow, at sun-up," Aram replied. "You, Thom, and I are going to see Rahm Imrid."

Startled by this astonishing announcement, Marcus stared. "My lord?"

"We are going to Farenaire, Marcus," Aram replied. "To the council."

"Just we three?"

Aram nodded. "Yes."

Marcus swallowed and hesitated. "May I ask to what end, my lord?"

Aram's icy green eyes hardened. "It is time Waren's son sat the high throne of Elam. With the council in session, this is as good a time as we could seek."

Marcus slid his gaze sideways to Findaen, who simply raised his eyebrows and made a slight shrug. It was immediately apparent to the young prince that no one in the room besides him questioned this astounding and bluntly stated intent on the part of their leader. Marcus looked back at Aram. ""There are thousands of Rahm's soldiers along the road between the gates and the palace, my lord. How will we reach Farenaire? Even if we go through the back door – at Basura, for instance – we will still be very far north, with much hostile territory between us and the palace."

Aram shook his head slightly. "We will not be entering Elam through a back way. We're going through the front door, to use your words. We are going through the gates and southward along the main road."

Marcus felt his eyes widen. "My lord, I –"

Lord Aram's demeanor darkened and hardened further as he cut him off. "We are not at war with Elam or its men-at-arms – we are at odds with its illegitimate ruler only. We will move through the land quickly – so quickly that they cannot warn those ahead of us of our coming. You and Thom will stay behind me as we journey, Marcus, at all times until we reach the palace and the issue is resolved. Believe me when I say that we are not likely to be challenged along the way." He shrugged. "If challenged, I will destroy only as many as is required to gain passage. This I promise."

Marcus gazed at him in astonishment. "We are going to pass through the length of Elam?"

"It is the quickest way to accomplish that which must be done." Aram answered and then he waited for Marcus to respond to this enigmatic statement, but the young prince could only stare. Aram watched him for a moment longer and then nodded. "Go with Findaen, then. Be back at this fortress before sunset tomorrow with both you and your mount fully armored – Thom and Norgen as well – and with a week's ration of food and water for each of you. The horses will find sustenance and water along the way."

Marcus gazed back at him, and then swallowed and inclined his head. "As you say, my lord." He turned as in a daze and followed Findaen from the room.

As they rode eastward through the gathering dusk, Marcus turned to Findaen. "What does he mean to do?"

Findaen glanced over. "You heard him – he means to place you upon the throne of Elam."

"But how will he accomplish such a thing with just the three of us? Indeed, how will he accomplish such a thing at all?"

"I cannot answer that," Findaen admitted. "But I doubt that you and Thom will be needed for whatever it is he has in mind." He considered for a moment. "I can only say that since he slew the dragons, Lord Aram is a different man. Harder, more certain of things – and more sure of what he can accomplish with the weapon perhaps. And if he declares that he will pass through the length of Elam?" Findaen shrugged and grinned across at Marcus. "Then he will pass through the length of Elam. You may depend upon it."

Marcus stared forward, into the gathering night. "And I'm to go with him."

"So it would seem, my friend."

6.

The eastern sky was pink, but the sun was yet below the horizon when, two days later, Aram, Marcus, and Thom splashed their mounts across the rapids above the islands in the Broad and headed westward across the cool prairie. Thaniel, Phagan, and Norgen were fully armored. For protection, Aram wore his armor from the Mountain of Kelven beneath his gold-trimmed armor of black from Regamun Mediar which he wore for effect.

When Marcus complained that the layers of thin steel that covered his body rendered movement, and even riding, difficult, Aram was adamant.

"You must be protected at all times – I cannot have you die," he stated bluntly. "And there will be no time to halt and put it on or remove it as we go. What we do in the south of Elam must be done quickly." He turned his hard gaze upon the young prince. "My plans for the coming year require that a friend sits upon Elam's throne."

Marcus did not respond. He felt that he did not dare question Lord Aram further as to his "plans". Findaen was right; a change had occurred in the kingly man riding ahead of him and Thom. Something unforeseen was afoot. Enormous changes were about to unfold in the world. Just what, Marcus did not know, but it was apparent that he would have an unobstructed view of whatever it was that Aram intended.

The sun rose and began to chase them across the surface of the world. Leaving the grasslands before mid-morning, they went up and around the southern flanks of Burning Mountain and made their way down through the valley of the dry lake. Despite the fact that Aram and Thaniel kept up a blistering pace, the sun overtook them before they reached the borders of Cumberland. In early afternoon, they passed by the town at the edge of the hills, openly, straight along the main road. The citizenry gazed open-mouthed upon the mounted men as they passed by them and then turned southward along the main road that ran through the heartland of Cumberland and toward the distant Gates of Elam.

Aram seldom spoke to Marcus or Thom throughout the day, but he conferred often with Alvern the eagle, in the skies high overhead. Alvern's grandson, Kipwing, had been left behind, in the skies above the hills to the north of Aram's valley, watching over Ka'en.

Aram did not close his mind during these conversations with Alvern, so his companions were aware of the information that the eagle imparted about traffic on the road ahead and relative distances to the Gates of Elam as well as any obstructions to their passage. But as yet, there were none. The road ahead remained clear, and nothing occurred to delay or hinder them.

Darkness found them far south in Cumberland though the Gates had not yet hove into view. An hour after sunset, as the night deepened and they found an area where the lights of villages and farmhouses were widely scattered, Aram and Thaniel turned aside, toward the banks of a small stream so that the horses might quench their thirst. Marcus and Thom and their mounts followed.

Aram removed his helmet and breathed deeply of the cool night air. Thom moved Norgen close to Aram and Thaniel. When the king looked over at him, Thom inclined his head in respect but then posed his blunt question. "My lord – is it true as Prince Marcus tells me that we are to go southward through the land of Elam all the way to Farenaire?"

"Yes," Aram replied simply, and his voice and features, lit by starlight, were placid, unconcerned. "We are."

Thom watched him with narrowed eyes. "Just we three – all the way southward through Elam? All the way to Rahm's palace?"

Aram nodded. The expression upon his face did not change.

Thom hesitated and looked away for a long moment before turning back. "My lord – I have seen what can be done with that weapon you bear. But there are many miles and thousands of troops between us and the palace. They are not dragons, I grant you, but they are numerous, and their commanders, by and large, are loyal to Elam's current High Prince."

34

Aram replaced his helmet, lifted the visor, and met Thom's gaze. "No; they are not dragons. And if their commanders must be slain in order to avoid conflict with the men-of-arms of Elam, then I will slay them. I hope not to find such killing expedient. Nonetheless hear me, Thom. Nothing – and no one – will prevent us from going to the south. I assure you of this, captain. You must trust me on this point. We will go all the way to Farenaire. I only require that you do two things for me."

Thom studied Aram's stern, cold countenance for a moment. And in that moment, he believed. He nodded. "Whatever you need, my lord – I will do."

"The first thing that I require," Aram told him, "is that you protect the prince. I need Marcus to reach the palace alive and well. If ever we are assaulted and separated, if only by a few yards; look to his safety. Remove him far from any harm. Phagan and Norgen are both very fleet of foot and will get you both away quickly. Do you understand?"

"I do," Thom affirmed, though a frown troubled his brow. "But what about you, my lord – if we are attacked?"

Aram shook his helmeted head slightly. "I cannot be harmed, captain; you may be assured of this. You must understand this and believe it if you are to protect the prince."

Aram turned his head sharply and looked into the night as the brush moved and crackled in the darkness off to his right, but it was only a farmer's ox going to the stream for water. Nonetheless, Aram remained alert for a moment longer, peering into the gloom.

"And the second thing?" Thom inquired.

Satisfied that there was no need for alarm, Aram looked back at him. "You are a captain of Elam, are you not?"

"I was," Thom corrected him. "Rahm's takeover of the troops became too much for me, and I resigned."

"Were there others that felt as you do?"

Thom frowned. "In the army? Yes – many."

"Did some of those others remain in service?" Aram asked.

"Some, yes," Thom replied and he shrugged. "Many have nothing else to do – or know of nothing else to do."

"So, then," Aram persisted, "Rahm's control of the army may not be as firm as he thinks?"

Thom laughed. "Men like him are never loved – nor are they respected as much as they like to think, especially by the boys in uniform."

"That's the second thing, captain."

"My lord?"

"Once Rahm is removed and Marcus is on the throne, you must reorganize the forces of Elam," Aram explained. "Find those that will readily accede to the altered order of things and place them in the various commands while removing those tied too closely to Rahm."

Thom stared. "You want *me* to do this? But I am – *was* – only a captain."

"I will decide what you are," Aram stated bluntly. "You have been to battle and acquitted yourself with courage upon the field. Besides that, you have shown yourself capable of making sound decisions. *And I trust you.* The forces of Elam must have competent new leadership that is loyal to Prince Marcus. You must do this for me – and for him."

Thom felt a thrill go through him. "You are going to depose Rahm, are you not, my lord? And make Marcus High Prince in Elam? Marcus stated this to me, and I heard the rumor at the fortress, but now I believe that I hear the very truth of it from you."

"We are going to remove Rahm Imrid," Aram confirmed, and then he continued on with the earlier conversation. "So – do you know of commanders that can be trusted?"

Thom looked away again, directing an unseen grin of delight out into the twilight. But then, after a moment, he suppressed his emotions, considered Aram's question, and nodded. "There are a few men left in the palace guard who, I think, can be trusted." He looked back at Aram. "It's as good a place as any to start."

Aram watched him closely. "You'll do it, then?"

"I'll do anything for Marcus, my lord."

"Good," Aram said simply.

They slept on horseback that night in a stand of trees in a bend of the stream some distance off the road. After the discussion with Thom ended, Aram went silent. Other than to inquire as to how Marcus and Thom were enduring the ride, and to advise them to get what rest they could, he did not speak further of the events ahead.

36

Before sun-up they moved back out onto the thoroughfare and continued on toward the south. As on the previous day, Aram spoke little to his companions, conferring almost exclusively with Alvern, high overhead. Neither he nor the great eagle, however, closed their communion to Marcus and Thom, so the two men were made aware of what was happening upon the road to their front.

Aram made no effort to avoid traffic, for it was all of a local nature. None of it had any apparent connection either to Elam or to the grim lord of the north. Late in the morning, before the sun found its apex, they spied the mighty gates rising up before them. Aram turned aside into the shade of a copse of trees, and gazed south.

They were close enough to see that the enormous gates were closed. Only a smaller aperture in the massive construct on the right was open, just enough to allow oxcarts and foot traffic to pass through. On the road, one lone oxcart moved toward them about halfway between their position and the gates.

"How many people are upon the road close to the gates?" Aram asked Alvern.

"There is one cart that comes toward you," the eagle replied, "and one about to pass through which will move your way as well. Otherwise, there is only foot traffic to the south, but much of it goes away from the gates. None of it, I think, will come through to the north."

"Good." Aram looked over at Marcus. "Did you hear?"

Marcus swallowed and nodded.

Aram's gaze moved on. "Thom?"

"I heard, Lord Aram."

"We will wait until the oxcart at the gates moves through and gets some distance along the road toward us before we move. I have no wish to involve the citizenry."

Marcus stared at him and dared to ask the question. "Just exactly what are we going to do, Lord Aram?"

Aram indicated the distant wall. "We are going through."

"They won't just let us pass, you know."

Without looking over, keeping his attention upon the gates, Aram smiled a small, grim smile that was hidden in the depths of his headgear. "I don't intend to seek permission."

While they waited on the oxcart spoken of by Alvern to appear through the opening in the gates and come along the road,

37

Aram studied the towers in the great wall to either side of the Gates of Elam. There were many men up there, moving around. According to Alvern, there were soldiers on the ground as well, manning the gates. And there undoubtedly would be Elamite officials of some kind, representatives of the throne, monitoring the traffic as it passed through.

About a half-mile west of the gates, to their right, there was a massive arch in the bottom of the wall, through which a river flowed. And there were towers to either side of the stream also, but they were far enough away that Aram gave the men in them little thought.

To the left, toward the hills, there was another tower, also about a half-mile distant, also too far away to accord any concern. Aram looked back at the gates. The cart had come through the small opening in the massive right-hand gate and was trundling slowly toward them.

Aram watched it closely. As soon as it cleared arrow-shot distance of the towers, he meant to move.

"What is immediately beyond the gates – upon the ground?" He asked Alvern.

"There are several buildings, both large and small, clustered near the gates," Alvern replied. "Men come from some of the smaller structures to meet with those that pass through the gates."

"Soldiers?" Aram asked.

"Yes, my lord. There are barracks to both sides of the road."

"How many men?"

"More than ten, but less than a hundred," the eagle replied.

Aram nodded. "Manageable," he said.

Thom leaned forward and looked at Aram, indicating the gates with his hand. "You know that they can see us sitting here, my lord – do you not?"

Aram kept his attention upon the gates. "It will not matter, captain."

Thom frowned at this and looked over and met Marcus' eyes. Marcus raised his eyebrows but remained silent.

The oxcart was now some way north of the gates.

"It is time," Aram said. He spoke to Thaniel and they went out into the road and the big horse cantered toward the south. Marcus and Thom and their mounts fell in close behind.

About a half-mile from the gates, Thaniel halted and Aram looked back over his shoulder. "When the gates are open," he said, "we will go through quickly. Once on the other side, Thaniel and I will turn and face the gates, and deal with any Elamite troops attempting to engage. The four of you will pass beyond us and go rapidly toward the south, out of the range of their archers upon the walls. Do you understand?"

The two men nodded in affirmation.

"It will be best to let the horses have their heads," Aram continued. "Thaniel knows my mind and what I intend. He will instruct Phagan and Norgen." He met each man's eyes for a long moment. "I will not require your aid," he stated plainly. "Your only duty is to get beyond the gates to a safe distance. I need the both of you to reach Farenaire unharmed. Do you understand this?"

Marcus frowned but replied, "I understand."

Thom gazed back at Aram with his face set in lines of seriousness. "If there is trouble, I would like to be of service, my lord, if I may."

Aram watched him for a moment but then shook his head. "If trouble arises, do as I require; take care of the prince. But I think there will be very little trouble for us here. And remember to let the horses have their heads."

He turned away and glanced up at the sun, rising towards mid-day. There were a few puffy clouds here and there, but none close enough to that bright disc to hinder the work of the Sword. Without looking back again, he lowered his visor and urged Thaniel forward.

"Let's go."

Aram drew the Sword and extended it above his head, holding the blade's fire in check as Thaniel picked up the pace and sped toward the gates. Its song arose and very quickly, under the undiluted influence of the sun, became a shriek of latent power.

The driver of the oxcart, seeing a trio of armored men on armored horses bearing down upon him, abandoned the cart and dove for a nearby farmer's ditch. The ox continued nervously on for just a moment before it, too, left the road and ran down the embankment into the fields. The cart's wheels mired in a drainage ditch and it jolted to a halt, but the frightened animal broke its traces and galloped away to the east.

Upon the walls, the soldiers of Elam had crowded next to the parapet on the near side, staring down upon the approaching horses. Some of those sentinels shouted warnings to the men on the ground. There were archers among the men on the walls and these troops began preparing to loose arrows down upon the road.

About a quarter-mile from the gates, while they were still well beyond arrowshot, Aram swung the Sword in an arc along the top of the wall and released its power. Fire, searing hot and crackling, sizzled through the air, jagged and terrifying, just above the heads of those gathered there.

On the instant, those helmeted heads disappeared, as if the parapet was abruptly abandoned.

Giving the Sword a few moments to gather more strength from the sun, Aram then swung it back again the other way, this time grazing the top of that turreted stonework, causing smoke to puff and bits of stone to be dislodged.

Then he lifted the Sword again and checked its fire, to let it gain power from the sunlight pouring down upon it. Thaniel drove hard toward the gates with the other horses right behind him. A hundred feet from the massive gates at the entrance to Elam, Aram lowered the weapon and pointed it at the gate on the right, toward the smaller opening, and unleashed the concentrated power. Flame leapt out and smashed into the right-hand gate, blowing a large hole in it next to the opening.

With a groan, the enormous gate buckled and heaved and then bent inward, creating another gaping hole, this one between it and the gate on the left. Thaniel and Aram drove through, followed closely by the others. Beyond the gate, along the road leading to Elam's interior, barracks and other official buildings crowded next to the thoroughfare. That stretch of road, however, was rapidly clearing of traffic and people as folk pelted off it to either side, away from the blasted gate and the huge metal-clad beast that pounded through the gap that had quite suddenly and with frightening effect appeared within it.

As Thaniel spun and slid to a stop, Marcus and Thom and their mounts rushed past. Aram twirled the Sword over his head, letting the fire flow through unchecked, creating a vortex of flame in the air above him.

No one stood to challenge the man in the black armor who was mounted on a fearsome beast and seemed to wield the power of lightning. The road and its adjoining walkways and alleyways quickly became empty as everyone within range of the Sword's fire and howling song sought refuge.

After a few moments Aram checked the flame of the Sword long enough to gather fire, and then he swung the blade at the top of the wall and released it, in case anyone up there still retained a shred of foolish bravado. Then he sheathed the Sword, pushed up the visor of his helmet, and stood tall in the stirrups.

"*Show yourselves,*" he commanded.

Other than a frightened face, here and there, that peered out at him for just a moment from a window or doorway back along the side streets and alleyways, no official or soldier appeared to ask him his business in the land of Elam.

He glanced up at the wall, where two or three pairs of eyes peered above the turrets only to disappear again when his gaze fell upon them, and then looked around at the apparently abandoned buildings to either side. He could see no one but he had no doubt that he was seen from the shadowed interiors.

He reached for the Sword and spoke harshly. "Whoever is in charge of this gate – show yourself to me at once or I will hunt you *and burn you to ash.*"

After another few moments devoid of acknowledgement or movement, a sturdy man of medium height, clad in the blue and gold of an Elamite officer, stepped hesitantly into view, appearing from around a corner of the barracks immediately to Aram's left. The man halted, trembling, near the entrance to the alleyway from which he had appeared, like a rabbit terrified of straying too far from the dark safety of its hole.

Before the man could speak or Aram could ask his name, he heard Thom exclaim from behind him,

"Jothan!"

The man froze and stared at the mounted men beyond Aram. "Is that you, Captain Sota?"

Aram turned in the saddle and looked at Thom as well. "You know this man?"

Thom lifted his visor and nodded. "I trained him at infantry camp, my lord. Jothan was a good recruit – and I assume is a good

41

soldier." Then, as he noted the epaulets on Jothan's shoulders, he corrected himself, "Officer, I should say. And a captain as well, I see. What are you doing here at the gate, Jothan?"

Jothan slid his cautious gaze sideways to Aram for a moment before answering. "I am the officer in charge here, captain," he told Thom. He hesitated again, once more looking warily at Aram. "Why are you here, Thom?"

Thom indicated Aram with his gauntleted hand. "This is Lord Aram, Jothan – the king of the alliance of free peoples. He has come to change things in Elam." Thom's next words proved that Aram's demonstration with the Sword had lain to rest any doubts he might have harbored about the intent and ability of the man he had followed into Elam. "Rahm Imrid will be deposed, and Marcus, son of Waren, will be elevated. Gather your men, captain, and present them upon the road. Lord Aram will tell you all you need to know."

Aram watched Thom for a long moment, as if gauging the captain's altered thinking and then he nodded his approval before turning back to the Elamite officer.

"Do as he says – and do it quickly."

Jothan bent his body forward until it became almost a bow. "At once, sir – *my lord* – at once." And he went shouting down the various avenues that ran off from the main road, calling his troops out to stand before the man who had just destroyed their age-old belief in the invincibility of the Gates of Elam.

When his troops had gathered and had formed up in the road behind Jothan, facing Aram, the order was passed to the men atop the wall to lay down their weapons, show themselves, and pay heed to the words of the menacing stranger.

Aram looked them over and then spoke.

"Rahm Imrid," he said, and his voice boomed out loud and clear among the buildings and echoed up along the vast ramparts of the wall, "is no longer High Prince in Elam. He is hereby removed and Marcus, son of Waren, sits in his stead." He gazed at them through the visor opening of his black helmet. "Tell this to everyone you see and meet, and to everyone that passes through theses gates. *Marcus, son of Waren, is High Prince in Elam.*"

He bent his hard eyes down upon Jothan. "Thom Sota is hereby elevated to the rank of general of the armies of Elam. In future, your orders will come from him, captain. Do you hear and understand?"

Jothan swallowed and nodded, still recovering from the display of awful power and stunned by the abrupt alteration of the landscape of his homeland, wrought in but an instant by this strange and terrifying man with the fiery blade that was mounted on an armored beast.

"I-I understand, my lord."

Aram nodded. "I will return alone within the week and will pass out through these gates. By the time I return, Marcus will sit the high throne and Rahm will be no more. You, captain, will remain at your post and attend to your duties. General Sota will contact you in due time."

Jothan stared, his features awash in astonishment. "Yes, sir."

Aram let his gaze rove slowly among the gathered soldiers and was satisfied by what he saw in their eyes.

Speaking to Thaniel, he turned the horse and they drove southward away from the gates and into the ancient land of Elam, followed by Marcus and Thom.

7.

Rahm Imrid sat very still and erect upon the high throne and watched as the members of the Council of the Great Houses entered the hall and found their ways to their seats upon the left-hand side, beneath the high windows. Try as he might, he could not read the general mood. Most of the elders of the land of Elam were stoic and stone-faced, even those he counted among his closest allies.

Despite his best efforts at containment, news of the military disaster in the north, wrought upon the fields of Basura, had been widely disseminated.

When the few thousand that had escaped from the action before Tobol fled to the south and encountered their reinforcements coming north along the main road, the survivors told their tales of beast-borne marauders, and panic had taken them all, including the reinforcing body. The entire lot had scurried back into the south. The officers, as terror-stricken as the men, had utterly failed to contain either their troops or the tale of defeat they bore with them.

Consequently, the ruin of Rahm's attempt to subdue Basura was well-known throughout Elam.

Acting quickly, Rahm had succeeded in separating the bulk of the defeated soldiers from society and ensconcing them in the various military installations near to Farenaire. And he had personally questioned those officers that had escaped from Basura.

That which he discovered brought to his recollection Marcus' tales of the barbarians Edverch met upon the plains of The Land Beyond the Gates in the spring. Apparently, men on armored beasts – the so-called horses of ancient legend – had attacked Slan upon his undefended northern flank and swept the army from the field.

Rahm always suspected that Marcus, when he disappeared from the landscape of Elam proper, had gone into Basura. Evidently, he had also gone even farther eastward and made contact with the barbarians, somehow gaining a sort of alliance with that rough and vicious lot of uncivilized denizens of the desolate lands of the east. The High Prince clearly remembered the tone of respect that had subconsciously entered Marcus' voice when he spoke of the leader of those wild folk.

Basura, then, undoubtedly with Marcus' help, had apparently enlisted those eastern people to aid in their revolt against the throne. Riding their villainous beasts, they had smashed into Slan's northern flank unexpectedly at dawn.

And Slan had not seen it coming.

Once he'd gained a full understanding of that which had occurred in the north, Rahm had two thoughts.

First – and this rather surprised him – he desperately wanted to discover a means of wresting some of those here-to-fore unknown beasts from the barbarians and put them to work bearing his own troops into battle.

Secondly, Edverch had been entirely wrong about Slan. The newly-appointed general – now apparently either dead or captured – though possessed of quite proper political attitudes, had nonetheless been incapable of leading men to victory. Slan had obviously been an utter fool, pressing carelessly eastward in search of glory and reward rather than minding proper military method.

Upon reflection, Rahm decided that he'd have been better served to send Edverch into Basura. The old general lacked the raw confidence displayed by Slan, but that would have only made him more cautious and might have saved the army. As a consequence, whether Edverch's caution had resulted in victory or stalemate, it would not have led to a complete rout of the forces of the throne. The High Prince would perhaps have been spared from dealing with the ensuing political embarrassment and possible dissension from his less loyal allies on the Council.

As soon as he understood the military aspects of the disaster in Basura, Rahm took immediate steps to rectify the situation. Even now twenty-five thousand troops were headed northward along the main road, bound for the rebellious countryside of the traitorous province. The rest of the nation's troops, at least those whose loyalty to the High Prince was reasonably certain, were summoned to the fortifications around the palace, in case Cinnabar or Berezan, or any of the other Houses whose fealty to the throne was suspect, decided to act rashly.

The troops going north had been placed under the command of Trebor Arrabi, a full general from House Antona. General Arrabi appeared capable enough, possessed a solid reputation for loyalty, and seemed to welcome the opportunity to restore the confidence and the honor of Elam's forces.

House Antona was not closely allied to the throne, but neither had its leading family shown any inclination to buck the prevailing political winds. Antona was on the extreme east of Elam, just north of Soroba's home province. It was a land of quiet farmlands, small in both population and geographic size, politically unimportant.

It was commendable then that a son of such a land had risen to the rank of full general. The impression Rahm had of Trebor Arrabi was that of stolid devotion to duty and an unwillingness to question orders.

When made to understand the nature of that which had occurred before Tobol, and pressed to state his own intentions, based upon that knowledge, Arrabi was clear and decisive.

He intended to march into Basura with his troops in the form of a square, he told the High Prince, with the bulk of his troops positioned on the leading edge and along both sides. The rear side of the square would be reserves, ready to move ahead or to the left or right as the situation demanded.

When informed that the enemy that had driven Slan's men from the field was mounted upon armored beasts, Arrabi blinked, looked down at his boots and thought for a moment. When next he looked up, it was to render this assessment – "These mounted warriors must have been a frightening sight, Your Highness, I am sure. But if invincible; why employ a flanking maneuver? Why not simply attack head-on, with the Basuran contingent on line with them?"

When Rahm did not immediately respond, Arrabi continued, "I intend to construct defensive fixtures which can be moved forward as the men advance. These beasts are quite tall according to that which I've been told. Still, they must approach across the ground as any other cadre of troops. A barrier of perhaps four or five feet in height, made of sharpened poles, will undoubtedly render their charge somewhat less impressive."

Upon hearing the description of this scheme, the devising of which demonstrated that Arrabi had given thought to that which had occurred in the north, and finding the reasoning sound, Rahm had inwardly approved of his choice of a general and then asked, "What will you do at Tobol?"

Arrabi inclined his head slightly. "I will, of course, do what you command, Your Highness. If you wish, I will assault the city, or we can besiege them and starve them out."

The High Prince had watched him in silence for a moment. "Alright," he said finally. "Go to Basura. When you arrive before the walls of Tobol, you may inform me of the situation to your front and to either flank, and I will send instruction."

Arrabi bowed. "I am at your service, Your Highness."

Satisfied, Rahm stood. "Go – bring Basura back into the fold."

That had been one week ago. By now Arrabi and his troops would be well north, probably nearing the gates of Calom Malpas.

Feeling at least somewhat comfortable with the military situation, Rahm now had to deal with the political. So far, none of the Great Houses, even those led by families opposed to Rahm's policies, had made any overt movement toward rebellion.

Some of them no doubt considered him weakened by recent events and were simply biding their time, while watching for an opportunity to subvert his will.

Rahm, on the other hand, knew himself now to be properly enlightened as to the dangers of military action – and aware of the fact that there were more enemies abroad in the world than first he'd thought.

He was, therefore, wiser.

Besides, the more he pondered, the more convinced he became that Slan had been a fool. The man had been so focused on the glory attendant upon bringing down a Basuran city that he had neglected basic military precepts.

By every account, the unexpected assault upon Slan's forces by mounted barbarians, though unquestionably terrifying and fierce, had been accomplished with a force that numbered in the mere hundreds. Had Slan's flank been defended, and the troops protected by proper defensive works as General Arrabi described, the attack would have ended at least somewhat differently, perhaps even with the barbarians routed and defeated.

The High Prince understood one basic concept of human nature very well – and that was that, in politics, an overt display of confidence trumped the uncertainty brought on by reverses every time. He fully intended to display confidence today, in front of the council. Nor would it be mere bravado – if anything, Rahm learned lessons quickly, and learned them well.

His political enemies, whatever their secret thoughts, would nonetheless be made hesitant to act upon those thoughts. Besides, despite the recent disaster in the north, those that opposed him were yet scattered, their lands and Houses divided by distance. It was those Houses that sat the political fence that he must convince of the need for continuity – one reason he had reached out to Antona when looking for a general to lead his army back into the north.

Rahm knew instinctively that he must be decisive – and act decisively. He also knew that he must maintain an appearance of normality within Farenaire and the palace, and thereby keep the reversal he'd suffered in Basura as far out of sight, and out of mind, as possible. For this reason, the palace guard stood solemnly to his right, in a solid formation upon the southern wall beneath the high windows, with their pikes held erect, resplendent in their blue and gold uniforms, and shining helms.

Once the councilors were settled in their places, he turned in his throne to face them and spoke candidly.

"The force sent northward under the command of General Slan has suffered defeat," he admitted and then went on to state what he intended should be the official view. "House Basura has blatantly attacked the forces of Mother Elam and with the aid of barbaric troops from the east, killed and captured many men – our own sons and brothers."

He let this statement settle in their ears for a moment.

Then, rising, he descended the steps that fronted the throne and walked out before the gallery of councilors. Turning to face them, he spread his arms wide. His face took on an expression of supreme sorrow.

"Those men were sent north to persuade the people of Basura to abandon the nefarious acts of the treasonous family that rules that House and return to the common fold. I do not know by what means the traitorous rulers of Basura convinced their people to continue in lawlessness – or how they bought the aid of rough, wild, uncouth folk from the wastelands. But this I will say." He held up his hand, as if to swear an oath.

"There must now be war. It cannot be avoided." He waited to see the effect of this statement on those seated in front of him.

Leeton Cinnabar refused to meet his gaze, along with a scattering of others. Most of the councilors gazed back at him stoically. Here and there, however – mostly from those who had profited by association with him, or those who feared him – there were nods of subservient agreement.

Kavnaugh Berezan met his gaze straight on but Rahm could not read the councilor's face. Councilor Berezan ruled the province from which had come Olyeg Kraine, recently named as a traitor to the throne by the High Prince himself. Kavnaugh's features, framed by short black hair and a thick beard of the same color, were as bland and still as calm water as he stared back at the man who ruled all of Elam.

If there was little trace of loyalty exhibited there, upon the face of Berezan; neither could Rahm detect the hint of treasonous intent. He moved his attention on to the others, meeting every set of eyes that deigned to look back at him.

Then he clasped his hands behind his back and continued.

"General Zelrod Slan," he stated, "whether he be now a prisoner or perhaps even dead somewhere upon the traitorous countryside of Basura –" Here he inclined his head toward Councilor Slan, the disgraced general's father and leader of House Valrie – "and who will be missed, did not take proper precautions upon the emplacement of his front lines. The Basuran traitors and their wicked allies recognized this fact and took advantage."

He nodded his head in subdued acknowledgement of the truth. "Elam's men-at-arms have suffered a setback." He stared at the floor in apparent sorrow for a long moment and then lifted his chin. "But our purpose remains unchanged. The world beyond the gates of Elam grows ever more dangerous – as the actions of these wild eastern folk demonstrate. Elam must face the challenges of a more dangerous world united in purpose and intent."

He started to form his hand into a fist, and then thought better of it. Folding his hands once more behind his back, he let his features grow solemn. "Eventually, we will have to confront these barbarians and learn *their* intent. If they mean to expand their control into Elam, they will be stopped and then destroyed." He loosed his hands and held up a cautionary finger. "First, however, we must deal with Basura. I have never wished to engage in conflict with our own citizens, but the people of that province must be persuaded of the foolishness of those that lead them astray."

Letting his gaze rove among the gallery of councilors once again, Rahm then turned and went back up the steps to his throne. He sat and looked with solemn expression over at the leaders of the Great Houses of Elam. "I have already taken measures to show House Basura the error into which it has fallen."

He leaned toward the gallery. "You will wish to discuss these matters amongst yourselves," he admitted boldly. "I ask you to take the rest of this day and the morrow for such discussions – we will meet here again on the second day from today."

With that, and without inviting discourse, he stood, turned his back on them, and left the chamber.

8.

Aram gave Thaniel his head as they went southward and the great horse established a blistering pace but one that all three horses could maintain.

The road was wide and well-paved with small pea-sized gravel that over time had been pounded hard and rendered level by the traffic that trod atop it. They passed through several small towns and villages, none of which were gated or guarded, without stopping or slowing to interact with the astonished citizenry that gaped as they drove through and went on into the south.

As they plunged ever southward, deeper into the wide green land, the mountains to the west drew further away even while the foothills that lay beneath those higher peaks dropped down and came gradually eastward until they crowded the river, which now flowed generally nearer the road.

The sun had fallen halfway down the sky to their right, toward the western horizon, when they came to a section that was familiar to Aram. He glanced leftward, toward the east, as they crossed the bridge spanning the River Shosk, into the devastated land of Basura where ruined farms and burned buildings dotted the once-lush landscape. He knew that over there to the east there were people that would be greatly relieved to learn what it was that he meant to do. Still, though, he did not stop, nor turn aside to speak to them, but let Thaniel keep driving toward the south.

They passed more small villages and way stations along the thoroughfare, and occasional travelers who turned their oxcarts off the road and into the surrounding fields when the strangers on horseback thundered down the road upon them. Aram ignored them and everything else and kept Thaniel moving. If the prince that ruled this great land possessed any means of rapid communication that might warn him of impending danger, he meant to override it.

He intended to arrive at the palace in Farenaire unexpected.

As the late evening sun slid down to sit upon the western mountains, the myriad structures of a substantial city began to rise up on the southern horizon. Aram glanced back at Marcus who correctly interpreted the inquisitive look of his lord. The young prince indicated the approaching town with his chin.

"Calom Malpas," he said.

Aram examined the road ahead and behind. Traffic had been light all day and at the moment there was no one in sight in either direction. Looking around, he sought a place of refuge for the night. Tended fields pushed up against the road from the east, and farms and outbuildings clustered darkly on the horizon. West of the road, however, the ground sloped away toward the river which along this stretch of highway was verged by untended meadowland. He glanced over at the sun. More than half of that great orb had already slid behind the mountains.

"Turn here, Thaniel," Aram said. "Let us go into the trees along the river. There is grass there for you and your people."

The horse slowed and turned off the road and pounded down through the tall grass and into the line of trees that lined the banks of the river. The great river of Elam flowed gently here; looping slowly in wide arcs; though there were also occasional stretches of rapids followed by long deep pools as the great stream fell ever so gradually toward the distant sea.

One of these pools lay immediately to their front as the river angled toward them and then bent gently away once more. Along the near shore of this slow-moving stretch of water there was a strip of sand perhaps twenty feet wide. Aram looked around at the sand bar, and then glanced back up toward the road, barely visible now in the dusk beyond the thick trees. He nodded.

"Let's get down and loosen our muscles," he told Marcus and Thom and he pointed at the bar of sand. "We can get a few hours rest away from the saddle upon that sand."

He removed his helmet and laid it aside upon a rock. Then he stretched his back and looked at Thaniel. "It will be necessary for the sun to be up and in the sky before we pass through Calom Malpas," he told the horse. "You might as well have some relief from the weight of that steel." He motioned to Marcus and Thom. "Let us give ourselves and the horses a night out of armor. We'll stash it in the trees. They can spend the night on the grass between us and the road."

After the horses were relieved of their burden of metal and released, Aram shed his own armor and started a fire on the narrow beach, close to the trees and next to a bank of rocks that had been piled there by past floodwaters. "We might as well be warm," he stated.

Thom sat down close to the fire and peered up into the hills on the far side of the river. Then he looked over at Aram.

"And if we're spotted?"

Aram shook his head. "It will not matter, captain."

Thom frowned. "You said this before, Lord Aram, up at the gates – that it wouldn't matter if we were seen." He looked back toward the road and then turned his suspicious gaze once more to the darkening hills opposite. "We are deep in hostile territory here."

Aram shook his head again. "No, Thom – we are in Elam, your homeland and that of Marcus." He indicated the surrounding countryside, and made a point of gesturing toward the far side of the river. "No one about us is the enemy; only him who sits the throne. And he will not sit there much longer."

Thom would have liked to pursue the topic, but Aram rose and went into the trees in search of more wood to feed to the fire. After staring after him for a moment, Thom looked over at Marcus, shrugged, and went into the trees also to help with gathering fuel.

Later, after they had eaten and were seated upon the sand around the fire, Aram studied the slow heavy current of the river that flowed past their campsite.

He looked over at Marcus.

"Rivers usually have names," he said.

"It's called the Sunder," Marcus told him.

"Will we follow it all the way south to the palace?"

Marcus nodded. "Mostly," he said. "We will cross over it just north of the junction where the road goes west to Farenaire."

Aram turned to watch the water for a moment longer and then stretched out with his feet toward the fire. "Let us rest," he told the others. "I want to be up before dawn to prepare the horses. We must be at the gates of Calom Malpas as soon as there is enough sun to empower the Sword."

They rose in the early twilight and by the time the sun began to show above the eastern horizon, were back upon the pavement of the road, cantering slowly southward toward the city to their front.

Aram glanced over at the emerging disc of the rising sun and then looked back at Thom and Marcus.

"Same plan as at the northern gates," he said. "Stay behind me and let the horses have their head. I will get us through and into the city quickly. Unless we are confronted, we will not stop, but go straight on through to the other side." He turned back to his front as they neared the city. "If there are troops in sizeable numbers, we will halt long enough that I may speak to them and then we will go on." He looked eastward at the rising body of the sun as he drew the Sword. "But I will tell them only what is needed, no more. I want to go far today."

Washing the Sword in the light of the new day, Aram spoke to Thaniel and the horse broke into a gallop.

The gates of Calom Malpas were open and there was an oxcart just coming through as the three mounted men stormed up. Seeing the armored beasts bearing down upon him, the driver of the cart abandoned his seat, bounded back through the gates, and leapt to the left out of sight. The terrified ox bolted off the road, dragging the bouncing cart behind him.

A man dressed in official-looking garb, and flanked by two soldiers, appeared in the road beyond the gates, just inside the city, staring toward the north in order to discover what it was that had so frightened the farmer.

Aram lowered the Sword and released its flame into the sky above the profile of the city's skyline. He was careful to hold the tangent of the crackling fire higher than the level of the rooftops. Nonetheless, deep inside the town, beyond the limits of his control, one of the lightning-like bolts arced downward and struck the roof of a building taller than its neighbors, blasting the tiles into shards and setting the roof of that building aflame.

At this, the official and his companions abandoned the road and dove for the verge, out of sight.

Thaniel, followed by the others, thundered through the open gates.

There was no large military presence as there had been at the gates in the north, so Aram twirled the flaming Sword over his head to prevent any possible foolish attempts at bravery and kept going on toward the city's interior.

Though businesses lined the road to either side; at this early hour, few people were in the streets. Proprietors of the various shops peered in terror from windows and partially opened doors as the three mounted men swept past. Very shortly, they passed the building with the burning roof, which lay along a side street that ran westward.

A few minutes more and they entered an open sort of square, bounded on all sides by large, tall buildings. This broad, open area obviously lay at the heart of the city.

"Halt!" Aram told Thaniel.

The great horse slid to a stop. Aram stood up in the stirrups and swung the Sword in a wide arc, letting its fire sing and crackle overhead. Then he sheathed the blade and looked around. Though no one was in sight, the citizenry having scurried for shelter, he was nonetheless certain that he would be heard.

"Know this – all you who hear my words," he roared. "Rahm Imrid is hereby deposed. Marcus, son of Waren, sits the throne in his stead. *Hear me – Marcus, son of Waren, is High Prince in Elam.*"

He stood high in the stirrups for a moment longer, listening to the sound of his own voice echoing along the apparently deserted streets, and then he settled into the saddle and spoke to Thaniel.

"*Go.*"

There were more official representatives of the throne at work in and around the southern gates of Calom Malpas, along with a small contingent of soldiers. Aram employed the Sword once more, scattering these officials and troops that manned the southern gates, which were also open, and they drove through and out into the open countryside.

South of Calom Malpas, the landscape of Elam broadened out. The hills over to the east curved away and disappeared beyond the horizon toward a line of hazy, distant mountains. To their right, west of the road, the river meandered southward, coiling lazily among reeds and marshes. On both sides of the road, to the west and the east, well-tended farmland covered every foot of arable ground.

Villages and sizeable towns became more numerous. Secondary roads angled away from the main thoroughfare in both directions.

Traffic increased upon the road but Aram kept driving south, scattering oxcarts and foot traffic into the farmland on either side. Off to the southwest, on their right as they drove deeper into the country, dark gray mountains, like the chipped and broken teeth of a massive predator, rose into the sky. "The Iron Mountains," Marcus responded to a questioning look from Aram. Aram studied those distant gray and jagged peaks for a long moment, among whose high wild ramparts, rumor suggested, hid the wizard, Da'nisam, who had created the gun and given it to Keegan. Then he looked back to the front, into the south of Elam.

Ahead the land rolled gently away toward the distant ocean.

Abruptly, just as they were speeding through a gentle region of large holdings of farmland where the river broadened out and looped in long slow arcs toward the south, Alvern's voice came down out of the blue. "There is a large body of men moving toward you along the road, my lord."

"How many?" Aram asked.

"Many," the eagle replied. "As many as I have ever seen in one place at one time."

Hearing this, Thom moved Norgen up beside Aram and Thaniel. "What do we do now, my lord?"

Aram looked over. "We are going to Farenaire, Thom," he replied calmly. "It matters not what stands between."

Thom gazed back with narrowed eyes for a moment and then simply nodded his head and fell back into place beside Marcus.

A mile further on, now several miles south of Calom Malpas, they topped a rise in the road and gained an unobstructed view of the countryside of southern Elam. Without prompting from Aram, Thaniel slid to a halt.

Darkening the road for miles, coming straight toward them, there were thousands of blue and gold clad troops, their helmets and the tips of their pikes gleaming in the sun. The front rank was barely a half-mile distant. Seeing the mounted men suddenly appear atop the rise, the long columns ground down slowly, like a gigantic snake bunching its muscles, and stopped. Aram studied them and then looked over at Thom.

"Recognize anyone?"

Thom leaned forward in the saddle and gazed intently at the foremost ranks of the vast Elamite army. Then, after a moment, he nodded.

"It's a long way, but that officer in front there looks like General Arrabi."

"How well do you know him?" Asked Aram.

Thom considered and then shook his head. "Not well. He was at officer training school when I was there – I think he was a sub-general then. As far as I knew him, which as I said was not well, I always thought him a solid soldier and a good man."

Aram gazed ahead for some time. Then he looked back over at Thom. "Is – *was* – he devoted to Rahm, do you think?"

Thom shook his head once more as a slight smile touched his face. "No more than any of us were, my lord. Like me, I think, he was simply dedicated to the army. Few men in the officer corps – or the ranks, for that matter – love Rahm Imrid."

Aram nodded and reached back for the Sword. "Alright," he stated, "I won't kill him then until we determine where his loyalties lie now. Let's go."

He spoke to Thaniel and the horse lunged forward. Holding the weapon above his head, he let it collect power from the sun, now well up in the sky. As they bore down upon the long column of men, the Elamite general, Arrabi, rapidly deployed his foremost ranks forward, positioning the troops across the pavement with pikes and lances lowered and ready to receive their charge.

Back along the column, other officers followed his lead, spreading the men wide. By the time Aram and his companions were within thirty yards of the front ranks, they were facing endless ranks of troops in defensive posture.

The Sword was howling, latent with power.

Aram lowered the blade.

Remembering the blazing rooftop in the town behind him, and having no desire to kill any of those gathered before him, he raised it slightly before releasing its power.

With a crackling roar, fire shot from the tip of the Sword.

As flame leapt from the end of the blade and sizzled and snapped through the air above the Elamite army, blazing with golden potency, hot and sharp with fearsome magic, the troops fell to the earth in terror as one man, abandoning any thought of defense.

Aram waved the Sword back and forth in the air above the massed ranks of troops, giving the lightning-fire time to accomplish its full measure of frightening the men that cowered on the ground beneath it.

"Halt, Thaniel," Aram commanded.

The great horse slid to a stop upon the pavement. Aram held the Sword aloft, letting flame flow through it unchecked, flaring high into the sky like bursts of power from the surface of the sun itself, and stood up tall in the stirrups. Infusing his words with rock-hard harshness, he raised his voice above the keening of the Sword.

"*Lay down your arms – or you die.*"

Many of the men had fallen to the earth atop their lances. Those that could now pulled them loose and flung them aside. Most simply lay where they were, covering their ears against the sound of the Sword's fury and hiding their eyes from its awesome power.

Aram looked back along the long line of men, watching for any signs of resistance. Seeing none, he nevertheless held the Sword high and lowered his gaze to find the man identified by Thom Sota as General Arrabi. The general was crouched down upon one knee with his hand above his forehead, shielding his eyes from the blazing fire of the Sword.

"I am not an enemy of Elam," Aram told him. "And I have no desire to slay her sons. But tell your men to abandon arms, general – *or I will kill you all.*"

Arrabi gazed up at Aram for a long moment. Then he placed his hands over his ears to mute the sound of the Sword as his eyes streamed. "Who are you?"

"*Now!*" Said Aram, ignoring the question.

Shakily, Arrabi got to his feet, though he kept his head bent forward with his hands still protecting his ears. "Lay down arms," he commanded of the officers nearest him. "Pass the word – *everyone* – lay down arms. Do it now!"

Aram held the Sword out for a moment longer, lowering it a bit to let the flame sizzle and crackle in the air overhead back along the line of troops, causing any that had gained their feet to once again dive for the cover of the weeds and ditches along the roadside. Then, deliberately, he sheathed it and raised the eye guard of his helmet. He looked down and met the frightened eyes of the Elamite officer.

"You are Arrabi?"

Arrabi pulled his hands away from the sides of his head, rubbed at his temples, and then wiped his streaming eyes. Slowly, shaking, he straightened up to stand before Aram as he nodded in assent. "I am."

Aram quickly and quietly took the man's measure. Though obviously discomfited – indeed, stricken – by the awesome display of power from the weapon borne by the terrible stranger mounted on the armored beast, he nonetheless found the courage to stand and face Aram squarely.

"Please," Arrabi asked of Aram. "Spare my men."

Though impressed by the selfless nature of the general's first request, Aram ignored it and continued to gaze into Arrabi's eyes.

"To whom do you owe your allegiance?" He asked bluntly.

The general's eyes widened at the arcane and unexpected demand of this query. He looked down at the pavement, swallowed, and considered the question for a long moment as he attempted to slow his breathing and still his rapidly pounding heart. Then, he looked back up at Aram.

"I swore allegiance to the flag of Elam," he replied.

"And what of Rahm Imrid?"

Arrabi hesitated. "High Prince Rahm sits the throne of Elam. Therefore ... he is due my faithful service."

Scowling fiercely, Aram leaned toward him and tendered another question, his tone low and harsh. "And if he is removed from the throne of this land?"

Arrabi blinked the remnants of moisture from his eyes and stared. Something like the ghost of a secret hope passed through the depths of his brown orbs as he gazed at Aram. "My allegiance is to Elam," he replied stubbornly. "He who sits the throne is due my faithful service."

Aram watched him for a moment longer until he was satisfied that he properly comprehended the man's meaning. Then he looked back along the column of men, some of whom had also once again found the courage to regain their feet though none had the nerve to retrieve his weapon.

"Where do you lead such a large body of men as this?" Aram demanded.

Arrabi swallowed once more. "To Basura."

Aram's eyes narrowed and hardened. "Chancellor Heglund Basura is a particular friend of mine," he said in a soft, dangerous voice.

The general hesitated once more. His eyes flicked away for a moment toward the unknown, helmeted companions of this strange and terrifying man before coming back to Aram's face. "Those were my orders from High Prince Rahm," he explained warily. "I only –" He discovered that he had no good answer beyond the enunciation of his mission from his prince and his voice trailed off.

"And if Rahm were no longer High Prince of this land?" Aram repeated the demand.

Arrabi drew himself up to his full height, daring the wrath of the stranger. "Then I await orders from him who comes after."

Aram leaned forward once more. "And if he who comes after be Marcus, son of Waren?"

Arrabi stared and then frowned in confusion. "I have seen Marcus, sir – forgive me, but you are not he."

"No," Aram laughed harshly, "I am not he. But he is with me and very soon he will sit the throne."

Arrabi started and glanced back at Aram's companions, both of whose identities were obscured by facial armor. He studied the two of them and then brought his gaze back to Aram. "I am a general of the army of Elam, sir. I confess to a lack of interest in all things political." He hesitated and looked around at the two subordinate officers that stood near him. "This also I confess. I have no great love of Rahm Imrid. I serve Elam and Elam alone."

After making this statement, he watched his subordinates closely until they too, both of them, nodded in agreement.

"Hear me then," Aram told them. "I go even now to depose Rahm Imrid. Marcus, son of Waren, will rule in his stead before the sun sets on the morrow."

Arrabi wiped at his eyes again and stared up at him. Slowly he nodded. "May I inquire as to your identity, sir? Are you he that rules in the far north of the world?"

"You speak as to Manon, the ally of Rahm?"

Arrabi drew in a hesitant breath. "I do."

Aram smiled grimly. "No – I am not Manon. I am the enemy of Manon." He leaned over Thaniel's head and spoke in hard tones. "I am Aram, ruler of Regamun Mediar, the ancient city of Joktan the

60

king. I have come to set you and your daughters free of the malice of Manon and of his foul minion that now sits upon the throne of Elam."

His voice grew harder. "You and your men, general, will stand aside and let us pass. Do so, and none of you will come to harm. Do it not and you will all die."

Arrabi gazed back for a moment and then turned and barked orders to his subordinates. "Clear the road. Let these men pass."

As the command began working its way back along the immense column, Arrabi looked up at Aram. "Do you mean what you say, sir? – that none of our daughters will ever again be torn from their families and borne away into the north?"

"Never again, general," Aram assured him and then he looked at Arrabi with pity as understanding came. "You have lost someone? A daughter, perhaps?"

Arrabi shook his head. "My sister," he said. "Long ago."

"The vile trade in human women perpetrated by Rahm Imrid ends with his fall from the throne," Aram told him.

Arrabi gazed back at the man upon the horse, and then he nodded his head in recognition of the new age that had come into his homeland with this strange man's arrival. "What do I do with this army?" He asked.

"Do you know Thom Sota?" Aram asked.

General Arrabi frowned in remembrance and then nodded. "I once knew a Captain Sota. He left the army some years ago."

"The very one," Aram agreed. "He has been in my army for some time now. He has seen action in the field and acquitted himself bravely and honorably. And he is no longer a captain, general. He is a commanding general. After tomorrow, in fact, your orders will come directly from him. Do you understand?"

Arrabi's eyes widened at this surprising news, but he nodded in acquiescence. "I understand, my lord. And I will obey."

Aram glanced to either side of the road, noting the wide grass verge between the roadside and the edge of the farmers' fields.

"There is room here, as long as you keep your troops near to the road. You may encamp here and await General Sota's orders." He held his hand up in caution. "I warn you to prevent your men from disturbing the fields of private citizens overmuch. From this day forward, citizens are to be treated with utmost respect. Do you understand this as well?"

Arrabi nodded in immediate agreement. "I understand and will obey." He continued to attend respectfully to Aram, but his eyes flicked away once more toward Aram's two companions. "Is Prince Marcus really with you, my lord?"

"He is," Aram assured him. "And he will sit the throne of Elam by sunset tomorrow." He looked closely at Arrabi. "You say that you have seen him?"

"I have," Arrabi affirmed.

Aram thought for a moment longer and then he turned in the saddle and looked at Marcus. "Your Highness?"

Marcus met his gaze and then deliberately reached up and removed his helmet.

Arrabi sucked in a startled breath and drew himself up to his full height. "I assure you, Your Highness – you will ever have my full and faithful service."

"Thank you, General Arrabi," Marcus replied. "I will never forget this."

Aram nodded his approval and then looked back at Arrabi. "Thank you, general." He looked southward along the road, where the Elamite troops were busily clearing the pavement to allow passage, and then brought his gaze back to Arrabi's face. Raising his hand in salute, he said simply, "Until we meet again, then."

Arrabi returned the salute. "Until our next meeting, my lord." Then he bowed to Marcus. "Welcome home, Your Highness."

Aram spoke to Thaniel and the great horse charged forward and swept southward along the road, followed by Marcus and Phagan, Thom and Norgen, galloping between seemingly endless lines of troops.

They passed through the army and continued southward into the very heart of southern Elam. Off to the southwest, the gray teeth of the Iron Mountains dominated the skyline, coming closer mile by mile. Around them, the vast green richness of southern Elam, with its countless square miles of farmland, and its many villages and towns, spread away from both sides of the road to the west and east.

While the Iron Mountains rose higher in the southwest, the distant hazy mountains off to the east gradually moved beyond the curve of the earth and faded into a green horizon of rolling farmland. Overhead, the sun wheeled through the apex of the sky and began to decline toward the west as they thundered south through villages and towns where the citizenry shrunk back into their doorways and alleyways and gazed at them in wonder, marveling at what this trio of armored men upon armored beasts could possibly mean.

Finally, as the sun fell down to touch the tops of those gray peaks in the southwest, Aram looked back at Marcus. "How far to Farenaire?"

Marcus glanced over toward the Iron Mountains drawing up on their right, looked around at the countryside where the shadows grew long on the east sides of trees and buildings, and then peered forward along the road. "I believe that we will be at the junction by nightfall, my lord."

"Is there a town at the junction?"

Marcus nodded in reply. "Mayfield is there."

"What lies between us and Mayfield?" Aram asked.

Marcus shrugged. "Mostly, more farmland." Then he raised his right hand and indicated Elam's river, flowing broad and slow a half-mile away upon their right. "The river turns eastward a few miles south and there is a bridge."

"Is there a village near the bridge?"

"No, only more farms."

Aram considered this as Thaniel continued surging into the south. He glanced over at the sun, already sliding down behind that sharp-toothed horizon. Then he looked back at Marcus. "We will camp near this bridge. I want to reach Farenaire at mid-morning."

"As you wish, my lord," Marcus replied. "The bridge over the Sunder is but a few miles north of Mayfield which is no more than two hours east of Farenaire."

9.

On the morning of the appointed day to hear the council's thoughts on his call to war, High Prince Rahm Imrid ate a quiet breakfast, dressed into his most impressive robes and went out into the council chamber where the palace guard once more stood in a solemn row along the right-hand wall. Climbing the four steps to the throne, he sat and nodded to his aide to summon the councilors from their chambers in the boarding houses that lined the avenue in front of the palace.

Minutes later, the heads of the Great Houses began filing into the hall. He watched them as he had two days earlier. On this day, those he counted among his closest allies met his gaze and nodded gravely. Most of the rest inclined their heads respectfully toward the throne and then found their places in the gallery. Cinnabar, Berezan, and certain others gave him but a passing glance and went stoically to their seats.

The various attitudes on display were a reprise of those of nearly every other council for the whole of Rahm's rule.

Rahm smiled to himself, satisfied that at last, perhaps, things were returning to normal. As the councilors sat and looked toward him expectantly, he centered his attention on the parchment upon his lap, which in fact was meaningless. He wanted to make them wait; show that he was still the master in a room filled with disciples. As he made a show of examining the document, he listened to the quiet conversations, but heard nothing untoward.

Finally, satisfied that enough time had passed, he laid the parchment aside and looked at the gathered heads of the Great Houses of Elam.

"My friends," he said. "Lessons have been learned by this court, hard lessons." He moved his hand expansively. "And out in the broad countryside of our beloved land, lines have been drawn." He held up the hand. "But, as your High Prince, I promise that our future will be one of prosperity and unity – and dissension will be dealt with to whatever length is necessary."

Rising, he prepared to descend the steps but was suddenly knocked back against the throne as the doors to the palace were blown inward by a tremendous blast.

Fire sizzled into the hall, snapping into the wall above the throne. One of the great wooden doors came loose with a loud crash, falling inward and sliding across the floor, mowing down several of the guards.

The councilors abandoned their chairs and dove for cover, cowering in the spaces around their seats, staring toward the doors with wide, frightened eyes.

Into the hall burst an enormous metal-clad beast. Upon the beast's back rode a man dressed in gold-trimmed black armor, and in his right hand he held a shining sword from which flame sizzled and crackled.

10.

Aram had awakened that morning while the sky in the east showed just a hint of pink. Blinking the sleep from his eyes, he sat up and gazed around in the gloom.

Thom and Marcus still slept, though Thom stirred restlessly toward wakefulness. Thaniel was down on the gravel by the river with his nose lowered into the water. Rising, Aram went down over the grassy bank onto the gravel bar to stand beside the horse.

"Good morning, my lord," the horse said quietly.

"Good morning, my friend. Do you understand what I intend to do when we get to the palace in Farenaire?" Aram asked him.

The horse raised his streaming muzzle and looked at him. "I do," he replied. "Of course. Why? Are there special instructions for me?"

"No." Aram shook his head. "You know my mind as well as anyone. I mean for you to bear me straight into the hall. Just stay near me once inside and watch for treachery."

The horse gazed at him for a moment and then gave his reply. "I always do, my friend," he said.

Aram reached out and laid one hand on the horse's massive shoulder. "Yes, I know."

Thaniel swung his head around and looked eastward, where the sky was beginning to brighten toward morning. Then he turned back to Aram. "After our young friend is seated upon the throne of Elam – what then?"

"Then we go home and spend a quiet winter in the valley."

"And after the winter is past?" The horse persisted.

Aram treated Thaniel to a grim smile. "Then I will accept Manon's invitation and go to his tower."

"Just we two?"

Aram glanced over sharply. "There is no need for you to go. I will only need you to bring me near to him."

"Where you go, I will go," Thaniel replied in a fierce voice. "I want my part in vengeance."

Aram watched him without speaking for several minutes. "I will need you to bear me into the north – to his valley," he said then. "It may not be possible for you to enter the tower."

"I will go as far as I can," the horse insisted. "But will we not lead an army to his gates?"

Aram shrugged. "There is no need to endanger the life of anyone else. He wants this Sword – I saw it in his eyes when he spoke to me in the Deep Darkness." He gazed across the river and then raised his eyes and stared into the darkness of the northern sky. "I believe it to be his great weakness. His lust for it will allow me into his presence. If I can get close to him and pierce him with this blade – it will destroy him, of that I am certain."

"If this be your wish, I will wait outside – but nearby," the horse replied as he followed Aram's lead and gazed into the north. But then he turned his head to look fully at Aram. "I have been thinking, my lord. You told me on the day that the dragons slew my father and mother that vengeance would not cost my life. But neither do I wish for vengeance at the cost of yours. How will you escape once he is slain?"

Aram shook his head and started to speak but then closed his mouth and stared into the low trees just now taking shape in the morning twilight beyond the dark current of the Sunder. After a long moment of silence, he said, "I must trust in the Sword of Heaven. The Sword will get me in – and the Sword will get me out."

"Are you certain of this?" The horse persisted.

Aram started to shrug, but then just shook his head. "No, but I must have hope, do I not?" He looked at Thaniel. "I want to live. I have reason to live, and I will try very hard to make it so." He sighed and turned away and looked once more toward the north. "But whether I live or die, I must destroy him."

"I have thought about that as well," Thaniel said. "Why must he die?"

Surprised by this, Aram looked at him sharply. "How else can this end?" He demanded.

Thaniel met his gaze and then swung his head away and gazed across the river. "Can we not simply fence him in?" He asked. "Why cannot we destroy his armies – render him powerless; and then place a guard around his tower?" He looked back at Aram. "He would be a prisoner, nothing more."

Aram felt a small flame of hope flicker into life in his mind as he considered this. But then, as quickly as it had ignited, it flickered weakly and winked out. He shook his head. "Manon's real power is not in his armies, my friend. He is strong – very strong – in himself. Even without minions to do his bidding, he would nonetheless find a means of troubling the world. Armies will not contain him." He sighed again. "No, he must die; and I must slay him."

The horse kept his gaze directed away as he replied. "If you say this be true; then I trust you. Just do not die, Aram. I cannot imagine a world without you in it. Indeed, I cannot live in such a world."

Aram started to laugh but then stopped himself. He watched Thaniel for a long moment but the horse did not turn toward him. Aram said then, "You were alive in the world long before I came into it, my friend."

"Yes," the horse agreed, as at last he swung his head around to look at Aram. His large dark eyes were grave. "But your coming into the world changed everything. You must live to finish that which you have begun."

Above the eastern horizon, the morning brightened further. Behind them, up on the bank beneath the arching bridge, Marcus and Thom stirred. Thaniel backed away from the river's edge. "Let us go and place a friend upon the throne of Elam," he said. "That will leave us free to resolve these other matters."

Aram smiled as he nodded. "Just so," he agreed.

The sun rose above the horizon as they clattered through the streets of Mayfield and turned west upon the broad, smooth track that would take them to Farenaire. Ahead of them the Iron Mountains rose up vast, dark, and forbidding, despite the fact that they were fully lit by the luminance of the new day's sun.

Less than an hour later, Farenaire showed ahead of them, clustered upon the low hills that tumbled up at the feet of those dark mountains.

Aram spoke to Thaniel and the horse came to a halt in the roadway. Aram turned around in the saddle and looked at the sun. The great disc was fully in the sky but still low, near to the horizon. He motioned for Marcus and Thom to come up alongside him.

"Are there many troops in the town?" He asked them both.

Thom nodded. "Marcus can answer as to how many guards are in the palace itself, but Rahm keeps a sizeable contingent quartered in the fort just to the south of the city."

Aram nodded and looked over at Marcus.

"The palace was not designed to be military in nature, so there is no parapet and there are no towers," the young prince told him. "But Rahm is very cognizant of his personal safety, so he keeps a company of guards near the doors and several more inside the hall itself."

"Twenty troops – fifty – or a hundred – how many are there?" Aram insisted.

Marcus thought for a moment. "About forty," he replied. "Twenty or so are stationed outside by the doors and approximately the same inside the hall. At least that was his wont in the past. I have not been to the palace in several months," he reminded Aram.

Aram brushed this aside. "Describe the interior of the hall."

Marcus folded his hands on the pommel of the saddle and considered. "It is an ancient building – built many hundreds of years ago by an ancestor of mine named –"

Aram held up his hand and smiled thinly. "I care nothing of its history, Marcus, for the moment at least. Tell me of its layout."

Marcus grinned sheepishly and nodded. "The interior is about a hundred feet long and nearly as wide. If you stand inside the doors, looking toward the throne which sits against the back wall, the councilors sit to the right, upon tiered seats, the most important on the first, lower tier, and the others behind. There are three tiers of seats. Behind them are tall windows.

"To the left is an opposing wall, also with high windows. The guards stand there, facing the councilors. There are many tapestries hanging just above them, between them and the windows, depicting scenes from the lives of previous High Princes of Elam. The throne, as I stated, is at the far end, raised up to just above the level of the topmost tier of the councilors' seats.

"There is a door immediately behind the throne which leads into Rahm's private quarters. Overhead is a skylight."

Aram looked at him sharply. "A skylight? How large is this skylight?"

"It's quite large," the young prince responded. "Brammen – the High Prince who built the hall – wanted that the whole interior be lit by natural light."

Aram nodded and glanced once more at the sun, climbing the sky behind them. Then he looked back at Marcus. "Tell me about the entrance."

"There are two double doors on the near side, looking eastward along the main street of Farenaire."

"So the main street ends at the hall?"

Marcus nodded. "The hall of the High Prince is the whole reason for the existence of the town."

"Are the doors tall enough to allow Thaniel ingress?" Aram asked.

Marcus frowned and looked at him for a long moment and seemed to want to ask a question of his own, but then simply nodded. "They are quite tall indeed. I believe that you could ride Thaniel right through into the hall if you wanted, my lord."

"Good," Aram replied. "That is what I intend to do."

Ignoring Marcus' wide eyes and raised eyebrows, he looked again at the sun. "Does this road lead onto the main road and thence up to the doors of the palace?"

Marcus nodded. "Yes, my lord; this road becomes the main street of Farenaire once it enters the town. It ends at the palace."

"And the councilors are there now – inside the hall?"

Marcus pivoted in the saddle and took his own view of the rising sun. Slowly, he nodded. "They should enter the hall within the hour, my lord. The morning session usually begins after breakfast."

Aram looked over at Thom. "Will the troops from the fort be inside the city itself? In the streets?"

After considering the question, Thom shook his head. "Not in times past – not to my knowledge. Certainly not at this time of day." He shrugged his shoulders and chuckled. "Besides, those particular troops are not known for their toughness. Being part of the High Prince's 'personal army' was always understood to be an easy post."

"Alright," Aram said. "Here is what I mean to do. I intend to go through the doors – Thaniel will bear me in. You two will follow close behind and ride into the hall as well." He looked at Marcus. "Once inside, you will turn to the right and dismount next to door closest to where the council sits. Show your face only when I give you the sign." Then he turned to Thom. "Stay mounted if you think it necessary, general, but I want you to take immediate command of the palace guard. I have no doubt that they will be somewhat frightened by events and therefore submissive to your will."

Both men nodded in silent understanding. Marcus cast a furtive glance at Thom and then asked Aram, "What do you mean to do with Rahm, my lord?"

Aram looked at him sharply. "He murdered your family, Your Highness – he requires judgment and there must be retribution. As a consequence, he will not survive the day. Elam is your land, Your Highness, and the palace is rightly *your* house. One does not leave a poisonous snake alive to wander at will in his own house."

"But, that means that you intend –" Marcus stared. "My lord – *we have laws in Elam*. They have stood for thousands of years and govern the actions of every citizen from the High Prince down to the least of us."

"I understand this," Aram agreed. "But I am not subject to your laws, my friend. Nor, it seems to me, is Rahm Imrid, at least in his mind." His eyes narrowed. "And we are at war. Manon will not wait while we take care to abide by every letter of your ancestors' edicts. I will not slay Rahm for any crime he has committed against you, Basura, or even the land of Elam itself. None of that is within my purview. No – I will destroy him because he is allied with my enemy, and is therefore my enemy and subject to my laws. Nothing in writ or word will dissuade me. Do you understand this?"

Marcus swallowed and stared for a moment longer. Finally, without speaking further, he nodded.

Turning his attention back to the city a few miles to his front, Aram sat for some while longer in silence as the sun climbed higher behind him. Then he lowered the eye guard on his helmet and urged Thaniel forward. "It is time," he said.

Thaniel lunged ahead and pounded westward along the center of the road, followed closely by the others. There was little traffic moving upon the streets of the capitol city of Elam as they drove into town and began to ascend toward the grand palace upon the low hill at the other end of the main thoroughfare.

Those citizens that were abroad, upon seeing three armored and mounted warriors thundering into their town, bolted for doors and alleyways, anywhere out of the way of these dangerous-looking men and their terrifying beasts.

The palace of the High Prince of Elam rose up before them. An impressive structure, it sat atop the highest point in the town which sat at the feet of the foothills of the distant Iron Mountains. The lines of the structure were simple yet elegant, with fluted buttresses on each corner. It was built of a pale tan stone that shone faintly gold in the morning sun. A second story of the structure, fronted by a balustrade and veranda that stretched across the whole of its front, rose above and just behind the main hall that jutted out from the main part of the palace toward the avenue. This part that jutted out, which contained the Hall of Councilors, was in itself very impressive, and was fronted by a massive pair of doors. Above the twin doors, there was a large round window made of colored glass.

Two hundred yards from the palace, as Thaniel galloped through a district comprised of businesses that crowded the main road, Aram drew the Sword and held it high, up into the sunlight.

In front of the palace, there were a dozen or so soldiers at their posts, half standing to one side of the wide, tall doors and half to the other side. Seeing the approaching horses and their riders, these men momentarily attempted to adopt defensive positions even as they subconsciously slid away to either side. Then, their tenuous courage giving away completely, they leapt out of the path of the black and massive armored horse that led the others, driving down upon them.

For it immediately became obvious that this great armored beast and its rider intended to charge right into them; maybe even intended to crash through the palace doors.

At the corners of the palace, the two groups tried once more to summon bravery and make some sort of stand.

Fifty yards from the doors, Aram lowered the Sword.

"Move aside or die!" He shouted and let loose a flash of fire.

This was too much for men whose duties up to this point had been to stand about and look impressive. As one man, they dove for the alleyways to either side of the palace.

72

Aram aimed the Sword at the center, where the doors came together, and released almost all of the accumulated power stored in the blade, a great bolt of flame.

With a flash of fire and a loud Bang! the doors blew inward. The door on the left, which had received the worst of it, came off its hinges and slid into the interior where it found the row of guards standing in a line next to the wall, knocking most of them off their feet, injuring several, and breaking the leg of at least one.

Thaniel charged up the steps and into the hall, sliding to a halt near the middle of the floor. Phagan slid in as well and spun to the right, depositing Marcus next to the door. Norgen and Thom moved up next and halted a bit behind Aram on his left.

Holding the balance of the blade's fire in check, Aram quickly took stock of the interior of the hall. To his front, a man he assumed to be Rahm Imrid sat hunched against the high back of his throne, staring at Aram with rounded eyes. To the right, forty or fifty men in fine robes cowered in their seats. Lacking anything substantial behind which they might hide, these men all attempted, with limited success, to make themselves small.

To Aram's left, there were about twenty soldiers, the bulk of whom had risen to their feet and stood clumped up together, gazing at him in fear and wonder. A few held their lances pointed in his general direction but none seemed willing to confront him. One man writhed in obvious pain upon the floor, holding his left leg, which lay at an odd angle.

Aram lowered the Sword at the guards and let a bit a flame leap to its end where it snapped and popped.

"*Lay down your weapons or I will destroy you all.*"

Twenty lances clattered immediately to the floor.

Aram looked over at Thom. "Take command of these men, General." He moved the blade, indicating the injured man. "And see to their wounded."

There was still power stored in the blade. Needing a means of release, Aram looked up at the skylight. It was a relatively simple affair, built of crossed beams with squares of thick glass between.

He chose one of the transparent squares above his head, aimed the Sword up toward it, and released the rest of its flame.

As the bolt of golden lightning shot out through the skylight in the ceiling, shattering the glass and sizzling into the sky above the palace, the man upon the throne cringed and the councilors tried in vain to make themselves even smaller.

Aram dismounted and sheathed the Sword. Raising the eye-guard in his helmet, he looked toward the councilors. *"Sit."*

There was a moment of terrified bustling while the leaders of Elam regained their seats. During this moment, Aram turned away from them and studied Rahm Imrid. The High Prince of Elam, though frightened and confused by the events of the preceding minute, seemed to grasp that if he did not try to regain a measure of control over the situation in his hall, the fullness of his life's work in rising to rule over the greatest nation on earth teetered on the very edge of a precipice.

Finding a scrap from a deeply buried reservoir of courage, Rahm rose to his feet and stood on the top step before his throne.

"Who are you?" He demanded in a loud yet shaking voice. "How dare you invade my hall in this manner?"

Without answering, Aram took one step toward him. Rahm flinched and stumbled, and only just managed to stay on his feet.

Aram lifted his gauntleted right hand and pointed a finger at him. "Speak again, without invitation," he stated harshly, "and you lose your tongue."

Then he lowered his hand and turned away from the cringing Rahm to face the councilors, most of whom shrank from beneath his gaze.

"Your High Prince wishes to know my name," he told them. "No doubt you desire to know it as well."

He studied them for a moment, letting his gaze rove over them, noting which of them attempted to meet his eyes openly despite their fear and which of them shared Rahm Imrid's stark terror – terror born of the conviction that this frightening man was very likely not a friend of Elam's current ruler.

"I am Aram, Lord of the North." Noting the widening of many of the sets of eyes that stared back at him from the gallery, he shook his head. "No, I am not he that steals your daughters from you to give to his vile beasts. I am not he that sends those same vile beasts to enslave your neighbors and ravage their lands."

He lifted the accusing finger once more and pointed to his left, centering it again upon Rahm. "I am the enemy of Manon the Grim – he whom your High Prince names as an ally."

Slowly, deliberately, he lowered the arm and turned to face Rahm. He moved one step closer and halted.

"Tell me, *Your Highness*; how did your brother, Waren, die?" He asked. "What were the circumstances of his death?"

The High Prince's gaze flitted back and forth, looking for aid in his ruined hall. There was none to be found. Thom had gathered the guards together, disarmed them, and piled their weapons over near the far wall. None showed any impulse toward resistance. On the other side of the room, his councilors, the heads of the Great Houses, some of whom feared him, some of whom detested him, and nearly all of whom hated him, sat silent and unmoving in the fearsome presence of the armor-clad stranger.

Rahm Imrid was trapped, like a rat cornered in his own hole, with the serpent not just at the door but already inside.

With courage born of desperation, he dared to meet Aram's eyes. "M-my brother died of illness," he answered. "Something got into the water supply."

Aram nodded. "Just so," he agreed softly. "Something was indeed placed into the palace water supply. And this 'something' is known as nectar of niessuh. Hurack Soroba placed it there."

There were scattered gasps from the gallery at this statement but its effect upon Rahm Imrid was to give him the perception of an opportunity to slide free of the coils of the serpent and convince the predator to focus his sharp attention upon another.

Who this man was that named himself "Aram" and had entered his hall with such violence, Rahm did not know. Whether he was a friend of Waren's come seeking revenge for the decade-old loss of comradeship or if he was a hitherto unknown enemy of Hurack Soroba did not matter at the moment.

If the stranger's desire was as simple as revenge and he already had seized upon Soroba as a likely culprit, Rahm was more than willing to aid him in turning his attention to his former compatriot. *Anything to get this man to leave his hall.* Corrective security measures could be taken later.

"Yes – I'd always suspected it," Rahm blurted out. "Soroba was a changed man after he allied with Manon – deceptive and untrustworthy." Cautiously, he turned away from Aram to look at the gallery. "If what this man states be true, then this I swear – I will arrest Soroba upon his return to Elam and we will discover the truth of the matter."

He turned back toward Aram to find the unknown "Lord of the North" gazing directly at him. Flinching at what he saw in those fierce green eyes, he nonetheless plowed forward. "I promise you, sir," he told Aram, "we will find the truth of your assertion and exact justice."

Aram took another step toward him, causing the Prince to shrink ever so slightly back into his throne.

Aram halted and spread his hands. "I have already found the truth and exacted justice," he told Rahm. "Soroba lies dead, along with his contingent of beasts, upon the southern edge of the great plains of the north."

Rahm's eyes widened in alarm at this statement and his terror returned. "I-I am very glad to hear that justice was visited upon him," he stammered. "But – if the matter has been rectified, sir – then ..... what do you seek here?"

Aram watched him with cold eyes for a long moment and then pivoted back to the gallery of councilors. "Before he died, Hurack Soroba admitted to me that the reason for the murder of High Prince Waren and his family was this – Manon wished for Rahm to sit the throne of Elam, for that would render Elam more compliant to his designs upon the world."

After hearing this accusation, Rahm breathed heavily for a moment and then managed to shout out, "*Lies!*"

Aram looked over at him. "Which of these assertions do you declare to be a lie, sir?"

The High Prince's breath came fast and haltingly. "*All of them.* I swear I had nothing to do with the death of my brother!"

Aram turned to face him and took another step toward the throne. "The dying testimony of Hurack Soroba directly contradicts you – and you name him a liar?"

"I – yes, I do."

Aram was now less than ten feet from the throne. He watched Rahm in silence for another long moment and then turned back to the gallery of councilors. "Many of you know Hurack Soroba – or *knew* him. He swore that Rahm Imrid knew of his brother's impending murder, along with that of nearly his entire family, and approved of it."

He let silence fall for a moment and then continued. "I know what I believe to be true, and will act upon that truth whatever any of you decides. Nonetheless, I will put it to you to consider." His hard eyes swept the gallery. "*Which of you think that Soroba lied?*"

More than thirty pairs of eyes gazed back at him, all of them completely engrossed in the drama of the moment – and utterly terrified, all of them wondering if what this fierce stranger intended next would directly touch them.

Fixing them with sharpened eyes, Aram pressed them. "Who lied? – Rahm Imrid or Hurack Soroba? *Speak.*"

Silence fell once more and thickened inside the hall.

After a time, during which Aram watched them in silence, ignoring Rahm, one of the councilors cleared his throat and stood. This man was strongly built, of average height, with short, thick, black hair and a short beard of the same color. He drew in a deep breath, shot one quick glance down the hall at Rahm, and then addressed Aram.

"I do not know you, sir, nor do I know what you intend here today as it concerns me and my fellows on the council. But this I will say, whatever happens to me – Rahm Imrid murdered his brother." The man looked again toward the High Prince, drew in another breath, and plunged on. "Understand – I have no regard for Hurack Soroba. He was as vile a man as ever walked the earth. But if he says that Rahm was complicit in the death of Waren and his family, I believe him, for I have thought this for some time without proof or witness."

"Who are you?" Aram asked the man.

"I am Kavnaugh Berezan, head of House Berezan."

Aram turned to face him and watched him closely. "Do you know Marcus, son of Waren?"

Berezan nodded. "I know him, sir – or at least I did, before he disappeared." He cast a dark scowl in the direction of the High Prince. "I have often wondered if Rahm Imrid has slain him as well."

Aram nodded. "More than just you have shared that fear." He turned back to face the gallery straight on and let his gaze move among the other councilors. "Tell me," he said. "How many of you believe Rahm Imrid to be innocent in the deaths of Waren Imrid and his family? I will accept your silence as belief in his guilt."

Silence fell and lengthened.

None spoke or rose to defend their ruler in the face of the tall, dangerous "Lord of the North".

Aram pivoted away from them and faced the throne.

Rahm Imrid's features were ashen. While Aram's attention was focused upon the gallery of councilors, the High Prince had feverishly searched his mind for some means of extricating himself from the alarming situation into which he had been placed but had found nothing. The rat was back in the corner of his hole and the attention of the serpent had fallen full upon him once more.

Aram walked slowly, deliberately, toward him, making the High Prince flinch and attempt to meld with the high back of his throne.

"It seems," Aram stated softly as he stalked toward Rahm Imrid, "that none of your closest advisors believes you innocent of murder." He held up his hand, cutting off Rahm's protestations. "You have been adjudged guilty by those that know you best."

He halted five feet from the bottom of the steps below where Rahm tried desperately to slink back into the recesses of his throne. "But hear this – I do not hereby condemn you for the murder of your brother, in which I have no doubt you were complicit," Aram told him. He shook his head and his voice became quieter. "Nor do I condemn you for the crimes committed in your name against your own people in the towns and villages of Basura. All those things are the province of others."

At this, a tiny measure of hope seeped into Rahm Imrid's eyes, replacing an equally small bit of the terror that had taken up residence there.

Aram continued to watch him, resisting the urge to look back toward Marcus, still fully armored and as yet unrevealed, standing by the door. "As Prince Marcus recently reminded me, this land has its own laws – laws to which I am not subject and which I may not enforce. And I accept that judgment."

With this declaration, the High Prince sat up a bit straighter. Desperate hope began to brighten the dark corners of his face. His eyes narrowed toward normal size and a hint of the old shrewdness showed in their depths.

Aram's next words dashed it all. "That for which I condemn you is perhaps not worse than those particular crimes, but it afflicts the world at large in a most despicable manner."

He moved forward and came to the bottom of the steps that led up to the throne. His eyes hardened further, making Rahm Imrid shrink away from him. "I condemn you for the enslavement and the deaths of thousands of the daughters of Elam – lives you sacrificed willingly that Manon the Grim might increase his vile minions and you could rule this land in the stead of a much better man than you have ever been – your brother."

He climbed up two steps, to within sword's reach of the terrified man upon the throne. "The monsters produced from the wombs of the daughters of your own people have caused death and destruction throughout the world of men – and is therefore a crime against humankind itself. It is for that crime that I judge you unworthy to rule – *or even to live.*"

It was in that moment that Aram realized that he had not brought a steel sword with him on the journey into Elam. The only weapon at his disposal was the Sword of Heaven. He had no desire to do further harm to the hall that he intended to leave in the care of his young friend, Marcus.

Nor did he wish to inflict a terrible scene of gruesomeness upon those watching. But there was no alternative.

He must, he realized, make quick work of it.

There was a moment of thick, intense quiet as he and Rahm Imrid faced each other.

Then Rahm's eyes flew wide, as if in that awful moment he finally understood that his life had just been declared forfeit by the man standing before him.

He threw up his hands. "You *cannot* –!"

"I can," Aram said.

Quickly, he drew the Sword and pierced the body of the man on the throne, leaving it in him for just a moment to make certain that death attended it.

But he left it too long.

Initially, when the blade pierced him, Rahm made a small bleating sound, like that of a sheep or a rabbit, but then he gasped, his mouth flew open, blood gushed forth.

An instant later his body burst into flame. Aram quickly pulled the Sword free, but it was too late to avoid the hideousness that he had wished to avoid.

The flames engulfed Rahm's body, even as he writhed and died, destroying him utterly. Within moments his flesh, his bones, and his clothing were entirely consumed, leaving only a smoldering heap of ash.

Astonished by the suddenness and completeness of the man's destruction, Aram stepped back and sheathed the blade.

11.

As he watched the fire consume Rahm's mortal remains, reducing him to ash, Aram became afraid that the fire would spread, setting the wooden throne aflame, sweeping through the great hall itself. He needn't have worried. Fortunately, and for reasons Aram could not fathom, the flame remained entirely contained in Rahm Imrid's person. When he was gone, the fire died out. Moments later, the smoke began to dissipate as well.

Aram turned and walked once more to the center of the room where he pivoted to face the gallery of councilors.

Shock registered on every face and more than a few were given completely over to horror.

By this time there was nothing to see upon the seat of the throne but smoldering ash and a dark stain caused by the intensity of the fire. The wide eyes of every head of the Great Houses of Elam gradually turned away from that stunning sight and focused again on the man that had just ended the criminal reign of Rahm Imrid.

Aram gave them a long moment in which to fully grasp that which had just occurred, then,

"I know none of you," he stated calmly. "I know not whether you are good men or bad, honest men or no." He let his gaze rove the gallery. "I have no political standing in this land nor do I wish it. Nonetheless," he said, "I require something of you."

He went silent and waited.

There followed a few moments of confusion as the councilors gradually realized that he did not mean to continue. Did he mean for them to guess at the nature of his "requirement"? As the silence lengthened, they looked around at each other in uncertainty. Then, over to the left, a tall, thin, elderly man with white hair and a long white beard rose to his feet.

Aram turned his gaze upon him but said nothing.

The tall man nervously cleared his throat. "You stated that you require a thing from us, sir. Then you said nothing further. May I – may we – ask what it is that you seek from us?"

"What is your name?" Aram asked him.

"I am named Leeton Cinnabar, head of House Cinnabar," the man replied.

Aram waved one hand toward the throne. "A loyal supporter of High Prince Rahm Imrid?"

The man flushed and drew himself up to his full and rather impressive height. "*Never!*" He glanced around at his fellows and then brought his eyes back to Aram. "Whatever you do with the rest of us, sir, I will say this – I am glad that he is gone."

Aram looked at him intently, until he was certain of the veracity of the elderly man's declaration. Then, satisfied, "And what is your standing on this council?" He asked him.

"I am the first in age and the second in time served behind Heglund Basura," Cinnabar replied. "As such, I would be next in line to be named Chancellor should Chancellor Basura retire from that post." He hesitated and looked down for a moment. When he looked up once more, his features were constricted with anger. "I should say, sir, that such would be my standing if the ancient ways were observed. But Rahm Imrid abandoned the old ways. After Heglund Basura ceased coming to the council, Rahm Imrid largely ignored protocol."

He turned his eyes upon the now quiet pile of ash. A look of intense revulsion crossed his face. "I suspect the former High Prince took council with no one except his own ambition."

When Aram did not respond, Cinnabar looked around at his companions once more and then, once again, cleared his throat. "I ask you again, sir, with respect – what is it that you require of us? Do you require our obeisance?"

"No," Aram answered. "I require the resolution to a question. Namely – it is this. Upon the death of Rahm Imrid, who will rightly ascend to the throne of this land?"

Cinnabar did not hesitate. "Were he here, Marcus, son of Waren, would rightly rule in his uncle's – I should say his *father's* – stead."

Aram nodded and glanced around the gallery. "And what say the rest of you?" He demanded. "What say you all?"

Kavnaugh Berezan stood. "Leeton is right," he said. "The throne of Elam rightly belongs to Waren's son, Marcus." He hesitated and glanced over at Cinnabar. "I must tell you, however, that we have not seen Marcus in some time, nor has there been news of him. Some of us greatly fear that Rahm slew his nephew in secret."

Aram nodded. "I understand this; nevertheless I must hear the consensus of this council. If he lives, does Marcus, son of Waren, inherit the throne of Elam? Or is there another?"

Berezan shook his head. "There is no other. Every member of Waren's family died in the palace tragedy – except for Rahm and Marcus."

Aram held up his hand. "Thank you, sir; but I wish to hear the consensus of this council. If he lives – does Marcus ascend?"

Several voices spoke at once. "He does."

Seated near the center of the gallery, a short, stocky councilor glanced around and then rose. He was dressed in layers of finery, purple and blue. Chains of gold fastened his cloak across his ample torso, stretching in gleaming splendor from button to button.

"I agree," he began, meeting Aram's gaze cautiously, "That if he lives, Marcus Imrid inherits the rule of Elam." He glanced to either side before bringing his wary gaze back to Aram. "But if he does not live – or cannot be found, there is a process by which this council chooses a successor. It has occurred twice before in the history of this land." He hesitated and cleared his throat.

Grasping the wide lapels of his cloak with either hand, he continued, watching Aram with expressions of both shrewdness and caution fighting for control of his features. "You stated, sir, that you seek no standing in this land." He hesitated again. "Does this mean that you will leave the matter with us where – as you yourself admitted – it rightly resides?"

"I want to hear the consensus of the council," Aram reminded him.

The portly man blinked and glanced to either side, self-importantly. "But I believe you have heard the consensus, sir. If Marcus lives, he ascend the steps, if he does not –"

"What is your name?" Aram interrupted him.

The man's sense of his own importance expanded as he gave his reply. "I am Bordo Bufor, first son of House Waurph, and as such mayor of Calom Malpas, a fine city of some substance in the north of this land."

Aram nodded without expression. "I know of Calom Malpas," he stated. "And what is your standing in this chamber, sir? Why do you feel as if you can speak for the council?"

Bufor blinked his heavy-lidded eyes again, several times in rapid succession. "I did not mean – it's just that the High Prince and I –" His voice trailed off as his gaze fell involuntarily upon the pile of ash on the seat of the throne.

"I meant what I said, Bordo Bufor," Aram stated quietly. "I wish to hear the consensus of this council – not one man's opinion of that consensus." He smiled thinly. "I suspect, however, that your name is one I will want to remember."

Bufor puffed out his chest momentarily at this, but then his perceptive gaze caught the look in Aram's eyes. His own gaze flicked once more toward the dusty remains of the former High Prince and he sat down rather abruptly.

Aram then polled the members of the council one by one, making them say their names and rendering a sure judgment upon the identity of Rahm's rightful successor.

To a man, they expressed the conviction that Marcus, if he could be found alive, would rightly take the reins of Elam. All stated it willingly, some eagerly, and some grudgingly. Many stated it matter-of-factly, as if the general view of the council was more important to them, and carried more weight with them, than any personal consideration.

When each had spoken, Aram let silence fall. The morning sun climbed toward noon, its rays finding their way down into the hall through the skylight with its one shattered pane.

"Marcus is alive," he said then. "And I know where he may be found. He will come in time and stand upon this very spot where I now stand – and you will name him High Prince of Elam."

There were audible gasps from the gallery at this remark and Leeton Cinnabar came to his feet.

"Is he nearby?" The old man asked.

Aram held up his hand. "Patience. There is one thing yet that I require of each of you."

Cinnabar frowned but returned to his seat and went silent. All of them watched Aram expectantly.

Aram stepped close to the foremost tier of seats and spoke in harsh tones. "Prince Marcus is alive and will reveal himself at his own volition." He let his hard gaze rove over the assembled leaders of Elam, letting it linger on each of those whose support of Marcus had been expressed in less than enthusiastic manner.

"Hear this warning," he went on, and his voice grew harsher. "High Prince Marcus is my friend. You have witnessed my power – but a small portion of it. Remember well what you have seen here today. Beyond the borders of your land, my word is law. Betray Marcus – any one of you – and I will return and I will find you. I will destroy you. *I will burn you to ash.*"

At this blunt threat, the widened eyes of every councilor went involuntarily to the powdery remains of Rahm Imrid.

"Now," Aram went on. "How will the change in the fortunes of Elam be announced throughout the land? Is there a process by which the people are notified of the ascension of a new High Prince?" He looked expectantly at Cinnabar and Berezan.

It was Berezan that answered. "There are heralds, official mouthpieces of the throne that dwell in Farenaire. They will be sent forth into the land – each with a writ from the Chancellor of this council." He looked over at Leeton Cinnabar. "Which, in the absence of Heglund Basura, must be you, my friend."

Aram looked at Councilor Cinnabar as well. "Do it then," he commanded. "Sign the writ and send it forth. Do so at once."

Cinnabar stood but then hesitated and looked at Aram. "And you will produce Prince Marcus?"

"High Prince Marcus," Aram corrected him, and with that he turned and looked toward the armored man standing to the left of the entrance to the hall. "Your Highness?"

Marcus reached up and removed his helmet.

The entire gallery came to its feet, all of them uttering exclamations of amazement, and many of joy.

As Marcus walked toward the center of the room, Aram inclined his head in respect and moved aside. "Forgive the damage done to your hall, Your Highness," He stated in a voice that all could hear. "I did not intend to add to the sum of those things requiring repair. And now, by your leave, I will say farewell."

Marcus halted in surprise and gazed at him, for the moment ignoring the gallery of men that had just become his councilors. "You are leaving us, my lord?"

"I am needed elsewhere, as you know well." Aram responded. "I am no longer needed here. I wish to return to my own land and see to my affairs there." He looked up at the broken skylight and then at the ruined entrance at the front of the hall. "Again, my friend, I am sorry for the damage done here today."

Marcus waved his hand dismissively. "It is nothing. There are other things in Elam in greater need of repair. We are – all of us – greatly in your debt, my lord."

Aram inclined his head to the young High Prince once more. "Then by your gracious leave, Your Highness, I will say farewell."

After meeting Aram's eyes for a long moment, Marcus bowed his own head in reply. "Of course, my lord. I thank you for this – and for all that you have done for me. I wish that you would stay for a time that you might enjoy the hospitality of my house. But if you say that you cannot; then I understand."

Aram shook his head. "I cannot."

Marcus watched him for a moment longer and then bowed. "Thank you, my lord. Journey well."

"Call upon me at need, my friend," Aram replied and then he moved toward where Thaniel had gone to stand by the door. As he did so, he looked at Thom and raised his hand in salute. "Until we meet again, General."

Thom inclined his head and returned the salute. "Travel well, my lord."

Aram led Thaniel out of the hall and down the steps where he mounted up and they went eastward toward the distant main road. Citizens stood in doorways and peered from windows, watching his exit from their town open-mouthed.

Aram sent a thought skyward. "Go ahead of me, if you will, Lord Alvern, and examine the road that I will travel as I leave this land. If there is nothing which requires a warning for my attention, then go on into the north, onto the plains. See if there are any slave trains of the grim lord near enough to Cumberland that I may disrupt them. If there are – return and tell me so."

"You will attack them singly, my lord?" The eagle asked.

"I will."

"And you do not require that I watch the road before you as you journey forth from Elam?"

"I do not think there will be any trouble, my friend."

"Then I will do as you wish, my lord," Alvern replied.

After reaching the junction at Mayfield, Thaniel turned to the left and drove northward with his might. Before evening fell, they once again made contact with General Arrabi, bivouacked near the road with his soldiers where Aram had left him on the previous day.

"High Prince Marcus sits the throne of Elam," Aram informed the general. "Rahm Imrid is no more. The heralds will announce this throughout the land in the coming days."

"What are your orders, my lord?" Arrabi asked.

Aram shook his head. "Wait upon General Sota – he will inform you of his needs in due time. I must go and see to my own affairs. Farewell, general."

"Farewell, my lord."

And so Aram went back northward through the vast green countryside of Elam and toward its distant gates, passing through Calom Malpas and many smaller villages and towns, leaving behind an astonished populace and an event that came to be known in the lore of that land as *The Day That Death Rode the Length of Elam.*

12.

Three days after the death of Rahm Imrid and the ascension of High Prince Marcus, as Aram passed through the great gates and out into Cumberland, he once more sought the sky for contact with Alvern.

The eagle answered immediately. "There are no slave trains anywhere in Aniza or on the south of the plains. I inquired of the hawks in this region and they told me that all such traffic ceased after the slaying of Soroba."

This surprised Aram. "There has been no slave traffic at all?"

"None, my lord."

"Any movement of the enemy's armies?"

"No," Alvern replied.

"What of the weather, and the coming of winter – what do the hawks say of this?" Aram asked.

"There is snow in Vallenvale," the eagle told him. "And also on the hills to the north of Bracken."

"Thank you, my friend."

Puzzling over Manon's suspension of the slave traffic, and wondering if it was a direct result of his confrontation with, and killing of, Hurack Soroba, Aram nonetheless happily turned eastward when he reached the north of Cumberland. Upon his journey from Marcus' Great Hall, he had considered turning aside to inform the House of Basura of the change that had been wrought, but in the end decided that joyful news such as that would travel quickly enough. Besides, he had no wish to rob Marcus of passing along the glad tidings himself.

As he rode north through Cumberland, he'd had the same thoughts about Governor Kitchell. In the end, he decided to leave that to Marcus as well. And so, reaching the bend in the road by the town next to the hills, he turned eastward up the valley of the dry lake, toward Burning Mountain and home.

On his last night upon the road before he would reach the fortress on the banks of the Broad, he camped in a hollow of the hills to the southwest of Burning Mountain. Satisfied that there were no enemies nearby, he gathered dead branches from the junipers and started a fire, made kolfa, and seated himself on a rock close to the flames. As the twilight faded, Thaniel, who'd been grazing along the banks of a small stream that tumbled out of the hills, came to stand facing him from just beyond the fire.

Sensing that the horse wished to speak, Aram looked up at him. "What is it, my friend?"

"I have had time to think about the deaths of my parents," Thaniel stated without preamble. "And my thinking has been altered somewhat."

"Altered?" Aram frowned at him. "In what way?"

"That morning by the river, when we were south in Elam, you told me that there was no need for anyone but you and I to go and face Manon."

Aram nodded as he sipped at his kolfa. "I did say this," he affirmed.

"I believe you are wrong – and that I was also wrong in my desire to go and face him at once after the deaths of my parents. I confess that grief over their loss muddled my judgment."

"Why do you think I am wrong?" Aram asked quietly.

"Because he will not allow you to simply come to him and bring the instrument of his destruction so near."

"How do you know this?"

"I don't know it," Thaniel replied. "I should have said that I believe that he will not allow it."

Aram looked down as a small log rolled free of the flames. He pushed it back into the fire with his boot and then looked up once more. "The grim lord stated that I could come to him and we could settle all this between the two of us."

"He is a liar." Thaniel said.

Aram nodded. "I do not dispute it." Then he moved his hand, indicating the sword above his back. "But he wants this – indeed, he greatly desires it – and that desire may render him careless."

"He is a god, Aram – however careless he may be; he would find a means of advantage over you." The horse lowered his head to gaze at Aram more closely. "Hear me, my brother – you cannot face him alone. I believe that his offer to you is more than a lie – it is a trick. There are tens of thousands of servants at his disposal. Were we to enter his valley alone, he would command them to surround us as he did at the bloody stream. Even with the aid of the Guardians, this time he would not fail. He would slay us both."

Aram looked hard at the horse; his eyes sharp and bright in the glow from the fire. "Have you not seen what this Sword can do?"

"No," the horse answered stoutly. "I have only seen what *you* are able to do with it. Imagine that you were slain, and it passed from your hand to his. What then?"

Aram shook his head. "The Astra would not allow it."

"You say so – and I believe it to be true. But can we be certain of it?" Before Aram could respond, Thaniel went on, "We must reduce his armies if we can; and then he will be the one hopelessly surrounded, at the mercy of his enemies, and not you, my lord."

Unable to dispute the wisdom of this assertion, Aram looked down and watched the flames devour the wood in silence for a while. Then, without looking up, keeping his gaze upon the fire, he asked, "Alright, my friend – what do you say that we should do?"

"We must take the army north with us in the spring. We must meet the grim lord's strength with strength," Thaniel replied. "Manon's forces must be diminished. And the reduction of his power must be the work of all the people of the earth. The world must be united in the fight for its freedom."

Aram remained silent for a time, and then, "Joktan gave to me this same advice," he admitted and then he sighed. "I am so weary of the killing, Thaniel. I am so tired of death." As he spoke, he waved a hand back toward the darkness behind him, toward the southwest. "Even the death of Rahm Imrid, who I was determined to kill – and who deserved killing – gave me sorrow and no pleasure."

Thaniel shifted his weight and spoke quietly. "I know this, my friend," he said. "And I am sorry that so much of it falls to you. Were it a burden that I could lift from your shoulders, I would do so."

Aram sighed once more, deeply, and stared out into the night. "All I have ever wanted is to live in quiet and in peace with Ka'en and my family." With that, he ceased speaking; his thoughts went out to a distance, across the plains, beyond the hills, and down into a green and pleasant valley. After a moment, his features gave themselves over to what was almost a smile. He sipped at his kolfa as he allowed himself to ponder the dream he'd just described as if it were reality.

He thought of the tiny sky-blue eyes of his daughter and his smile grew pensive and soft. The weariness of travel and the soreness in his muscles faded before that pleasant image. Even the chill air of the deepening night momentarily surrendered its struggle with the fire.

Thaniel waited, silent, patient, and understanding until Aram retrieved his attention from the shapeless darkness beyond the influence of the flame and brought it back once more to the horse standing before him.

"My friend," the horse stated solemnly. "Forgive me for being the one to state that which we both know, but a life of peace and freedom – for you or for any of us – will require more death and more killing, perhaps much more."

Aram relinquished the last vestiges of pleasant thoughts and looked up at Thaniel. "I know – and I already count my own life as forfeit, if it becomes necessary," he agreed. "But I hate the idea that so many others will die as well."

"Those others have dreams of peace and freedom just as you," the horse told him. "And like you they know the cost."

Aram met his eyes. "Do they?"

Thaniel shifted his weight again, this time in irritation. "Ask yourself, my friend – do you not think that other men know what will happen to those they love if Manon and his foul minions are not destroyed or driven from the earth? What do you think? Would those men rather that their wives be made widows and their children orphaned, but made free of his evil – or that their wives be slain, their sons enslaved, and their daughters fed to his loathsome beasts?"

Aram looked down and stared into the fire. After a moment he sighed. "We have so few men. His armies are easily eight or ten times our own in strength."

"There is Elam now," Thaniel reminded him.

Aram shook his head. "I meant what I said to the council. I have no standing in that land. Nor do I wish it."

"But Marcus swore fealty to you, my lord – I heard him do so. And with his fealty now comes Elam and its strength. And from that which I hear of their numbers, there are many thousands at his command."

Aram shook his head again. "I absolved him of that vow of fealty when he ascended the throne of Elam."

"Now that part of things," Thaniel returned caustically, "I did not hear."

Aram looked up. "I am certain that it was implied."

"No – it was not, except perhaps in your mind." The horse lifted his head and looked out and gazed into the darkness of the hills behind Aram toward the southwest. "You gave Marcus his land. He will not deny you his strength."

Aram reached out and placed more wood onto the flames. "Well, let us go home," he said, ending the discussion. "Let us enjoy the quiet of winter and then we will see what next year brings."

The two of them arose early and wended eastward, reaching the fortress by mid-morning of the next day. Findaen, Wamlak, and Jonwood met them at the river.

"What news out of Elam, my lord?" Findaen asked.

"Marcus sits upon the throne," Aram replied simply. "He is now High Prince. A friend governs that land now."

Findaen raised his eyebrows even as a slight smile touched his mouth, but said nothing.

Wamlak and Jonwood stared, but like Findaen, reached the conclusion that whatever astonishing event had occurred to alter the circumstances of that distant land so dramatically, they would have to hear of it from others. Lord Aram, who no doubt had precipitated that "event", would not speak of it.

After they'd all been ferried across, as he dismounted, Aram looked around at the others. "Manon suspended his slave trains," he told them. "What does this mean, I wonder?"

In response, Jonwood grinned a savage grin. "Maybe because he has discovered that whoever he sends south doesn't usually come back."

"Perhaps." Aram smiled tightly and then looked at Findaen. "Where are Boman, Matibar, Edwar, and Andar?"

Findaen glanced onto the prairie at the many rows of tents. "They have been staying in the camp with their men, my lord."

"Are they among them now?"

"Yes."

"Can they be easily found and brought to the fortress?" Aram asked.

"Boman and Andar were together at breakfast not an hour ago," Wamlak told him, pointing to the north side of the fortress, toward the rows of tents that belonged to Duridia. "They have probably not gone far."

Aram looked at him and nodded. "Bring them, and send someone for Matibar and Edwar. And find Donnick and the other captains." He looked up at the sun, rising toward mid-morning. "Tell them to make haste, if they will. I wish to confer with them and then go toward home. I want to be in Regamun Mediar before sunset on the morrow."

Within the hour, the leaders of the armies of the east were gathered in the war room, along with Donnick and the captains. Aram informed them shortly of that which had occurred in Elam, ignoring the many raised eyebrows that were exchanged and the surreptitious looks of satisfaction that worked their way around the table.

"Now," he went on, "Alvern tells me that the enemy has made no move to come southward, and that winter has come to the northern regions. It will soon come here. It seems clear that there will be no more fighting before the spring." He looked over at Findaen. "How are we fixed for firewood and food for the men?"

"Dane and his men bring more fuel for the fires out of the green hills two or three times a week, my lord," Findaen told him. "And Kinwerd sends word from Stell that the harvest is in, and that it was plentiful. We can send for that which we need whenever we wish. Lamont brought supplies with them as you know. With the excess harvest from here, from across the river, and from Stell, there should be plenty for the army." He looked across the table at Boman. "Governor Boman has arranged for the surplus harvest from Duridia to be brought north as well."

Aram studied the table top for a moment and then looked up at Boman. "Lamont is far away and Seneca is an impossible distance, but perhaps your men could go to their homes for the winter."

The Governor stiffened and immediately shook his head in disagreement. "It cannot be right, my lord, for my men to winter at home among their families while these men from the east encamp in the elements." He shook his head again, vehemently. "No, my lord; Duridia will stay with the army."

Aram met his gaze. "I meant no offense, Governor; it's just that we must gather supplies to go north with us in the spring as well. The less that is consumed through the winter here, the better." He hesitated and then admitted, "Also, I confess that I wish for no man to be disheartened by separation from those he loves, especially when they are so near in miles."

The expression upon Boman's features remained impassive, as was usual for the quietly competent governor of Duridia. "As for supplies, my lord, we are all of us aware that it is as much for the campaign of the spring as it is for sustenance through the winter that stores are required. Word has come that the harvest in Duridia was ample; there will be enough." After a moment, he went on. "As for the other thing – we came north not to fight one battle, but to fight all that are necessary until this war is won. No man of Duridia will become disheartened, or seek to return home until final victory is accomplished."

Aram inclined his head. "Thank you, Governor." He looked around at the others. "Thank you all." He folded his hands upon the table. "Alright, now to other practical matters. Winter is not usually very harsh south of the Green Hills – still, there will be periods of cold and some snow." He turned back to Boman. "How are the temporary shelters holding up?"

It was Edwar that laughed and replied. "They are something a bit more than 'temporary' now, my lord. Since returning from the battle, the men have taken an interest in their lodgings, knowing that they will winter in them. Many are now more wood than canvass."

Findaen nodded his head in agreement and waved a hand toward the unseen prairie outside. "It is more like a town out there now than an encampment. Dane has been bringing poles down out of the hills with every shipment of firewood, which the men have placed in the earth surrounding their tents, rendering them as more substantial protection against the elements."

Timmon leaned forward. "We have even partially enclosed the latrines and banked the streets to shed the rain." He grinned. "All this encampment needs now is a proper name."

"Streets?" Aram chuckled. "It seems I have not been around much lately." But then he nodded. "I am glad to hear it. Alright, we will all winter here at the fortress then."

From the other end of the table, Nikolus cleared his throat and frowned at him. "*We*, my lord?"

Aram frowned in turn. "Yes – well, not Lady Ka'en. She and our child will stay in Derosa."

He was surprised to see the expressions of disapproval and consternation that immediately rendered themselves upon the faces of his commanders at this statement.

"What is it?" He asked of them, his frown deepening.

Hesitant silence greeted this question.

Finally, when no one else spoke, Andar leaned forward and grinned at him. "Forgive the impertinence, my lord, but you are not welcome here."

Aram's frowned deepened further, becoming an expression of irritated confusion. "What do you mean?"

Findaen turned to him and spoke evenly. "Lord Aram, we all know the sacrifices you make on behalf of all of us and our peoples. As you said – there will be no more fighting before the spring." He reached out and put his hand on Aram's shoulder. "Go home, my friend. Go home to Regamun Mediar and take a well-deserved rest with your family."

Continuing before Aram could respond, he waved his hand around the table. "We will be fine here – and quite busy. There are men to be trained, a few wounded yet in the infirmary, and armor to be made and fitted." He dropped the hand back to table, folded both his hands in front of him, and met Aram's fierce gaze squarely. "Go home, my lord. We promise that your army will be fit and ready to fight when next you need it."

At this, there arose a chorus of assent. Mallet seemed on the verge of tears as he spoke. "Go home, Lord Aram, and get to know your wee one. We'll manage everything here."

Abashed, regretting the moment of annoyance, Aram nodded his thanks. "I am grateful," he told the assembled leaders. Fighting down an abrupt surge of emotion, he said, "Lord Alvern and Kipwing will be in the skies above us, and the hawks will remain on alert all the way north to Vallenvale and Bracken. I will come at once if there is any alarm."

"Unless you are sorely needed, my lord," Mallet stated, "we will take care of any alarm that arises without finding it necessary to disturb your rest."

"Here, here," Edwar agreed.

The meeting wound down on that note and Aram took his leave of everyone present.

The sun had risen to within an hour of mid-day when he was once again in the saddle and he and Thaniel were wending their way eastward around the limits of the camp.

Aram glanced up at the sun. "Can we make it near to the summit of the green hills by dark?" He asked Thaniel. "I want to be home before evening tomorrow."

Thaniel lengthened his stride and his great hooves began to eat up the ground. "We can," he replied.

13.

As autumn waned toward winter, Aram and Ka'en spent their days in leisurely manner; walking the porch and the avenue while carrying their daughter, going up the valley as often as possible to visit with Borlus and Hilla before the time came for the bears to go to their winter's sleep. It occurred to Aram one day as they sat in the sun next to the orchard that these were the happiest, most pleasant days he had ever known.

He began to hope that time would continue to pass in that uneventful manner right into and through the winter.

One morning he stood alone on the porch in the hour after sunrise and gazed northward where far away there was new snow whitening the tops of the highest peaks. Ka'en and Mae were yet inside having breakfast. He turned to look the other way and found a familiar hooded specter standing next to the top of the stairway, facing him.

Aram inclined his head in surprise. "Lord Joktan."

"Good morning, my son," the ghost replied.

"What may I do for you, my lord?" Aram asked him.

Joktan turned his hooded head for a moment and looked toward the east where the body of the sun had just cleared the tops of the hills.

"The pass to the high plains is still open," he said, turning back toward Aram. "Goreg seeks an audience with you."

Aram frowned. "Goreg?" Then memory came. "Ah, the wolf, Durlrang's son."

"Yes – with the death of his father he is now chief of all the wolves of that country."

Aram looked back toward the city for a moment before once again facing Joktan. "What is it that he requires of me?"

"That is not my affair," the ancient king answered. "I want you to come to the high plains as well – and my need, I dare say, outweighs his in importance."

"Your need?" Aram glanced toward the east. It was as Joktan stated; though there was snow on the peaks off to the north, those on the east of the valley were yet free of wintery deposits. He nodded. "I will come, of course. What is your need?"

Joktan shook his head. "It is not my benefit that I seek, but yours, my son."

"Mine?"

"Yes." With that, Joktan began to fade. "You will come?"

"I will."

"Soon?" The king persisted, even as he shimmered on the edge of visibility.

"Tomorrow," Aram promised.

"I will await you then. Bring a shovel – you will need it." And Joktan was gone.

Frowning at this last instruction, Aram nonetheless turned and descended the stairs to find Thaniel and inform him that they would be making a journey on the following day. Afterward, he turned back toward the city and his family.

"Why does Joktan need to see you now – and why there?" Ka'en asked him.

Aram shrugged as he looked down at Mae, cooing in the crook of his arm. "I don't know what Joktan wants, but Goreg – Durlrang's son – seeks an audience as well," he answered. He looked up and met her eyes with a reassuring smile. "I won't be gone but a few days."

"If it storms while you are away," she protested, "you might be trapped there until spring."

He shook his head. "The Sword will melt any snow that might fall in the pass. Don't worry – I will be back as I promised."

Before the sun cleared the eastern hills the next morning, Aram and Thaniel were already across the river and climbing through the forests toward the pass. The sky was clear but the air was brisk and grew ever colder as they gained altitude. Off to the north, the sky had a hazy look, as if in that direction a storm was taking shape.

They crossed the mountains and camped near the meadow where Aram had saved Florm's life so long ago, but neither of them remarked upon that incident. Florm and Ashal's deaths were still too fresh, too painful.

Late the next morning, they came to the area of troubled ground where the battle for Rigar Pyrannis had been fought and lost. Joktan was already there, corporeal, seated next to the fire pit, gazing down into the earth. He looked up as Aram dismounted.

"Did you bring a shovel?"

Reaching into his pack, Aram produced it. "I did."

But the ancient king was in no hurry to set Aram to whatever task required the use of that particular instrument. He motioned toward the pit. "Let's have a fire and share a cup of kolfa."

After freeing Thaniel to leave the region of troubled ground and go graze down next to the river, Aram gathered wood and built a fire. After the kolfa boiled, he poured two cups and handed one to his ancient ancestor.

"Why the shovel, my lord?" He asked.

"Patience," Joktan responded shortly. Then he gazed at Aram with a wry smile playing about his mouth. "I confess that I did not anticipate your solution as it concerns Elam, simply riding into that land and killing its ruler," he said, and then he held up his hand to prevent Aram's response. "But I heartily approve – a much better solution than a civil war."

His eyes went upward to the hilt of the Sword. "You begin to understand the power of that thing, do you not? I was nervous, I confess, when you went so boldly through the entirety of Elam. But I should not have been. I watched you slay the dragons with it, after all." Then his gaze came back down to Aram's face and the wry smile had gone, to be replaced with an odd expression of concern. "It is becoming rather difficult to tell where you end and that unearthly weapon begins."

He sipped at his kolfa and frowned at his descendent. "Is it becoming a problem for you?"

"The Sword?" Aram frowned back at him and shook his head. "No, no problem. It is just a weapon, after all – a powerful weapon, as you say, my lord – but a just weapon nonetheless."

"And you control it? It does not control you?"

Aram met his gaze coolly. "I control it."

There was a silence and then Joktan smiled again and nodded with satisfaction. "I am beginning to think that you will live, after all, when you face the enemy."

Aram dropped his gaze down into the flames. "That is my hope, my lord."

Joktan studied him for another long moment. "You are a king, you know. Everyone that knows you sees it."

Aram nodded as he watched the fire consume the dry wood. "I know."

"Still, my son; you are in a very odd situation for a king," Joktan went on.

Aram looked up, curious. "Why? How so?"

"Despite the fact that everyone knows it and accepts it; there is no one but me, a dead monarch, to affirm your kingship," Joktan replied. "There is a process, you know, for ascending to rule at Regamun Mediar." He frowned at his own words, stared down into the flames and continued in a quiet tone. "At least there was – once."

Aram shrugged. "Once Manon is destroyed, it will simply be that I am king – if I survive. I have little interest in process."

"I know this about you," Joktan agreed. "Nonetheless, you should at least have the symbol of authority."

Aram gazed at him quizzically. "Symbol?"

The ancient king looked down and examined the grass that surrounded him. "I told you once that my blood is in this soil, my bones beneath this earth." He leaned a bit to his left and patted the ground. "The symbol is here, too. It is also beneath this earth. It fell some short distance from me upon my death, but it is still here. Hence the shovel."

Aram looked at him with the light of understanding in his eyes. "And you want me to dig it up."

"More than that, my son." Joktan's features were a study in solemnity. "I want you to have it. And I want you to wear it. You are my heir – and you are now king. The crown cannot stay here – it must go with you always."

"A crown?"

Joktan looked at him and chuckled. "Don't worry – it is a relatively simple thing. It will adorn your brow nicely." He finished his kolfa and looked up at the sun, rising high in the morning, and then stood. "We might as well begin," he said.

Grasping the shovel, Aram stood and moved around to stand next to Joktan. He looked at the king, frowning. "Are you certain this is necessary? Your bones are here, my lord – I would not wish to disturb them."

"It is necessary," Joktan replied and he indicated the spot on the ground he had patted earlier. "Have no fear – as I stated; when my body fell, the crown landed away from me. You will not disturb my bones. Dig here."

It was at that moment, as Aram sank the bit of the tool into the soil, that the strangeness of the situation struck him. He hesitated and looked over at Joktan. "This feels odd to me," he admitted, speaking his feelings aloud, though quietly.

Joktan threw back his head and laughed outright. Then he gazed at Aram, grinning. "There is no one upon the earth that is stranger than you, Aram," he declared. Moving his foot, he tapped the ground. "This is important. And it is necessary. Dig."

Aram began to remove the earth from the spot indicated by Joktan. When the hole was a bit less than two feet deep, Joktan reached out and laid a cold hand on Aram's arm. "Careful now, you are almost there. It is made of pure gold, and can be damaged. Move the shovel out a bit, push it deep, and lift the earth in one large clump."

Aram complied and as he lifted the clump of damp earth, something caught the sun and gleamed.

"Yes, there it is," Joktan stated, and there was strong emotion in his voice. "Clean it up, remove the earth, and let us see it."

Laying the shovel aside, Aram knocked the dirt away from the exhumed symbol of those that ruled for thousands of years at Regamun Mediar. It was a simple golden circlet. On one side, at the front, there was a raised portion of three triangular points, with the center point being the tallest of the three. Embossed in the middle of this center piece, in the widest area, there was a circle with tiny lines extending off from it in eight places, as if it was intended to signify the body of the sun.

After Aram had cleaned the earth from it with his sleeve, Joktan studied it for a moment and then looked at Aram. "Put it on your head," he insisted. "Let us see if it will properly fit the place where it belongs."

Aram turned it over and over in his hands, admiring the simple elegance of the thing. But after a moment, he shook his head. "No. Forgive me, my lord; I cannot wear it now. I will carry it with me always, but I will not wear it until Manon is no more."

Joktan gazed at him for a moment in disapproving silence. Then he turned his head away and looked out over the fading green of the autumnal landscape of the high plains. After a few moments more, he sighed and nodded. "Alright," he said quietly. "I suppose that is what I expected of you." He turned back and spoke earnestly. "But bear it with you always – it is the symbol of your birthright. And when Manon is defeated, *put it on.*"

Aram met his eyes. "When Manon is no more," he agreed, "I will wear it."

He went to his pack and stowed the crown carefully, and then he went back and replaced the soil he had dug up. Joktan was seated once again in his accustomed spot. Aram sat down as well and indicated the pot resting on the coals. "More kolfa, my lord?"

Joktan nodded. "We have time, I think, before the wolves arrive."

Aram looked across at him. "I had forgotten about them," he admitted. "What do they require of me, do you think?"

Joktan shrugged. "That is their concern," he replied. "And yours, of course. But I do not know. Anyway, they are coming and will be here soon, and then you can ask them."

They shared another cup and talked of general things, with Joktan once again finding good humor arising from Aram's actions in deposing Rahm Imrid. "That was a great thing," he said, more than once. "Would that the distance was not so great and I had been able to be there to see it."

Just after mid-day, Thaniel, still down near the river, lifted his head and focused his attention upon the high ground to the north. "Wolves," he told Aram.

Arm stood and looked off toward the north and immediately sucked in an astonished breath.

Over the slope of the hill came Durlrang.

Only it was not Durlrang.

The wolf leading the pack that came over the crest was large and black, and moved with a somber confidence. For just a moment,

Aram felt emotion rise in him at the sight of Durlrang's son – the very image of his father.

For that's who it was. Durlrang's son.

The wolf stopped some feet away from Aram and bent his head over to the ground, in which action he was joined by all his people.

"I am Goreg, master," the black wolf said. "Son of Durlrang. I seek an audience with you, if possible."

The voice reminded Aram of Durlrang as well; the inflections in his tone were, if anything, fiercer. Perhaps it was because of his youth.

"I am pleased to meet you, Goreg, son of Durlrang," Aram replied. "Your father was a great friend.' He looked away as he felt emotion stir within him. "A very great friend." Gathering himself, he looked back at Goreg. "What do you require of me?"

"Require?" This word seemed to trouble Goreg. "I am not worthy to require anything of you, master." He gazed at Aram for a long moment and then cast a brief glance at Joktan. "Do I interrupt?"

"No. Ask of me what you will."

Goreg met Aram's gaze. "I am told that the enemy sent great beasts into your valley and that it was one of these beasts that slew my father."

"You heard correctly," Aram affirmed.

"I am also told," Goreg continued, "that you slew these beasts, master."

Aram nodded. "I slew them. They are both dead."

"But the enemy that sent them still lives?"

"He does." Aram answered as he studied the wolf closely. The animal seemed agitated by strong emotion. "Why did you seek this audience, Goreg?"

Goreg glanced around at the wolves with him, perhaps ten in all. Then he met Aram's gaze once more. "You will fight against the evil one?"

Aram nodded. "Until he is no more."

"We wish to go and fight him with you."

Aram gazed at Goreg in surprise. "You wish to fight with us?"

"I want to avenge my father," Goreg stated. "And if possible, I would like to stand in his stead in service to you, master."

Aram frowned. "But who will remain here to watch over your people?"

"No one, master. If you will have us, we will all go to war with you."

"All?"

"If you will have us," Goreg repeated.

Aram looked the company over once more. "How many are there in your band now, Goreg?"

"Nearly two hundred."

Aram considered this. Slowly, he nodded as he came to a decision. "There are plenty of woodlands with food in the west where your people may winter with plenty," he said.

He knelt down and looked into the wolf's eyes. Deep inside those dark brown orbs, there shone the same clear determination that had been resident in his father's gaze. Aram nodded. "Bring your band," he told Goreg. "We will face the enemy together."

Goreg bent his head to the earth. "I am most grateful to you, master." Then he looked up. "When do you return to the west?"

"On the morrow," Aram replied.

"We will be here in the morning, master."

Aram raised his hand in salute. "You will be most welcome, you and all your people."

Joktan watched them leave and then looked at Aram. "What are your plans?"

Aram sat down and replenished the fire, even though the day had warmed. "A quiet winter," he said.

"And in the spring?"

Aram kept his gaze directed downward into the flames. "A quiet winter first, my lord. In the spring I will go to bring justice upon Manon."

"With the army?"

Aram looked up and gazed at his ancestor. After a moment, he nodded. "Yes, I will take the army."

"Elam as well?"

Aram lowered his eyes from the shrewd gaze of the ancient king. "What Elam will or will not do is the province of High Prince Marcus," he said.

Joktan stirred impatiently, even angrily. "He is your vassal, Aram; you made him so when he was elevated by your actions. You may insist upon his strength going north with you. I believe, my son, that you *must do so*. Without Elam's strength, you are too badly outnumbered."

Aram looked up then and smiled thinly. "I have discovered something important, my lord," he replied. "It is that I am truly never outnumbered. This Sword will bring parity to almost any situation. I will draw his army out into the sunlight and I will destroy it."

"I have seen the ground where you will face that army," Joktan stated and he shook his head. "There is very little sunlight in that land."

"I know – I have also seen it," Aram replied, and then he shrugged. "The grim lord may not wait for me to come to his door. He may very well send his armies into the south to prevent us – where there *is* sunlight. I intend to follow the snowmelt north. If it takes all summer and many battles; I will reduce his armies bit by bit."

Joktan was silent for a moment, then, "Would you like me to talk to Marcus?"

Aram looked at him sharply. "No, my lord, I would not. Marcus is a good man and will join me if asked. But there is much for him to set right in his own land."

"This is true," Joktan agreed. "But the winter should suffice to accomplish any 'setting right'. I know what you told the council – Marcus' labors will be made much the easier because those that would be inclined to oppose him will not do so out of fear of you."

Joktan drew in a breath and let it out. Then he leaned toward Aram and spoke earnestly. "Send an emissary to Elam, I beg of you. Say only that you intend to go north in the spring to meet the enemy. If Marcus is as honorable as you believe him to be, he will do what is right."

Aram gazed down into the fire and considered. Then, after a moment, he nodded. "I will send an emissary." He looked up again. "But I will make no demand of him, my lord. No one should enter this fight unless he does so willingly."

"And this is how you will seek to govern?" Joktan asked. "This is how you will act as king?"

"If I survive Manon's destruction," Aram affirmed, "I will attempt to govern without coercion."

105

Joktan's eyes narrowed. "It is not coercion to insist upon the aid of those who owe you everything."

Aram watched him for a moment, his face a study in sobriety. "I don't intend to collect on debts, my lord – except from the grim lord himself. He owes much for all the evil he has done, and he will pay. Everyone else must be truly free."

He looked around the high plains, where the grass was gradually fading from the last vestiges of summer's green to tan. Turning his head further, he gazed eastward, toward the distant, unseen Inland Sea. Sorrow made its way onto his face.

"All I ever wanted," he stated quietly, "was to live someplace out of the way, in peace and relative solitude, with her." He looked up as a cloud passed before the face of the sun. "I never wanted to be king, I never sought a destiny or a crown; I only wanted her."

Joktan grimaced at these words even as he nodded. "I know, my son, I know. But you are strong – stronger than anyone I have ever known." He waited until Aram looked at him before continuing. "Whether it be destiny or no, Aram; it is the doom of the strong to bear the troubles of the world. It has ever been so, and will always be so."

At that, Aram dropped his gaze. "Forgive me, my lord. I did not mean to complain." He sighed and looked up once more. His eyes were sharp and hard. "Have no fear – I will accomplish that which it has become my destiny to do."

"If I could lift this burden from you, I would do so," Joktan told him in solemn tones.

Aram shook his head and smiled slightly. "The burden is mine, my lord; and I will bear it to the end. As I said – I did not mean to complain."

They talked about other things then, pleasant things, and the day wore away. Aram gathered more wood as the sun sank toward the western hills and he and his ancient ancestor communed deep into the night.

Finally, hours after the Glittering Sword of God had dropped out of sight beyond the western horizon, Aram stretched and rose to lay out his bedroll. Joktan looked up at him. "I will go with you now, if you have no objection, all the way to – to the end of things."

Aram met his eyes. "I have no objection, my lord. I will be grateful to have your counsel."

"Goodnight then, my son."

"Goodnight, my lord."

The wolves arrived at dawn and together Aram, Thaniel, and Goreg and his band went west. At mid-day on the next day, Aram parted from the wolves at the end of the avenue, sending them southward into the green hills to winter among more amenable surroundings than these wolves of the high country had ever known. Leorg went with them to show them the way.

14.

Through the waning weeks of autumn and into the first days of winter, as the snow finally fell upon the pass to the east and then began to make its way inexorably toward the valley floor, Aram and Ka'en passed peaceful days and nights, often sitting up with Eoarl and Dunna into the wee hours. On these occasions, Mae was often passed from one pair of gentle hands to another. To Aram, it felt like family and like home.

He never talked of the spring and what it might bring and no one else in that company broached the subject. He did not send the emissary to Elam, intending to do so toward the end of winter. He wanted to give Marcus as much time as he needed to consolidate his governorship of Elam.

Then, one crisp mid-day, Aram went walking on the porch with Mae bundled up in his arms, to find Alvern there, preening his feathers.

The eagle looked up as Aram came out through the damaged arches where the last of the dragons had died.

Aram went toward him. "Lord Alvern – what brings you down to earth this fine day?"

"Forgive me for troubling your peace, Lord Aram, but I have news. Some time ago, High Prince Marcus of Elam requested that three horses be sent to him in Elam with the intent that they bear riders into Wallensia." The eagle paused but when Aram tendered no response, he went on, "Findaen thought not to trouble you, my lord, so horses were found that had not chosen riders and were willing to make the journey."

Alvern paused to run his beak along the tip of a wing feather. "The horses returned today with Prince Marcus and Captain Thom.

They and three companions await you at the fortress, seeking audience. What shall I tell them?"

Aram pulled Mae close as a cool breeze freshened out of the northwest, frowned down at the ancient pavement of the porch for a long moment, and then glanced up at the sun, high in the southern sky. "Tell them that I arrive at the fortress by sunset tomorrow."

"At once, my lord." Alvern spread his wings and lifted up, accelerating away toward the green hills.

Aram turned toward the city to find Ka'en standing just behind him. As she reached out her arms to receive her daughter, she smiled softly up into his eyes. "I know," she said, "you must be off again. But you will hurry back to us?"

He looked off to the north, scanning the sky for clouds. "It seems that I am never to be left in peace," he grumbled, "until winter sets in with its strength and prevents travel."

But then he sighed. "This summons from Marcus, however, cannot be ignored. If there is trouble in Elam, in the resolution of which I can lend him aid, then it will be worth my time. I will find Thaniel and go now, and be back in four days' time, five at the most."

Within the hour, he and the great horse had crossed the rivers and were wending up toward the top of the long ridge to the south of the valley. Once again, they camped near the spring where they had camped so long ago on the eve of that first battle. A few hours before morning, the temperature dropped sharply and the wind came out of the north and whistled over the crest, moaning as it moved down the long ridges, as if wounded as it went by the bare branches of the trees.

Aram started a fire and sat near it with his cloak pulled tight and tried to nap until the dawn. But when dawn came, the sun did not show, except as a wan ghost behind gray and thickening clouds.

The sun had passed through the middle of a darkly overcast day that promised a demonstration of winter's strength by the time Aram and Thaniel swung around the vast array of tents and rode up to the walls of the fortress. Fires burned bright and hot everywhere along the avenues of that temporary "town".

Wamlak was near the door at the foot of the stairs that led up to the war room, his cloak wrapped tightly to his throat. Torches were already lit along the stairway leading up.

The archer bowed. "Welcome, Lord Aram. High Prince Marcus and his company are upstairs."

"How are things in the camp?" Aram asked him. "Is there enough food and fuel for heat and cooking?"

Wamlak nodded. "Dane brought the excess harvest north from both sides of the river and Arthrus' boys bring wood out of the hills every day. There is no lack."

"Good," Aram acknowledged, and then he looked back as he started up the stairs. "Captain – be sure that the men working in the green hills know that there are wolves in those forests now – but that they are allied with us."

"Yes, my lord, we know about them. We have already made contact. Their leader, named Goreg, looks much like –" Wamlak caught himself. His eyes went wide and he seemed not to know how to finish the sentence.

"Yes – he is Durlrang's son," Aram said simply. "Thank you, Wamlak."

Marcus was seated at the table with Findaen, Andar, Boman, Edwar, Thom Sota, Amund Basura, Kavnaugh Berezan, and Olyeg Kraine when Aram entered. To his surprise, Suven the tailor was there as well. They all stood.

Marcus inclined his head to Aram. "Greetings, my lord; pray forgive me for disturbing your rest."

Aram waved this away as he nodded to the other occupants of the room. Then he looked back at Marcus.

"What can I do for you, Your Highness?"

Marcus' blue eyes were serious. "I will be as blunt as I have often known you to be, my lord. I have come, along with my Chancellor and my generals, to declare fealty to your banner, and renew to you our oath of fidelity. This oath binds to your cause, and to your command, the will of the people and the arms of Elam."

The young High Prince bowed low before Aram and then straightened up. As he did so, he held out a rolled piece of cloth. "You are our king," he said. "And ever will be. This is the standard of the land of Elam. I give it to you as a token of our fidelity, and as a sign that when you go to war, Elam and all its strength goes with you. Your standard will fly above the soldiers of Elam whenever we are upon the field. It will be placed upon each staff in superior position to that of my homeland."

Aram gazed upon him, astonished at the clarity and fervor of the young Prince's words. Briefly, he wondered if Joktan were truly nearby to witness this – and if this was what the ancient king had foreseen.

He reached out one hand to take the rolled-up flag. The other he extended to the Prince.

"I thank you, Marcus. The free peoples of the world thank you." He turned his eyes upon the roll of cloth in his hand. "And with this, the whole of the world is at last united against tyranny." Then, as Marcus' words of intent registered in their fullness, he frowned at the youthful High Prince. "Upon *each staff*, Your Highness?" He shook his head. "I possess but the one standard only."

In response, Marcus indicated Suven. "I am told that this gentleman understands its configuration."

Aram looked at the tailor, treating the older man to a grateful smile, and then nodded in assent. "He aided Ka'en in the making of the standard that flies above this fortress."

"Then if you are agreeable, my lord," Marcus continued. "I will pay him to create as many more as are needed, based upon the pattern of the first."

Aram shook his head. "If you really mean to do this, Your Highness," he replied. "I will see that Suven, and anyone that aids him in this endeavor, are properly recompensed."

With obvious temerity, but with his chin nonetheless lifted in determination, Suven stepped forward. "Forgive me, my lord," he stated, addressing Aram, "but we did not discuss payment when the prince inquired as to my knowledge and my services." He paused and dared to meet Aram's gaze. "No payment is wanted. I am too old to go to war, perhaps, but I can yet render a service to our cause. If you will provide me with the materials; I will gladly make a royal standard for every staff in Elam."

He drew in a deep breath. "But to be as blunt as the High Prince – I will accept no money for my labor in this."

Boman stepped up beside Suven. "I shall be blunt also, Lord Aram. Every flagstaff of Duridia will require a standard as well."

"As will those of Lamont," Edwar interjected.

"Seneca, too," Andar said, and he grinned at Suven. "A lot of work for you, my friend."

Aram frowned and studied the tailor. "Can you make so many over the course of the winter?" He asked.

Suven inclined his head in firm assent. "Yes, my lord. When I was approached about this matter, I took steps to engage every willing seamstress in Derosa. The royal standards will be ready before the spring."

Aram's frown took on a puzzled aspect. "When were you approached about this matter, my friend?"

Suven glanced at Marcus. "A week ago, my lord – when the High Prince first came."

Aram looked around. "You all discussed this – and agree?"

He was answered with a grin and a nod from each. After a moment, he nodded his own head in reply. "That is settled, then." He looked at Findaen. "Materials?"

Findaen's grin widened. "Arthrus left for Durck three days ago."

"I thank you all," Aram said quietly. Then he turned once more toward Marcus. "As this seems to be a day for engaging in bluntness – may I inquire as to the extent of Elam's strength of arms, Your Highness?"

Marcus glanced over at Kraine. "General Kraine is better able to answer that question than I, my lord. What is the measure of our strength, Olyeg?"

Olyeg inclined his head first to Marcus and then to Aram. "It is good to see you again, my lord. The men under arms in the land of Elam," he went on, "number something more than eighty-two thousand, including surgeons and those that are trained to supply the men who do the fighting."

Boman's eyes went wide at this and Andar whistled low. Findaen came to his feet. "That makes our numbers almost one hundred thousand," he declared in amazement. He turned to Aram. "With such a number, Lord Aram, we will match the grim lord man-for-man."

Aram nodded briefly and turned narrowed eyes upon Marcus. "And your council – what do they think of this? I ask you to forgive the question, Your Highness, but you yourself told me once that you have laws that govern even the actions of the High Prince."

"May I ask a question of my own first, my lord?"

Frowning, Aram nodded.

"Do you intend to go to war?" Marcus asked.

"Yes, in the spring," Aram replied. "I mean to follow the snow into the north, push his armies to the foot of his tower and engage him there, and destroy him. I mean to end this in the coming year."

A light came into Marcus' eye and he nodded with decision. "Then Elam is at your command, my lord. But my Chancellor may tell you the particulars of the feelings of the council better than I." He turned to Amund. "Chancellor?"

Aram looked at the eldest son of House Basura and his frown deepened. "What has happened to your father, Amund? Was he not Chancellor?"

Amund nodded. "I am pleased to stand in your presence once again, Lord Aram. Yes – my father was Chancellor. High Prince Marcus asked him to continue in that post but my father deferred out of deference to his age." He hesitated and smiled slightly. "Also, as you well know, my lord, the last few years have been difficult times in our province. He wished to devote the years that are left to him in the restoration of our land's peace and prosperity."

He inclined his head. "Thanks to you, my lord, those difficult times have passed and my father may attend to the welfare of our people as it pleases him to do." Looking up once more, he continued. "When my father declined to continue as Chancellor, the post fell by right of age and length of service to Leeton Cinnabar, but that worthy gentleman declined for much the same reasons as had my own father."

He indicated Kavnaugh Berezan with one hand. "Which left Kavnaugh next in line – but, since he has had experience in the army; once he found that we were likely going to war under your banner, he opted for a position in the military. At that point, Marcus was free to choose whom he would. He chose me, and I accepted gladly."

"I am pleased," Aram replied. "Now – what of the feelings of the rest of the councilors? In particular, what does Bordo Bufor think of all this?"

To Aram's surprise, this caused the men from Elam to throw back their heads as one and laugh aloud. As Amund regained control, he grinned at Aram. "For one thing – he is utterly terrified of you, my lord, as is everyone fortunate enough to witness your actions in the palace on that day. Would that I had been allowed to be numbered among those fortunate few."

He gave himself over to laughter for another moment, and then went on. "Also, whatever his ideas for personal advancement upon the death of Rahm, they were put to rest when you produced Marcus in the hall. In the end, Bufor – like all the rest of Rahm's closest allies, decided that their wealth and position were of much greater importance than any political aspirations they may have held. Bordo will be content to remain mayor of Calom Malpas, drink his fine wines, and enjoy the company of his foolish women – and continue to dress far better than anyone else in the great hall."

Aram smiled and turned back to Marcus. "So there is no dissent?"

"None, my lord," the young prince assured him. He hesitated and a look of wonder came over his face. "It is as if the whole of the land of Elam has awakened after a very long night that was filled with sinister shadows and darkest terrors." Then his features hardened. "We have placed soldiers, battalion strength, at all the entrances to Elam and Cumberland, including the passages to Aniza and the gap into the plains at the end of the valley below the black mountain. The grim lord's slave trains will never again enter our borders."

"Well done," Aram commended him. "But Alvern tells me that the hawks report no movement of slave trains anywhere along the roads leading north."

Marcus looked relieved. "That is good news indeed."

"I think Manon knows that we are coming to him – and he is drawing in all his power," Aram stated. "He is preparing for the final confrontation."

"So be it," the young High Prince of Elam responded. Marcus seemed to have aged since his ascension and his new-found maturity was evident in that moment. He inclined his head. "Elam is at your command," he said to Aram. "What are your orders, my lord?"

"One hundred thousand men will consume much food," Aram told him. "If there is excess to be found, it should be gathered and laid in store for the coming campaign. And we will need oxcarts to bear those stores north that the army may draw upon them at need. I have money – will your farmers sell us what we need?"

Marcus held up his hand. "My lord, my people have since the beginning of time prepared for times of want. Every Great House has as much as a year's supply of stores laid aside."

Aram looked at Amund. "I remember that your father told me this."

"The time has come that they are needed, my lord," Marcus went on, "and since time of war is one consideration for this practice, the goods will be used for the purpose of feeding the army as it goes to war." Marcus glanced at Amund and lowered his hand. "And since the children of my land have been made free from the threat of enslavement and transport into horror, the farmers and merchants – whose daughters they were – will gladly provide oxcarts for our use. There will be no payment sought or accepted."

He inclined his head in respect. "I thank you for your offer of money, my lord, but we are all in this together and must all pay our share." He straightened up and met Aram's gaze. "I speak for Elam. We are at your disposal; lead us where you will."

Aram let his gaze move slowly among the Elamite delegation, noting the same conviction on every face as was evident on that of their High Prince.

He nodded and focused his attention once again on Marcus. "Meet me in Cumberland – with your army fully supplied for a six month campaign – when the trees of that land turn green with the departure of winter. I want to stand before the tower of Manon with all our combined strength by the advent of summer."

Marcus bowed low. "Elam will be there, Lord Aram."

"Thank you, Marcus," Aram replied warmly.

They supped together and talked long of the campaign to come, while outside, the cold wind swept across the prairie though as yet it brought with it no snow. In the morning, Marcus and his company forded the river and went back westward while Aram and Thaniel bade the others farewell and rode northeast into the icy wind.

And finally, it snowed; though much more fell to earth in the valley to the north of the green hills than southward upon the plains of Wallensia. And with that storm, the winter came and life grew quiet. Eoarl, Dunna, and Cala stayed in the house with Aram and Ka'en. As the winter deepened and snow accumulated in the valley outside, Mae flourished at her mother's breast, and they spent many pleasant evenings gathered close to the fire.

No one talked of the coming spring.

The winter passed slowly. Though it was not as severe as some that had been known in that valley, it was severe enough. All was calm and quiet and Aram was happier than he had ever been able to be.

Storms came and snow fell, followed by periods of sunny days, crisp and cold. It began to seem as if this time of peace and contentment would go on forever and never find an end. The old year turned into the new without anyone noticing.

Then one morning, as Aram slogged through the snow south of the avenue to bring Thaniel some of the apples that Arthrus had brought with him after Aram's orchards were devastated by the dragons, the breeze arose out of the south. Rain fell from scudding clouds that scurried northward in short bands of sodden gray.

Aram stopped and looked about him at the low places where the snow had turned to slush and the ice on the scattered pools was becoming rotten. Then he lifted his gaze and looked southward, toward the green hills. Showing here and there among the gray trunks, there were bare patches of earth.

Nothing was green as yet, spring still stayed in the south far beyond the hills, but it was apparent that winter was loosening its grip.

Soon, from the broad plains south of those green hills, spring would rise up and send its first hesitant feelers north.

His heart grew solemn even as his thoughts hardened, and his destiny, unheeded for these few months, stirred and came to the forefront of his mind.

The time of quiet, rest, and peace was ending.

He found Thaniel on the far side of a small rise where the snow was shallower and the horse was more easily able to get at the grass beneath.

Thaniel looked up as he topped the hill.

"It is warmer this morning, Lord Aram," the horse stated.

Aram nodded, frowning. "I brought you a few of the apples."

Thaniel munched on one of the treats and studied Aram closely. He lifted his head and looked into the north. Then he swung around and gazed southward. "I am very sorry for you, my friend," he said at last. "But spring is coming."

Aram looked that way as well, toward the hills to the south. "It is," he agreed. "It will have already arrived in Elam. Marcus will be bringing his troops north." He met Thaniel's gaze. "It is time that we did what has to be done."

"I am sorry," the horse repeated.

Aram turned and looked toward the city. One lone beam of sunlight rent the cloud cover and bathed the central part of the city in a multi-hued glow. Reaching out, he laid his hand on Thaniel's broad shoulder. "We will leave within the week," he said simply.

And then he dropped his hand and turned his steps toward home.

That evening, as they sat by the fire and listened to another of Eoarl's stories of his childhood, romping through the fields near his ancestral home with the brother that had died in his youth, Ka'en noticed Aram's pensive attitude.

She did not speak to him of that which she knew to be the focus of his thoughts, but simply moved closer to him and handed him the tiny girl who had fallen asleep while nursing.

Later, Aram abruptly realized that the older man was no longer speaking and that the room had gone silent. He looked up to find Eoarl's gaze fixed upon him.

"You haven't heard a word I've said in the last hour, have you, lad?" The farmer asked gently.

Aram looked back at him with regret. "I apologize, Eoarl," he said. "I meant no rudeness."

Eoarl waved it away. "With apologies to your lady, Lord Aram; we all know where your thoughts have gone." He lifted his chin and indicated the unseen valley beyond the walls. "Spring is coming along out there, isn't it?"

"Soon," Aram acknowledged quietly. "There was a good bit of warmish rain this morning, and the snow is getting soft."

Eoarl stared into the fire for a long moment and then lifted his glass and drained it, turning his head to gaze at Aram with an expression of fierce determination upon his face. "I'm going with you, lad."

"What –?" Aram looked back at the older man in confusion. "Where?"

Eoarl reached over and held his glass to the end of the barrel and turned the spigot. "To war," he replied. "I'm going with you – and with my son – to this war."

Aram stared at him and then opened his mouth to protest but the older man cut him off.

"It's true," Eoarl said, "that I have seen sixty-two years come and go, but I am as strong as many another man in the ranks. I was in the army in my time, and I know the use of a sword and a lance." He touched his wife gently to prevent her protests. "It is also true that I have never been to battle, but that is the case for many others who follow you, including every man out of Elam, is it not?"

"It is," Aram admitted. "Still –"

The old farmer held one hand up toward him, palm outward, and then lifted the glass he'd just filled and drained it dry in one attempt. He set it down firmly and his eyes hardened.

"I'm going," he said.

Aram hesitated due to the vehemence of Eoarl's words, but then a glance at the look of fright evident on Dunna's face told him to try once more. "But I need to you to protect Lady Ka'en and Miss Dunna – and Cala," he suggested.

Immediately, Eoarl shook his head and indicated Gorfang, asleep near the fire. "That wolf over there will do a finer job of that than I could ever do – as has already been demonstrated," he said.

He turned aside then and looked long at his wife, his eyes going soft with affection, "I'll be alright, Dunnie girl; don't you worry. Besides, by going along, I will be better able to look after our boy, won't I?" He patted her hand gently and then he looked over and met Aram's gaze. "I'm going, lad – and there's an end on it."

Silence fell and then Aram said, "You'll need a sword. I put some of the best aside long ago when I first came to this valley. Of course, I have had little use for them since. We will go up to the armory in the morning and you may choose whichever one you like."

He considered the older man for another long moment.

"Will you ride?" He asked.

Eoarl gazed back, frowning. "A horse?"

Aram nodded.

Eoarl turned his frown upon the fire and thought for a time. Then he shook his head.

"No," he stated. "I'll be infantry. Muray is infantry – I would rather be there with my boy, in the thick of it."

Dunna sucked in a breath at this, but Eoarl turned his placid eyes upon her. "Don't you worry, Dunnie girl," he told her once more. "I will return in one piece, I promise. Where do you think Muray gets his toughness?" He smiled at his own words. "Well, most of that he got from you, my girl, I'll grant you – but his stubbornness came from me."

Dunna didn't speak, but her black eyes misted over and she reached out and took his hand.

After a moment, Eoarl retrieved his glass and reached across for Aram's. Once more, he extended his hand toward the barrel.

After that, the evening turned quiet. There was little to say that was not better kept as an unspoken thought.

Ka'en found Aram, early the next morning, standing at the southern end of the great porch, looking southward, watching another band of gray cloud break like water around the sharp southern end of the black mountain and spill out over the valley. He turned as she came up.

"Where is Mae?"

Ka'en took his hand and stood close to him. "Dunna has her."

"I have to go," he said.

"I know." She turned her head and looked up at him. "Can we come with you?"

He frowned down at her. "You and Mae?"

She nodded. "Yes – and Gorfang."

To her surprise, he did not immediately refuse, but turned to gaze once more toward the distant green hills as he considered her request. After a long moment, he shook his head.

"No," he said, and there was regret in his voice. "If things go badly, as well they might, I want you and Mae far away from there."

"I do not mean that we will go to the battle, my love, but we can be nearby." She lifted her chin. "It will give you strength to know that your wife and child are there with you."

He shook his head again. "No – rather, it would render me vulnerable." He pulled her close. "I love you – and Mae, and I will miss you terribly, but I will not take those I love into danger ever again."

She laid her head on his shoulder. "There will be injured," she told him. "I could help Bertrain and the others."

Again, he hesitated. He thought of the Sword and how he had come to learn a measure of control over its immense power. Now, more than any time since he'd accepted the doom of confronting

119

Manon, he felt that there was at least some hope that he would find a way to survive the encounter.

And it was this hope that decided him. So, again, after a moment, he shook his head.

"No, my love," he said. "You will stay and I will go and do what needs to be done, and then, when it is over, I will return to you and I will never leave you again."

She leaned back and looked up into his eyes. Her own lovely, topaz eyes were wide and soft, limpid with secret fear. "You *will* return to me, won't you?"

He met her gaze with firm eyes. "I will return."

She hid her face in his chest. "I cannot live if you die."

As she spoke these words, in his heart the flame of hope brightened and became more substantial than it had ever been.

Out of that bright flame of hope there grew an iron-willed determination.

I will live.

Gently, he pushed her away and made her look at him. "I will not die, my love. If anyone, ever, tells you that I have died, he will be the liar." He grasped her shoulders and spoke firmly. "I will go now, and I will end this. And when it is over, and Manon is no more, I will come home and I will never leave you again."

Moisture filled her eyes and overflowed. But they were tears of trust and hope, and not of fear.

15.

The day that Aram and Eoarl left the valley for the fortress, the sun shone warm in a clear sky, and it seemed a harbinger of good things.

Eoarl was riding Huram, who had been sent for by way of Inico the falcon. Aram had informed the horse that once he had delivered Eoarl to the fortress he would return to the valley and stay with Ka'en. The horse had protested but Aram was adamant.

"It may be that an emergency will arise and Mistress Ka'en may have need of you. I will not leave her without the benefit of your strength and speed," Aram told him. And in the end, out of his strong sense of duty and his affection for Lady Ka'en, Huram agreed.

They camped at the edge of the plains and arrived at the fortress in the late morning. The fortress was alive with activity. Troops marched and wheeled upon the grasslands, horses moved in unified lines. To the west, north of the fortress upon the heights near the river, targets had been set up and the bowmen from Seneca were teaching the basics of archery to willing men from Wallensia, Lamont, and Duridia.

South of the fortress, winding down through the swale toward the river, there were long lines of oxcarts, loaded with supplies. At the banks of the Broad, the carts were lined up end-to-end, and the ferry made unceasing trips back and forth across the heavy current, moving men and material over the near-floodtide of spring.

Wamlak stood at the entrance to the fortress when Aram rode up and swung down. "How soon will the army be across the river and ready to march to Cumberland? And is there any word from Elam?" He asked the captain.

"The army will be across the river within the week," Wamlak replied, and then he grinned and indicated the stairs leading up. "Elam is here, already – at least the High Prince and some of his companions, anyway."

This surprised Aram. "Indeed? Thank you, captain."

Marcus, along with Amund and his three generals, Olyeg Kraine, Thom Sota, and Kavnaugh Berezan were seated at the table in the war room with Findaen, Boman, Matibar, Edwar, and Andar when Aram entered. Governor Kitchell was there, as well. Upon seeing him enter the room, they all rose to their feet.

Aram greeted them all and then bade them sit. When he had also taken a chair, he looked around. "Wamlak tells me that we will be across the river and moving west within the week. Is this your assessment also?"

It was Boman that replied. "Yes – at the rate that men and material are crossing the Broad," he told Aram, "we will be fully across six days from today."

Aram nodded. "Good," he said, and looked at Marcus. "And Elam?"

Marcus inclined his head to him. "Our armies will be upon the plains of Cumberland within the week as well, my lord," he said. "And there are trains loaded with six months' worth of supplies."

"Thank you, Your Highness," Aram responded, and he turned to Findaen. "Are we supplied for that length of time also?"

"We are, my lord," Findaen answered. "Arthrus and Dane have done the calculations, and believe that we are properly supplied to the end of summer."

Marcus held up his hand, gaining his attention. "My lord," he said, "you need have no worry about sufficient supplies. To the southwest of Elam lies the land of Vergon. For time out of mind – before Rahm, that is – that land was a close ally, nearly a vassal, of Elam.

"Now that Rahm is gone, Lady Stefia, Princess of Vergon has re-established relations with us. When she found that we were going to war with Manon, she offered of her stores to go with us, including oxcarts and drivers." He held up his hand. "They are not military men, mind you, but will aid us in any way you deem necessary."

"What is Vergon's quarrel with Manon?" Aram asked. "Why would they aid us in this way?"

Marcus nodded, almost as if he had been expecting the question. "Lady Stefia's brother, Ujen, was Prince of Aniza, and was slaughtered when Manon's beasts ravaged that land." He shook his head and smiled grimly. "She hates Manon even more than she hated Rahm."

"Alright, Your Highness." Aram said. "I would ask you to give the Lady Stefia my regards when next you meet with her."

"I will do so, Lord Aram," Marcus assured him, and then he went on. "There is one thing more – Vergon has long been the seat of intellectual endeavor. I was sent to study there in the academy at Sulan as a youth. Vergon has historically produced skilled surgeons of very high quality. Lady Stefia has sent every one of these surgeons that she could spare to us along with the supply wagons."

Amazed at this piece of unexpectedly good news, Aram gazed at the young prince with a smile of admiration. "You have done well, Marcus," he said, forgetting the use of the young man's title in the warmth of the moment. "You have a very good friend in the Princess – and I am glad that you are our friend."

Marcus flushed. "I owe you everything, my lord."

Aram's smile went away, and he shook his head solemnly. "You owe me nothing," he said.

Then he looked around at the others. "Thanks to all your efforts, and Prince Marcus' friend, we seem to be well supplied and moving out in good order." He looked at Findaen. "What about the gun?" He asked.

Findaen grinned. "Your man, Timmon, has shown a great proclivity for the use of that thing, my lord. He intends to seek permission to be placed in charge of it when on the field."

"He's a very clever man," Aram agreed. "Does Arthrus concur with Timmon's opinion of his prowess?"

"He does."

"And do you?" Aram persisted.

Findaen laughed. "Timmon destroys every target we construct with no more than three or four shots from that thing."

Aram nodded. "Good. How is it moved?"

"My lord?"

"How is the cart containing the gun to be transported north – and once upon the field, how will it be moved about as needed?"

Findaen frowned. "By oxen, of course."

Aram shook his head at that. "Oxen may transport it into the north but are too slow to manage it upon the field. If we need to reposition the gun during the course of battle, it must be done quickly. I will talk to Thaniel and inquire as to the possibility of his people aiding us in the matter."

He looked over at Marcus. "How are your troops organized, Your Highness?"

Marcus, in turn, looked at Olyeg. "By your leave, my lord; I will defer that question to General Kraine."

When Aram's gaze settled on him, Olyeg nodded and replied to Aram's inquiry. "Elam's forces are organized into six divisions, my lord, each under command of a general and two sub-generals. Beneath the sub-generals, the forces are divided into four units, each of whom has its commander. Below those commanders, every group of two hundred men is under the direct command of a captain."

Aram nodded. "And are you satisfied with the skills of those in command of the various units?"

Olyeg hesitated. "As much as I can be, my lord, but of course none of us – except for General Sota – has seen action upon the field. I command one division myself. It is hard to know how any of us will behave when steel meets steel until we have actually experienced it."

"This is undoubtedly true," Aram agreed thoughtfully. He looked at Marcus for a moment and then returned his gaze to Kraine. "Which is why, general, I request your permission to meet with your commanders, that I may reach my own conclusions. Do you object to this?"

"No, my lord, of course not," Kraine responded. "In point of fact, I assumed that you would wish to do so."

Aram looked at Marcus once more; then moved his gaze on to Thom Sota and Kavnaugh Berezan before once again addressing Olyeg. "Elam will be the largest contingent by far upon the field," he told the general. "But it is also untested."

He hesitated and looked at Findaen. "Where are Donnick and Nikolus?" He asked.

"Nikolus is working with the new horse-borne riders from Duridia, Lamont, and Seneca," he said. "And Donnick is overseeing the movement of troops across the river with Dane and Arthrus."

Aram nodded and turned back to Kraine. "You said that you command one of the divisions, general?"

"I do, as does General Berezan and General Sota."

"Are there officers you can promote to command of divisions to replace you, Thom, and Kavnaugh?" Aram asked.

Olyeg started – as did the other men mentioned – and he frowned. "Yes, there are other men of competence, my lord – if you think it necessary."

"I want to split Elam into two equal forces, general," Aram explained to Olyeg, as he moved his hands apart upon the table. "Of three divisions each. I want you in command of one half, and General Berezan in command of the other – rather than having each of you bound to the actions of a single division. These two large but untested forces will anchor the flanks of our army upon the field."

Olyeg's frown deepened. "What of General Sota?"

"I need him elsewhere," Aram explained. He looked around at all those assembled. "I have not seen the ground where we will meet the forces of the grim lord," he admitted. "When I have seen it, I will place General Berezan and his force on the side where the flank is most secure – where the enemy is least likely to attempt an assault upon the end of our line."

He brought his hands back together. "Next to him, at our center, will be Boman and his Duridians, and Edwar with Lamont. Olyeg with the other half of Elam will then deploy to the side of the field where the danger of a flanking attempt might be greater. In any event, Duridia and Lamont will stand at our center – for they *are* tested."

Findaen leaned forward, frowning at Aram. "What of Wallensia, my lord? I know that we are small, but we have seen battle. Donnick and his troops performed especially well at Bloody Stream."

Aram nodded. "Wallensia, with Mallet in command, will be positioned upon Olyeg's flank, where the possibility of being flanked is greatest, whether it be to the left or to the right."

Findaen stared at him. "Mallet? Mallet will be in command? But what of General Donnick?"

Once again, Aram moved his hands apart for a small space. "Where Elam and Duridia on one side of the field, and Elam and Lamont upon the other, come together, Donnick and Thom will be placed in general command of the troops in their vicinity. Donnick will command where Elam and Duridia come together, and Thom will be in command where Elam and Lamont come together. The other commanders in their vicinity – whoever they may be – will be instructed to defer to their judgment. I need those two potentially weak points to be made strong, and the presence of a commander who has been in battle will help to accomplish that end."

He looked around, and met the gaze of every man at the table. "These two men have shown their mettle – as well as their steadiness in the face of the enemy. Does anyone disagree with me on this point?"

After a moment, Olyeg Kraine nodded solemnly. "I think it a wise decision, my lord."

At this, everyone nodded in agreement.

Matibar, however, though he also inclined his head to attest to the soundness of Aram's strategy, maintained a frown upon his taciturn features though he did not speak.

Aram watched him for a moment. "Captain?"

Before speaking that which was on his mind, Matibar looked at Andar, who, as a reply to the unspoken question, spread his hands and shrugged. "You are in command of our military, captain – do not defer to me in these matters."

Matibar nodded his thanks, and looked back at Aram. "My lord, it is apparent that you have decided upon the placement of every contingent except that of Seneca. How do you intend to use us?"

In response, Aram addressed Andar. "It is true that Captain Matibar will command Seneca upon the field, sir?"

Andar nodded. "He is trained for it – I am not."

Aram turned back to Matibar. "I want you to break your troops into three units, captain," he told the Senecan. "You will position one unit at the center – where I want you to be in command – and the others behind our right half and our left."

Aram moved his hands upon the table. "I hope to deploy the army in such a way as to be able to place your troops on higher ground behind our lines where you will have clear lines of sight to the front.

"The enemy, from his vantage opposite, may discern what he thinks is a weak point in our deployment, and he may mass troops there – at that place, wherever it may be upon the line. It will fall to you and your archers to concentrate the two units nearest that point and weaken him as he makes his assault."

Aram paused for a moment and then went on. "If the enemy perceives no weak point and assaults the line equally along it, I will need you to weaken him all along the front, paying special attention to his lashers. It is my hope that those beasts will deploy in a line behind, rather than among his lesser troops. If so, this would give your archers clearer lines of sight to diminish those among the enemy that will be our most treacherous foes.

"As the battle proceeds, there will be times when our line is in danger of being breached. With you and your archers upon the high ground, it may be that you can use your weapons to prevent the breach. Thaniel and I will go to those places as well – as we are needed."

Matibar nodded, but a frown asserted itself once more upon his face. "My lord, each of our archers is supplied with four full quivers of arrows. When these are exhausted, Seneca will not want to remain behind the lines while others bear the brunt."

"I understand, captain," Aram told him. "You and your men have all been equipped with swords from the armory?"

"We have, my lord."

"Then when your missiles are gone; I will leave you to act as a reserve – put your troops into the line wherever they are needed, captain. By that time, I am sure, conditions will have become chaotic at one or more points along our lines, and we will need you to bring order to that chaos, if you can."

Aram then invited a general discussion of his overall strategy, answering questions, and asking them as well. In the end, everyone agreed that his disposition of the forces of the free world was best, and the various commanders consulted with each other to make certain that his vision was equally comprehended by all.

As the day began to wane toward late afternoon, Aram concluded the meeting by saying, "Manon's tower is a thousand miles, perhaps more to the north, beyond the limit of the great plains. The army will be on the march for two months, maybe longer. Every ten days, we will rest from the march, but upon those days of rest, we will array into lines of battle so that the men will get to know those beside whom they will stand in the face of the enemy."

There was general assent to this, and then Aram rose. "Let us go then," he said. "Let us get across the river, unite with Elam and Cumberland, and then march into the north together to do that which must be done."

Seventeen days later, Boman and Duridia, at the head of the grand alliance of free men, left the rolling prairie of Cumberland and trooped onto the road leading through the gap toward the plains, and the great army began its march into the north to decide the fate of the world.

16.

Aram sat on Thaniel and gazed ahead at the large slave holding that spread out upon both sides of the main road just north of the battlefield of Bloody Stream. Behind him, the grand army of the free peoples of the world stretched all the way back onto the rolling green hills of Cumberland. Behind that, along all the roads leading back into Elam and up the valley of the dry lake, thousands of oxcarts, filled with supplies wormed their way forward.

A chill breeze came down out of the north, across the wide, flat lands and made Aram tug at the collar of his cloak. Spring was only now feeling its way across the hills to their rear and into the vast plains. Behind and above him, the sun shone wan and dim through a thin, high overcast. He leaned forward, peering at the settlement and then looked to his right, at Matibar, and to his left, at Wamlak.

"I see no lashers," he stated.

"No," they both agreed, almost as one.

"There aren't many people about, either," Wamlak asserted.

Aram sent a query skyward to Alvern. Kipwing was farther north, scouting ahead along the road the army would travel upon as it went to war, but his venerable grandfather was above Aram and would be so for the duration of the march.

"If there are lashers in the village," Alvern replied to Aram, "they are hiding inside the huts, for I see none of their kind below me."

Wamlak grinned. "Hiding won't do them much good."

Aram smiled but shook his head in abrupt conviction. "They are not hiding," he said. "There are none here. Manon knows that we are coming and he is drawing in all his power."

129

Looking down, he spoke to Thaniel. "Let us go see if I am right."

The village was larger than it had appeared from a distance, though most of the structures nearest the road were of ancient construct and had been either burned or otherwise damaged at some point in the past. The slave huts were clustered along the edge of the ancient town, between its ruined buildings and the fields.

Aram kept his hand on his shoulder, near the hilt of the Sword, but no enemy appeared to confront them as they rode slowly into the town.

Nor did any of the slaves come out to greet them.

"Where is everyone?" Matibar asked, looking around.

Wamlak chuckled as he pulled at his collar. "Staying out of the cold, I imagine," he replied.

Aram turned in the saddle and looked back along the road, where Boman and the Duridians, the leading edge of the army, crested a rise not more than a mile behind them.

He shook his head. "If there were any of the enemy here, they fled northward yesterday or perhaps even before that." He indicated the leading elements of the army coming up the road behind them. "They won't stay to confront such power without the fullness of Manon's might beside them."

He swung down out of the saddle, though he kept his hand near the hilt of the blade. "Let's find the inhabitants of this town – if they are yet here."

On foot, leaving the horses in the road, they moved along a ruined street of the ancient town and made their way out to where the huts began.

Aram stopped. "Hello!" He called.

There was no answer but that of the chill wind whistling among the drab and dreary profile of the huts. Aram looked around, frowning. Was the village deserted? Had Manon recalled his slaves farther north, when he took his servants to him?

"We mean you no harm," he called again. "Come out."

He motioned to Wamlak and Matibar. "Check that hut over there – I'll check this one. Beware of treachery," he warned them.

At that moment, a scarecrow figure appeared warily in the doorway of the hut immediately to Aram's front. It was a man, thin and ragged, so thin, in fact, as to appear emaciated.

Realizing that he was fully exposed to these armed strangers, the man slid sideways and peered at them around the corner of the doorframe. "Who-who are you?"

"I am Aram, the enemy of Manon the Grim," Aram replied. "What is your name?"

The man stared at Aram. "You are the enemy of the grim lord?"

"I am – my army and I go to destroy him even now. What is your name?" He asked again.

The man emerged from the hut's dark interior slowly and cautiously, blinking his eyes against the light. "I am named Hured."

Aram studied him closely, noting the lack of energy and the curiously swollen aspect of the middle part of his terribly thin body. "Are you the elder?" He asked.

"No – Aluren is elder of this village. I am a member of the village council but no more. He is the elder."

"What has happened here? Is there sickness in this village?" Aram asked. "And where are your overlords?"

Hured was too fatigued – or unwell – to reply to, or perhaps even comprehend that many questions, so, with an effort, he focused upon the last. "The great lasher came and took the overlords away, along with our grain and milcush."

"They went north after collecting the harvest?"

Hured shook his head weakly. "This was after the collection of the harvest. The great lasher came with wagons and took much of our winter's stores."

Abruptly, understanding came to Aram; and with it came an explanation of the villager's thinness and lassitude. Anger rose hard and sharp in him as once again Aram examined the man's poor condition. "They took your winter's food?"

"All but a small portion," Hured confirmed.

Aram worked to keep his voice gentle, devoid of any hint of the fury that was blazing within him as he asked, "How many people are in this village?"

Hured shook his head. "I am not certain. About five hundred, I think, though more than a few have died." He looked down at the ground as if in guilt. "We have rationed the stores – tried to make the food last the winter, so there will be something to plant." He

131

looked up with tears streaming down his face. "We killed and ate the oxen during the last snow."

Aram drew in a calming breath and let it out again slowly. He glanced around. "Where is the granary?"

Hured tried to lift a hand and indicate the direction, but it was a futile attempt. "North," he said. "At the edge of the village, just on the east side of the road."

"Go back and rest," Aram told Hured, and then he looked at Matibar and Wamlak. "Let's find the granary and see for ourselves."

They went back to the road, mounted up and went to the northern edge of the village. The granary was very large, much larger than that in the village of Aram's youth. This had been a big and productive slave-holding. The building was round, perhaps fifty feet across and twelve feet high, and separated into two halves by a center wall. There were high windows spaced around the wall, each protected on the outside by a slanted extrusion that prevented rain from entering even as they let in a bit of light. There was a five-foot-high retaining wall just inside the main doorway, connected to the center wall, beyond which, on either side, was stored the harvest.

There was nothing in the room on the left. On the right, in the middle of this vast structure, in a pitiful mound upon the floor, there was perhaps an amount equal to fifteen or twenty bushels of grain. Beside it, there was another smaller mound of some rounded, reddish-brown substance that was unknown to Aram. He stared at the miserable pile. It was hardly enough to feed five hundred people for a week, let alone plant the many fields that went away from this village in all directions.

Aram glanced at Matibar and Wamlak and saw in their eyes the same anger that burned in him.

"We must help these people, my lord," Matibar said.

Aram nodded without hesitation and turned to Wamlak. "Ride back – find High Prince Marcus. Bring him to me at once."

Wamlak nodded wordlessly and went back to Braska, mounted up, and the two of them pounded back toward the south. After he'd gone, Aram looked once more at the pitiful stock of food, and then he and Matibar went back to where they'd left Hured.

Aram reached inside his pack and produced a piece of bread. "Eat this," he commanded Hured. "Then I want you to find Elder

Aluren and have him bring the village together in the center, by the road – all those still able to walk. Will you do it?"

Hured stared down at the bread in disbelief. Then he looked up at Aram with moist eyes. "May I give this to my wife and children instead?"

Aram nodded without speaking and reached inside his pack again, emptying the entire contents into Hured's hands. "You need strength as well. Give what you need to your family, but eat some yourself – then go do as I require."

Hured bowed stiffly and nearly fell. Matibar caught him and held him upright. The villager nodded his thanks to Matibar and then looked at Aram. "At once, my lord," he said, and despite the dry, wispy appearance of the skin on his face, and the sunken aridness of his eyes, tears of gratitude appeared and overflowed down his cheeks.

As Aram and Matibar sat on their mounts in the road at the center of the village, Aram worked at tamping down the anger he felt for the actions of Manon's minions, along with the pity for these helpless people that mingled with that fury. He needed to be cold and clear in his thoughts as he considered the problems before him.

Matibar looked over at him and frowned. "Is the Scourge trying to waste these people, or does he do this in an attempt to slow our progress?"

Aram thought for a moment and then nodded his head. "Both, I suspect," he answered. "Manon knows we are coming and that this conflict will decide everything – in his favor, he thinks. So, he is pulling in all his strength in order to ensure victory." But then a frown creased his brow and he looked over at the Senecan captain quizzically. "But why take all the food? Why run the risk of having no future crops upon which to draw supplies for his armies? Does he prepare for a siege? Or does he expect to plunder the whole of the world for his needs after defeating us?"

Then the frown went away and a look of suspicion came into his eyes. "Or does he think that if he succeeds in wresting this weapon from my hand that he will have no further use of his armies – and consequently of these slaves?"

As he pondered this new possibility, he looked away and turned his gaze northward, staring with hard eyes up the roadway toward his unseen enemy, far away beyond the horizon.

Matibar, however, kept his gaze fixed upon the king. "Can he do it, my lord?" He asked after a moment.

Aram turned and frowned at him. "Do what?"

Matibar lifted his chin, indicating the hilt of the Sword. "Wrest that weapon from your hand – can he do it?"

Aram met his gaze for a long moment. "When I meet Manon," he said then, "This Sword will pierce him. I will drive it into him. His hands will have no strength left in them to wrest anything from anyone – ever again."

Matibar looked away for an instant and then looked back. "You told me once that the weapon was an heirloom of your line. I have talked with Wamlak and others, my lord, and I know that you went to a mysterious place in order to gain possession of it. I know that it is powerful beyond imagining." He hesitated and glanced away once more. "If the Scourge were to gain possession of it –"

Aram shook his head. "Fear not, captain. The Sword has Guardians other than me, and they will not allow Manon to take it up. Should I fail, they will take it from the earth and move it far beyond his reach." His eyes narrowed and he looked once more into the north. "The possibility of my failure is the reason we must destroy his armies now, in the battle that is before us, that we may leave him without the full measure of his power."

Matibar had turned back and was gazing at him intently. "These other 'guardians' of the weapon, of which you speak – they are more powerful than the Scourge?"

Aram thought for a moment and then nodded in assent. "Yes, at least I believe them to be."

Matibar's frown deepened upon his brow. "Then why do not they take up the weapon and destroy the Scourge? Why lay this burden upon a man – even a man such as you?"

A dry, slight smile, utterly devoid of amusement, came upon Aram's face. "You are not the first to ask that question, captain," he replied. "I have often asked it myself, always without resolution." He shrugged. "The answer to that lies with the Maker alone. I only know this – the Sword is in my hand. It falls to me to put it to its intended purpose."

Matibar continued to watch him closely. "The destruction of the Scourge – that is its intended purpose?"

Aram nodded. "That is the sole reason it is upon the earth, captain."

Matibar met his gaze for a moment longer and then nodded and looked into north, his dark eyes sweeping along that unfamiliar horizon. "I will do everything in my power to aid you, my lord."

The first of the villagers began to straggle up, timidly, slowly, painfully, and warily. They had heard the rumors, wrought that very day that these men on beasts were come to rescue them, but long experience had taught them that those who were strong were not disposed to come among them for benign purposes.

So, despite the small flames of hope that flickered in each starving breast, they hung back as they arrived at the road, gazing up at Aram and Matibar with more wariness than hope. These tall, fearsome men in armor, mounted upon even more fearsome beasts, had commanded them to come, so they came. Such was their lot.

As Aram looked around at them, his eye fell upon an older man with gray hair that leaned heavily upon a staff. Two others stood near him, as if by wont.

Aram dismounted and walked slowly toward this man. "Are you Aluren?" He asked.

The man flinched as Aram drew near, and glanced furtively at each of his companions. "I am Aluren, my lord."

Aram inclined his head and spoke firmly but quietly. "I am Aram, lord of the free lands of the east and south. We have come to make you free."

Aluren blinked, but made no reply. He eyes went flat and he simply gazed at Aram as if without comprehension. "Free?"

Aram swept his hand around to indicate the village. "The grim lord has removed all his servants from this place – and has taken your food. Is this not so?"

"Yes," Aluren admitted. "It is so."

Aram indicated Matibar, seated upon Yvan behind him and then pointed back down the road. "It is because of us that he has done this. Our army will begin to pass through this village within the hour." He looked around at the villagers, who were still gathering, shuffling in from among the ruined buildings of the ancient town.

"Behind the army, there are carts filled with grain and other foods. We will leave you enough to feed you until harvest, and give you seed to plant." He indicated the road. "Our army will pass along

135

this road for the next day or more as we go north to vanquish the grim lord. The carts with the seed and food will follow behind."

After watching the approach of the leading elements of the army for a moment, he turned back to Aluren. "Empty your granary," he commanded of the elder, in a tone that brooked no dissent. "Distribute the grain among every family." He studied the pitiful folk that had slunk out of their dreary huts to hear him on this chill, late winter day. "Regain your strength," he stated kindly. "You are our people, and we will let you starve no longer."

The people continued to stare at him, most of them in confusion, unresponsive, though a few looked at their fellows with the smallest glimmer of hope brightening their dulled eyes.

Watching them, Aram knew that the truth of their changed circumstances would dawn on them but slowly. It was useless to try and convince them of it at this moment. "Go," he said to Aluren. "Distribute the food to every family."

Aluren stared at him for another long moment and then swallowed and nodded. "At once, my lord."

Aram mounted up on Thaniel again and he and Matibar went back to the south end of the village to watch the army come toward them. As the leading elements of Duridia arrived at the village and began to pass through, Boman, riding ahead of his troops on Stennar, raised his hand in salute.

"Continue on, Lord Aram?"

Aram raised his own hand in reply. "Continue on, Governor; there is no enemy about. Lord Alvern is above you, and Kipwing and the others scout ahead. They will warn you of any danger. Have you seen Marcus?"

"No – Captain Wamlak asked the same question not a half-hour ago. Is there a problem?"

Aram nodded. "These people are starving. Manon took their winter's supply in advance of our passage."

"Bastard," Boman growled, and said no more, but his hands made fists as he continued on, leading his troops northward through the burned and crumbled-down town.

Duridia had already passed by and the foremost troops of Elam were flowing past when Marcus came pounding up on Phagan, accompanied by Wamlak. The young High Prince nodded to Matibar and then looked at Aram. "You wanted to see me, my lord?"

136

"You told me once that your people keep a year's supply of food-stocks laid up whenever possible."

"Yes."

"And your troops brought six months' worth of those stores with them?" Aram asked.

"As I told you, Lord Aram," Marcus affirmed.

"So there are six months more laid up in the storehouses of Elam, are there not?"

"Yes, my lord – what –?"

Aram nodded shortly. "I want to buy as much of it as you will spare – if you will sell it to me."

Marcus frowned at him. "As I stated before, my lord, the army may have it all." He shrugged, though his frown stayed. "It must be rotated through the stores at the end of each year anyway – only grain crops may be held over for any length of time; the rest is returned to the fields each winter – and the farmers of my homeland are already into this year's planting. So – you may have it all, my lord. We need no payment."

Aram shook his head. "It is not for the army," he said and then hesitated, looking out over the plains, "though, of course, we will have to replace that which we distribute as we go north."

"Distribute?" Marcus asked.

Aram swept his hand around the village, taking in the plains beyond as well. "These people are starving, Your Highness. Manon took their food-stores after the end of last year's harvest. I suspect that we will discover that it is the same with all the people of the plains."

Marcus' eyes widened. "Is he abandoning his slaves? Why would he do such a thing?"

Aram shrugged. "Apparently, he feels that he will have no further use of them – one way or the other. Also, it is likely that he intends to distract us, and slow the movement this army; perhaps weaken us by means of that distraction." Aram met the eyes of the young prince. "Which is why I need you to do something for me – if you will, Marcus."

"Anything, my lord."

"I mean to keep these people alive, if at all possible – give them food and seed to plant from the stores of the army. I would like to replace those stores from Elam's surplus." Aram looked at the young prince closely. "A voice of authority will be required to bring the stores out of Elam in order to replenish that which we will disperse to the people of the plains as we go north. *Your voice*, Your Highness."

Marcus stared. "You want me to leave the army?"

Aram shook his head. "Only for a while, Marcus – only as long as it takes to give instruction to whomever you entrust with the task of gathering the extra stores and bringing them out of Elam." He smiled at his young friend. "I promise not to leave you out of the action, but I need this done. I will not allow these people to be lost. As we go north, I will have Arthrus distribute that which we can spare, saving enough to get the army to the tower and feed it there for two weeks."

He leaned toward Marcus and spoke earnestly. "The army must not lack, either. Take whatever men you need. Find Dane and take him with you. He is very good at such organization – tell him it is my wish. Will you do this?"

Marcus looked around at the ruin of the ancient town, noting here and there the emaciated citizens shuffling back toward their respective huts. His frown left his features, his eyes grew sad, and he nodded. "I will see it done, my lord."

After Marcus left, Aram turned to Wamlak. "Nikolus and his cavalry are back at the middle of the column?"

Wamlak nodded. "As you instructed, my lord."

"And your mounted archers? – where are they?"

"With the cavalry."

Aram looked westward, out across the wide vastness of the plains. "There are many villages out to the west," he told Wamlak. "I want you to gather extra supplies of food and take your mounted men, swing to the west of the column, find those other villages. Pass this same instruction along to Nikolus – tell him to divide his cavalry, sending Ruben out as well. Between the three of you, you should be able to find and save many."

He thought for a moment longer and then shook his head. "You cannot save them all," he admitted. "The plains extend far to the west." He turned a severe gaze upon the captain. "I want you to go no farther to the west than a day or two from the main road and this army. It is yet cool here and you will be able to carry little in the way of shelter. Leave what food you can with whatever villagers you discover and return. I want to see Nikolus, Ruben, and you every third or fourth day."

Wamlak looked west, out across the seemingly endless rolling prairie, still brown and tan with the freezing stain of winter. "Is there fuel for fire out there, my lord?"

Aram nodded. "Some. There are willows along the smaller streams and trees by the larger rivers. Why?"

Wamlak looked at him. "I don't mind going without shelter, my lord – as long as we can start a fire each night. We can go much further west, if you like."

At this, Aram shook his head immediately. "You cannot carry enough food for such long journeys – for yourself or to do the villagers any good. And we must retain enough to feed the army." He fixed his gaze upon the western horizon and thought for a moment longer. Then he shook his head once more. "Take as much food as you can carry – leave an extra portion with the westernmost village every second day and then return quickly. Instruct the villagers to send word to the west that people are to migrate eastward toward food." He sighed deeply. "Whatever we do, we cannot save them all," he said again.

Wamlak nodded his understanding and turned toward the rear, but Aram stopped him.

"Manon may move against us," Aram told the captain. "If word comes of this – I will send an eagle, probably Lord Alvern, to find you and Nikolus. Keep your mind open. Pass this along to Captain Nikolus."

"Yes, my lord."

As Wamlak pounded away to the south, Matibar and Yvan wheeled away as well. "I will go along, my lord, if you agree."

Aram thought for a moment and then nodded. "For now, captain. In ten days, however, we will begin to accustom the men to forming lines of battle. I will need you with the army then."

"As you wish, my lord."

17.

It was the same with all of Manon's former slaves, all the way along, as the army marched northward. Their food stores had been raided before winter, and all were starving. In some villages, where the wisdom of rationing had not prevailed, or perhaps where hope had been surrendered entirely, death was widespread.

In a few villages, not a soul had survived.

Bodies were often stacked in an unused hut – unburied due to the weakness of the survivors and the hardness of the frozen ground. With temperatures rising, Aram gave instructions to his commanders to send details into the villages near the road and properly dispose of the dead.

Aram grew deeply disturbed at the amount of death they encountered as they progressed northward along the eastern edge of the plains. Unwilling himself to take the time from the army or from his main order of business in order to roam off the road to the west, across the vastness of the plains to seek out every village, Aram instructed Wamlak and Nikolus to go ever farther into the west. In doing so, it became necessary that the mounted men ignore those villages nearer the road.

To bring a measure of relief to these, Arthrus was instructed to gather a contingent of willing men and oxcart drivers and go a day west of the army, help whoever he discovered, and then return. Before going south with Marcus, Dane calculated the stores needed by the army for two months. All the rest, Aram surrendered to Arthrus and the cavalry for use in their mission of mercy.

Ten days north of Cumberland, they camped near the southwestern edge of the hills that separated the valley of the river that flowed by the field from which Aram had fled the bonds of slavery and the long valley to the north along whose southern slopes he had been transported.

A broad-topped, gentle-sloped ridge extended for several miles out into the grasslands from the verge of these hills. It was suitable ground for Aram to begin teaching his army to deploy.

The next day, while Aram and Thaniel stood upon the top of another small yet higher ridge that jutted out from those same hills, observing, the various commanders of the army worked at forming a line of battle across the plains. On this day, Kavnaugh Berezan's half of the Elamites were being deployed to the left – on the western wing of the army – while Olyeg Kraine's were lined up on the right, east of the Duridians and Lamontans, who formed up at the army's center. Mallet and the Derosans anchored the eastern flank.

It did not go well.

Aram had placed a post in the ground about two miles west of the road, signifying the point that represented the middle of the left flank of the army, where Elam would deploy west of Duridia. The Elamites formed up well enough for the first several hundred yards of their triple-ranked line of battle. Then, all semblance of order dissipated. When the second division of Kavnaugh's half of the army came on line, they spread too thin, causing the third division to expand completely through the ground meant to be occupied by Boman's force of Duridians and all the way to the post, nearer the road, that Aram had driven into the ground to signify the center of the army itself.

Donnick went to work, re-aligning the troops of Elam, so that Boman could deploy in the center, and then Edwar and Lamont came on line. Once General Kraine's half of Elam began to form, there was more work for Thom Sota, who, soldiers later claimed, invented an entirely new vocabulary of curses that day.

The difference in experience between the men of Elam and the eastern troops, all of whom had seen battle at least once, was obvious. Three hours passed before the commanders were satisfied. Then Matibar and his Senecan archers filed into position behind the main body. For the moment, Aram left the gun on the road, although Boleson and Javeir, the two horses that had volunteered to move the gun upon the field, were hitched to it in place of the oxen and they and Timmon practiced moving it forward and back, and angling it slightly left or right.

The cavalry was not on hand to participate.

But the infantry was the spine of the army. If the spine could not form and hold, it mattered little what cavalry would do, anyway.

Aram glanced up at the sun, already nearing the apex of the sky. He wanted this day to be restful, for he intended to drive the army north on the morrow. Rather than making the men repeat the entirety of the maneuver, he instead had the army move back twenty paces and then return into position. Hopefully this would give the men at least a rudimentary feel for how they would form up when it mattered.

When the men were on line for the second time, Aram rode down and faced them, letting Thaniel move slowly along the line in each direction while he examined what his army would look like to the foe.

An hour later, he sent them to their tents, to eat and rest, and to tend to any physical difficulties brought on by ten days of hard marching.

For ten days more, they tramped steadily northward. Word came down from Alvern that there was still no sign of Manon or his forces, anywhere upon the road that verged the eastern edge of the great plains all the way north to Bracken.

Nikolus, Ruben, Wamlak, and Arthrus continued with all diligence to seek out and aid the people of the plains, scattered across the vast grasslands to the west, where spring was just now beginning to replace winter's gold with a hint of green.

Often, their reports of what they found were so disheartening as to cause Aram to pace back and forth outside his tent deep into the night, venting his silent despair into the chill air.

Just south of the river that flowed out of the long valley, Aram ordered the army deployed once more. On this occasion, after casting about in indecision, leaning first one way and then the other, Aram decided to have the army reverse its order of deployment, with Kavnaugh upon the right, and Mallet upon the extreme left. For until he examined the ground on which they would face the forces of the enemy, the ultimate configuration of the army was in doubt.

Despite the efforts of the commanders, this attempt at forming lines of battle went worse than the previous, ten days earlier. Once again, Aram let the army stand on line for a half-hour and then sent the men to rest.

The next time, ten days north of that great stream, near the jumbled line of hills that marked the northern verge of the long valley, things went somewhat better. Ten days after that, it went so smoothly as to quell Thom Sota's penchant for colorful language. He was even heard to grudgingly admit, "That's fine, boys, just fine." Aram watched with growing satisfaction. His soldiers were gradually evolving into veteran campaigners.

Their thoughts were becoming focused on the task ahead, and this translated into camaraderie and order, which in turn would ultimately help them to stand and face the enemy's steel.

Northward across the plains, as they entered into country where winters were ever harsh, the incidence of disease, starvation, and death increased among the villages of those in thrall to Manon. Alvern received word that Marcus had succeeded in filling another wagon train with food and was even now coming northward through the gap in the hills near Cumberland with all speed.

Aram took stock of his supplies and released another measure of food from them to be distributed. The greenish tint to the ground that rolled westward from the road told him that spring was coming to the north of the world. The people would need something to plant as well as to eat.

After crossing the river that flowed out of the long valley and passing the edge of the hills, the road angled westward, curving out into the flat lands. Six weeks into the march, they came to another broad river, coiling slowly to the west. Alvern informed him that this was, in fact, the Secesh, which at this distance from Vallenvale, was a substantial stream indeed. On the northern side of that mighty current, Aram gave the order to deploy yet again, for the fifth time since the march began.

Perhaps it was the ever-increasing proximity to the dark stronghold of the enemy, but the army performed the necessary maneuvers with greater determination, skill, and success than ever. The grim lord of the world, who thus far had shown no inclination to leave his fortress and come south to face Aram and his army upon the open ground, came nearer with every step.

Over the next week, the road rose up through a line of small, rocky hills that extended out into the flatlands before curving back on a tangent just east of due north, where it then descended toward another broad land, which was also greening up beneath the strengthening sun. The sky grew increasingly hazy and a slight odor of brimstone pervaded the air here. When the wind sharpened out of the dark heights to the north, the odor became amplified and the eyes stung.

This, Aram abruptly realized, was the land of Bracken.

One mid-day, he sat upon Thaniel atop a rise and gazed into the north. Along that dark horizon there were darker mountains jutting up. Even at this distance, he could see that two or three of those taller peaks spewed smoke into the sky. Try as he might, however, his eye could not resolve the tower he had last looked upon through the glass from the heights of Kelven's mountain.

Speaking to Thaniel, they went on, down the road where it curved out onto the plains once more, this time angling westward and then bending back until finally it straightened out and ran almost on perfect alignment into the north. Surprisingly, the people of the villages of Bracken had fared somewhat better than their fellow slaves further south. Though their stores had been raided, they had not been left in such dire circumstances as most of the others.

Aram puzzled over this. Did the grim lord feel a measure of pity for those that had labored in his chains so much longer than any of his other servants? He dismissed that thought immediately. More likely, Manon had simply filled his storehouses to overflowing and found no need of further goods. Or perhaps, after all, he had decided that he might find use for a few healthy, living slaves sometime in the future.

In any event, the people that clustered together in their fields or shrunk away from the road to watch the vast serpentine line of armed men wind past them and tramp off toward the north seemed in much better shape than those slaves further south.

Before they had traversed half of Bracken, Marcus arrived to inform Aram that the oxcarts with the extra food were yet two weeks behind the army.

"I'll send Kipwing to summon Nikolus and Wamlak," Aram told the High Prince. "The stores of the army are low, but the horses might serve to ferry the supplies from your oxcarts to those of Arthrus if it becomes necessary."

He squinted northward, peering into the smoky haze along the horizon. "You've done well, Marcus. As you can see, we are getting close to our destination."

Marcus looked to the north as well and then stared up into the increasingly murky sky. "What a miserable place this is."

Over the next week, as they began to leave Bracken behind, the road passed through another line of rocky hills that tumbled down out of the east to immerse themselves in the plains. Beyond those hills was yet another valley though not so wide as to render itself as a plain. It was just a valley through which flowed a small stream lined with willows and a few trees, all bearing the green of new leaves despite the thin sunshine that struggled to find its way through the smoke-filled overcast that grew heavier with every mile.

As Thaniel crested the rise in the road, the hills began to fall away to his right and Aram looked into the north, beyond the valley to a horizon defined by much higher ground. Though hills clustered along its base, this higher ground was something else entirely. Dark and rocky, the height curved away in both directions, as if it might be the lip of a caldera.

Aram raised his eyes further and gazed into the sooty sky above the curve of dark, rocky high ground.

And there it was, rising up to pierce the clouds.

The black serpent's fang tower that was the dwelling place of the enemy of all free people.

Manon's lair.

The dark tower of Morkendril.

Swinging off the road, Aram brought Thaniel to a halt and studied the tower. Even through the haze, he could see that it was gleaming black. He could not see its base, only about the top half or two-thirds of the structure. Where it came into view, just above the horizon, it was already narrowing. As it soared into the firmament, it narrowed further, until ending far above in a fine, sharp point, like a needle.

The shape was familiar to him – he'd viewed a much smaller version of this same structure far away to the south, in Panax.

Duridia came up, boots tramping along the roadway. Boman and his mount moved out of line to come and stand next to Thaniel. The governor also studied the tower for a long moment and then glanced over at Aram. "That is where we are going, I assume."

Aram nodded. "Alvern reports that his forces have not moved from his valley, Governor." He lifted one hand and indicated the high ground to their front. "If he refuses to come out and remains in place, we may find ourselves positioned to advantage atop or perhaps beyond that highest ridge. I will know better when I have been up there and examined the ground."

He glanced back at the sun, just now slipping down to the west, and then he turned to look forward along the road, which was altered in substance here where it approached the tower of the grim lord. From Cumberland north, it had been broad and smooth, composed of ancient stone set down long ago, in another age of the world.

Here, the roadway was yet broad, but the surface was newer, smoother, and the pavement was made up of shining black rock. Aram pointed along it.

"Let us reach the northern base of these hills by evening," he told Boman. "The army may encamp along the roadway going back through the hills into Bracken. I will go ahead of you and stay the night between you and the stronghold of the enemy and send the wolves abroad among the hills. In the morning I will cross the small valley and climb to the top of that high ground and see how the ground lies before his tower, and if possible, how he has disposed his strength."

Boman nodded as he moved away to the road and rejoined his men. "I'll stand pickets in a semi-circle to our front through the night," he called back, to Aram's approving nod.

Aram spoke to Thaniel and the great horse surged ahead, making for the last remaining hills that rose between them and that place where the fate of the world would soon be decided. Leorg and Shingka left him to go east and gather Padrik, Goreg, and the rest of the wolves. Those people had gone northward in small bands through higher ground to the east, where food might be found for them. They had shadowed the long column for nearly two months; now they were to be gathered together in order to disperse them into the high ground ahead of the army.

Aram slept in the saddle in the shelter of a rock outcropping just off the road near a small, tumbling stream, the waters of which were stained pale yellowish brown but which the horse nonetheless declared to be drinkable. The morning sun found him and Thaniel atop a rise, gazing back southward down the gleaming black surface of the road into the small valley, little more than a mile-wide, grassy swale through which a sizeable stream of slow-moving brackish water flowed from east to west. Down there, Boman and his troops from the southern plains were beginning to stir.

He bent his thoughts to the sky. "Lord Alvern?"

He listened for some time but there was no answer as the sun began to climb the sky to the east. Concern grew in him as the silence from the sky overhead lengthened.

"Lord Alvern?"

"Forgive me, my lord," came the reply then. "We have been engaged in driving away Bezathog and his kin."

"Bezathog?"

"He is the lord of vultures. He and his kind serve the enemy."

Aram frowned upward. "Have any of you suffered injury?"

"None, my lord," the eagle responded. "The vultures have been driven away, across the mountains to the east of the valley of the enemy. And Manon yet keeps his forces positioned close to his tower."

Aram's frown deepened as he returned his gaze to earth. "Does he send no scouts toward us?"

"No, my lord. He does not."

"Alright, Thaniel," Aram said to the horse. "Let us go and see."

Thaniel turned northward and they descended and passed through the bottom of another small swale and followed the road up where it ran through a shallow cut into the higher ground beyond. The road curved gently this way and that to accommodate uneven places in the slopes of the hills that tumbled up toward the even higher ground that Aram had spied from the valley behind him. Viewed from up close, this highest ground was apparently indeed the lip of a large crater or rounded valley, for it curved gently away in both directions, gradually bending northward out of sight to either side.

Finally, they came out of the hills onto a long, broad, fairly gentle slope that rose to the horizon.

Ascending along one last smooth stretch of the gleaming black road they spied to their front where the road cut through this highest ground in a straight line and then bent down out of sight as it fell toward whatever lay beyond. Far away, through that cut, Aram could just make out the icy heights of distant mountains.

They crested the slight rise in the road where it passed through the cut and Aram brought Thaniel to a halt.

Immediately to his front, the road ran down a very gradual slope and out onto level ground.

The valley of Morkendril lay spread out before him.

At its heart lay a vast cluster of stone structures. These were comprised mostly of enormous concentric circles of interconnected huts that spread out from the base of the tower, separated by narrow streets. The distance too great for certainty, but to Aram's eye it appeared that most of these huts looked to be of a size that would serve as the dwelling places of small groups of gray men or perhaps three or four lashers. Some buildings, however, especially on the outskirts of the city, were of much larger construct.

Rising from the center of everything was the mighty tower. Aram was obliged to lean his head back as he peered upward in order to see the top of it, nearly lost in the haze far overhead. At its base, sweeping out from it on four sides, there were other, smaller towers, and while these were also round, they were squat, blunt, and topped with crenellated turrets. Each was connected to the main structure by strong heavily-built walls of black stone.

The main tower, the seat of him who named himself Lord of the World, appeared to have sprung straight from the earth, smooth, gleaming, black, or maybe it had been punched up and through the skin of the earth, like the serpent's fang it resembled. The odd thought came that perhaps it was the spike at the end of an impossibly huge dragon's tail. For just a moment, Aram had a vision of a vast, heavy-bodied creature, inhabiting a deep warren in the barren ground, slumbering in the earth just beneath this desolate valley.

He lowered his attention to the city at the tower's base and then brought his gaze back along the road toward him.

The distance was perhaps three miles from where the road gained the floor of the valley to where the stone structures of the city of the enemy began. Between where he and Thaniel stood and the stone huts of the city of Morkendril began there was nothing but barren and apparently gravelly ground. Then something else, near to the edge of the city, caught his eye. He leaned forward and peered toward the near side of the vast cluster of buildings.

There was a dark line there, in the small of the distance, just at the edge of the buildings that might have been the vast ranks of an army, deployed to defend the city. If this was, in fact, true, his eye could not resolve it to his satisfaction. He sent the query skyward.

"Yes," Alvern replied, "the full forces of the grim lord are deployed at the very edge of the city."

"Do they move?"

There was a moment's hesitation before the eagle gave his response. "They do not."

Aram nodded to himself, satisfied. If Manon meant to meet him in battle, the grim lord was evidently content to do so at the very heart of his domain.

He glanced over at the sun climbing the morning and then bent his thoughts skyward once again. "Tell Boman that his troops are to remove toward the far side of the small valley, where they will spread out into the hills and encamp," he instructed Alvern. "This will make room for Berezan to move through and camp next to the hills.

"In fact, I want as much of the army as is possible to come up and encamp in that valley which will serve as our base of operations. Tell Boman that the water is good, despite its appearance. Send word that I want him and the other commanders to join me here upon this ridge as soon as they may – as soon as their troops are moving forward."

"I will instruct them, my lord."

While he waited, Aram rode out onto the slope to study the ground. The top of the ridge that had seemed to be quite defined when he had viewed it from the valley to the south and consequently had appeared to possess a sharp-edged summit, did not. It was, in fact, rather broad at the top where it crested and sloped away rather gently into the valley.

Aram found this fact somewhat disappointing. He had hoped to position his troops upon advantageous earth where the enemy – if they could be coaxed to attack – would be obliged to assault him up a steep grade.

And he meant to lure them out if at all possible. He had no intention of confronting the power of Manon upon the open floor of the valley.

To their left, along the top of the ridge to the west, a mile or so from where they stood, the slope steepened as it bent back to the north beneath the flanks of a great mountain that rose there. The lower slopes of this mountain, from whose top a tendril of smoke rose into the sky, knifed down through the slope and onto the valley floor in a jumble of jagged, impassable rockslides, effectively cutting off the gentle ridge. Aram noted this harsh ground with satisfaction. He would anchor his greenest flank, Kavnaugh Berezan's Elamites, there, up against the ragged slopes of that mountain.

He looked the other way, to his right toward the east, and felt the sharp pang of dismay.

That way, the top of the ridge over which the road passed before spilling into the valley continued on around in a gradual swing to the north; its slopes remaining fairly constant in height and pitch. But less than a mile from where the road cut through the ridge, where he and Thaniel now stood, there was obvious difficulty. Aram had come to believe that the roadway would be very near the center of his lines, if not the exact center.

But where to the west the ground gave him a place to anchor that wing of his army, to the east the terrain was not so charitable. While the main ridge that comprised the crater rim continued curving on around into the north, becoming gradually and then severely more steep and jagged, there was a small secondary ridge that jutted out into the valley, ending about a hundred yards further on in a small hillock.

If he placed his right flank upon the main ridge, his lines would extend beyond the point where this small secondary ridge jutted out, giving the enemy an avenue of attack into that wing of his army.

Rising at the end of the secondary ridge and expanding out for perhaps another hundred yards into the valley, the rounded hill defined the extent of that ridge as it bent into the valley. The top of this small hill was just about the same distance from the roadway as was the place at the far end of his lines where his flank would be relatively secure, anchored beneath the rugged mountain on the west.

Aram now knew – and his heart sank at the knowledge – just where Mallet and his small band of Wallensians would be deployed.

He was bent forward in the saddle, studying the distant hill, pondering the lay of this troubling piece of ground, when the wolves flowed over the top of the ridge and came down to join him.

"We are all here, master," Leorg told him.

Aram nodded. "Good." He moved his arm indicating the surrounding hills to the rear of the ridge. "Patrol all this area while the army moves up," he instructed them, and then looked both ways along the sloping ground. "Including this ground, especially during the dark hours, for this is where I hope to meet the enemy and I want to keep possession of it if at all possible." He bent a severe gaze upon Leorg and all the rest of them. "Stay out of the valley. Alvern and his kin will watch that in daylight. Secure this slope but do not enter the valley floor. Patrol in groups of five or more," he ordered. "I want no one moving alone in hostile country."

"Yes, master."

After the wolves moved away, Aram looked down at Thaniel. "Walk out to the top of that little hill there," he said. "I want to see what may be done."

The horse began to move but spoke the question as he did so. "What may be done?" He asked.

"In order to defend it," Aram explained. "I cannot let the enemy gain possession of it and occupy it; he would split my right wing. If possible, I will have to anchor my right flank on its summit." He went silent for a moment and then spoke low, as if to himself. "May the Maker help Mallet," he muttered.

The hill was far worse, logistically, than it had appeared from a distance. Rounding up at the end of the smaller secondary ridge where it extruded into the valley, the hill sloped away rather gently on all sides, including into a small canyon that the extrusion formed between the hillock and the main rim of the crater.

Despite the fact that the slopes leading up to the main ridge out of the depths of the small, narrow canyon were steep enough to be easily defended, perhaps by wolves, the back portion of the hillside that dropped into it was not. Consequently, Aram would be required to split the right end of his line. Not only was it necessary to defend the hill but he would have to position troops upon the ridge behind, at least for the distance of two hundred yards or so to the

151

point where yet another smoking mountain had sent streams of jagged rock sloping down onto the valley floor.

He had hoped to give the wolves freedom to roam beyond both ends of his lines, in order to detect and prevent secret assaults and to exploit any opportunities they might discover. Now, however, it would likely be necessary to anchor them to the area of the ridge above the canyon created by the extrusion, and to place the very end of his right wing upon the hill. Mallet would be forced to defend on at least three of four sides. Even with the wolves to aid him and archers positioned to give him cover, it would be a daunting, even terrifying, prospect.

Aram dismounted and walked the hill, going to the right to peer down into the small canyon and then to his left to survey the hillsides that sloped away into the valley. Then, standing at the rounded summit he turned and studied the main rim of the crater above and behind him.

He had hoped to anchor both ends of his line in a manner that would render any attempt at a flanking maneuver by the enemy a difficult thing. Instead he found that his right flank would be bent away from the main line of battle and exposed on three sides.

He trusted Mallet and the Wallensians; they had faced the enemy more than once and come away the victor each time, but here, upon this small hill, he would ask more of them than ever before.

Perhaps this time, he thought, he would ask too much.

The hill and the jutting ridge of which it was the final extension were both too constricted to allow room for the cavalry to maneuver effectively, so Nikolus could not be called upon to help. As he let his gaze rove along the main ridge behind, Aram realized that his only recourse was indeed to place the wolves there, buttressed by a contingent of Matibar's archers. Still, if the enemy studied his deployment and decided to exploit this weakness, Aram himself might be called upon to help defend this ground, leaving most of the rest of the battlefield dangerously out of his view.

In an agony of uncertainty, he turned and gazed down over the slope that fell away toward the valley floor. Could he position his army lower upon that rocky incline? Was there perhaps a more defensible line to be executed closer to the valley floor?

But even as he entertained this thought, his eyes informed him of its futility. Unless he moved his forces all the way to the level valley floor itself, this little hill – or its lower slopes – would become his right flank. And the lower he would go, the more difficulties this minor projection of ground presented.

He rejected outright the idea of defending the valley floor.

Down there, both his flanks would be hopelessly exposed.

The sun climbed ever higher while he prowled the hilltop in doubt. Finally, without satisfying himself as to the means of making his eastern flank more secure, he decided to go back toward the center.

As he mounted up, he uttered his doubts to Thaniel. "Mallet is in for a hard time if the enemy decides to push with his strength here."

"He will hold," the horse answered. "Even if he does not, and the enemy takes the hill, we could trap him on this narrow ridge by sending the wolves to his rear."

"Perhaps." Aram nodded at the possibility rendered by this statement. "True; with the wolves behind him it would be a difficult flanking assault for the enemy. Still, if he gained that hill in strength enough to resist the wolves, he could then chip away at this end of our line and reduce us piece by piece."

As the horse regained the main ridge and began to move westward along it, Aram let his gaze sweep down and over the sloping ground where upon the morrow his army would very likely face the enemy. "Give me your thoughts – where is the weak point?" He asked the horse.

"The hill to the east is difficult, but it is at the end of our lines. The road where it cuts through the ridge at the center is the true weak point," Thaniel replied without hesitation. "If he can pierce our forces there, he may roll us up in both directions. Manon is wise; he will know this. He will send his power against that place."

Aram looked ahead, at the wide, smooth, black roadway that rose up the slope from the valley floor. After a moment, he nodded. "Yes, but you and I – and the Sword – will be there in the middle, my friend," Aram told him.

Thaniel returned his answer, once again without hesitation. "Then it is become strong," he replied.

When they reached the road, Boman, Matibar, and Berezan were there, sitting on their mounts atop the ridge just to the west of the cut. All three were gazing in silence at the fearsome tower that reared up from the heart of the dark valley to their front.

Matibar looked over at him as he and Thaniel fell into line beside them. "The Scourge dwells there – in that black tower?"

"He does," Aram assured him.

"Then why would he turn his wrath – as he did in ancient times – upon Seneca?" The captain wondered. "We are almost at the other end of the world from him."

"Yes," Aram agreed, "but you stood with Joktan against him and he could not abide what he considered rebellion against his rule. Besides, the grim lord lusts for all – for everything that there is, even the stars."

Boman was leaning forward in the saddle, peering at the vast city that surrounded the base of the tower. "Where is his army? I can make out nothing."

"It is there," Aram responded. "It may be hidden among the buildings – or it may be lined up close to the city, looking at us even now as it was not three hours ago. The distance is too great for my eyes as well."

After a moment, Matibar nodded his head. "There is a long, dark line upon the plain just at this edge of the city. I believe it to be his army."

"Open your minds," Aram commanded, and he sent a thought skyward, to Alvern. "Where is the might of the enemy, Lord Alvern? Does it yet stand before his city?"

"It does. There are many lashers and gray men there, very many, in a line," the eagle responded. "Shall I look closer?"

"*No*, do not approach his tower, my friend. Remember his treachery of long ago."

"I do remember, Lord Aram," Alvern answered. "It is the reason I have forbade the lords of the air to approach any closer than the sky above the ridge on which you stand."

Aram nodded. "Very wise." He looked around at the three commanders. "That line of men and lashers is undoubtedly the full strength of Manon."

Berezan pulled his gaze away and looked over at Aram. "Will we assault him there – upon the plain before the city? For if his

154

troops remain where they stand; then the enemy expects us to come to him."

Aram shook his head slowly and then looked left and right along the ridge. "I would rather face him here, where he must climb this slope to meet us." He looked back at the others. "What are your thoughts?"

"We must hold the high ground," Boman answered at once.

Matibar nodded in agreement. "We should meet him here."

Aram looked at the Elamite. "General?"

Berezan stared at the dark valley for a long moment and then met Aram's gaze. "What if he doesn't come out?"

Aram turned and looked north. "The whole of the world lies to our rear, so we have access to supplies," he replied. "The grim lord does not. His armies may last a few months, perhaps even for the most of a year on that which he has laid up, but no longer. He knows this. Eventually, his stores will be empty, and then he will have to come out, and he will be weaker."

Boman looked at him with narrowed eyes. "Do you think he means to withstand a siege?"

Aram shook his head. "No. We are here where he wants us. He expected us, even wanted us to come. I believe that he will send his strength against us."

Matibar turned his gaze upward and stared at the heights of the massive, fang-like tower. "It is rumored that the Scourge has other powers than his armies," he said.

"Yes," Aram admitted. "But we have another power as well – one that he desires greatly. He will come out and try to take it."

Matibar looked at him. "You speak of the strange sword that you bear."

"Yes."

"And he would sacrifice his armies to gain it?"

"Yes; I think that he would," Aram replied, and then he bent a thoughtful gaze upon the distant dark city. "It may be that Manon will wish to settle this between him and me – make his army stand aside so that I may go in unto him. It may be that he wishes to have no fight here at all."

Boman shook his head vehemently. "It would be a trap, my lord. Were he to separate you from us, he could send his forces to overwhelm you – then he would have the Sword, and we would not have you."

Aram smiled slightly. "Which is why I will not accept the offer if it is made, Governor." The smile faded. "I am afraid that we must engage his army first, destroy it if possible. Then I will go and face him."

Berezan turned and looked behind him and then studied the ridge in both directions. "If he sends his army out, my lord," he said after a moment, "then we should meet him here, on this high ground, as Governor Boman stated."

Aram nodded. "He will come out."

The sun was almost directly overhead when more hooves resounded upon the black road. Edwar, Olyeg Kraine, Thom Sota, Findaen, Mallet, and Jonwood with Donnick behind him on Colrad pounded through the cut. Their mounts slid to a stop as the valley floor came into view. For a long moment, they all stared ahead of them and up at the heights of the black tower.

Mallet growled beneath his breath and shook his massive, eight-foot-long lance – which he had long ago named "Lasherbane" – at the distant menacing structure.

"At last," he stated through gritted teeth, "we come to the end of it."

Ignoring that, Aram looked at Findaen. "Where are Nikolus and Wamlak?" He asked.

Findaen replied without looking over. His gaze was fixed ahead and high in the sky above him, upon the tower that pierced the smoky firmament. "They went east, into Bracken, my lord," he replied, "to find any that need aid." Finally, he yanked his gaze away from the gleaming tower and looked over at Aram. "High Prince Marcus went to recall them. Is this where we fight?"

Aram waited to return an answer to this query until all of them looked at him. Then he waved one hand, indicating the ridge that ran east and west. "Look over this ground, and then give me your thoughts," was his reply. Centering his attention upon Edwar, he asked, "Your troops are at the rear of the army?"

Edwar pulled his gaze away from the dark tower before him and nodded. "Yes, my lord."

"How long before the whole of your force arrives in the small valley behind us?"

156

Edwar considered and then shook his head. "The column stretches back almost to the borders of Bracken, my lord. My men will reach the near edge of the hills south of the valley by nightfall. If they are roused early – along with the men of General Kraine that are on the road ahead of them, we may fully enter that valley before midmorning on the morrow."

Aram moved his attention to Olyeg Kraine. "Do you agree with that assessment, General?"

Kraine nodded. "The majority of my troops will enter the small valley by evening, but many of them will camp upon the road this night."

"Where are your troops, general?" He inquired of Berezan.

"In the valley, my lord," Berezan replied. "They will encamp at the base of these hills behind us this evening."

"Duridia is already in the valley, as you know," Boman told Aram, "and we are moving up behind General Berezan."

"Wallensia is immediately behind Boman, my lord," Mallet stated.

Aram looked back at Olyeg Kraine, who nodded. "My troops are immediately behind Wallensia. The main body will move within the valley by evening."

"And Lamont will encamp upon the road this night, as I told you, my lord; but will move as soon as the way clears to our front," Edwar told him.

"Seneca is with Lamont," Matibar stated, when Aram looked at him.

Aram acknowledged all this and turned to Boman. "Is there room in that valley, do you think, for you, General Berezan, Mallet, and the main part of General Kraine's people?" He asked.

Boman considered and then nodded. "We have agreed to spread our columns, my lord, and extend the camps into the high ground on either side of the valley as necessary."

Aram turned and looked once more at the distant dim line of *power* that stood before the city of Morkendril. "Alright," he said. "The wolves will patrol this slope throughout the night, and Thaniel and I will encamp here on this ridge, near the road."

He glanced eastward at the jutting little hill, and realized that despite his doubts, he would deploy his army here, along the top of the ridge. There was no acceptable alternative. He looked over at

Berezan. "Rouse your men before dawn, general," he said. "Make certain that they are fed and on the move by sun-up." He indicated the ridge running away to their left, toward the west and the shattered slopes of the volcano a mile or so distant. "You will anchor your flank against that dark mountain and deploy toward this road in a line of three ranks, perhaps thirty paces below the crest – with your archers to the rear."

As Berezan nodded his understanding, Aram moved his gaze to Boman. "You will follow him to this spot and position your men to the west of this road, Governor. Mallet and Wallensia, General Kraine, with his half of Elam, and Edwar and Lamont will move to the right of the road behind you. Once General Berezan is in place you will move left and close the gap between him and you and when Lamont is in place, they will move forward and close upon your right."

He then settled his gaze upon Olyeg Kraine. "Your men will arrive here sometime after mid-morning, general, and will move toward the east into position along the top of the ridge to the right of Edwar, with your right flank touching Mallet and his men, who will deploy as I will instruct him shortly. Once you are fully on line, and Lamont is in position, move down the slope until you are aligned with the rest of the army. Do not delay; for the enemy may decide to strike at us when we are without your strength." He lifted his eyes and his arm and pointed toward the east. "Your flank, Olyeg, should be anchored near where that ridge juts out into the valley."

Olyeg nodded his head, his mouth set in a hard line. "We will be here before you expect us, Lord Aram, of this I assure you."

"Thank you, general," Aram replied. He waited for a moment and then continued. "I want the front rank of all troops positioned thirty paces below the brow of the ridge, upon this slope. He moved his hand upward. "Seneca will deploy in three contingents upon the ridge, one in the center, one over on the east, and another to the west, above and behind the main line. The cavalry will roam the field to lend aid as needed." He looked at Donnick and Thom. "Generals Shurtan and Sota must be here at sun-up, in order to aid the army in its deployment."

Both men inclined their heads in comprehension.

Aram held up a cautionary finger. "It is my hope that I have calculated the distances along this slope correctly to facilitate the proper deployment of our strength. Nonetheless, in order to make certain that we present a solid front to the enemy, you will all hold a good measure of your troops in reserve until the line is formed – in the event that your line must be lengthened either to the right or the left."

Pointing first to the west and then back to the east, he said, "I want our front to extend from the slopes of that mountain to the point where that small ridge juts out into the valley. On our left, General Berezan and Governor Boman will deploy their troops in order as was practiced during the crossing of the plains. It will be on our right that adjustments may have to be affected once the men of Elam, Lamont, and Wallensia are on line – either to lengthen our lines or to shorten them."

He let his gaze sweep them all. "Questions?"

Kraine was gazing eastward. He lifted his hand and pointed. "My right flank will deploy where the ridge splits?"

"Yes," Aram answered. "And will extend perhaps a hundred yards beyond."

Kraine turned an obviously worried eye upon him. "And when the enemy gains possession of the ridge that juts out toward that small hill, my lord?"

"Wallensia will be tasked with that problem, general," Aram replied, "and the wolves will be there, along with a contingent of Senecan archers." He nodded solemnly; acknowledging the Elamite general's instincts. "You are wise to recognize the difficulties of our right flank. You will, no doubt, wish to keep a force in reserve upon your right."

Mallet looked at him with narrowed eyes, frowning. "What of Wallensia's task, my lord?"

"One moment, please, Mallet," Aram answered and he looked at the others while the big man's frown strengthened upon his face.

"Does everyone understand what I expect of him and his men?" Aram asked.

There were silent nods all around.

"Then take the time to examine the ground that has been assigned to you. Verify my measure of the ground, and discuss with the commander to your right and your left any issues that you suspect might arise. I will return shortly."

Aram looked at Mallet.

"Come with me, if you will, my friend," he said. Speaking to Thaniel, they went eastward along the rim to the point where the extrusion angled northeastward into the valley. Reaching the place where the two areas of high ground diverged, Aram halted, dismounted, and signaled for Mallet to do the same. "Walk with me," he said.

On foot, the two of them went out the extruding ridge to the rounded brow of the small hill.

Aram gave the big man a few moments to examine the ground and then he spoke. "We must defend this hill, my friend," he said, "for it can be used as a direct route into our right flank."

He indicated the rim of the caldera behind them to the south, which continued on around in a gradual curve toward the north. "The wolves will hold that ground – along with a contingent of Captain Matibar's archers." He turned away and gazed down the sloping sides of the hill that fell away into the valley. "But our flank must be here."

Comprehension dawned upon the features of the big man, and this expression of understanding was followed immediately by a posture of grim determination.

He looked at Aram. "This is Wallensia's task, is it not, my lord – holding this hill?"

Aram nodded as he met Mallet's eyes. "It is, and it will not be an easy one. It may very well be impossible. But if the enemy were to push you back, or overrun you, he would have direct access to our right flank." He pointed back toward the main ridge. "And if he gained that ridge, he would roll us up to the west and we could not prevent it."

He watched the big man's face for a long, quiet moment.

"Can you hold this hill?" He asked.

Mallet turned in a slow circle, in a careful examination of the ground. He walked over and gazed down into the canyon behind and then returned to study the slopes that fell into the valley ahead.

Finally, he stared at the tower for a while.

Neither man spoke. A cold, restless wind picked up and blew sharply out of the north, feeling as though it came directly off the icy slopes of the mountains beyond the dark valley.

Then, Mallet pivoted to face Aram.

Saying nothing, the big man lifted his lance, Lasherbane, upended it, and drove it deep into the gravelly top of the hill. Then he rose to his full height and met the gaze of his king, the man who had led them here, the man he had sworn to follow into the underearth if required – the man he was convinced was not a man at all, but a god.

"This is my post, my lord," he told Aram. "You have entrusted it to me, and I will not abandon it. When the enemy comes, whether it be tomorrow, or the next day, or the next, they will find me here and ready for them. And at the end of that day, whether I am alive or whether I am dead – *I will be at this post.*"

Aram watched him for a long moment.

"Mallet, my old friend –"

"Yes, my lord?"

"Be alive."

18.

After giving his generals several hours to examine the ground upon which they would deploy their troops and prepare to meet the enemy, Aram sent them back to oversee the task of getting the bulk of the army as close to the chosen battlefield as possible before the end of the day. Then he called in Leorg, Shingka, Padrik, and Goreg, and gave them their orders for the coming day. Afterward, "Patrol this ridge," he instructed them. "Watch it throughout the night – from the flanks of that western mountain to that upon the east. Do not allow the enemy to surprise us."

"They will not get past us undiscovered, my lord," Leorg assured him, and the wolves loped away in small groups to do his bidding, Leorg and Shingka, with Goreg and his kin toward the east, and Padrik and his kin to the west.

Then Aram was left alone upon the ridge as the sun declined toward the horizon. He lifted his gaze from a final examination of the ridge top and looked long at the gleaming black tower of his enemy. He felt certain that the baleful eye of the grim lord was upon him as well at that moment.

"We are here," he told Thaniel. "What will he do?"

The horse was silent for a time, and then he said, "The grim lord will send forth his power, Aram. What else can he do? Unless he were to come out and face you between the lines, alone, he must attempt to drive this army away. Though he be a god – he and all his minions are now besieged. All his strength is here, and all that of the world is at his door. He will fight. He can do nothing else."

Aram considered that for a moment, and then nodded. "That is my hope. I cannot help but suspect, however, that he intends mischief which we cannot foresee. Why else would he surrender this ground to us, and give us time – as he apparently intends – to deploy our strength upon it?"

"I do not know the answer to that, Lord Aram, but as to the possibility of mischief?" The horse snorted with contempt. "What can he do to us that you cannot answer? You are stronger, whether you – or he and his forces – know it or not."

Aram smiled. "Would that I possessed your certainty."

Thaniel was silent for a moment, and then he said, "You will destroy him, my lord – either upon the morrow, or the next day; whenever he can summon the courage to face you."

Aram looked around as the thin, cold breeze picked up once more and blew out of the mountains to the north of the valley. "The wolves will patrol this ground throughout the night," he told the horse. "Let us get out of this wind and camp on the other side, where we might have a fire – if I can discover wood for it in this desolate place."

They went back up and over the cut and onto the south side of the rim, where Aram found a sheltered ravine and gathered a few sticks of dead brush to make a fire. As he sat near the small flame and ate a cold supper, he looked down upon the valley to the south and saw many fires burning in the night.

How many of those men, he wondered, would be alive to sit by another fire after tomorrow, or perhaps the day beyond that? And would they prevail, once the grim lord sent his thousands out to meet them? Many times, Aram had heard the advice of others – that such thoughts should not trouble a commander – but it was of no use. He could not dismiss the nagging suspicion that there had been a better way to resolve all this.

Perhaps, after all, he should have accepted Manon's offer to come alone, and settle it between the two of them.

But that "solution", as Thaniel had stated with such certainty, was most likely a trap.

He shook his head, as if to empty his mind of doubt.

Still, he could not shake the feeling that there was something he had missed. The army had been unopposed, all the way up across the plains. Manon had seemed content to pull in all of his power and wait to be confronted here, as if inviting a siege.

Why?

He could find no good answer to that simple, short question.

Tomorrow, if the grim lord sent his power out to meet them, then, perhaps, he would know.

He pulled his cloak more tightly around him and lay down next to the tiny fire, which even now was burning down to ash. The golden armor would keep him sufficiently warm. The urge for a fire was nothing more than the need to find comfort in the brightness of a flame, small solace in the thick, bitter darkness that covered this part of the world.

He gazed up at the smoky, starless sky for a time and then closed his eyes and thought of Ka'en, and his young daughter.

Would he ever see them again?

The pang of that sentiment turned his thoughts to the Sword. He had discovered – quite without knowing how – a means of controlling its fire. Could he gather enough power from this veiled sun of the north, and hold it in check long enough to blast the god into obscurity from a safe distance?

Manon would no doubt resist the dissolution of his body with all his might, even when pierced by the blade. Could he use the god's resistance to bodily destruction to find time to flee to a safe distance after driving the Sword into him?

And what was, in fact, a safe distance?

Aram had witnessed the awful result of a god's dissolution once before. The entire valley atop Kelven's mountain had been blasted into ruin by the obliteration of that god's body.

Once wounded, could Manon resist destruction long enough for Aram to run so far? And would he? Or, realizing that his end was upon him, would the god desire to take his destroyer with him into eternity?

He frowned up at the murky sky. How would he survive the meeting he had come so far to seek? There had to be a way; his heart told him so, but where was it to be found? There was only one day, perhaps two, to resolve the greatest difficulty he had ever – or would ever – face.

Sleep did not come readily.

At times during the night, he would doze off, only to be brought sharply awake, sometimes by the feeling of doom hanging above his head; at others, it would be to thoughts that Ka'en and Mae were in danger, unprotected by him, far off to the southeast. Other times, it was simply the wailing of the wind through the rocks of the barren hillside that startled him to alertness.

The last time he awoke from a short period of slumber, it was to the tramping of boots, coming up the road. In the east, the sky had grown pale with a hint of pink. He got to his feet and located the dark bulk of Thaniel in the gloom.

"It is time to dress you into your armor, my friend."

"I am ready, Lord Aram," the horse replied.

After outfitting the horse, Aram also put on his black armor over the golden armor from the mountain. The hood, he left through his belt. For the next several hours, at least, it was more important that he see and hear clearly, especially if Manon sent out his army.

The sound of boots pounding along the road intensified and as the light strengthened, Aram could see the soldiers at the head of the long column, marching four abreast, winding up the long slow curve toward the cut that would bring them to the battlefield.

Aram spoke to Thaniel once more and he and the horse went straight up and over, halting upon the crest to gaze down into the valley. Except for the heights of the tower, the top of which had already found the first rays of the sun, the valley was dark, lost in the shadows of the volcanos and the crater rim to the east.

Padrik came up out of the twilight to his left.

"Anything to report?" He asked the wolf.

"Nothing, master. The enemy did not come onto this slope during the night."

Aram nodded. "Stay alert. It will take most of the morning for the army to deploy into lines. The enemy may see an opportunity while we are not ready to receive him." He looked down at the shadowy form of the wolf. "I meant what I told you and your people yesterday – stay off the valley floor."

"As you wish, master."

Moments later, Leorg and Shingka appeared from the east to give a similar report. Though Manon obviously knew that they were here, he had not sent any probe toward them.

As he sat upon the ridge awaiting the leading elements of his army, Aram pondered this and spoke his doubts once again to the horse. "Is the grim lord content to have a straight fight – strength against strength, here upon this ground? Has he at last found a measure of honor?"

Thaniel was silent for a moment. Then, "Though I cannot know the mind of Manon, I believe that you are looking at this only from your position, Aram – which is that of a man who thinks that he has driven his enemy to ground. You forget that Manon may want us here, in exactly this place."

Aram frowned. "What do you mean?"

"Just this – we are all here, all of his enemies. And the grim lord no doubts trusts that his might can overwhelm us, even upon this higher ground," Thaniel replied. "By allowing us to come to him and gather before his gates, he may think to destroy us all, without having to send his minions to hunt us across the face of the earth. He may be as anxious as you are to resolve the issue once and forever."

Aram gazed forward as the light strengthened upon the valley floor below, gradually resolving the huts and other buildings surrounding the base of the distant tower. "Do you believe that he can do as you suggest?"

"I do not know Manon's mind, as I stated, Aram," Thaniel answered. "I simply relate what is logical." Then he snorted. "But if, in fact, my belief in his intent is accurate, then he will be sorely disappointed today. The men of the earth will fight – as they have already shown." He blew another great blast from his nostrils. "Besides that, my friend, you are here with us – and you are stronger than he."

"He is a god," Aram reminded him.

"Yes," the horse agreed, "he is. Still, you are stronger."

Aram looked to his right as Kavnaugh Berezan and the leading ranks of his half of the strength of Elam spilled through the cut. Officers shouted orders and the soldiers of that great land began swinging around toward the west, tramping across the slope just below where he and Thaniel stood watching them. Every so often along the line there marched a standard bearer. On each pole, the blue and gold of Elam's flag hung in the second position, beneath the horsehead standard of the king.

Most of them had their heads turned to the right, gazing northward at the dark valley and its massive, gleaming tower. This was their first sight of the wicked place where sisters, cousins, and even daughters had been transported after being yanked from the bosoms of their families. In some of those hearts there burned the hope that – despite what they'd been told by their new High Prince –

today might not be just the day of reckoning for him who had stolen those women, but release and freedom for the women as well.

After staring into the valley, many of them looked the other way, up the slope toward the man they had come to know as king, beneath whose standard they now marched. Discovering their monarch's gaze upon them, several raised a hand in salute. Aram nodded in reply.

For the next hour, Berezan's forty thousand troops erupted from behind the near wall of the cut, swung left off the road and tramped off toward the west. Marching near the last of them came Donnick, tall and stoic as ever. Saluting Aram briefly, he glanced out toward the valley and then calmly kept on, speaking low every now and then to those who walked near him.

When the front ranks of those troops came up against the rockslide, a mile or more to the west, they turned and began forming up, facing the valley – into which the first rays of morning finally had begun to find their way.

Immediately behind the last ranks of Elam, Boman came through the gap, mounted on Stennar, and then the men of Duridia came through and began to move to the left as well. As Boman's commanders knew as well as anyone upon the field how to deploy their men in preparation for battle, Boman and Stennar moved away and came up the hill to stand beside Aram and Thaniel. The governor saluted Aram and then peered into the valley.

"He still does not come forth?"

Aram shook his head. "No, Governor, and he is missing an opportunity here while we form our lines – one neither you nor I would let slip by."

"Perhaps after all, he means for us to come to him," Boman suggested.

"Perhaps," Aram agreed, "but I would rather fight here." He lifted his hand and indicated the distant city that spread out darkly from the base of the even darker tower. "Who knows what machines of war he hides among those buildings? That is a discovery I do not intend to make."

Boman looked over at him. "And if he doesn't come out?"

"We will await him here," Aram replied. "If he does not come today, we will encamp upon the south slope tonight and challenge him again tomorrow."

Boman hesitated. "Forgive me, my lord, but if he does not come out tomorrow – or the next day, or the next?"

Turning toward the Duridian, Aram met his gaze. "Tell me – what are your thoughts in such an occurrence, Governor?"

Boman shook his head. "You are far more experienced in the matters of war than am I, my lord."

"Perhaps that is so," Aram agreed. "Nonetheless, I trust your judgment. It was not an idle question." He looked back toward the valley. "If he does not come out – if he never comes out – what do we do?"

Boman swept his gaze back and forth across the valley between their position and the massive city sprawling at the base of the tower. "We could test his resolve to stay in place," he said. "Send in Wamlak's mounted archers, close enough to launch some darts among his troops. They might inflict some damage upon him and because they are mounted they will find it easier to fall back quickly should he begin to move forward."

Aram considered that for a moment and then nodded. "It may be that we can do something to entice him to come out. I do not want to face him upon ground that he has prepared. The grim lord is powerful and exceedingly wicked – I do not doubt that there are some nasty surprises hidden in that city."

They sat in silence while Boman's men continued to pour rapidly through the gap and form lines of battle to their front. The right wing of that line extended eastward from Berezan's right flank and moved ever nearer the road as the stolid southerners marched leftward and then wheeled into place, facing the dark valley below.

The governor examined his troops, which by now stretched across the slope in front of them and nearly touched the gleaming pavement of the road. He looked over at Aram. "I should see to my commanders," he said.

At that moment, the sun, though veiled by the ever-present smoke and haze, fell full upon the valley. Boman leaned forward, squinting through the growing light. Lifting his hand, he pointed.

"Maybe, after all, he means to come," he said.

Aram narrowed his eyes and squinted at the distant city. Instantly, he realized that the governor saw correctly. The dark line that had stood before the city on the previous day had formed once more and slowly, inexorably, distance was opening up between that line and the mass of stone structures behind it.

Manon, after all, was coming forth to meet them.

Aram looked to his right, where the last of Duridia had come through the gap and formed up, their right flank almost touching the road. Mallet and his Wallensians were marching through, swinging off the road to the right and toward the top of the distant rounded hill. The big man was marching along with his troops, with Markris the horse that he usually rode keeping time alongside the column. The fierce Jonwood rode Colrad at the head.

The Wallensians were through in less than half an hour, and then Olyeg Kraine and his half of Elam's forces began spilling out of the cut and following Mallet and his band toward the east. Like all those that came before, the marching troops turned their heads as one and gazed down upon the dark valley of the foe. Kraine looked over, raised his hand in a quick salute to Aram and then continued to move eastward with his men, determined to form up quickly and with good order.

Aram looked back toward Morkendril.

There was no doubt now. The broad, dark line of Manon's might was moving slowly away from the city and coming toward them, though the enemy seemed to be in no great hurry. In fact, the forward movement of Manon's army appeared almost deliberately sluggish. At the rate they were coming, and with three miles or more of ground to cross, Aram estimated that those many thousands would not be at the base of the slope for at least two hours.

An hour later, with the dark line of the enemy only halfway to the base of the slope, Elam was not yet through. Behind them, and yet to come, there were the men from Lamont, who would, with Boman and Duridia, form the center of his line. Last of all, there was Matibar and Seneca – his weapons of distance, whose skills he would need in the first moments of the coming battle.

Timmon and the gun would come behind them.

And Nikolus and his cavalry – who, Kipwing assured him, were on the move toward the front – were still not present.

The sun climbed inexorably up the hazy morning sky as his troops continued to pour four abreast through the cut. Down on the plain, dark power approached. And it seemed to Aram's eye that the enemy forces had accelerated their movement.

169

Anxiety began to foment within him. He looked to his right and spied Thom Sota, marching with the rearward ranks of Kraine's troops.

"Is Lamont behind you, Thom?" He called.

Sota nodded. "Entering the gap now, my lord."

Aram looked back to his front.

The thick, dark line of lashers and gray men had crossed more than half the distance from the tower to the base of the slope. They were yet too far away for him to see individual soldiers, but near enough that he could make out the taller, larger forms of the lashers in the rear ranks of the approaching enemy.

Just then, with a thunder of hooves, Nikolus and the cavalry, accompanied by Wamlak and his mounted archers, came over the crest of the rim behind Aram. Braska slid to a halt and Wamlak grinned over at Aram. "I hope we're not too late," he said. "I'd hate to miss the fun."

Aram smiled slightly and then looked at Nikolus and pointed down the slope, to the open ground in front of Boman's Duridians.

"Get in front of Boman and examine the ground the enemy must climb," he told him. "Send Ruben to the east in front of General Kraine. Wamlak – you go to the west to Kavnaugh's front. Bring me reports of any advantages the enemy may find and use to assault our position. Also, your presence in front of the army will give the enemy something to consider, perhaps slow him, while Edwar comes up."

Nikolus nodded and took his troops to the right, followed by Wamlak, around the end of Boman's line and out onto the slope. The horsemen split into three groups and diverged across the face of the slope.

The men of Lamont were spilling from the cut and filling the gap between Duridia and Kraine's Elamites when Findaen, Marcus, and Andar pounded through the cut on their mounts and galloped over to Aram and Thaniel. Hilgarn rode behind them, bearing the standard that Ka'en had made for him.

For once, the features of the young "Eldest" of Seneca were utterly devoid of mirth as he saluted Aram. "Matibar and Seneca will be here in less than an hour, my lord," he said.

Aram nodded. "Thank you, Your Worthiness. Tell Matibar to deploy his archers in three groups as we planned – one to the west behind Kavnaugh, and one here, just to the right of the center behind Edwar. The other contingent must deploy over to the right to Olyeg's rear; and at least a hundred must move further to the right to cover Mallet's position. His position is somewhat forward of the line and is badly exposed."

Andar glanced to his right, toward the east, and then nodded his head and went back through the cut to find his captain.

Findaen gained Aram's attention. "Where do you want me, my lord – with Mallet?"

Aram shook his head. "No, Fin; you must stay with me. Our line is more than two miles wide. Andaran is very fast. I will need you to help me maintain contact with all commanders."

Findaen scowled. "Are you trying to keep me out of the fight, my lord?"

"I am not trying to protect your life, Fin," Aram told him bluntly. "My need is real. Besides, when things grow confused – as they will – you will find plenty to keep you occupied, as will I."

"And as for me, my lord –?" Marcus inquired.

"Elam will need to see you after we make contact with the enemy, Your Highness, that they may know that you are with them." He moved his hand left and then right. "Your countrymen are split upon this field. Kavnaugh is to the left and Kraine is to the right." He looked out and gauged the progress of the enemy for a moment, and then he looked back at Marcus.

"I would have you speak with them now, both left and right, for they are in position, and the enemy comes."

"And when the battle begins, my lord?" Marcus asked. His features clouded. "Would you have me be no more than a provider of encouragement?"

Aram turned in the saddle and looked at him. "You cede too much authority to me, Your Highness," he told the young prince, and his eyes were hard. "There are more of your people upon this field than those of any other principality. They are *your people*, and they will need encouragement and much more once the enemy makes contact. Go where you will this day, young man. Do whatever – in your judgment – your people require. You need not consult me. Understood?"

Nodding somberly, Marcus spoke to Phagan and they moved away to the west.

Findaen watched him go. "Forgive me, my lord, but your words and your tone were harsh, were they not?"

"War is harsh," Aram replied. "Today will be a harsh day. Our friend Marcus is young and inexperienced and he governs a land that is broad and rich, prone to all the ills of humankind. To rule such a land requires a firm hand." He leaned forward and peered down the slope for a time before continuing.

"War," he said, "will ever be a hard and deadly business. Prince Marcus needs to make his own decisions and learn to trust in his own judgment. After today, our good, young friend will no longer be so young or so inexperienced. If we win this battle, and he survives, the events here today will help to provide a good amount of that much-needed firmness of hand."

A small wry smile moved across Findaen's face as he looked over at Aram. "I was wrong. You are a fine king, my friend."

Aram made no reply as he looked over to his right toward the road. "Look," he said. "Edwar is nearly through and in position."

Findaen nodded. "Matibar will not be far behind."

After that, the two men more closely bound to each other by blood and friendship than perhaps any others upon the field sat in silence and watched the thick, dark line of Manon's army approach. Aram attempted to judge the strength of those that came toward him across the floor of the valley.

There were at least eighty thousand, perhaps as many as a hundred thousand. As soon as Seneca arrived, he would field more than ninety thousand troops of his own. Of course, the presence of lashers in the enemy host created more than a little inequality, but he hoped to remedy some of that with the missiles of the Senecans. Those tremendous archers from the east with their arrows tipped with malsite should be able, he hoped, to greatly reduce the numbers of Manon's beasts – through injury and even death – that would reach his lines.

That thought made him impatient and he looked over at Findaen. "See where Matibar is, will you, Fin? Tell him that I need him as soon as he may arrive. Timmon and his gun are behind them. Tell him it is time to exchange oxen for horses and deploy upon the road once Seneca is through."

Findaen nodded, spoke to Andaran and the two of them went back through the cut toward the rear.

Just then, Nikolus, Ruben, and Wamlak returned from their reconnaissance in front of the army.

"Where are your troops?" Aram asked.

Nikolus pointed. "We left them out in front, in position with lances at the ready, until you wish them to be placed elsewhere, my lord."

Aram nodded. "What is your assessment of the ground?"

"It is not as level as it might appear, my lord," Nikolus said. "Nor is it as gently sloped as it seems. There are ravines all along the slope which become more pronounced as they near the valley floor. I believe the enemy will find it difficult to maintain order as he tries to negotiate them."

"Good," Aram replied. "I wish him the most difficult of days. And dis-advantages to us?" He asked.

At this, Wamlak pointed to the left, toward the place where Donnick was in command of the mixed forces of Elam and Duridia. "There is one very serious, in my judgment at least."

"What is it – and where is it?" Aram glanced at the army of Manon, now approaching to within a half-mile or less of the base of the slope. "Tell me quickly."

Wamlak once again indicated the left of the long line, where Kavnaugh's forces were deployed. "In front of Elam, there is a sort of shelf that extends in front of our lines."

"Shelf?"

Nikolus moved his hand across in front of his body. "A level place – if it slopes away at all, the angle is not severe. If the enemy can reach that flat ground in force, they will be fighting us on equal terms."

Aram looked left. "It is to Kavnaugh's front, before Elam?"

"Yes, my lord, but also in front of Duridia's extreme left, right where those two forces come together. The widest, most dangerous part is directly in front of Donnick."

Aram stared long and hard, and then looked over at Ruben. "You will be on our left this day?"

"Yes, my lord, behind Kavnaugh."

"Warn Donnick, even though I am certain the general has already seen the danger. Then instruct Kavnaugh that he is to send as many of his reserves as he can spare over to his extreme right. Tell him this instruction comes directly from me."

"I will place my troop in reserve behind Donnick as well, my lord," Ruben stated. "Unless you need me to be elsewhere?"

Aram nodded. "Do so, captain – if the enemy breaks through, we will need the shocking power that your horses can provide to drive them back and heal the breach. And make Kavnaugh aware of the danger to Donnick's front so that he will not hesitate to send his reserves that way."

"Yes, my lord."

As Ruben rode away, Aram asked, "What about our right?"

Nikolus shook his head. "Nothing very troubling, other than a few gentle slopes where the enemy will find better footing than at other points and may try to concentrate his forces. There is Mallet's hill, of course. And that is a very weak position – as you know, my lord. I do not know how he will hold if the enemy storms it in sufficient numbers, and it will be nearly impossible for the cavalry to maneuver there and lend him aid."

Aram grimaced in agreement. "Yes. But the wolves will be there, and I will help him hold – if I am not badly needed elsewhere. Also, Matibar will place a contingent of his archers on the ridge behind."

Wamlak laughed and smiled grimly. "Those archers will do some damage for sure. I wish we had ten thousand of them."

"As do I," Aram agreed. "Still, we have three thousand, and that may suffice." He glanced once more toward the plain below and then looked toward the gap where Lamont was still coming through. "I should have asked Seneca to march nearer the front."

Nikolus looked down at the valley and then met Aram's eyes. "I will go see if they are getting close, if you wish, my lord."

Aram hesitated but then shook his head. "No. I sent Findaen to hurry them. Go back to your troops and bring them through. I don't wish the cavalry to be exposed for any longer than necessary."

"Seneca cannot be far away, my lord. If needed, the cavalry will do what we can to delay the approach of the enemy."

Aram shook his head. "As you say, Seneca should be here in time. We will need you here when the battle commences. There is no reason to weaken your forces with unnecessary casualties. I want your troop strong and sound so that you may drive back any breakthrough of the enemy."

"I understand." With that, Nikolus and Jared wheeled and went back through the lines to collect their men.

Wamlak started to follow but then halted and looked back. "What of my archers when the battle begins?" He asked Aram. "Do we stay with Nikolus and Jared?"

Aram shook his head. "No. Nikolus and Jared will deploy to the right of the road, Ruben and Varen to the left. I want you in the middle, here on the heights, where you can see most of the field." He looked hard at him. "I trust your judgment, captain – go where you are needed, wherever your missiles will benefit our front."

Wamlak inclined his head. "Thank you, my lord." And he and Braska went back out front to gather his mounted archers.

Aram stood up in the stirrups and gazed to the east and then back to the west along the front. Then he sat back and watched the oncoming enemy. There was nothing else to be done. The army was situated to his satisfaction, pending the arrival of Seneca upon the field.

The long dark line of Manon's power was now approaching the base of the slope, coming close enough that his eye could resolve the individual forms of lashers and gray men. The enemy was not yet near enough, however, that he could judge the disposition and strength of the various components of the army that would soon climb the slope to his front and crash into his own.

Once more, his attention was drawn to his right as Findaen returned with Edwar and Matibar.

Edwar turned in the saddle and indicated the last of his troops just now exiting the cut. Then he looked at Aram. "Lamont is here, my lord."

Aram nodded. "Anchor your left flank across the road and next to Boman, captain. I will stay here behind your left. Wamlak's archers will remain here as well."

As Edwar wheeled to rejoin his men, Aram looked at Matibar. The taciturn captain inclined his head.

"Seneca is here as well, my lord, to stand with you against the Scourge. Shall we deploy as you stated earlier?"

"Yes." Aram pointed toward the enemy. "How close do they need to come for you to cause them damage?"

Matibar studied the approaching host and then examined the ground between them and the line of allied troops. He looked back at Aram. "Let them traverse half the distance of that slope and we can begin to kill them."

Aram frowned. "Are you confident of your accuracy at that distance, captain?"

Matibar looked back down the incline for a long moment, searching left and right across the slope. Then, he nodded firmly. "We will begin to slay them when they cross half that distance and come to within three hundred yards of our lines."

"How many arrows per each of your archers, captain?"

"Each man carries ten in his primary quiver, and ten more in a secondary quiver," Matibar replied. "And there are approximately another hundred thousand in the supply wagons – about thirty more per archer. The wagons will be placed as near to the front as possible, with mounted riders to keep the men in the lines supplied."

"How near are those wagons?"

Matibar turned and looked at the road where his men were following Lamont through the cut. "Immediately behind the men, my lord, in front of the food wagons."

"Alright." Aram pointed up the slope behind him toward the top of the ridge, twenty yards or so away. "Deploy your men along the top as we agreed, captain. Place one-third behind our left and one-third behind our right, with the remainder here in the middle, upon ground where they have a good view of the foe and may do the most damage."

He held up his hand. "Instruct your men to ignore the gray men among the enemy host, and focus upon the lashers." He looked hard at the approaching enemy lines once again. "I believe that those beasts are deployed entirely in the rear of the enemy host. We will know as they come closer. I want as few of their number as possible to reach our lines. Also; send a contingent to the right to cover Mallet upon that hill at the east end of our lines. His position must not be overrun."

Aram stared down the slope for a long moment and then looked once more at Matibar, meeting the Senecan's dark brown eyes. He had always respected the captain; lately that respect had become something more – a genuine appreciation for the taciturn captain and his many fine qualities. "We will need every one of your arrows this day, captain," he said, "but save a few until the enemy closes upon us – so that you can aid those places in the line that may weaken in the face of the foe."

"And when our arrows are gone?"

"Then we will need your swords."

Matibar looked away and gazed at the dark tower. As he did so, his mouth tightened into a hard line. After a long moment, he looked back at Aram. "Seneca is here, Lord Aram, in whatever capacity is required. We will expend our arrows and then employ our swords and expend our blood – whatever is needed to bring the end of the Scourge upon him. Vengeance is owed my people for a terrible and ancient wrong. Today, we will exact it."

He inclined his head respectfully. "I will bring my men into position quickly, my lord." Speaking to Yvan, he turned away.

"Where is Andar?" Aram called after him.

Matibar halted and looked back. "He is on foot, in the line, among the men. I could not dissuade him."

Aram met the captain's gaze for a long moment and then nodded shortly. "Tell His Worthiness that I wish him to be alive at the end of it."

"I will tell him."

An hour later, Aram's army was fully deployed, including Timmon and the cannon which were in place upon the road behind Edwar's left.

The enemy was at the base of the slope.

Aram started, as did all those to his front, as a deep bass note, as from an enormous horn, sounded from the direction of the tower. The dark line of the grim lord's host halted and stood still, unmoving, at the base of the slope. The deep note echoed away along the ridge and faded into the hills.

Silence fell.

19.

Manon stood in the opening high in his tower and gazed at the forces of the man, Aram, that had deployed along the top of the southern rim of the valley of Morkendril. Aram had positioned his army to either side of the road that came out of the south, crossed the ridge, descended the slope, and ran across the valley toward the tower.

At last, the god thought, *the end – and the beginning – of all things has come.*

For the weapon was there, too, with the man.

He could feel it.

Into that object, that small, strange piece of unearthly metal, his enemies among the Brethren had poured their strength. Then, as the fools they were, they had given that immense, combined power into the hands of a man, hoping that he would do what they feared to do; confront the Lord of the World – soon to be Lord of All – and pierce him with that strange blade, bringing about his destruction.

Manon smiled to himself.

Fools.

They were all of them fools, worthy kindred of Kelven, that pathetic ghost that haunted his great mountain in the east.

The Brethren had concentrated their power in an attempt to destroy him that was strongest among them, believing that they acted in the interests of all the lesser species and with the blessing of their "Maker". Instead, they had let come within his grasp all that he needed to ascend to supremacy.

There was now only to manipulate the man and bring him into the tower.

But that must be done carefully.

The man had shown himself resistant to manipulation. He must be made to think that he was working his own will when at last he came into the presence of his god.

For a brief moment, Manon's smile took on a grim, regretful aspect. Would that he could open his door now and the man would come in. However, were he to do so too soon the god was convinced, based upon his observation of the man, that Aram would sense deception.

And so there must be a battle.

There must be blood.

Much blood.

It was not the thought of carnage that troubled the grim lord. No; the lives of small creatures were of no import.

The god was more than willing to see the life of those lesser than him spilled in abundance – the future that he foresaw for the universe did not include their kind in any event.

So let them die here.

But he had grown impatient to possess the weapon.

He wanted that small bit of metal, lusted for it, the repository of his foolish enemies' strength; strength that he would soon absorb, and by doing so, become invincible.

This thought generated impatience.

And it was this impatience that he must resist. He must be circumspect and deliberate.

Still, he was pleased, very pleased.

For after today, the man, as foolish as those whose bidding he did, would come to him and bring the weapon within reach.

And then everything would change.

To this end, Manon reached out with his obsidian gaze and studied the disposition of the man's army more closely.

Aram had deployed his army advantageously upon the high ground. And Seneca, those vile archers from the edge of the world that had caused Manon much trouble in past ages, were there with him. The Lord of the World's minions would be forced to make their assault up the slope, beneath the withering missiles of Seneca. In such conditions, even the god's first children would find themselves hindered greatly, injured, and slain; Manon knew this from prior experience with the vile spawn of Felspar.

But many would reach the lines nonetheless and there would be great slaughter on both sides.

It was imperative that there be slaughter.

Or Aram might become suspicious. And he must not be made to suspect manipulation.

He must retain the will and the desire to enter the tower.

One thing – the man must enter the tower alone, without his ethereal companions, or difficulties arose. The Astra that travelled with him must not enter this place. Manon had often puzzled over those creatures and their strange powers. Even odder was their alliance with him who named himself "Maker".

Did they not know that their "master" was a fraud? Had they arisen after him and been fooled like all the others?

In the end, perhaps, it did not matter. Reports confirmed that those creatures had avoided contact with the weapon during the battle where Vulgur had died.

So – they feared it as well.

Its power must be enormous.

All Manon had to do was wrest the weapon from Aram – which he was certain of doing – and the Astra would be made to submit to him as well.

Or die.

20.

Once Seneca was in position and Nikolus and Jared with the cavalry had come back through the lines to deploy behind Aram's right and his left, a strange silence descended over the slope of the caldera. Almost two hundred thousand belligerents gazed at each other across something less than a thousand yards of rocky, sloping ground.

The sun was approaching zenith in a hazy sky, filled as it was with the smoky ejections of at least three volcanos. A cool breeze stirred out of the north, whipping up puffs of dust as it rushed across the valley floor and rose up the slope.

The silence was heavy but not complete. Up and down the line men and horses shifted nervously. Some soldiers drummed their fingers against the shafts of their spikes and lances or the hilts of their swords. Uneasy laughter arose from various places along the front. All these small noises blended together to create a quiet that was not truly silent but rustled low, tense and expectant.

Down upon the plain, standing at the edge of the slope, the enemy still did not move.

Aram watched them for a moment longer and then, "Go out in front of the men," he told Thaniel. "Then move to the left. I want to ride the length of our lines and speak to the men."

As Thaniel went toward the western end of Aram's army, pushed up against the steep, jagged flanks of the smoking mountain, he met as many of his soldiers gazes as he could. All along the line, the flags of the various companies of Duridia, Lamont, and Elam snapped in the chill breeze. Suspended on the lanyard above each was the horsehead standard of Aram's ancestors.

Coming near the end of the line, Aram told Thaniel to stop and face the line. He raised his voice.

"We hold the high ground," he told the soldiers. "The enemy is at a dis-advantage. Take courage from this and be strong." He lifted his hand and pointed behind them. "Your archers will damage the foe ere they reach this line. And Seneca is here as well – they will slay many of the grim lord's beasts. And the lesser soldiers of the enemy – the gray men – are no match for those that I see here before me."

He folded his hands across the pommel of the saddle. "Obey your commanders, let those of you with spikes deploy them when directed, and use the enemy's weight against him when he comes near enough to put your pikes and lances to proper use. You have the advantage of the high ground," he repeated, "and that fact will stand this army in very good stead."

He went silent for a moment, meeting many of the pairs of eyes that stared back at him.

"We fight today for the freedom of the world – for our wives, our sons and daughters, our families, and those that will come after us." He made a fist and held it out in front of him. "Together, we are stronger than any enemy. Be brave, be strong, hold the line, and we will prevail."

As Thaniel moved along the line, he repeated words similar to these to every segment of the army until he came out at last to the top of the small hill where Wallensia and Mallet held the army's most vulnerable flank. Jonwood stood near the big man, holding his sword in his left hand, gazing with fierce eyes down the slope at the enemy as he listened to his lord.

"We have known each other a long time," Aram told the men of Derosa. "We have met the enemy together; you and I, and we have always won the day." He leaned forward and spoke low, earnestly. "We have become brothers in arms, and brothers in blood. Be strong this day, my brothers, and once again we will win the day."

He looked long into Mallet's gaze and met Jonwood's eyes for a long moment when the small compact man looked up at him. Then he saluted them all and he and Thaniel went back toward the middle.

Before he reached the road, the deep bass note sounded once more from the direction of Morkendril.

Aram turned his head to look down the hill.

The long dark line of the enemy began to move.

Thaniel reached the roadway where he halted and turned to look down the slope as well. The great horse ejected breath from his nostrils in a low, shuddering sound, almost a growl.

Aram did not respond to this but lifted his eyes and gazed narrowly at the gleaming black tower.

We will slay every one of these your servants, vile enemy, he stated under his breath, *and then I will come for you.*

As the sun slid into zenith, the breeze from the north faltered and died.

A deep low rumble began to make itself known to every listening ear – the sound of thousands of boots impacting the rocky floor of the valley.

There was no sound from the enemy other than this muted, rhythmic, earth-bound thunder. The enemy host reached the slope and began to climb the angle of the incline, and then there were shouts and roars from lashers as they attempted to keep their lines in order.

Along the ranks of soldiers from all parts of the free world, men looked at their nearest companions, nodded, swallowed, and gave and received encouragement.

"Here we go," some said.

Others opted for the simple phrase, "I am with you," which was answered every time with, "and I am with you."

Standing in the middle of the road, Thaniel turned his head and cocked one eye upward.

"You will get little fire from this sun, Aram," he said.

Aram glanced up at the dim sun, glowing feebly through the smoky overcast. "It will matter little," he replied. "There will likely be no time to gather flame even if it were possible. Today, my friend, we must be everywhere, in the thick of it – wherever the enemy threatens a breakthrough."

"And when it is over," the horse said, "we go to bring justice upon the grim lord." It was a statement.

Aram nodded but did not reply.

The rumble of pounding boots and thick, clawed feet grew in strength and volume.

Up the slope came the full force of Manon's might.

The battle for the future of the world was at hand.

21.

All that knew him described Kavnaugh Berezan as quiet and steady. Deliberate and intense, but calm.

Now, facing battle for the first time, watching the grim ranks of the enemy approach his lines in force, Berezan clasped his hands together behind his back and drew in a deep breath.

He did not feel calm at all.

It was not so much that he had never seen action upon a field of battle; it was that none of those young men standing in a long line to either side of him had done so, either. Together, he and they were about to gain experience in that deadliest and bloodiest of arenas. He glanced each way along the line, trying to gauge the general mood.

Would they hold?

What would they do when those gigantic monsters that he could see there at the rear of the enemy host approached the line?

Would they fight or would they run?

They were all of them well-trained, and each of them had willingly marched hundreds of miles across the surface of the world to stand here, upon this desolate, rocky ridge where, very soon, they would be joined by death's specter. No man among them, Kavnaugh thought, would have done so just to then flee when the conflict they had all been preparing to enjoin came upon them.

He believed that in fact they would fight, but would the next hour justify that belief?

Desertions had occurred along the way on the march out of Elam. Early on, most of those had been for reasons of sheer laziness, an unwillingness to endure the hard tramp northward. Later, there had been those few that, having come to an understanding that at the end of this long trek their very lives would be placed in certain and serious jeopardy, found that they simply could not face that bleak possibility.

The code of conduct that governed the military of Elam stated that desertion was to be punished by death. It was an old law, written for those that had never known – or were ever likely to know – war. Still, it was the law of the land.

Lord Aram had countermanded it, though not for reasons of mercy but of pragmatism.

"I only want those who are willing to fight," he told his various commanders. "Better that those who will run, run now. It is preferable that they leave us now than when we are standing face-to-face with the enemy – when they might inspire others to fail as well."

And some, a few, had run.

Still, the vast majority of the uniformed men of his homeland had come all the way to this cold ridge top, either to avenge their women that had been sent to this awful place, or simply because it was their duty to come.

Now they were here.

And the enemy approached.

Moving to the right end of his lines where his troops joined with Duridia, Berezan found General Donnick, the placid Wallensian who, by all accounts, had acquitted himself so admirably in more than one battle.

Nodding a greeting, he said, "This is it, I suppose."

"They are but minutes away, general," Donnick replied.

Berezan glanced down the slope before looking back at Donnick. "Any last instructions?"

Donnick shook his head. "No; this is the time when training must take over. I've seen it before – the initial shock is accompanied by death and injury, which engenders fury, and it is that fury from which the men will draw strength." Donnick looked at him closely. "Are you alright, general?"

"Nervous," Berezan admitted. "I'm just hoping that my boys will stand and fight."

Donnick looked along the line toward the west. "They will fight, general. They know why the army came here – and each of them knows why *he* is here." He looked back and met Berezan's eyes. "As Lord Aram so prudently foresaw, those that would run away have already done so. Duty and honor are powerful things, my friend, and they are to be found in the hearts of all these good men. Duty and honor brought them here and will keep them in the line when it matters."

He looked down the slope. "And it will matter in less than an hour."

Berezan looked toward the enemy as well and watched their progress for a moment. Then he inclined his head respectfully to Donnick. "Thank you, general. I will see you after."

"See you afterward, sir," Donnick agreed.

Berezan moved back along the long line until he was positioned at about the center of the Elamite portion of this half of the army, near where he had placed his reserves.

"Alright, boys," he said, lifting his voice. "Let us show these bastards how Elam fights."

His front ranks were three deep. Behind them, he had kept a few thousand in reserve, to plug holes or exploit opportunities. The archers were behind the main lines, too, and would act as reserves as well, when either their missiles were expended or when the enemy had closed upon the main line.

Every tenth or twelfth man in that forward line had been issued a "spike", one of those oddly short and heavy lances that had been designed by Lord Aram's engineers. After having examined one of those weapons and comprehending its purpose, Berezan couldn't help but wish that every man of Elam had one in his possession as the enemy came up the hill toward them.

But there were only so many spikes available to be issued to his Elamites. General Berezan would have to depend upon his archers to reduce the enemy as much as possible before impact.

He turned his head and looked further up the ridge, at the Senecan archers positioned behind his right. There were more than a thousand of those solemn, capable men from the east and their missiles were tipped with strange blue-green stone that penetrated almost anything. Berezan had witnessed a demonstration and had been impressed and amazed.

Those men would certainly do damage to the foe when he came within range. And their range far exceeded that of Berezan's Elamite archers. Every one of the Senecans had an arrow nocked in his long bow, and they were all of them staring intently down the slope toward the valley and the approaching enemy.

Berezan studied them with a measure of astonishment for a long moment. As far as he knew, those men of the east had not known battle either. How could they stand here, facing an enemy for the first time, and exhibit such stolid focus upon the task at hand? He looked back to the front and saw the reason for those eastern warriors' intense interest in what was occurring upon that sloping ground.

The enemy was nearly within range of their missiles.

He drew his sword and moved up to stand with his men.

22.

After Kavnaugh Berezan went back toward the west, Donnick studied the men of both Elam and Duridia that stood near him and was satisfied by what he saw. It was as he'd told Berezan – these men, the Duridians who had seen action before, and the men of Elam, though green and untested, would fight.

There was fear, of course, raw and palpable; but underlying that emotion, as was evident on every face, there was determination to do what they had come here to do – to set the world free from evil. Donnick moved back and forth just behind the ranks, several yards to the left, behind Elam, and then back to his right, behind Duridia.

"Stay strong, men," he stated repeatedly in his quiet voice. "I have met these people before, and they will run this time just as they did that time. Hold the line, stay focused, put your weight into your pikes when the enemy comes close. Right is with us, the king is with us, his sword of power is with us. Stay strong, men, and we will win the day."

As he walked back and forth, he studied the ground to the front of his troops, over which the enemy must cross to reach them. In front of Duridia, there were a series of shallow ravines that cut into the hillside as it sloped away. Though not severe, these would nonetheless hinder the enemy's progress and cohesion. In any event, Duridia had shown its mettle in the Battle of Bloody Stream. And Boman was there.

Donnick was not worried about Duridia.

But in front of the extreme right of the Elamite contingent, however, where he now stood, there was an area of level ground – a sort of shelf – that extended out from his lines for perhaps fifty yards before breaking over and sloping more severely toward the valley floor. Once the ranks of the enemy gained that stretch of ground, they would be more or less on level with the far right wing of the Elamite lines. If Manon massed his strength there, on that shelf, things would become dangerous very quickly.

And he could not move men forward to defend that ground. The front lines of the army must retain their order. If he pushed that segment of the line forward in order to defend the edge of that shelf, a bulge would be created in the allied lines; the men defending it would rapidly become exposed to attack from three sides. If they gave way and tumbled backward, the integrity of the front lines would then be compromised, perhaps without remedy.

No, Donnick would have to keep his attention centered here, upon that piece of treacherously gentle ground, more than anyplace else along the line.

He had a feeling that he would be needed here more than he would over to his right, where Elam and Duridia came together.

The sound of the enemy's advance up the slope became more pronounced. Donnick backed away from his lines for several paces and studied the disposition of his troops. Nowhere could he see any cause for correction.

He looked beyond his men, toward the enemy.

They would soon be within the range of the Senecan archers, positioned upslope over to his left, behind Berezan.

He gave the command for his small contingent of reserves to move up behind the men facing the shelf of level ground.

The he collected his pike and moved into the ranks.

189

23.

Donnick perhaps was not worried about Duridia, to his right, but Boman, in command of those men that had slain the mighty Vulgur, was not so sanguine.

Because of the disposition of the army upon the slope, his lines ended at the edge of the black-paved road that sloped into the valley. Edwar's Lamontans touched his flank there, at the edge of the roadway from whence they then stretched across the pavement and went toward the east.

Boman did not like the road. He didn't like it at all.

To him, it seemed like the perfect conduit for a massed assault upon the front lines of the army by an enemy determined to break through. Whereas the ranks of the enemy might find difficult going out upon the rocky slopes to either side; the road was smooth and its angle of incline was gentle.

"That is precisely where I would attack this line," Boman muttered to himself more than once.

But that tangent of smooth access was under the control of Lamont. True, Lord Aram was there, but the king would very likely roam back and forth across the whole of the ridge, wherever he felt he was needed. And if he and his Sword were not there when the enemy had the same idea about the road as Boman – what then?

He'd already moved his own reserves as far right – toward the road – as he dared.

He turned his head and looked back up into the cut, where the road passed through the ridge. Timmon was there, with several men, positioning Keegan's gun, running out the chains and chocking the wheels of the cart that bore it. Three horses were with Timmon, two of whom were helping to maneuver the heavy weapon. The other was his mount, Bonhie.

The gun would undoubtedly be an asset, were the enemy to attempt a break-through, for the amount of carnage it could inflict was impressive; but it came with its own set of logistical issues. For one thing, it could only be fired at intervals of several minutes. Timmon's clever management of the gun had shortened the time between discharges by impressive amounts – still, it was but an intermittent tool for doing damage to the enemy.

For another thing, the friendly troops to the front had to swing aside and give way every time the gun was fired. This tactic had been practiced by every unit on Lamont's left once Lord Aram had decided which forces would stand at the center of his army. The chosen troops had behaved impressively, shunting aside to allow the gun to fire and then re-establishing position quickly – but that had been merely practice, accomplished without the deadly steel of the enemy driving upon them.

How would they behave now?

There was also a contingent of Senecan archers upon the ridge behind, half of their company positioned on Boman's side of the road, with half on the other, and their presence no doubt added another layer of protection for the army's center. Still, the black road was so damnably wide and smooth and gently sloped. He could not help but believe that, sooner or later, the enemy would make a very determined push up that gleaming ebony tangent.

Unable to contain his agitation, the governor went to his right to discover which Lamontan commander was in charge there, at the left of Edwar's lines. Coming close, he was both gratified and dismayed to see that it was Muray.

The stout young Lamontan commander, with his enormous bristling red beard, steely blue eyes, and growlingly harsh voice was hobbling back and forth across the pavement of the road, from one side to the other. As he performed this act of ceaseless prowling, he snarled low to himself, halting in the middle of the pavement on every pass, by turns staring at the gun and then gazing down that smooth blackness at the approaching enemy.

Boman went up to him in time for Muray to glance over, see him, and wave one belligerent hand down the pavement.

"You see this, Governor?" He growled. "Do you see this? My left flank is right here – right where I would assault this army was I

191

the enemy. *My flank*," he repeated. "I know that there is nothing to be done, but damn this ground!"

Garnering a substantial measure of satisfaction from the fact that another commander, especially one as tough and clever as Muray, shared his concern about the road, Boman nonetheless spoke soothingly. "Lord Aram is here, right behind you, commander. I heard him tell Nikolus to stay near the center. A thousand of those Senecan archers are here as well. Also, Timmon and his cannon are deployed upon the road behind you." The governor laughed and pointed down the road at Muray's front ranks. "Those boys will have to move aside on the quick if he decides to light that thing up, you know."

Muray nodded. "Well – that's all fine and good, but in the end, it will be pikes as do the job."

"You're right," Boman agreed, as his smile faded. "Look, Muray – I have moved my reserves close – if the day proves that they are wanted here. Call upon them at your need, even if I am engaged elsewhere. I have informed Commander Jefna of the possibility that you might have need of him."

Muray bent his fierce gaze upon him. "A-ha! I knew I was right about this damnable road – you see it, too, don't you?"

Boman looked down the pavement and nodded. "I always saw this as a weak point," he admitted. Then he grinned at Muray. "But that was before I knew you were here. Now I am not so worried."

But then Boman's good humor faded as he gazed at Muray. "How is your leg, commander? You won't take unnecessary chances this day, will you now?"

Muray leaned on his pike, glowered darkly at the Duridian for a moment; and then his foul mood faded and he grinned. "I already have a mother, Governor, and she worries enough for all of us. I will be fine. The leg is stiff but usable –" He pointed down the road without looking "– as some of those bastards will learn this very day." He frowned then and peered at Boman closely. "I have very few reserves that are allotted to me, Governor. May I truly have those men, if needed?"

"You may consider them yours as of this moment, Muray," Boman replied, and he nodded. "Yes," he repeated, "you may have them; for I do think that you will need them."

"How many are they?" Muray inquired.

"About six hundred."

Muray looked thoughtfully at both sides of the road; then he also nodded his head. "They will more than double my depth upon the road and a good way to either side. You mean it, Governor – I can have them?"

"You may have them," Boman reiterated. "I confess that I will feel better about it. I will send them closer to you at once."

Muray pushed himself erect and held out his hand. "Thank you, sir."

Boman shook the proffered hand. "See you after," he said.

"See you after, Governor," Muray agreed.

After dispatching Jefna with the reserves to report to Muray, Boman went back to the center of his lines feeling much less agitated than before his foray to the right. He still felt as though the road was the weakest point, here in the center of the army, but knowing that Muray was there, and that his reserves would be lent to a competent soldier allowed him to concentrate more fully upon his own front.

He looked intently back down the slope, beyond the lines of his men in order to gauge the progress of the enemy, just as a Senecan captain's voice rose in sharp command to his right rear, on the ridge top at the center of the army.

The voice sounded very much like it belonged to Matibar.

"Loose!" The voice shouted.

24.

Standing in the third rank, at nearly the middle of Muray's regiment, several yards east of the road, Eoarl watched his son hobble fiercely back and forth across the gleaming black pavement, cursing and exhorting his men to *hold*, to *steady up*, and to *stand firm* as the enemy came up the hill toward them. Despite the imminence of danger inherent in the moment, Eoarl smiled with pride as he saw his only son for the first time as others saw him – tough, smart, and competent.

Weeks earlier, Muray had discovered the presence of his father among the troops of his regiment as they were being ferried across the river below the walls of the fortress.

The young commander stepped into the line of men waiting to board the transport across the great river, blocking his father from moving forward.

"My ken! What are you doing here?"

Eoarl raised his chin. "Step aside, lad – I'm going north with you."

Just as adamantly, Muray shook his head. "No, ken – you're not going. You're too – too –"

"What – old? *I'll not be too old to handle the likes of you, my boy.*" Eoarl narrowed his eyes and reached for the hilt of the sword Lord Aram had given him, rendering the gesture only half in jest. Though his mouth adopted a wry smile, his eyes were hard and serious. "Do you really want to settle it here, like this, laddie?"

Muray looked closely at his father. "Is this about my leg, dad? If it is – you needn't worry about me; I'll be fine. I won't have you worrying over me – or fighting for me."

Eoarl shook his head. "Not fighting for you, son." But then he hesitated to consider his own words. "Well, in a way," he said, "I suppose I am fighting for you, but I'm fighting for your mother, too. And for Lamont, and for the freedom of the world." He lifted his hand and pointed at the man sitting upon the black horse on the high ground to the north of the crossing.

"As much as anything," he said. "I will be fighting for him – the king."

Muray glanced up and then returned his sharp gaze to his father's face. He was silent for a long moment. Then; he nodded.

"Alright, ken – you can go, but you'll be in the third rank."

Eoarl treated his son to a smile. "Third rank will be fine, lad."

Muray, Eoarl had discovered upon the long, hard trek north, was held in high esteem by his men. In fact, regard for their fierce captain bordered on reverence. He was the only man of them who had slain a lasher single-handed.

And he was a good commander. During the practice runs as they were crossing the plains, Muray's men had always been the first of all Lamont's forces to form up properly. He cursed them, shouted at them, and drove them, but he took care of their welfare, too, always making certain that any lack that he discovered among his ranks on the great march north was managed immediately.

In fact, Eoarl had learned several surprising things on that seemingly endless journey. Not only did the men in the ranks of Lamont revere their tough, irascible commander, but they held odd beliefs about another man that Eoarl was certain that he knew better than any of them.

One evening as he returned from the management of certain personal, private business at the edge of the encampment, he found several of his fellow-soldiers embroiled in argument.

"Captain Mallet declares him to be a god," a wiry man by the name of Larley stated with angry intensity to a large, red-headed and red-bearded behemoth named Mitchom. "And he's known him longer than anyone."

"He's not known him longer than Captain Wamlak – and that worthy gentleman declares that Lord Aram is one of the ancients," Mitchom returned with the same intensity.

"You're a pair of dim-witted fools," broke in Sevard. "He is heir to the ancient kings, no more nor less – though I grant you that such a thing is a whole world's worth of *more*."

Just then Muray came to the fire in search of his father and the hope of a quiet smoke. As their commander stepped into the glow of the fire, the men stiffened and ceased their squabbling.

Muray looked around at them, his fierce blue eyes blazing in the light of the dancing flame.

"Whatever Lord Aram is," he stated in a dangerously low and quiet voice, "his fight is with Manon. *Ours* is with the many, many thousands that serve that great, grim, black-hearted bastard. *That* will be our work – Lord Aram has entrusted it to us. So you all better get into the proper frame of mind about it – leave the rest to those with more sense and education than you lot."

Now, the enemy approached, and Muray had his men on line and in the proper frame of mind. Watching him, Eoarl found himself given to a curious thought, though one that was not incongruous to the moment.

I hope this fine son of mine lives beyond this day, he thought, *for he would no doubt give Dunnie and me an equally fine grandson someday.*

25.

Edwar stood in the center of his lines and gazed out at the slope that fell away toward the valley, up which the enemy even now approached. His stomach tensed as he watched them come. Despite Lord Aram's satisfaction with how he and Lamont had acquitted themselves during the battle of the southern plains, he knew that disaster had been but a step away that day.

His line had buckled in several places, had been pierced in more than one; and it was his troops that had created the gap at the center that so nearly led to ruin. More often than he should, perhaps, he entertained the thought that it was only the intervention of the wolves that had saved his side of the field that day.

He never enunciated these doubts to anyone – certainly not to the men – but he held them nonetheless.

And now they were about to be tested once more.

This time, the wolves were far away, over to the right behind Mallet, guarding the most vulnerable end of the line. Edwar and his six thousand held the right half of the center of the line. Worst of all was the fact that his left flank extended across the road, which his instincts told him was very likely as vulnerable a place as that little hill of Mallet's.

Once, he glanced away from the approaching host and saw Boman talking with Muray who was gesturing with agitated hands down that very avenue of danger that so worried Edwar. Muray saw the danger clearly, which was the reason Edwar had put him there in the first place.

Unwilling to try Muray's nerves any further with interference from his commander, Edwar decided to let him and Boman sort it out between them. Besides, Lord Aram was there. And Timmon was there with his cannon. That dangerous tangent was in as good and capable hands as there were upon the field.

Edwar had problems enough to his front.

As Manon's army came closer, he could see that a solid line of the great beasts called lashers marched behind the gray men, driving them forward. Lamont had not faced any of those terrible and frightening creatures during the last battle.

They would surely face them today.

He looked to his left again and his heart lifted a little. Boman had evidently sent Muray his reserves. Several hundred of those stout men of the south plains were moving into position behind Muray's Lamontans.

He returned his attention to the downslope. The front ranks of the enemy were but a few hundred yards away, the long dark line of gray men and beasts undulating a bit as they encountered uneven places in the terrain. Looking along his line, he saw no cause for concern that his men would do anything other than to stand and fight. They had faced this enemy before, after all, and had held the field at the end of it.

Those men scattered along the front in possession of spikes had the weapons in their hands, at the ready. He found himself wishing once more that he had not been constrained to share his portion of spikes with the rest of the army. It was only fair and right that he had done so, of course; still, he was certain he would miss those odd but deadly weapons in the next several minutes.

The muted thunder of enemy boots strengthened. He turned his gaze toward them and moved forward to be nearer his men. The enemy was near enough now that Edwar could resolve faces and figures in the first rank.

From behind him and to the left, just above Muray's position at the center of the army, a Senecan captain's voice rose in sudden, sharp command.

"Nock arrows!" The Senecan ordered.

A moment passed.

"Loose!" He shouted. "Gauge your distance! Focus upon the beasts alone!"

And then again, "Nock arrows! Loose!"

A cloud of deadly missiles whined over Edwar and his troops. He looked up, fascinated, as those instruments of death and injury screamed through the air and began to fall toward the enemy. If the words of the Senecan commander had been clearly heard, every one of those implements of death was intended for a lasher.

Good enough, he thought, *there will be a few less of those monsters now.*

26.

Matibar watched the enemy come up the slope with intent and narrowed eyes. He had longed for this day, hungered for it, when he and his compatriots would join with the rest of humankind against the wickedness of the Scourge.

Throughout his life, the young captain had often doubted the version of Seneca's history that was peddled by the Elders in Mulbar. In his secret thoughts – and he often felt that he was the only man in his land that entertained such ideas – he believed that, whatever had actually occurred in ancient times, the quasi-religious edicts from the old men of the grove served merely to maintain their hold upon the people and countryside of his homeland.

Thinking himself alone in his doubts, he nonetheless was certain that the history of his people was something quite different from that which was espoused by the elders.

The idea that his most ancient ancestors had been punished nearly to extinction for the casual sin of building great cities had seemed worse than implausible – it was offensive to him.

Why had the Maker allowed – nay, had commanded, if the elders were to be believed – the near-destruction of a great and industrious people because they wished to live in cities of stone?

The very idea offended Matibar's pragmatic mind.

Secretly, he believed that the Maker had not been in any way involved in the horror that had been visited upon his people in ancient times. Against all the teachings of those that governed his society, Matibar became convinced that it had been the vile work of the Scourge alone, conceived in his own dark heart, and carried out by his beasts.

Then Aram had come, and that kingly man's version of that which had been Seneca's part in the affairs of ancient times made sense and rang with the sound of truth. More importantly, it gave Matibar something for which he had always longed, and believed that he deserved – pride in his ancestry.

Now, he was here, facing the same enemy that his forebears had faced. And he stood here in concert with a king who was the scion of Seneca's ancient ally.

This day mattered to Matibar greatly, more perhaps than any other day in his life.

He loved his family, his wife and his children, and he hoped that whatever this day brought, it would conclude in such a way that would allow him to return to them. He did not wish to leave his young wife widowed and his children orphaned. If, however, the day was not fated to end with him alive and standing; even if he knew with certainty that this day would be his last upon the earth, he would choose to be nowhere else.

Vengeance for a terrible and ancient wrong was called for, and Matibar intended to be instrumental in exacting it.

The part of Seneca's ancient history that he had come to know as true, not only because Lord Aram told him of it, but because it was widely known to be true by many learned people – like the scholar Willar in Sunderland, in Lamont – was that the Scourge had sent his beasts among the forests of Seneca unexpectedly, while Seneca's forces were unaware and scattered to their various homes and cities.

Nowhere had they been able to unite their strength and face the deadly creatures in force.

It had been known, of course, that an uneasy truce, likely to be broken, existed between their ally, King Joktan, and the Scourge. But the Scourge had devastated the population of eagles, blinding the allied world, before he struck. Joktan was already dead when Manon had sent his terrible servants into Seneca's forests, killing with the intent of causing extinction and burning their cities. Only because many of the Senecans had been scattered abroad among their forests, in their villages and small towns; and the servants of the Scourge had focused mainly upon the cities, had a remnant managed to survive.

Today, however, Seneca's archers were united, with the enemy in plain view. There were no great trees here to shield the beasts as they advanced or to deflect an arrow and drive it astray.

The monsters were lined up, out in the open, ready to be slaughtered.

He bent his gaze even more intently down the slope as the front ranks of the enemy topped a rise in the hillside. Another hundred yards, and the archers of Seneca would strike the first blows to begin the battle that would decide the future of the world.

The captain's plan was to eliminate as many of the lashers as he could from engaging the Lamontan commander, Muray, at the army's center and then focus his archers leftward to aid Boman and Duridia. Then, he would turn them back to the right, to bring the same relief to Edwar and the rest of Lamont, saving the last few bolts in order to return his attention to the center – in case the enemy decided to force the issue up the pavement.

Andar was to the west, behind Elam. After Lord Aram had expressed his wishes for the deployment of Seneca's men, Matibar had presented his plans to Andar, only to see the features of His Worthiness dissolve into a grin.

"I'm a decent archer, captain – as you know – but I am not worthy to wear your boots here, in this place." The grin on Andar's handsome face went away. "You are captain of Seneca's strength, my friend. Here, upon this field, you do not seek my approval. You give the order – send me where you will – and I will obey."

Relieved, and gratified, Matibar watched him for a moment. "Will you consent to take command of the western contingent, Your Worthiness?"

Andar nodded. "I will."

Matibar indicated the ground at the top of the road, where it went through the cut. "When I loose here in the center, you and your men will do the same behind Elam. Focus upon the beasts alone – let us slay as many of those creatures as possible before they reach Lord Aram's lines." He thought for a moment and his face darkened as he looked at the prince of his people. "It may be that they will approach in companies, or perhaps in a line. If so, they will make our work here the easier. Let us *kill them all* if we can, Your Worthiness," he said.

Andar simply inclined his head once more. "I will watch for your signal, captain."

With that settled, Matibar had then sent Captain Findar, who was older and well-known for his steadiness, eastward with another thousand, to deploy behind the right half of the army as per Lord Aram's instructions.

Further east, upon the ridge behind Mallet, there were a hundred of Matibar's best – also at Lord Aram's behest. They were to prevent the big man and his Wallensians from being overrun, if at all possible.

Down the slope, the enemy neared the range of his archers.

As he had hoped, the beasts were approaching on a line.

"Nock arrows," he commanded.

Spread out to either side of him almost eleven hundred men put blue-green malsite-tipped missiles to the string and raised their long bows.

Matibar lifted his own bow and looked along the shaft and then lowered his gaze to the approaching enemy, judging the distance.

"Loose!" He shouted.

Smoothly and cleanly, slipping through the thin, cool air, the instruments of death flew forth, arced high, and began to descend.

For the briefest moment, Matibar watched their flight, to determine that he had correctly judged the gap between his men and the foe, and that his men had largely accomplished the same. Down the ridge and to his left, many voices were abruptly raised in a cheer.

Then, he repeated his command, "Nock arrows – loose!"

As the second volley rose toward the top of the arc, down the slope, the first volley fell among the lashers at the rear of the enemy ranks. Screams of pain and howls of anger and anguish arose from dozens of thick-muscled throats. Here and there, some of the great beasts crumpled without uttering a sound.

Death was making its first appearance upon the slopes of the caldera south of Morkendril.

Matibar sent the deadly darts flying again so that every Senecan released three into the enemy center; then, "Left," he said. "Gauge your distance."

And death found the ranks of those lashers approaching the Duridian line and Boman's front. Then, three arrows later, he turned his archers to the right in order to visit death and injury upon the lashers approaching Edwar.

Not every arrow found a mark, but most did. Lashers died, others suffered injuries too severe to allow them to continue. Even those that suffered damage and continued on would pose less of a challenge when they finally made contact.

Seneca was exacting its vengeance.

27.

Despite having recently been elevated to one of the highest ranks in Elam's army – and consequently Lord Aram's – Thom Sota had no intention of commanding from behind the lines.

Though no longer young, like most of the men around him, he was nonetheless still strong and reasonably agile. And he intended that his blade be one of the first to draw enemy blood.

Standing among the front ranks of the army at the point where Elam and Lamont came together, he grinned a hard, tight grin and made direct eye contact with as many of the soldiers around him as possible. When the enemy cleared a rise just down the slope and the missiles of the Senecan archers began falling among them, Thom drew his sword, stepped out in front of the lines, and raised his voice.

"Today," he told those within the sound of his words, "we bring justice upon Manon the Grim for all the misery he has caused our people." Lifting the tip of his sword, he pointed it at the men of Elam. "Many of you have lost sisters, daughters, some of you perhaps even the girl you had cast your eye upon to be your wife. All were lost to the evil of this tower behind me and the designs of the one who dwells there – and those of his puppet, Rahm Imrid the Evil, who now rots in the underearth."

Moving the sword once more he indicated the horse-head standard flying above the blue and gold of Elam and the silver and purple of Lamont.

"Look upon that flag," he commanded them. "It is the most ancient banner upon the earth, flown in olden times by the great kings as they resisted this same evil with our fathers. And we are here today, beneath that same flag, following a man who is mightier than all those great and ancient monarchs."

He moved his sword yet again, pointing westward, toward the center of the army as his words waxed toward the poetic. "Today we are led by Aram the King who bears with him the instrument of Manon's final destruction. I know that man – and have seen what he can do with the weapon he bears. Our work here, upon this rocky hillside, will ensure that he finds the chance to put that instrument to its intended use." He lowered his gaze, his eyes hardened, and he met the eyes of all those near him. "This is the most important day in any of our lives, the greatest day that any of us will ever know, for today will decide the fate of the world."

Pivoting, he pointed his sword at the tower, rising up dark and sinister from the desolate plain. "Now," he said, "for the first time in many centuries, the whole world is at war with evil – here, today, led by a king."

He lowered his sword and watched the approaching line of gray men and lashers for a moment before pivoting back to face his men. Thom's stirring words had caused every face to be riveted upon him, even though a few hundred yards away the minions of the enemy came nearer with each step.

"All that is needed," he continued, "is for us to aid Lord Aram and the rest of our comrades from all over the earth in removing this army so that he may go and evict the grim lord from his tower and from the world for all time."

His features and his tone grew solemn. "For the next hour, you and I – all of us – will be more than the best of friends. We will be brothers – no matter our disparate parentage. Brothers in arms we will be, and brothers in blood, shoulder to shoulder and steel to steel."

He let silence fall as he moved his gaze up and down the line of men, those from Lamont, and those of his homeland of Elam. Then he lifted his sword high just as a flight of arrows flew from the bows of the Senecan archers positioned upon the ridge behind them and began tracing an arc through the sky toward the foe.

"Today we bring justice to the earth!"

As the men erupted in a roar of approval, Thom stepped back into line, sheathed his sword and picked up his pike.

"Alright, boys," he said, and his deep baritone voice carried for a good distance both ways along the line. *"Here they come."*

28.

Olyeg Kraine wasted no time gazing down the slope as the enemy army began its approach up the incline. He was too busy moving along the lines of his men, checking the ground upon which each of his commander's regiment was deployed, straightening out bulges and indentations in the ranks, and making sure that each of his soldiers had room to work when the bloody hour came.

He was acutely aware that he had never commanded an army when faced with steel raised in anger against it; still, he felt calm and prepared. Though green, the men were well trained, well-armed, and well-armored. They would fight.

The contingent from Basura, two full regiments, was in his half of the Elamite army, near the center of those lines entrusted to Kraine, and he stopped to discuss the coming confrontation with Cole Tensee, Basura's commander.

Tensee was a large man with massive shoulders and hands as big as two of any normal man, and though young, was of a calm and serious disposition. Like Kraine, young Cole had chafed at not being allowed the opportunity to face the host that Slan had brought before the walls of Tobol.

Now, of course, many of those that had accompanied Slan into Basura were here, in these ranks, allied with him in facing a new foe.

Over time, on the march north, Cole had managed to make peace with that fact.

At this vital hour, his only desire was to make a difference in setting the world free from evil.

"Ready, are you, general?" Kraine asked him.

Tensee saluted. "We are, sir. Anxious to get to work."

For the first time since the horn had sounded from the tower, Olyeg looked down the slope at the approaching enemy. He shook his head. "You won't have long to wait – here they come."

He looked up into the stern face of the young commander. "Hold the line," he said, "and we will be alright."

"We will hold, general," Cole replied.

"Good man." Kraine briefly placed a hand on the younger man's shoulder and then moved on.

To Cole's east, nearly four thousand men from Cumberland, under the command of the Governor-general of that land, had been inserted into Kraine's forces. Kitchell had insisted that he be placed in regimental command, and Kraine, who had been Kitchell's friend since their youth, had agreed – on the condition that the Governor-general oversee the actions of his men from the rear, behind the ranks, as a concession to his tenuous health.

Now, as he came up behind the ranks of brown-and-green clad soldiers from The Land Beyond the Gates, Kitchell was nowhere to be seen. Frowning, Kraine glanced up and over the slope, but the Governor-general was not with his small band of reserves.

Finding a company commander by the name of Haarlan standing nearby, Kraine saluted him. "Where is your commander?"

Haarlan smiled a wry smile and pointed eastward, toward the center of the line. "You'll find him just there – in the front."

Giving a curt nod of his head at this alarming bit of news, Kraine moved rapidly toward the Cumberland center.

Kitchell was standing in the front rank with both his hands firmly grasping the shaft of his pike, the butt of which rested on the stony earth beside him. He was gazing down the slope, watching the approaching enemy, speaking quiet words of encouragement to the men standing near him.

Kraine cleared his throat loudly. When this failed to attract Kitchell's attention, he raised his voice and spoke firmly. "May I have a moment of your time, Governor?"

Kitchell looked back at him and frowned. "The enemy will be upon us in less than an hour, general," he replied. "I can give you but a moment."

Kraine bit off a sharp retort and let out a breath. "It won't take longer, Governor, I promise."

Nodding to the men behind him to stand aside and let him pass, Kitchell came out of the ranks and up to where Kraine stood, using his pike like a walking staff.

Kraine met his gaze for a long moment and spoke quietly. "You promised me, Kit, that you –"

Kitchell held up one trembling hand, cutting him off. The expression in his large blue eyes was both solemn and respectful. "We are old men now – you and me, Olyeg. My life has been as good a life as the Maker has ever granted to anyone." The shaking of his hand intensified as he pointed behind him, at the ranks of soldiers.

"The future of the whole world is about to be decided right here, upon this miserable rocky hillside." He shook his head firmly. "I won't be kept out of it."

Lowering the hand to the shaft of his pike, he turned his head and gazed along the line of his countrymen. "Many of those men are little more than boys, with their lives in front of them. Others have young wives and younger children." He brought his gaze back to Kraine's face and the blue eyes narrowed and hardened. "Men will die here today, Olyeg – more, probably, than we can abide."

He leaned toward his friend and spoke earnestly and almost pleadingly. "I may be one of them, but if by my death I can help to weaken the enemy and ensure that at least one of these young men returns home to live out his life – then that is what I will do with my last breath and my last bit of strength. *Don't deny me this, my old friend.*"

Kraine gazed back at him for a long moment and then looked past his childhood friend at the young men filling the rank and file of Cumberland, gazing longer at them. Then; slowly, giving vent to a sigh of reluctance, he nodded. "Alright. I will see you after, Kit."

Kitchell's eyes grew moist with gratitude as he turned away to rejoin his men. "I will see you after, Olyeg."

Moving along to the next regiment, one drawn mostly from southern and southeastern Elam, Kraine found Marteren Hulse in the midst of quietly exhorting his troops to "stand together, put your weight into your pikes when they come. You in the second and third ranks – when a man falls, move up, plug every hole; show the enemy a solid front."

Kraine hung back and waited for the sub-general to finish his exhortation and then he moved up to stand near Hulse. Together, they watched the enemy come. Kraine reached out and put a hand on Hulse's shoulder. "That's good advice – what you told the men," he said, and then he turned and indicated another regiment standing a bit behind the line.

"Evan Cinnabar's regiment of reserves is just there. He has been instructed to release them in companies of a hundred at a time." He glanced down the hill and then met Hulse's gaze. "If you get into trouble – send a runner to Cinnabar; tell him how many you need. Hold the line, Marteren, and we'll be alright."

Hulse saluted his commanding general solemnly. "We will hold, sir."

Both men turned to look up toward the ridge top as a voice shouted a command. A moment later there came the sharp twang of hundreds of bow strings.

A cloud of long, thin, deadly missiles flew over the lines and arced down toward the approaching host.

Kraine watched them sail toward the enemy to fall among that advancing, grim host and then looked once again at Hulse. "The Maker be with you," he said.

"And with you, sir."

29.

Mallet watched the long dark line of the enemy sweeping toward him with rising alarm. The end of that line of vicious intent extended far beyond the limits of the hill that he had promised Lord Aram he would hold to the very extent of his life. For perhaps the hundredth time, he bent anxious eyes upon the surrounding terrain, trying to decide which weak point – of the myriad of weak points – would ultimately prove to be the weakest.

The continuation of the main ridge that ran behind his position to the east fell over ever more sharply as it angled away and appeared to become far too steep for even a lasher to climb without great difficulty. Undoubtedly then, the enemy flank would turn toward this hump of scalable high ground and concentrate upon its slopes. It was becoming obvious to Mallet that all those extra ranks of the enemy would have to come right here, to this little mound of earth that had been entrusted to him.

His vow to hold unto death was beginning to look more like a prophecy than a promise.

He looked over at Jonwood, standing to his right, near where the hill sloped away due east toward the mouth of the small canyon that ran behind them. "Unless those Senecan archers and the wolves can help us out, we are going to very soon have more company than this ground will allow," he growled.

The compact little man grinned up at his giant companion. "Yes," he agreed with savage anticipation. "Won't it be fun?"

Mallet frowned and shook his head. "No, Jon – it will be hell to hold this hill."

Jonwood watched the big man's face for a moment as his grin faded. "The Senecans will help us," he assured Mallet. "You told me yourself that Captain Matibar drove one of those arrows straight through a post the size of a large tree." He shrugged. "And you know that the wolves will help. Shingka can kill a lasher by herself, and that big black wolf – the one that looks like Durlrang? – he seems ready to take on the whole enemy army by himself." His grin reappeared. "We'll be alright, my friend."

Mallet glanced back toward the archers from the east, and then let his gaze drift down over the rough slopes of the canyon where, here and there, one could just make out the shadow of a four-legged warrior lurking among the rocks.

But then his attention turned once more to the many thousands approaching his position across the floor of the valley. Manon's army was nearing the base of the hill. Farther west, in front of the main army, their grim companions were already ascending the slope. Mallet shook his head in uncertainty once more. "I don't know how many arrows those Senecans have with them, but I doubt it will be enough to make any great difference with that lot. There are so many."

Jonwood watched the dark host come and then reached out and laid his good hand on Mallet's arm. "Lord Aram won't forget us," he said.

In response, Mallet waved vaguely at the broad slope that stretched away to the west behind them. "Lord Aram has a whole army to worry over."

"He does," Jonwood agreed but then insisted, "Still – he will not forget his friends."

Down on the plain, the long lines of the grim gray host had reached the edge of the gentle slopes that led up toward the summit of the hill. As Mallet had foreseen, as the main force immediately below them halted at the base, the enemy flank began to curl in upon itself, hooking around the base of the hill.

They were – all of them – apparently intent on coming right up to the place where the small force of Wallensians held the right flank of the army of free people.

May the Maker help us, thought Mallet.

A voice rose in sharp, clear command behind them.

"Loose!" It said.

212

30.

Sitting on Jared at the extreme left of his half of the cavalry, right behind where Thom Sota had finished his exhortation to the men of Lamont and Elam, Nikolus watched the Senecan missiles fly overhead to drop among the ranks of the enemy. He smiled with satisfaction as here and there gaps appeared in that line of hulking monsters at the rear of Manon's army. Some of those gaps were large and long. Apparently, some groups of the eastern archers had found the range together, obliterating large chunks of the lasher ranks. Hundreds of those beasts went down, many of them never to rise again.

Still, the enemy came on, and there were thousands.

He glanced to his left, toward the road at the center, and then looked down at the back of Jared's head. "I want to talk with Timmon a moment – before things heat up," he told the horse.

As Jared swung away, Nikolus looked over at Stevven, his lieutenant. "I will return in a moment. Wait here."

"Yes, sir."

"What is the limit of mind-speak?" Nikolus asked Jared as the big brown horse cantered toward the center. "How far away can you hear the voice of another of your people?"

"Beyond the limits of this valley," Jared answered shortly. "Why do you ask this thing?"

"Can you hear even in the midst of battle?" Nikolus persisted.

Jared swung his head around. "Noise in the ears complicates communication – certainly. Still, if the communication is clear and specific, I will hear. Why?"

Nikolus looked up as they approached the wagon on the roadway that contained the cannon. "I fear this pavement, Jared, for it pierces our center like the business end of a lance. I know that

Lord Aram understands this and is here, but he will have much to consider this day – besides, nothing can be done about it, the road is here and cannot be moved. Bonhie is with Timmon, helping with the wagon. If Timmon or the company to his front that protects the roadway gets into trouble, I want Bonhie to be able to summon you and me – and the rest of the cavalry – to their aid."

"Do not fear, Nikolus," Jared replied. "Even in the midst of battle, I can hear. I will instruct Bonhie to call upon us, if needed."

"Thank you, my friend."

As they came up, Timmon was standing in front of the gun with his crew, gazing down the road. As Jared turned his head and spoke to Bonhie, Nikolus saluted the cannoneer.

"How goes it, Tim?"

The clever man from Aniza smiled a tight smile as he turned to look up at Nikolus. Lifting one hand, he pointed at the distant tower, rising dark and sinister above the barren plain. "That vicious bastard in that tower and his servants destroyed our homeland. *Today, we destroy both them and theirs.*"

Nikolus frowned at him. "You sound confident."

Timmon's smile left his face. "I believe in destiny, Nik; I always have. You remember my sense of unease in the years before the armies of the grim lord came into Aniza?"

"I do," the horseman admitted. "You always said evil times were coming."

Timmon nodded. "And evil times did come, didn't they?" He turned and looked down the long slope for a moment, watching the approach of the forces of the enemy, and then lifted his gaze to the heights of the tower rising beyond. "I believe everything happens for a reason," he continued, looking back up at his friend. "You and that horse found each other for a reason." He turned to look at the wagon anchored in the road behind him. "And that cannon came to me for a reason."

A strange light seemed to come into his eyes as he gazed first one way and then the other along the vast lines of the army that stretched away in both directions. The muscles along his jawline worked with emotion as he once again met Nikolus' eyes.

"*We're supposed to be here today, Nikolus.* This is where everything will end, and it is our destiny – both yours and mine – *to be here.*" He paused, looked away down the slope once more, and then nodded solemnly as his eyes filled with moisture. "I feel the hand of the Maker in all this – so, yes; I am confident."

Nikolus looked down the slope as well. The enemy was within a few hundred yards of the front lines. Even though the Senecan archers were busy thinning the ranks of the great beasts that brought up the rear of the enemy army, more than enough of those monsters would survive to bring havoc up the hill with them. He leaned down and held out his hand. "Have Bonhie summon Jared if you need us, my friend."

Timmon took the proffered hand, gripped it and held tight for a long moment. "This is our destiny," he repeated. "This is where the paths of our lives have led."

"I believe you," Nikolus said. "Stay safe."

"I will – you do the same."

31.

Aram leaned forward in the saddle and tried to gauge the amount of damage that Seneca was inflicting upon the ranks of the lashers. For nearly every missile released by those deadly archers, one of the great beasts stumbled, many fell, and in places sizeable gaps appeared in their ranks. It appeared that thousands were being removed from the ranks. But many got up again and came on; even injured, they would be formidable foes when they reached the lines of the waiting men.

As he watched that long dark line come toward him, the low rumbling thunder of their boots intensifying by the moment, Aram felt suddenly out of his depth. The size and scope of the imminent clash abruptly became crystal clear.

And in the context of that imminent, massive struggle, his part seemed to him to grow pale and diminish in importance.

The two armies about to come face to face upon this barren slope were approximately equal in size – his, he realized, might actually be numerically superior, especially now that the lasher ranks were being devastated by Seneca.

The presence of lashers in the opposing host that survived to reach the front negated his numerical superiority to a very great extent, whatever the number of beasts that lived through the deadly aerial assault. Still; even as he watched, their numbers were being continually reduced by the missiles of Seneca, and his heart lifted with every monster that dropped and didn't rise again.

Even so, many would survive, and there were more than enough gray men to occupy every soldier in his ranks.

Watching the many thousands coming up the slope, Aram had an epiphany. In that instant he comprehended the reason for his feeling of impotence. He was accustomed to being involved in much smaller confrontations, in which he and the Sword were able to make a dramatic difference upon the field.

Today, with nearly two hundred thousand combatants about to meet in the raw conflict of battle, any difference he would make would necessarily be confined to one small area of the field. Despite its awesome power, the influence of the weapon was limited to Aram's presence.

And the front stretched across three miles or more.

He could not be everywhere at once.

Today's outcome would be decided by the actions – and the strength and courage – of thousands of others, rather than by any single action on his part.

He drew in a deep breath and let it out slowly. Joktan had warned him that it would ultimately come to this.

Now it had.

He looked back and forth across the slope. Because of the ravine-riddled ground, the lines of the enemy had become more than a little disordered. Still, they came on, up and over the rocky slope. As another volley from Seneca fell among them, the lashers in the rear roared in fury and drove the lines of gray men harder.

Aram studied the lines of the foe immediately to his front and gauged the distance. They would soon come within the range of normal archery. Doubtless, there were archers among the ranks of the enemy as well. He looked up at the sun, glowing dim and wan above the layer of thick haze. The Sword would find little to use, he feared, from that pale disc.

Still, he drew it forth and held it up.

To his surprise, the song of the blade arose immediately, and within moments, tongues of flame appeared and began to ripple along its length. Submitting to the pull of the sun, he let it rise higher, turning it this way and that, in order that it might gather whatever it could from that shrouded orb.

When about a hundred yards separated the combatants, horns blared among the enemy ranks and the long line paused. In the rearward ranks of gray men the arching tips of bows appeared above the helmets of those in the front ranks.

"Sound cover!" Aram shouted and the bugles sounded their response, reverberating away to the east and west along the front.

Shields came up along the line as a dark cloud of arrows rose up from the ranks of the enemy and descended toward the waiting soldiers of the army of free men.

Aram stood up in the stirrups, with the Sword stretched aloft.

He watched the dark mass of arrows pass through the top of their arc and begin to descend; then he swung the Sword in a broad stroke through the falling cloud of missiles, releasing its accumulated fire a bit at a time. As the golden flame sizzled and leapt out from the end of the blade, it turned many of the black arrows to dust along the center of the lines.

But many more got through.

Out beyond the reach of the flame, farther to the east and west along the extent of the army, all the deadly darts of the enemy fell among the ranks of his men. And they brought death and injury down with them. Among Elam especially, deployed to the right and left flanks of the army, the missiles of the enemy did serious damage. Those soldiers had never known the terror of death raining from the sky. Some of those men, too many, were unprepared, and did not properly employ their shields.

Death and injury came among those men with the descent of the enemy's missiles.

Yells of surprise and terror mingled with screams of pain along that vast front. Here and there, the injured arose and began to hobble toward the rear, in places accompanied by those who were not injured but who were shocked into retreat by the first touch of death in their ranks. Most of these uninjured were cajoled back into the lines by their commanders, but a few could not be persuaded to return.

Ignoring this by-play, having seen it all before, Aram raised the Sword again in preparation for another volley from the enemy.

And it came.

And then came again.

Three times, Manon's archers released their darts into the waiting lines of men above them on the slope. Each time, death and injury came with those missiles.

Then, with a great concerted roar from the throats of many lashers, the dark host of the enemy rushed up the last hundred yards or so, moving with surprising speed over the rocky incline, lowering their pikes as they came.

"Prepare to meet the enemy!" Aram shouted, and heard his words echoed by commanders all along the front.

Ninety thousand pikes went a bit below the horizontal, pointed down toward the gray mass sweeping up the rocky slope.

The battle for the freedom of earth had begun.

32.

Many of the arrows that had fallen among Kavnaugh Berezan's troops had been poorly aimed and missed their intended targets, falling harmlessly either to the front or the rear of the main ranks. Most of the rest bounced off shields or imbedded themselves into rocky earth between soldiers. But of those that found his men, many wrought serious damage, killing more than a few men outright and wounding others.

"Wounded to the rear!" He roared. "The rest of you – reform the line! Reserves into the gaps – *now*!"

As the enemy charged up the rough slope toward his lines, he found his attention drawn away from the oddly mesmerizing view of the approach of that imminent threat by the need to repair the rifts in his front.

At the moment the enemy impacted his lines, he was looking away, toward the east, attempting with desperate speed to move a company of reserves into a fairly large gap that had appeared in his lines, where a concentrated cloud of arrows, whether by design or accident, had found his troops. This gap appeared just above the point where a ravine cut downward through the slope. Thankfully, this ravine slowed the enemy and gave him the time to plug the hole.

He was still looking toward the east, willing the company of reserves into place when the enemy slammed into his lines. The sudden eruption of sound that exploded in his left ear momentarily deafened him.

Shouts, yells, screams, howls of rage, pain, and fury; these all melded into a roar that seemed as if it would, by its suddenness and intensity, crack the very firmament above him.

Pivoting toward the front, gazing with widened eyes, he saw his lines buckle and recoil before the force of the enemy's assault.

Because of the disorder in the enemy ranks, caused by the rough ground over which they had made their final charge, the sudden pressure being exerted upon Berezan's front was uneven, in places concentrated, in others utterly lacking. In response, the line held in places and bent inward in others, taking on the sinuous configuration of a serpent.

For just a moment, as the line to his immediate front buckled toward him, Kavnaugh was tempted to employ his pike and get into that line, but almost instantly realized that his role as commander negated any such thoughts. For the next several minutes, his energies were entirely directed toward moving reserves forward, both to plug gaps that appeared when the line buckled and to try to reverse the pressure upon the concave aspects of his front.

"Forward, men!" He yelled again and again, sprinting back and forth along the straining line of men, at times pushing the third rank forward physically with his hands. "Drive them back! Hold the line!"

Men began to die, but the enemy was taking casualties as well. Screams of pain and roars of fury, often indicating the violent hand of death at work, rose up here and there above the general cacophony. These individual sounds seemed apart from the general noise of the battle, as if the souls of the dying felt compelled to give a separate and significant voice to their violent departure from earthly bounds.

But it was the unrelenting groan of thousands of men, gray men, and beasts, pushing, slashing, and heaving that swelled beyond the ability of human ears to bear, until it seemed to Berezan that all sound ceased and a strange, unearthly silence overlaid the roiling scenes of carnage before him.

Enveloped in the calming shroud of this bizarre cone of quiet, he moved like an automaton, directing wide-eyed and frightened reserves toward the front, exhorting them to, "get up – help your comrades – *hold this line!*"

Strangely, even the sound of his own voice failed to register, though every enunciation was delivered with great force, compelled by the deadly urgency of battle.

Finding a rare moment of calm in the enveloping storm of the conflict, Berezan raced to the top of a small knoll and peered both ways along his lines, looking for signs from any of his commanders that they were being pressed beyond endurance.

To the west, the ground in front of his troops was steep and rough, and the enemy was making little, if any, headway anywhere to the left of where he now stood. But to the east, toward the center of the army, the slope became gentler, and there, in several places, his lines had been pushed backward, up the slope. Every one of his commanders in that direction was screaming for reserves, and as they were fed into the lines, the slope above the front became ever more bare, deserted of friendly troops.

Kavnaugh Berezan was running out of pieces to put into play.

He turned and examined the front immediately before him. He still felt encased in an odd zone of silence, seemingly insulated from the noisome fury that raged yards away from him.

He could hear nothing, but his eyes told him that his troops, by and large, were fighting well, standing firm, while grappling hand-to-hand with the foe.

And his eyes told another surprising thing.

Behind the front lines of the enemy, the ranks of the large beasts known as lashers seemed to have thinned appreciably. He frowned at this abrupt comprehension. True – the archers of Seneca behind him and to the right had wreaked havoc among the numbers of those beasts, but surely not to the extent that was visible to him now. Now, there were only a few of those great beasts, scattered along the rearward ranks of the enemy. More were missing, surely, than had been brought down by the missiles of the warriors from the eastern woodlands.

He turned his head and looked eastward.

And there they were – the missing beasts.

The great monsters had moved to Kavnaugh's right and were concentrating their numbers upon the brow of a wide-topped ridge that ran out from his front a ways before tipping over and falling away toward the valley. There was no doubt of their intention.

They meant to pierce him there.

Instantly, he was sprinting toward the right of his lines, yelling at his few remaining reserves to – "get up, *get up* – bolster the line! *Those monsters are coming!*"

Before he could arrive at the scene of impending disaster, howls of pain and rage erupted from the massed company of beasts

222

upon the ridge. Finding another high point in the ground, fearing the worst, Berezan halted and looked.

And there were far fewer of those beasts now.

The sharp eye of Andar, the young prince of Seneca had seen them as well, and had discerned their intent. A storm of deadly missiles had found that cohort of Manon's monsters. And with the death that rained down from the sky, confusion found them as well. That which they had planned was in ruins. The beasts that remained upon their feet were milling about and beginning to disperse, fearing more of the deadly rain of arrows.

Berezan turned to shout his thanks up to the Senecan prince, and found himself face-to-face with that very same young man.

Andar grinned at him. "We're out of arrows now, general – but we have swords. Where do you need us?"

Berezan reached out gratefully and grasped the blonde-haired young prince's hand.

"Thank you, Your Worthiness – you saved us from disaster there!"

Andar's grin turned rueful. "Well, the day is young – where do you want us?" He asked once again.

Berezan turned and examined the field. To the west, above the rougher ground, his troops were holding the line well. Here, though, on the east end of his lines, in places, the line had thinned, battered to the point that splintered and shattered pikes had been abandoned, and men fought on savagely, with swords.

Kavnaugh looked at Andar and swept one hand toward the front. "I will leave your deployment to you, Your Worthiness – but it appears as if we need you right here."

Andar's grin widened. "Well, then – it's a good thing that here is where we are, is it not?"

Berezan looked at him curiously. "You seem strangely glad to be here, sir."

It was then, when the young man turned and gazed straight into his eyes, that Berezan saw the flinty hardness behind the blue eyes in the friendly, open face of the young prince.

"I assure you, general, that glad is not the proper word. But I will tell you this – today, *I would wish to be nowhere else in the world.*"

With that, Andar drew his sword and shouted at his troops. "To the front, men, with me!"

As the troop of Senecans went down the slope toward the fighting, Berezan glanced toward the east – and his heart froze in his chest.

Without turning away from that which had captured his attention, he shouted at Andar. "Are you certain you've no more arrows, sir?"

Andar glanced back as he sprinted toward the front, his grin still in place. "Sorry, general – but we've no more to give you. I'm afraid it's all sword work for us now."

But it wasn't his own lines that concerned Berezan at the moment. A few hundred yards to the east, on the broad shelf of smooth rock that extended in front of General Donnick's position, it looked as if the world of men was about to come to an end.

33.

Before the onrushing enemy closed upon his front, after the triple volley of arrows had come and gone and the wounded had been removed, Donnick stepped out in front of his lines, at the point where Elam and Duridia came together, and looked at the men that stood on either side of that line of demarcation. Fixing his gaze on the young man from Elam that stood in the foremost rank, Donnick asked him, "What is your name, son?"

"My name is Kevan, sir," the soldier replied shakily, his eyes flicking back and forth between Donnick and the charging gray host.

The general then looked at the man standing next to him, a stocky fair-haired soldier who hailed from the southern plains of far-off Duridia.

"And your name?"

"I am called Durayne, sir."

Donnick looked back and forth from Kevan to Durayne and then he spoke. "Alright, boys," he said, "today you two are not from different lands, with different princes. Today, you are brothers, men born alike of free earth and free parentage." He leaned toward them and his voice went low. "I want you to fight like brothers today. Shake hands and pledge your honor to one another."

After the two men had complied to this, gazing at each other, each swearing solemnly to defend the other, Donnick nodded and then inquired as to the identification of each man in the rank behind and then the rank behind that.

He looked from one side to the other, slowly, from Elam to Duridia. *"Say it,"* he commanded. "Say it with me – today we are brothers!"

Inspired by his words and their meaning, soldiers from very widely separated lands raised their fists and declared, "*Today we are brothers!*"

Satisfied, Donnick went back through the lines, turned to look down the hill and deliberately raised his voice once more, but kept his tone calm. "Steady, boys. Ready spikes. *Hold the line* – here they come."

As he waited for the enemy to reach him, Donnick looked each way along his lines once more. To his right, Duridia seemed stoic, tense, but solid – they had been in this position before, and knew what to expect. To Donnick's left, the men of Elam seemed much less sure of themselves, white-faced and skittish as the dark line of the enemy came on.

Still, though their knuckles seemed ready to burst from their straining hands, and their eyes were wide with fear, they remained at their post. They had not been in this situation before; nonetheless, each of them knew *why* he was here.

The enemy charged hard for the last thirty yards or so, lowering their pikes and rushing at the lines of waiting men. Except for the occasional roar of command from a lasher, however, that dark mass was silent. Donnick waited until the leading elements of that onrushing host were within twenty yards, then –

"Spikes!"

The short oddly-weighted spears sailed forth and into the ranks of the enemy. Because of the tight formation of the gray men, for nearly every one of those deadly spikes, a gray man went down, in places their bodies tripping up those that came behind.

"Now!" Donnick yelled. "Ready pikes – hold fast!"

Just over to his left, upon the level shelf that extended out from his lines, the enemy was coming on hard, the dark line forming a convex bulge as it approached him. He turned and found Sub-general Jonders with his company of reserves.

Pointing to his left, Donnick barked the command. "Get up, and get behind Dewit and his regiment!"

The sub-general immediately moved his company down the slope to get into position behind the place where the leading elements of the enemy would arrive within moments.

Donnick also moved leftward. Duridia, he knew would be alright. Not only were they experienced in battle, but the ground to their front was steep, rough, and broken. It was in front of Elam that things would rapidly get dicey, especially if the enemy commanders recognized the advantage that the level ground deferred upon them.

Donnick had little doubt that they already knew.

Coming up next to Jonders, he put a hand on the young sub-general's shoulder. Pointing toward the front with the other, he stated with as much calmness as he could muster, "I will need you right here, sub-general. Spread your men out, and plug any gaps that appear to your front. Do that and we'll be alright."

Jonders stared to the front, swallowed and nodded, "Right, sir."

The enemy smashed into the lines. At the point where the dark line of gray men had developed a convex shape as they crossed the level ground, Elam buckled and began to give way as pikes pierced flesh and men died.

Donnick put his hand once again on Jonders' shoulder and pushed him forward. "Now, general – now!"

In response, Jonders shouted "Forward!" and his company of reserves showed their training, rushing headlong down the slope and into the rear ranks of their comrades, lowering their pikes into the enemy and buttressing the sagging line.

The timely arrival of Jonders' reserves fortified the line. Despite the horrific carnage in Elam's front ranks, the impetus of the enemy charge stalled and the line once again held solid, even as the two opposing forces pushed and strained at each other.

Donnick looked eastward, toward Duridia.

Duridia was holding.

Boman was there and he was capable, experienced, and steady. The men from the southern plains were fully engaged and taking casualties, but they were dealing death as well. Duridia would hold.

Donnick looked long enough to be sure that he was not needed anywhere to his right and then he looked back to Elam's front, out over the level shelf of rocky ground.

He sucked in a breath and held it.

A large clot of horned monsters were gathered out there.

Seneca had devastated the lines of the lashers as they had come up the slope, killing a high percentage of those loathsome beasts. However, many had survived the aerial onslaught – and now they were gathering out upon that level, open ground, obviously with every intention of storming Donnick's front. There were hundreds – nay, thousands, and more came from the right and left to swell their numbers by the moment.

Even as he watched, with his heart in his throat, another storm of arrows rained down upon that gathering clot of monsters. Over to the right, near the center, Matibar had seen the imminent danger and was working to mitigate it.

The Senecan captain sent his remaining missiles into that gathered host, killing and injuring many.

But there were too many.

It looked as if every lasher from across the whole of Elam's front had been gathered there.

And their response to the hail of deadly missiles from Seneca was to immediately turn toward the front, without waiting to form any semblance of order – and charge. As they did so, a horn sounded from among their ranks and the gray men fighting along Donnick's front abruptly disengaged, broke into two parts and peeled away; those to his left moving toward Kavnaugh and those to the right toward Boman.

His front was open, fully exposed to the onrushing mass of monsters.

Desperately, Donnick looked around for any remaining reserves, but there were none. Sheathing his sword and picking up an abandoned pike, he rushed down to insert himself into the line where the lashers would come. As he moved into a gap he heard the thunder of hooves behind him. He glanced back to find Marcus, High Prince of Elam, looking down at him from Phagan's back.

"Hold if you can, General – I'll get help!" The young prince shouted, and then he jerked his head to the right. "Look – here comes Wamlak with his troop!"

Turning his head, Donnick saw his son, Wamlak, and his mounted archers driving down the slope towards him.

As the horsemen came they released the last of their arrows into the onrushing lashers and then drew swords and lifted lances.

"Hold, father!" Wamlak yelled. "We are coming!"

34.

Boman also saw the danger that gathered upon the level ground in front of Donnick, but he had sent his reserves to the right, to aid Muray at the road. His own front was taking a beating. Though there were few lashers in the host that struggled with his men, the gray men there fought with a fierceness that belied their odd silence and seeming lack of emotion.

Desperately, he examined his lines for any men that could be relieved and sent to the left to aid Donnick.

But there were none. Everywhere, Boman's Duridians were fully engaged; to weaken any segment of his line would risk that which he feared would shortly befall Donnick. He looked up the slope to find Lord Aram, but the king was no longer there, in the center, where he had been shortly before. He and Thaniel could just be seen, going eastward behind the lines of Lamont beyond the road, driving rapidly away, apparently toward an imminent danger that had been espied on the east of the army.

A voice broke upon his ears.

Loose!" It shouted.

Boman looked up the slope. Matibar had his Senecans turned to the left, toward the danger that gathered in front of Donnick, and were employing their remaining missiles to mitigate it.

Then, sweeping down the slope in front of Matibar and his archers, Wamlak's mounted troop hove into view, charging toward Boman's left, toward Donnick. The mounted archers loosed their remaining arrows and drew swords and lances.

"Hold, father!" Wamlak shouted as he and his troop swept past Boman. "We are coming!"

Thinking that perhaps by the combined actions of Captains Matibar and Wamlak, Donnick would be saved; Boman returned his undivided attention back to his own struggles. His Duridians heaved and shoved against the vigor of the gray men, parrying with their shields as they thrust the deadly sharp steels of their pikes forward into the ranks of the enemy.

Though monstrous lashers roamed the line behind the ranks of the gray men, roaring commands, so far none of the great beasts had actually entered the fray. In fact, as Boman stopped for a moment to examine the behavior of the beasts, it abruptly occurred to him that their number had lessened beyond what he would have expected.

Seneca had dramatically thinned their numbers as they came up the hill, still there had been more that reached his lines than he now saw roaming the slope beyond the ranks of cursing, straining combatants.

Curious, he let his gaze rove back and forth along the front.

Then, he saw the reason for the reduction in numbers of the beasts that directly opposed Duridia.

Over to the right, upon the smooth pavement of the road, just out of reach of the Senecan missiles, three large groups of lashers milled about and gradually began to form into three separate and very deep lines of battle.

What he and Muray had feared all along was about to take place – Manon's great beasts meant to split the army of free men, right here, in the center.

Looking hard along his own front to make certain that his commanders had their struggling troops in hand, Boman then turned and sprinted toward the road and the right of his lines. As he ran, he looked up the hill and spied Matibar standing a few yards in front of his line of archers, gazing down the road toward the gathering clot of lashers.

"Do you still have arrows, captain?" Boman yelled up at him.

Matibar dropped his gaze for just a moment. "But two per archer," he replied, and then he turned and looked to his left, toward Donnick. "I must send one more volley to aid General Donnick," the captain stated tersely, "but I fear I will wish it back when that lot to our front charges up the road – as they will surely do."

Boman slowed and looked back toward Donnick, where pandemonium reigned and then glanced down the hill toward the beasts gathering upon the roadway. "Timmon has the cannon," he reminded Matibar.

Matibar nodded. "Yes – and we have our swords when the arrows are gone."

Briefly inclining his own head in reply, trusting the Senecan's judgment to do what he could, Boman picked up the pace and continued running toward the center. Just what *he* would do when he got there, he had no clear idea.

But things were unquestionably about to become perilous at the center of Lord Aram's army.

And Lord Aram was not there.

35.

As Aram sat on Thaniel's back, watching the enemy charge up the hill in the wake of their missile assault, he could not shake the feeling of irrelevance that had descended upon him. He had done all that he could to prepare his commanders and their men for that which they now faced. And the evidence of the men's willingness to fight was apparent in the way that spikes were launched into the foe, and how, upon the heels of that action, pikes were lowered into position to receive the enemy.

But it was all so *big.*

How and where could he and Thaniel make a difference? Mallet would very likely need him, but there were obvious points of weakness here along this front as well. He and Thaniel could not just simply choose a spot at random to enter the fray – the peculiar aid that could be rendered by him, his horse, and the Sword must be targeted.

Restless and anxious as the enemy closed upon his front, Aram nonetheless realized that he must be patient, allow the battle to develop, and then go where he was needed most – where he and the Sword would do the most good.

Standing in the stirrups as the gray men, driven by the lasher commanders that had survived Seneca's onslaught, crashed into the waiting army, he peered first this way and that, trying to gauge where he was needed.

As the fight erupted along the line, unevenly at first because of the disarray in the enemy lines, but then everywhere as the tens of thousands of gray men reached the front, the lines of Aram's army held. Though there was some initial buckling, reserves were sent in by the various commanders and the line held.

Aram stood higher and strained to see where the lashers might try to concentrate their power and break through. But their numbers had been reduced by Seneca's skill and prowess, and along most of the front, the great beasts remained in the rear, driving the gray men into the fray.

Then, off to his left, upon the level ground that had worried him earlier, a large group of lashers, hundreds of them, perhaps more than a thousand, began to gather. Almost immediately, however, Andar over on the left behind Elam, and Matibar here in the center, trained their remaining missiles upon them and began to wreak havoc among their company.

Those that survived that assault immediately turned and stormed toward the front, right at the point where Elam and Duridia came together and Donnick was in command.

Instinctively, Aram turned in the saddle, and prepared to send Thaniel in that direction.

Still, he hesitated, his mind filled with doubt over Mallet and that little hill, way over there on the right. It would not do to commit himself into the line here anywhere if it meant that his right flank was enveloped, shattered, and rolled up. It would be impossible to hold the field if that happened.

A few moments later, while Aram was still deciding whether Donnick's position was indeed the place where he would be needed most, Wamlak led his troops down the slope toward his father's lines. The horsemen expended their arrows into the charging lashers, and then drew forth lances and swords.

He was leaning leftward in the saddle, becoming increasingly intent on going to the front at that spot when Thaniel suddenly stiffened and swung his head to the right.

Aram looked down. "What is it?"

"It is Markris, my lord," the horse replied. "He states that Mallet is in imminent danger of being overrun."

Upon hearing this, all hesitation left him. "Go," he said, and as the horse plunged toward the eastern end of the field, he glanced back toward Findaen. "I am going to aid Mallet – Markris sends word that he is in danger. Go see about Donnick," he said. "See if he can hold until I return. Come and get me if his situation worsens."

Findaen nodded silently and he and Andaran peeled away to the west. Just at that moment, Matibar sent another volley into the lashers to Donnick's front. Aram looked back to see what effect the assault had upon the enemy. Many fell, but there were plenty left to wreak havoc upon the men of Elam, and contact was imminent. Wamlak was there now, almost to the lines of men surrounding his father.

He looked back toward the east as Thaniel drove to the right behind the lines of straining, shouting men. The situation to Donnick's front troubled him deeply. Leaving the road, with its obvious though so far unexecuted threat, worried him as well. At the same time, for many reasons, Mallet could not be abandoned.

And now, despite the dangers that crowded upon his army at many places, Aram felt right. He had never grown comfortable with simply being in command – he had to be engaged in the fight.

36.

When the enemy crashed into his front, Muray drew his sword and dove into the eruption of sound and fury, right at the place where two lashers roared at the gray men in front of them. He had slain one of those beasts before, and now he lusted for the chance to do it again. The thought, odd and unbidden, flashed through his mind at that moment that he was very much like Larnce, a farmhand that had once worked for his father.

Larnce was a large, very strong young man from the north of Lamont, from the rough hill country that tumbled up on the west of the great mountains above Condon. There were poisonous serpents in those hills, serpents whose venom reportedly could slay an ox. Despite the fact that they were seldom encountered, Larnce had been deathly afraid of them from his youth.

One hot summer day, as he labored to help his father and brothers bring in their crop of hay from the slopes of the rocky hills, he had stepped on one of those serpents and been bitten on the foot.

Ill and feverish for days, he had lingered near death while his mother fretted and cried over him, and begged his father to send for a doctor that could not have arrived on time in any circumstance.

But Larnce had survived. In the end, his constitution had matched his great size, and was better and stronger than the viper's sting.

Once he began to recover, Larnce grew even stronger than before. His father would often grin and state that, "That boy got something from that snake – what, I don't know, but he is stronger, bigger, and a better worker than ever."

One thing for certain, Larnce's fear of serpents was gone, having vanished with the act of surviving that which he had feared.

Now, Larnce was in these very lines, upon the rocky slope before the tower of the grim lord, somewhere over to Muray's right.

Muray, like Larnce, had survived a struggle with an opponent thought to be much stronger and deadlier; and though the lasher that he had slain wounded him severely, Muray became, if anything, fiercer in his desire to kill more of the beasts.

Now, with his men fully engaged and standing firm, Muray forced his way into the front lines, stabbing and slashing at the gray men that stood in his way, and felling any that replaced those that his sword disposed.

When the soldiers to either side of him realized that their commander fought with them, they redoubled their efforts. Within moments, a substantial gap appeared in the enemy lines, and there were no reserves to fill it.

Two lashers hove into view.

Muray twisted his sword free from the body of a gray man he'd just slain, sheathed the blade, and picked up a pike. He grinned a savage grin at the twin behemoths.

"Alright, big boys," he grunted. "Ready to taste of my steel, are you?"

The monster to Muray's left, though slightly behind the other as they came up, was larger than his comrade, and evidently anxious to rid the battle of this pesky human with the bushy red beard.

Shoving his companion aside, the lasher raised his halberd and brought it down and across in a slashing side stroke, designed to sever Muray's head from the rest of him.

To the beast's surprise, Muray stepped into the falling stroke, ducked down and shoved the butt of his pike into the rocky earth. Then, using it like a lever he thrust upward, intercepting the lasher's stroke and causing the broad blade of the halberd to ricochet off the shaft of the pike and sail upward.

The shaft of the pike shattered under the force of the blow and Muray's hands and arms vibrated painfully. Ignoring the pain, he quickly drew his sword and struck at the twisting body of the beast, driving the steel deep into the sinewy flesh below the rib cage, and then, with a savage twist, yanked it free. Brackish blood spewed and the beast gave vent to a howl of torment.

Seizing upon their commander's brave actions, those soldiers nearest him assaulted the lasher with hard thrusts from their pikes, and at least one man succeeded in piercing the great beast, causing him to lose his balance and tumble back down the slope whence he'd come. As he fell, the lasher collided with his companion, shoving him sideways. Roaring in anger, the second lasher regained his balance and spun to continue the attack.

But Muray and his men were ready.

"Come on, boys!" Muray shouted. "Give him the sharp end of your pikes!"

Emboldened by their success in driving off the first lasher, Muray's men lunged forward with their pikes, impaling the second beast in several places. As the lasher twisted and swung his halberd in an attempt to wrestle free of the offending steel, Muray leapt to the side and slashed at the meaty part of the beast's thigh.

Ducking around to the other side, he slashed at the other leg, his blade cutting deep just below the knee. Then whirling back the other way as his men strained to keep their pikes in the beast while avoiding the massive halberd, Muray stuck his blade deep into the meat of the thigh he'd slashed moments earlier and twisted with his might.

Something cracked, and the beast went down.

"Swords!" Yelled Muray. "Strike at his hands and arms. Kill him!"

Then he turned to face the first lasher, who'd managed to regain his feet and work his way back up the hill.

"Pike!" Muray yelled again, and someone thrust one into his hands.

Before the beast could rise to attack Muray upon the same level, Muray thrust the pike with his might. The beast swung the butt of his halberd and Muray missed, losing his balance and going to one knee. But his leadership had raised the blood of the men near him to feverish levels.

Other pikes assaulted the great beast. Some were thrust into his face, while others found exposed parts of his massive body. Having lost his own pike in the melee, Muray once again drew his sword and went to work on the lasher's arms and legs, sawing and hacking with his might.

Within moments, the beast was down and at their mercy.

The news flashed along the front like lightning.

Muray and his men have slain two lashers!

Where this incredible rumor went, courage seemed to go with it. Men's hearts were raised. *If Muray can do it, so can we.*

Muray and his men had created a gap in the enemy lines and now the fierce commander meant to exploit the opening. Shouting hoarse commands at his third rank, he moved men through the lines and formed them up, facing each way along the front. Directing his attention to the east first, he sent those men on a flanking maneuver into the ranks of gray men.

There was another lasher a short way along, and Muray raised his voice. "You know now that they can die, lads. *Forward –* and I will be with you in a moment!"

Then he pivoted and focused his attention on the men facing west.

His savage heart almost pounded to a stop.

He was looking at the road, in clear view a few dozen yards away.

Massed upon that road, preparing to charge straight into the heart of the army, was a clot of at least a hundred lashers.

37.

Edwar was heartened as he watched lashers fall by the score beneath the terrible assault of Senecan arrows. Again and again those deadly missiles rained upon them out of the sky. Beasts went down. Many never got up again. With each gap that opened up in the ranks of those great monsters, Edwar's spirit lifted a bit more.

His men had not faced those beasts at the Bloody Stream, and he was not anxious to meet many of them here. He gave the order to employ the spikes when the gray men were but twenty yards away, all the while wishing he had hundreds of the things and could use them upon the surviving beasts that trailed behind.

The slope in front of his lines was fairly steep and rough. When the enemy made contact, it was spotty at first and those men that felt the first brunt held, giving courage to those that still waited for the fateful moment to arrive.

"Hold, men – *hold!*" Edwar shouted as he roved back and forth behind his soldiers. "Lean your weight into your weapons."

The noise of the battle began abruptly, like an explosion, but quickly escalated further, into a horrific cacophony of grunts, curses, and screams of pain.

The steepness and roughness of the ground to the front aided his men greatly, but over to the right, on a ridge that ran out in front of Kaspar's troops, a group of lashers bunched up and punched through. Edwar yelled for reserves and sprinted that way, drawing his sword as he ran.

But Findar, positioned over to the right behind Elam, saw the danger, too, even across a distance of more than two hundred yards. Before Edwar could reach the breach, as the beasts began to lay about them with their massive halberds, killing and maiming with each stroke, the Senecan captain sent a concentrated volley of death into them.

By the time Edwar reached the clot of lashers, all were injured, many were down, and some were prone, kicking at the ground with their clawed feet in the final throes of death.

"Swords!" Screamed Edwar, as he brandished his own above his head. "Muray slew one of these beasts with his sword," he reminded the men nearby. "Upon them – *now*!"

And the men of Lamont fell upon the hapless lashers, all of whom were wounded by Findar's volley. Within minutes, they were dead, and the breach sealed.

A great shout went up, even as word came from the west.

Muray's men have slain two lashers!

Kaspar, his face fouled by brackish blood, grinned and lifted his sword high.

"Yes? Well, tell them – *we have slain eleven.*"

But there was little time for celebration. The enemy still pressed upon them all along the front.

"Back into line – form up the line!" Edwar yelled. When the line was reformed and the breach stopped, before he turned back toward the west and his own center, Edwar looked at the distant line of Senecan archers and raised his sword in salute.

Having averted disaster here on his right, Edwar found some high ground from which he could examine the whole of his front, in case there were other imminent dangers.

It was when he looked to the west, at Muray's position upon the road, that he knew disaster was not only imminent but upon them.

38.

Thom stood in the front rank of his troops as the enemy advanced upon them. Feeling a touch upon his shoulder, he looked to his right. A young Elamite by the name of Braden stood there, his pike in his other hand as he pointed to the rear.

"General," Braden suggested, "shouldn't you be back there?"

Thom grinned. "No more than you should be, son."

Braden glanced down the slope at the approaching enemy before looking back at Thom. "But what will we do if you are injured or ..... or slain?"

Thom's grin widened and grew savage.

"Then you will avenge me," he said.

Braden stared at him for a long moment, and then swallowed and nodded. "I'm glad you're here, sir."

"I would be nowhere else," Thom assured the young soldier. Then he looked down the slope. The enemy had picked up the pace and were coming on the run.

Thom raised his voice. "Ready spikes!"

After those unwieldy weapons had been employed and had pierced gaps here and there in the line of gray men, Thom looked at Braden before raising his voice once more. "Ready pikes!" He yelled, dropping his own down into position, grasping it firmly with both hands. "Here they come!"

There was little, if any, emotion in the slitted eyes of the gray-skinned soldiers that stared at Thom through the eye-guards of their helmets. But there was surprising strength in their muscle and sinew. As he blocked the pike that was thrust at him with his shield, Thom dropped his own and then abruptly brought it up, stepping into the stroke.

The gray soldier made no sound except for a guttural grunt as the sharp steel pierced him, but the black eyes widened for a moment in pain and then dulled. Thom twisted his pike and drew it out, falling back a half-step as he prepared to face the second enemy in line.

This one was quicker and cleverer than his fallen comrade. As Thom feinted to the side, lifting his shield with his left forearm, drawing back his pike for a killing stroke, the gray soldier moved the other way, and plunged his pike behind Thom's shield, and found the exposed flesh of his shield arm.

Pain erupted and blood spewed.

Gritting his teeth against the hot fire of a deep wound, Thom lunged to his left, bringing his weight to bear on the pike of his enemy. The gray man stumbled as he tried to raise his weapon and draw it back toward him. His leather shield fell open to his right, to Thom's left, as the gray man tried to regain his footing.

Thom struck.

Lifting his pike from the earth, he thrust it with his might into the belly of his opponent, leaning all his weight into the stroke. The pike went deep, scraped against something hard and unyielding, and then abruptly went deeper.

The gray soldier opened his mouth to emit a howl of agony.

But there was no sound. Only blood came forth in a gushing flood as he fell.

As he crumpled, he dragged down the gray man to his rear. Drawing back his weapon, Thom slew the fallen gray soldier with one stroke. And there was no lasher in the immediate area. Thom looked to his right and found Braden finishing off the last of his three opponents.

The line of the enemy was breached.

He turned to wave reinforcements into the gap, but as he did so, a strong hand fell upon his arm. It was Braden.

"No, general, you're wounded – bad by the amount of blood you're losing. Get to the rear, sir," the young soldier stated firmly. "We'll handle this."

Thom, who was in fact feeling a bit light-headed, nodded and turned away. "Get the men through," he told Braden. "Flank these bastards – but watch out for lashers."

"The word is that they've been killing lashers west along the line, sir," Braden replied.

"Have they now?" Thom nodded as he moved aside to let reserves flow into the gap. "Then let's do some of that here," he said.

Once behind the line, Thom looked down at his upper arm, where the gray man's pike had pierced him. Thankfully, the wound was with the grain of the muscle rather than against it. It was, however, apparently deep, and had found, if not a major artery, at least an important vein, for it was spewing blood. Moving east behind the straining line of soldiers, Thom found a surgeon tending to a man lying prone in a pool of blood.

The surgeon looked up and frowned at the sight of his commanding general holding his left arm while blood bubbled through his fingers. The surgeon, a man by the name of Ramstin, made to get to his feet immediately, but Thom reached out with his good hand and prevented him.

"Tend to that man first," he ordered.

Ramstin looked down, shook his head, and rose anyway. "I can do nothing more for him. He's gone," he told Thom. "Here – let me see your arm."

While the surgeon examined his wound, Thom watched the progress of his men. The gap he'd helped to create had been closed by the arrival of three lashers, but after dealing enough death to close the break in their line; the monsters had then driven gray men into place and moved once again to the rear.

"*Damn*," Thom muttered.

The surgeon stopped his work and looked at him. "Did I hurt you, general?"

Surprised, Thom twisted around to look at him. "What? No – but the enemy has pushed us back from an opportunity. How soon will you be finished with me?"

"It's quite a deep wound, sir, and you've lost a lot of blood," Ramstin replied. "You should go to the rear."

Thom shook his head. "I'm not going to the rear – I'm going back to the front. Are you done there yet?"

Ramstin watched him for a moment and then signaled to one of his subordinates, who brought him a small vial which he passed on to Thom. "If you're going back – you'll have to drink this, sir."

243

Thom held it up with his free hand and looked at it. "It was deeply golden in color and contained something that sparkled in the wan light of the shrouded sun. "What is this?"

"Honey and extract of goldenseal root."

Thom twisted around and glared at him. "What the hell is goldenseal root?"

Ramstin glared back. "I don't have time to give you a lesson in remedies, general. If you want to get back into the battle – *drink it.*"

Thom watched him for a moment longer and then tipped up the bottle, gagging over the contents but managing to get it down.

"Can I go now?"

Ramstin finished tying a knot in the bandage. "Go, sir – and the Maker go with you."

Thom sprinted down the slope a ways but then stopped and looked back at Ramstin, who was stooping over another soldier that had been given into his care.

"Thank you," he called.

The surgeon nodded and raised one hand but kept his attention on the wounded soldier before him.

As he hurried back to the front, Thom felt the "remedy" begin to have a surprisingly rapid effect upon him. Not only did a measure of his strength return, but he felt as if his senses were somehow heightened.

And with that return of strength and its accompanying surge of awareness, he found himself seized by a sudden and urgent need to kill a lasher. If the rumors that came along the line in the midst of battle held any truth, those great beasts were being killed elsewhere – and not by Lord Aram. No, the monsters had been slain by men, by soldiers of the line, working together to bring down the behemoths where they could.

And now Thom wanted his share of lasher blood.

Picking up a fallen pike, he worked his way along the line, studying the ground in front of his troops and gauging the ebb and flow of battle. Finally, he decided to insert himself into the fray opposite the point where a lasher commander was feeding reserves into his ranks. There was a depression in the slope that fell over into a steep-sided, rocky ravine a few feet from where the two lines of combatants struggled, strained and died; steepening sharply right behind the enemy ranks, and this rough earth placed the gray soldiers in difficulty and at a disadvantage.

The lasher was compelled to maintain the flow of reserves at this point because of the disadvantageous nature of the ground. His troops slipped, and slid, and faltered, and as a consequence were being slain in numbers that could not be sustained.

Thom recognized an opportunity when he saw one.

Gathering up a few reserves that stood nearby, waiting their turn to get into the fight, he formed them into a small company. "Follow me in," he told them. Looking to his right, he singled out three men. "You, you, and you – when we break through, turn to the right, and flank the enemy line. The rest of you go to the left with me." He worked his way into the front rank and raised his voice above the din.

"*Forward* – with me!"

Spurred onward by the presence of their commander, the men made a great push, driving the gray men backward and over the lip into the upper reaches of the ravine, pushing the lasher commander back as well, breaching the enemy line. As the men rushed forward to finish the enemy that had stumbled backward into the ravine, Thom shouted – "No! Ignore them – let others deal with them. Follow me! Take out the beast!"

The lasher had regained his feet by using his massive broad-bladed halberd as support, though because of the slant of the ground, he actually stood somewhat downhill from his approaching enemies. The beast's head was on level with Thom and his men.

The monster had not yet been able to bring his weapon up at the ready. Thom lowered the tip of his pike, aiming at the beast's broad chest. "Forward!"

As he rushed at the lasher, Thom raised the tip of his pike and lunged at the beast's head even as he yelled to his companions – "Go for his legs, *now*!"

The lasher responded to the threat posed by Thom's pike, lifting his halberd up in front of his body and swinging it to the right to deflect his enemy's blow. Focusing on Thom, while ignoring the weapons of those that accompanied him, was a fatal error on the part of the great beast. Even as Thom's strike was pushed aside, shattering the shaft, the sharp steel of Thom's companions found the lasher's thighs and bit deep, not only wounding the beast but driving him back and down into the ravine.

In a desperate attempt to keep his clawed feet beneath him, the monster dropped his weapon and reached down for the earth with his right hand.

The massive horned head was now at the level of Thom's shoulder.

Thom's pike had fallen away; his hands were free. Quickly drawing his sword, he lunged forward and drove the blade into the lasher's neck, just above the edge of his leather chest armor.

The lasher howled in fury and agony and grasped at the sword, but Thom twisted it with his might and jerked it free, instantly driving the blade forward again. This time, Thom's thrust drove the steel into the lasher's neck just above the previous wound. And this time he sawed sideways with the blade as he once again pulled it free.

Brackish blood poured forth in a flood.

The beast fell forward upon his face as a great cheer arose from the men in the line. And now the breach in the enemy line widened as the men of Elam and Lamont fought with renewed vigor. Thom began sending men right and left, into the exposed flanks of the enemy.

Another lasher approached, loping toward Thom and his men from the east. Thom took stock of the situation. Behind him, his troops were driving hard into the enemy flank. The ravine below him was empty; the gray men having climbed out and moved either to the right or left.

Alright, he thought, *we killed one of those beasts – we can kill another.*

"Pikes to the fore, close ranks!" He shouted. Thom looked around for something he could use as a weapon, having lost his pike in the struggle with the first lasher. He did not wish for his men to face this second beast without him. His left foot fell hard upon something that turned and rolled beneath it. He looked down.

A spike.

Somehow, one of those unwieldy weapons had fallen short of its mark or had been carried, perhaps unknowingly, to the front. He picked it up and examined it. It was whole, unbroken, the deadly tip still sharp.

He looked up. In front of him, his men had closed ranks, their pikes in position, as the lasher charged them. There was only a moment before the beast closed. Drawing back the weapon, Thom ran toward his men, launching the spike over them as the lasher closed. The weapon arced downward and caught the beast in his right leg. The sharp steel bit deep and the butt of the shaft of the weapon fell and imbedded itself into the earth, becoming an unbreakable impediment. The lasher stumbled and went down.

"Now!" Yelled Thom. "Attack! Don't let him up!"

The men jammed their steel into the body of the fallen lasher. The great beast roared in pain and tried to rise, but there were too many. And then Thom was there with his sword, hacking at the lasher's arms and then at the thickly muscled neck that held up the head. Within moments, it was over. Wasting no time on celebration, the troops retrieved their weapons from the body of the lasher and drove on.

The breach in the enemy lines widened further. The men of Elam and Lamont smelled victory – they had slain two of the monsters and had pierced the ranks of the enemy. Their blood was fully up. Thom glanced down the slope, but there were no reserves of the enemy visible below him.

"Onward!" He shouted, motioning to the right and the left. "*Drive them.*"

On Thom's part of the field, things were going well, indeed.

39.

Olyeg Kraine did his best to bury his nagging worries over his friend, Kitchell, and focused on maintaining the order of his lines as the enemy charged up the slope, smashing into his front in haphazard manner. The rough terrain, though not as bad here as elsewhere on the rim of the crater, nonetheless caused a measure of disorder in the lines of the enemy, and so contact was uneven all along the front. Kraine's lines buckled and sagged as the enemy made impact – but the effect was not constant; the line weakened here, but not there.

He was loath to send reserves in so soon, until he was certain of the places where his lines would, indeed, buckle and fold to a dangerous degree, something that at this moment could not be easily determined – not before the enemy made impact all along the front.

He ran from one commander to another back and forth along the line. "Hold! Reform that line!" He shouted again and again, as his lungs burned from the exertion and his old legs began to fail.

But his commanders responded – whether because of Kraine's exhortations or their own acumen – and soon, there was a relatively even front straining against the enemy – all of whom were now there, driven forward with vicious ferocity by their lasher overlords.

Kraine had placed several thousand soldiers in reserve. More than a third of these were positioned to his left, near where Thom Sota was in command, so he left those to the discretion of that younger man and focused upon the center and right of his lines.

Technically, Kitchell was in command of his right, but since the Governor-general had decided to join the fight in a personal way, the responsibility for Elam's extreme right had effectively fallen to young Marteren Hulse. Kraine trusted Hulse, both his nerve and his intelligence; still, he kept an eye trained on the right as he worried over his center.

In contrast to many of his younger compatriots, Olyeg Kraine was not surprised by the horrific noise and instant carnage of war. It was not that he'd known what exactly to expect; the only battle he'd witnessed had been very one-sided, when Lord Aram and his mounted troop had driven Slan from before the walls of Tobol.

It was simply that Kraine had lived long enough to witness death in its many forms, both natural and unnatural, so he had known in at least a general sense what would occur when two great companies of enemy combatants came together in violent collision. That which he saw happening along the rocky slope in front of him exceeded every expectation.

What surprised him most was that his men were holding their own, struggling and straining to push the enemy back and pierce him with their steel. Kraine's heart swelled at the sight, even as he swallowed down his emotion as broken, dead, and wounded men were transported away from the front in ever greater numbers as the first hour after contact waxed and waned, and began to wear away.

Despite his nagging concern over his friend, Kitchell, in the very front of things over to his right, Kraine's time, after the enemy made contact, was utterly consumed with gauging where along the front his reserves were needed most and directing them there.

The initial carnage was light but soon became terrific, both among his own men and those of the enemy, as soldiers gave in to the fury of battle. Gaps appeared with frightening regularity in Kraine's lines, especially where those lashers opposite injected themselves into the fray.

Findar of Seneca and his archers, positioned upon the ridge behind him, had saved a few of their arrows, and these they now employed in felling those great beasts wherever they threatened to break through. But these volleys came less and less, and finally not at all. The deadly missiles of the eastern warriors at last gave out.

Immediately after, Findar and his men presented themselves to Kraine, armed with swords.

"Where do you want us, general?"

"Thank you for your help thus far," Kraine answered, in way of reply, and then he turned to examine the front for a moment before looking back at Findar. "Do your men employ pikes?"

"The pike is not our weapon of choice, general," the Senecan responded, but he nodded as he did so. "However, we do understand the use of it. Do you have any to spare?"

Kraine waved one hand generally toward the front. "There are plenty there whose owners have no further use of them. Will your men fight as one or may I deploy them in companies?"

Findar shrugged as he looked toward the battle raging a few yards away with rising agitation and impatience. "We came to fight, general. Send us in however you wish – by companies if you so desire. My men know their unit commanders and will follow them when ordered." He turned and met Kraine's gaze as he also lifted a hand and indicated the front. "It seems that we can be of immediate use."

Kraine nodded. "Yes, you may." He looked closely at Findar. "This is my first experience of war," he admitted. "I know no more than you, captain. Divide your men up however you will and send them where you will – I trust to your judgment. There will be pikes on the ground at the front, but keep your swords close. If the day continues to progress as it has thus far, we will need every piece of sharp steel we possess."

Findar bowed. "As you will, general," and he immediately turned and began barking orders at his troop of Senecans, directing them to places where the line showed strain. Findar himself trotted toward the front with the last company. As he went, he turned his head and looked back at Kraine, raising one hand in salute.

Kraine nodded. "Thank you, sir," he said, though he doubted the Senecan heard above the noise of battle. Shortly afterward, Kraine sent in the last of Elam's reserves that were stationed on the left and went to the right in search of Kitchell.

40.

Kitchell ignored the pleas of men to both sides for him to go to the rear as he watched the enemy charge up the slope.

"I'm staying right here, boys," he said. "We'll meet them together, you and me – for Cumberland, for our families, for hearth and home – and for freedom."

After gaining permission from Olyeg to fight with his men, the Governor-general of Cumberland realized that he had told the truth about his need to fight.

Every man that stood upon this barren, rocky slope knew ultimately why he was here, but many of those men had other ideas as well of what this day should bring them should they survive. All fought for the requisites of duty and honor, because their country required it of them. Many, perhaps very many, fought for vengeance, for a sister, a daughter, or a friend.

But there were larger ambitions at work as well. Lord Aram, for instance, fought for his kingdom and for the right of those people who populated it to be and remain free. His aspirations were high and noble, as befitted his station. And there were many other princes here upon the field, whose causes were similar.

Kitchell's, perhaps, ought to have been like that, he knew.

But for him it was more personal.

He had told Olyeg the truth when he said that his life had been good and, if it ended here upon this stony ground, long enough. To either side of him, however, as he watched the enemy rush up the slope, were young men, some barely more than boys, with the biggest part of their life ahead of them if they survived this day.

And that is what this battle had become for the Governor-general of Cumberland – a mission to get as many of them home safe and as sound as possible. But even if just one survived because of his actions on this day, it would suffice. Young Sub-general Hulse, under whose command his own troops had now fallen, was better trained and clearer-eyed than Kitchell, and Kitchell was happy to stand aside, get into the line with the men, and let him command.

It was not that he had a death wish; he did not. Kitchell hoped to live and see his young grandchildren grow to maturity. But he also knew that none of the men of Cumberland had seen that which was about to transpire on this hazy day; and he meant to be in the line, with the men, whatever came to pass.

He was not as strong as he'd once been, nor as quick; still, he was strong enough, and one didn't need to be quick with a pike, only determined.

And Kitchell was determined.

The enemy was within twenty yards, their pikes down and at the ready.

"Spikes!" Kitchell shouted, as from either way along the line, other commanders rendered the same instruction.

Those with spikes drew back and hurled those odd weapons into the face of the onrushing foe. Many went down; some got to their feet again, others did not. Small gaps appeared in the lines of the enemy but these quickly went away as the gray men behind moved up to take the place of those that had fallen.

Another volley from the archers of Seneca sailed over the line, off to the left of Kitchell's position, to fall among the lashers at the rear there. In front of him the beasts that ranged along behind the charging gray men, driving them forward, remained unmolested.

"Pikes to the fore!" Kitchell yelled, and again this command echoed along the line.

There came an odd swooshing sound as thousands of pikes came down into position, pointing slightly downslope into the faces of the enemy. Kitchell quickly adjusted his shield, which was strapped to his left forearm, gripped his pike tightly, and took aim at a gray man whose narrow gaze seemed to be fixed on him in turn. At the last moment, Kitchell abruptly realized that his pike, in fact, was slightly longer than that of his foe, giving him an opportunity. Nor was this foe – or any of the enemy immediately before him, strangely enough – bearing a shield.

The enemy seemed intent on using the force of their charge to grant them advantage in the first moments of the conflict.

Cocking his left arm upward to lift his shield, Kitchell took a half-step forward and thrust with his might. He was rewarded with a grunt from the gray man as the pike pierced both his armor and his flesh. The black eyes widened, and the enemy soldier's pike fell and ground its steel tip into the rocky soil. The lean, hunched figure lost all forward momentum, impaled upon Kitchell's pike.

The Governor-general's muscles twanged and bunched from the effort, but he persisted, pushing his victim's body against the force of the enemy charge. Gray men following behind stumbled and faltered.

And a gap was created.

Forgetting for the moment that he did not fight alone, that thousands of friends and enemies alike surrounded him, Kitchell gave into the impetus of the kill and moved forward, intent on thrusting the ranks behind back down the hill, widening the gap, and creating further opportunity.

For a moment, it worked.

Though no longer young, Kitchell was yet strong. More gray men, to either side, stumbled and faltered. The gap grew wider.

Then, into the gap, stepped a lasher.

The monster fixed Kitchell with a malevolent gaze and raised his halberd.

Kitchell tried to wrest his pike loose from the body of the gray man he had slain and pushed backward, but to no avail.

The lasher's arm began its descent.

Abandoning the pike, the Governor-general of Cumberland lifted his shield with his left arm and reached for his sword with his right hand, yanking it from its scabbard and swinging it upward.

He was too slow.

The lasher's stroke smashed through his shield, severed his arm, and sliced deep into his body between his ribs and his hip. Blood poured forth in a flood, both from the stump of his arm and from the gash in his lower torso.

Kitchell stumbled. The hazy sun above grew suddenly darker as his strength left him in the rush of blood.

Still, in his last extremity, there was enough left in him to stoke the fires of fury. As he fell, he stabbed with the sword, though the blade was strangely heavy. The tip fell toward the earth as he shoved it toward the lasher. It missed the monster's thigh, brushed the leather shin-guard of the beast and then, the weight of Kitchell's dying body driving it downward, plunged into the great clawed foot, pinning it to the earth.

The lasher stumbled, lost his balance and went down to one knee, howling with pain and fury.

But his fury was nothing compared to that of the young men of Cumberland who had just witnessed the slaying of their beloved leader. As the beast attempted to use the butt of its halberd to roll Kitchell's body from his foot so that the blade might be dislodged, those young men, their blood fully up, saw opportunity.

Pikes plunged into him and swords hacked at his massive arms and clanged off the horns of his head.

With a great roar, the lasher attempted to rise, lifting his weapon to strike. But the sword was still lodged in his foot, pinning him in place. Down he went again upon one knee though his great steel blade was ready for action.

It was at this moment that a stout young man of Cumberland by the name of Wethurfurd stepped behind the beast and swung his sword with all his might at the base of the creature's neck. The steel bit deep, the massive head tipped unnaturally forward, and the beast let out another shriek of pain.

Wethurfurd struck once more.

And then again.

The great head came loose.

The lasher's body rolled away down the slope. As he went, the blade of his weapon tripped two gray men that fought beside him on his left. They went down as well.

The gap that had been created by Kitchell grew wider yet.

From his position behind and over to the right, Sub-general Marteren Hulse had turned from directing reserves into gaps of his own in order to check, yet again, on Cumberland's leader. With his heart in his throat, he witnessed the duel between Kitchell and the lasher. When Kitchell went down, Hulse began running toward the scene, drawing his sword as he went.

His soldier's mind saw the gap created in the enemy ranks, even as his eyes fell upon the terrible sight of Kitchell's body lying face down upon the slope in a widening pool of blood that thickened as it oozed downhill. As he sprinted toward the front, Hulse turned his head and saw Evan Cinnabar, who was directing the last of his reserves to the left.

"No, captain!" Hulse shouted as he slid to a halt on the gravelly slope. Cinnabar's head jerked around to look his way. Hulse pointed to his front. "There is a gap! Give me the last of your men and send them through! We'll turn the enemy here!"

Cinnabar glanced toward the indicated spot, immediately saw the truth of his commander's words and shouted for the last company of his troop to – "Belay that! Come with me! Forward!"

Hulse sprinted on into the gap where even now, the men of Cumberland were turning to the right and to the left, instinctively flanking their enemy.

Wethurfurd was leaning over Kitchell's body, tears streaming down his face.

Hulse grabbed him by the shoulder, making the young man look up. "Get some help – and get him out of here," he told him. "Then get back here and help me turn this flank."

Hulse knelt to put a finger upon Kitchell's neck, even though it was obvious that the Governor-general of Cumberland was no more. In the midst of battle, with pandemonium surrounding him on all sides, Marteren Hulse bowed his head for a moment in reverence and grief. Then he came to his feet and his eyes blazed.

As Cinnabar's troops came through the gap he formed them up and sent them left and then right, while placing a small group to watch the downslope for treachery. "Push them, boys!" He shouted, waving his sword above his head. "Push them!"

And so it was that Kitchell's desire to save the life of at least one young citizen of Cumberland was multiplied many times over, and victory was given to that part of the field where he fell.

41.

While the lines of the enemy were being pierced in front of Thom Sota and Marteren Hulse, over to the east upon the little round hill where Mallet stood with his band of Wallensians, things were rapidly going from very bad to very much worse.

As he had feared, the part of the enemy line that overlapped his position had elected not to attempt a climb up the steep, broken slope that extended beyond him to the east in an attempt to flank the army of humans, but had turned instead and enveloped his hill.

And up the slopes of that hill they came – in numbers that appeared irresistible. To the north, the enemy charged up the slopes in three ranks, but to the east and around the southeastern portion of the hillock, where the excess of their strength had gathered, they were eight or ten deep – and there were more than enough lashers in that host to chill any man's blood.

Mallet turned his right flank as well to meet this threat, even as he knew this act to be very likely a futile one. There were simply too many of the enemy.

"Go to the right, Jon," he told Jonwood. "Take every reserve – put them into the line."

When the enemy was something more than halfway up the hill, the Senecan archers standing on the main ridge behind went to work, targeting lashers. And they were deadly accurate. Mallet's spirits rose ever so slightly as he observed the carnage those eastern warriors inflicted upon the ranks of the great beasts. Even as he watched and drew courage from the spectacle, he knew that, sooner or later, probably before the enemy reached his pitifully small line, those men would use the last of their missiles.

Then the enemy would be here, and it would get savage.

As he was examining the shape of his deployment one last time before the enemy made contact, Mallet heard screams of pain and fear erupt from down the slope, from among the ranks of the enemy upon the right side of the hill, where it sloped away into the small dark canyon.

The wolves had entered the battle.

Mallet's spirits lifted a bit more.

Behind him, the Senecan archers, commanded by a tall, dark-haired young captain named Stevear, were making their presence count. Ignoring the gray men, as Matibar had instructed them, they were slaying and wounding the lashers by the score. Still, though, many of the monsters remained, driving their hordes of gray men up the slope – and how many more arrows, Mallet wondered, did those men of the east yet possess?

The sound of screams from the right and rear intensified, mixed with the low growl and eager yips of the wolves. The number of enemies that would shortly arrive at the top of the hill would be less – much less – than they had been.

But they were still very many.

Too many.

And they were nearly here.

"Spikes!" Roared Mallet. Even as he gave the command, he found himself wishing that every man in his troop was in possession of not one but two or even more of those blunt killing instruments. After watching to gauge the effect upon the enemy of those odd spears, he hoisted Lasherbane and inserted himself into the line, working his way into the forward rank at the point where there were still three or four lashers in a group coming up the hill.

"Now!" He shouted again. "Ready pikes! *Here they come.*"

Just before the enemy host impacted his front and his flank, Mallet roared out one more command.

"*Lean into it, boys – give them the steel!*"

The men of Wallensia, though daunted by the vastly superior numbers that they confronted, had nonetheless been in battle twice before. They could perhaps not all be called veterans, but they were all of them experienced in the terrible pageantry of battle and the attendant dark carnival of death. To a man, each obeyed his commander's exhortation and put all his weight into his weapon, pushing off the back foot, making the sharp end of his pike do that for which it had been designed.

There was one thing more that gave each of them courage, a small reservoir of savage hope.

It was a thought.

Lord Aram will come.

There was no buckling of the line here, upon the brow of this small hill.

There was instead a horrific collision of determined men and lasher-driven gray soldiery.

At the first, the determination and courage of the men of Derosa held, and the enemy took casualties in terrible percentages. Mallet swept the gray soldiers before him to the side and went for a great beast that driven those lesser creatures before him. The lasher sneered and swung his halberd, but though Mallet was smaller, he was not small. And he was quicker.

Rolling the lasher's stroke over the top of his shield, Mallet stepped close, crouched, and thrust upward with Lasherbane. The sharp end of that massive pike careened off the monster's hardened leather chest armor and went into the fleshy part of the beast's neck behind the jawline. Then the big man rose up out of his crouch and drove the steel upward with his might. The steel disappeared into the lasher's head.

The great beast died without uttering another sound.

Around Mallet a mighty cheer went up as his first kill hit the ground, rolling downslope and into the rear ranks of the enemy. Another lasher challenged him, and though this duel went on a bit longer, in the end, one more of Manon's beasts died.

But as the minutes wore away, free men, too, began to fall, many to never rise again. And they had not the numbers to sustain such casualties.

The angled, hook-shaped line of Wallensia became ever more exaggerated and sharply bent until, at the east end of the hill, comrades fought almost back-to-back. The only thing saving them at the moment was the actions of the wolves. Leorg, Shingka, Padrik, Goreg, with all their people continued to harry the foe. In the rearward ranks of the enemy host, Manon's troops fought facing away from the men upon the hilltop, contesting with the sharp teeth of wolves for their very lives.

Then, there was another respite granted to Mallet and his small company when Stevear and his Senecans joined the fray. Their missiles exhausted, the men from the east ran out the ridge to the extreme eastern end of Mallet's line where it hooked back above the canyon, drew their swords and assaulted the enemy upon his flank.

Soon, however, the Senecans were pushed back until they became Mallet's eastern wing, fighting desperately to keep the enemy from enveloping them.

And still, despite the savage aid of wolves and the added weight of the Senecan contingent, Mallet's company was pushed back further, casualties mounted higher, and the enemy pressed ever harder upon them. The strength and the will of Mallet's small band approached its breaking strain.

"Fall back – close the gaps!" Mallet roared for what seemed the hundredth time and as he obeyed his own command, his right shoulder pushed into something larger even than him. Startled, he turned his head.

Markris stood there, using his bulk to fill a gap in the line. Mallet shook his head and shouted above the din, forgetting in the heat of things that the horse could hear his thoughts. "No, my friend – get away! This is no place for a horse!"

"There is no one else to stand here," the horse replied. "If I go, who will guard your right?"

"We'll move back further, close the line to the rear," Mallet replied. "Please, my friend – you have no weapon."

"I have my hooves."

"*Please!*" Mallet pleaded.

Markris hesitated. "At least let me summon Thaniel. He will bring Lord Aram."

Mallet dropped back, keeping his pike to the fore, and glanced around. His line had doubled completely back upon itself. The company of Senecans actually faced toward the south, still fighting to keep the company from being flanked. But it was a losing battle. Flanked, they most certainly were – on all sides.

Mallet nodded. "Do it," he agreed.

Markris moved back, and Mallet eased backward as well, closing the gap.

"Is he calling for Lord Aram?" Jonwood asked breathlessly.

Mallet nodded again, without looking over as he thrust his pike into the chest of yet another gray soldier. "He is."

Jon had lost his pike and was fighting with his sword. His face was streaked with blood, most of it that of his enemies, but some of it his own.

"About time," he said.

And still the fighting went on, and on, against seemingly endless ranks of gray men and the occasional lasher. As Mallet parried the thrust of yet another giant creature and then sank his pike into the beast's side, twisting away and driving the monster to the ground, Jonwood directed a question at him.

"How many of those bastards have you taken down today?" He grunted, swinging his sword in time to relieve another of Manon's minions of his head.

"I've lost count," Mallet responded wearily. "Not enough."

"*Make way!*" A familiar voice shouted.

Mallet glanced around.

Aram and Thaniel were driving toward him along the top of the ridge, making for the far end of the hill where the enemy were strongest.

"Here, Lord Aram!" Mallet yelled and he leapt out of the way, dragging Jonwood with him.

Aram and Thaniel drove through the gap and into the enemy ranks, and the king lowered his sword and released a thunderous bolt of lightning-like fire into that grim host. Then he swung that unearthly weapon and scores of the enemy went down in a heap of blood and gore.

Jonwood looked up at Mallet and grinned. "See – I told you he wouldn't forget his friends."

42.

When the urgent call came from Markris, summoning him and Thaniel to Mallet's aid, Aram felt an odd sort of relief. Rather than having to choose a spot upon the field to inject himself into the battle, perhaps to the neglect and detriment of another place that needed him more, he was free now to get into the conflict, to strike the foe where he might do so to the salvation of his men.

As Thaniel charged eastward down the ridge behind the lines of straining, struggling men, he passed Nikolus and Jared, going the other way. Nikolus saluted him as they passed, but it was Jared who spoke.

"Varen states that we are needed to aid Donnick," the horse explained, to which Aram returned a terse reply.

"Go. I will come when I have relieved Mallet."

Ahead of him the hilltop where, according to Markris, Mallet fought against such terrible odds came into view. And it was as the horse had said.

Mallet and his band of Wallensians, joined by the company of Senecan archers, were hard-pressed. While the line still held as it ran out along the ridge toward the brow of the hillock, upon the small rounded summit itself the line of men had nearly collapsed, retreating until it held just the very brow of the hill. Mallet's band was now nearly surrounded on all sides by gray men and their lasher commanders.

Aram immediately saw where he could relieve the pressure upon this wing of his army. He held the Sword aloft, washing it in wan sunlight. "Go out to the east end of the hill," he told Thaniel. "Where Mallet and Jonwood stand together."

As Thaniel drove down upon the compact formation of men, Aram shouted at the top of his voice.

"Make way!"

Mallet jerked his head around, discerned Aram's intention, and leapt to the side, dragging Jonwood with him as a group of four lashers made to close the gap that opened up.

Thaniel charged through the gap and into the enemy.

"Turn left," Aram instructed the horse. Leaning out to the right side, Aram lowered the Sword and released the flame it had gathered.

Lightning flashed from the blade, smashing into the lashers, killing one instantly, knocking a second down and causing the others to twist away, stumbling into their own troops. As Thaniel crashed through the gray men, wounding many and killing two or three outright with the spikes of his armor, Aram leaned further and swept the blade through the body of the wounded lasher, severing the great torso. Then, as Thaniel surged onward, he kept the blade out, letting it slide through the bodies of multiple enemies, piling them in a devastated heap.

Then Thaniel was through and beyond, down the slope and among the wolves that harried the foe from the rear. Aram lifted the Sword again, letting it gather what power it could from the shrouded sun.

"Turn!" He yelled aloud, and the horse pivoted, digging his great hooves into the rocky hillside. The surviving lashers had spun to face him, and they had committed the grave error of forming up together. Thaniel charged and Aram lowered the blade once more.

This time, the fire slew them both.

The soldiers of the enemy here on the eastern slope of Mallet's hill were packed eight or ten deep, and many of them now turned and lifted their pikes, thrusting them at Thaniel.

Concerned that one of them might get in a lucky stroke and wound the horse, Aram told him, "Turn away, Thaniel – let's get clear and we'll go at them from below."

As Thaniel pivoted to go back down the hill, Aram swept the Sword through the forest of pikes that were leveled and thrust at them, ruining many. Then they were clear once again and back out among the circling wolves.

"Turn and hold a moment," Aram told Thaniel. "I want to see how things stand."

The horse pivoted again and halted, facing up the slope, breathing heavily from the exertions of the last few minutes. Aram stood tall in the stirrups, holding the Sword above his head, and examined the fighting just up the slope from where they stood. Already he could see that the intervention of his Sword and the horse had made a difference.

Thaniel's passage through the ranks of the enemy, combined with the death wrought by the Sword of Heaven, had disordered the enemy greatly. Mallet, Jonwood, and others had moved into the gap he and Thaniel had created in the line and were pushing the enemy in that area back down the slope, relieving the pressure on other parts of the line.

Still; more needed to be done to ensure the survival of Mallet and his troops.

Aram looked left, eastward, toward the depths of the small, rocky canyon. The gray men there were in the midst of a slow retreat in the face of increased pressure, having been apparently abandoned by their overlords. The enemy commanders in that quadrant, the very end of the enemy line, numbered three.

Oddly, these three lashers seemed to have lost all interest in taking the hill. Grouped in close formation, they were busily moving away, not down toward the floor of the valley, but eastward, along the jagged slope and away from the battle, using their halberds to defend against a company of four wolves that worried them as they went. The three beasts were obviously fleeing the fight.

Closer at hand, the wolves had attacked with renewed vigor, and Mallet's line of men atop the hill were now expanding their area of control. Aram looked westward, along the ridge leading toward the main bulk of the army.

A short distance away, there was a company of several lashers, five or six, sprinting toward him.

It was at that moment, as he was deciding on his next move, that it occurred to him that the Guardians had not shown themselves when he and Thaniel had smashed through the enemy host. They had not abandoned him – he could *feel* their presence. Yet they had done nothing.

Was it because of the proximity of Manon, he wondered? Or was it perhaps that the Sword had shown astonishing power, despite the timidity of the noonday sun?

The Sword, held high above his head, shrieked with power and fairly glowed with fire in the hazy sunlight. Aram glanced up at it curiously. Rather than blunting its power, the smoke-shrouded sun seemed to imbue it with greater strength than ever. Perhaps the particles of smoke and ash in the firmament enhanced in some way the effect of that great golden orb upon the blade.

Or maybe the Sword itself sensed that it was near its ultimate fated doom, just across the valley in the dark tower.

Whatever the reason, the blade seemed exalted.

When he dropped his gaze from the gleaming Sword to the battle raging atop the hill, Aram quickly took stock of how things stood. Mallet and his men were pressing forward, retaking bits of the ground they had lost. Still, though their lasher overlords were either slain or were deserting them, there were too many of the gray men in active lines of battle near the top of the hill. Mallet needed a bit more relief to turn the tide.

Aram glanced at the approaching group of lashers.

And then he knew what he would do.

"Go to the west, Thaniel," he told the horse. "Straight into those lashers."

The horse hesitated. "What of Mallet?"

In reply, Aram pivoted in the saddle, leveled the screaming blade, and released its fire into the clot of gray men gathered upon the eastern slopes of the hill. Terrible flame leapt forth and exploded with a massive burst of energy among the enemy soldiers, killing dozens outright, wounding many others, terrifying the rest.

Many broke and fled toward the valley floor.

Aram lifted the Sword once more. "Now," he said to Thaniel. "Let us go to the west and slay as many lashers as possible and bring relief to our lines – from here all the way to Berezan's Elamites."

Thaniel spun and drove away toward the west, but as he went, the great horse faltered, even stumbled, due to the ruggedness of the sloping ground.

"Careful, my friend," Aram cautioned him. "We cannot afford to have you go down."

"I will not go down, Aram," Thaniel responded gruffly.

Aram looked forward, along the lines of the enemy. Though their numbers had been diminished greatly by the Senecan missiles, there were still hundreds of the beasts scattered along the rear ranks of the enemy. At the moment though, curiously enough, most seemed content to act as commanders, driving the gray men forward into the human army.

Many others, however, in places where the free men had managed to pierce their lines, were actively involved in the fight. It mattered not, Aram intended to kill as many as possible, but because of the surprising potency of the Sword, slaying those fighting in close proximity to his own men presented a danger to his own troops. So he decided to slay those behind the lines and where feasible, weaken the enemy line in general.

When the flame from the blade was released into the gray men below Mallet's position, the group of six lashers running toward the hill hesitated and then turned and charged down across the angle of the slope straight toward Aram and Thaniel. Apparently, they thought their numbers sufficient to overwhelm the horse and rider, or perhaps they believed that Aram had exhausted the Sword's magic upon the gray men.

In either case, they were wrong.

"Turn to the right, downhill," Aram instructed Thaniel. "Go around them."

As the horse responded, angling down the slope and then turning westward again, the lashers altered course and charged down in an attempt to cut them off.

Aram lowered the blade and swept it across their formation, releasing its flame as he did so. Because he angled it downward in order to avoid some of its power from rebounding up the slope and endangering his own troops, the lightning stroke struck the lashers in the meaty parts of their thighs, severing their legs from their bodies, on the instant rendering each of them immobile. Brackish blood poured from the stumps of severed limbs as the monsters went down, screaming with pain, their lives draining away.

Aram raised the blade again and he and Thaniel went on.

As Thaniel pounded through a shallow ravine and to the top of the next ridge, Aram looked up the slope toward the battle. At that moment, they were passing below Elam, right where the brown and green of Cumberland filled the ranks. A gap had opened up in the enemy lines and Kitchell's troops were flanking the enemy toward both the east and the west.

Gratified by the sight, convinced that no aid was needed from him here, Aram looked forward for more targets of opportunity. Fifty yards away, just coming up and over the slope from the west, another group of lashers were herding a large reserve company of gray men toward the gap in front of Cumberland.

Another blast of terrible fire from the Sword of Heaven slew many of them and scattered the rest back down the slope toward the valley floor. The lashers that survived Aram's blast ran after them, though it was unclear whether they meant to corral the fleeing gray soldiers and bring them back into the conflict or were themselves in full retreat.

In any event, for the moment at least, they were removed from being a threat.

"Keep going to the west, Thaniel," Aram said.

"Should I get closer to the lines?" The horse asked him.

"No," Aram told him firmly. "I do not want the power of the Sword to endanger our own men, nor do I wish to bring you too close to the enemy. There are very many, and I do not intend to give them an opportunity to find a gap in your armor, my friend."

"I can stand a pin-prick or two, Aram," Thaniel argued with obvious irritation. "Other than killing two or three of the enemy below Mallet's hill, I have done nothing."

"You are doing what is needed," Aram told him bluntly. "This Sword is our best weapon today – it will fight for both of us."

On they went. Though the bodies of lashers littered the slope all along here, where Seneca had slaughtered them as they came up toward the battlefront, many more had survived and were engaged along the front, most as commanders behind the ranks of gray men.

Aram slew dozens more of the beasts as Thaniel charged toward the west, through ravines and up over the crests of ridges. As they went westward, toward the road at the center, the ground grew perceptibly gentler. Aram let Thaniel move upslope, closer to the actual conflict, so that he might more carefully target the flame from the blade, slaying both lashers and gray men while keeping the fire from recoiling upward and scorching his own men.

They passed Thom, and Aram was gratified to see that the tall general and his men had opened a wide gap in the enemy front and were working to exploit it. Further, there were the bodies of at least two lashers visible among the enemy fallen.

They began to pass underneath where Lamont was heavily engaged. The road was not much further ahead. Below Lamont's right flank, there was a rather deep ravine and Aram instructed Thaniel to angle to the right to minimize the effects of the slope as they climbed the higher ground opposite. For a few moments, because of the orientation of Thaniel's course, Aram was looking out across the valley almost directly at the distant tower.

He let his gaze run up the sleek lines of the structure, looking for the door or window that he knew was there, but his eye could not resolve it.

He held the Sword high as he glared at the gleaming tower.

See us, vile enemy – we are here.

I am here.

Then Thaniel turned and angled the other way as he climbed toward the crest on the far side of the ravine and gained the road. Aram turned his gaze away from Manon's tower and looked up the pavement toward the battle front. And his heart jumped.

Ice crystalized in his veins.

The road was filled with lashers. At least three separate companies of the huge beasts were deployed upon the black surface of the road. The group farthest from him and Thaniel, beyond those clustered nearer, and that was closest to the lines of battle, had formed up and was rapidly moving away, charging straight into the fray on Lamont's left flank.

43.

Timmon checked the holding chains of the cart that held the cannon for perhaps the hundredth time, first the left and then the right kicking them to see that the anchors held firm, even as he knew that any pressure from his booted foot was far too feeble to gauge their soundness. Then he looked forward once again. The gun was loaded and ready to fire, but for the moment, unneeded. Muray's men still held the road against a straining mass of gray men, who were ceaselessly hounded forward by their beastly overlords.

He kicked the right-hand chain once more and went to the back of the cart where Bonhie waited with the horses that would move the cart if it became necessary. The rest of his crew was there as well, standing bunched up together, nervously watching the action raging just yards away to their front.

For the moment, there was nothing for any of them to do.

Bonhie whinnied and Timmon held up a hand to stroke the horse on the side of the head.

"Easy, old girl," he said. "We'll be alright."

Bonhie was a mare, the only one of her gender present at the battle. Bonhie's mate had died during a particularly rough winter on the high plains four years ago. During that same difficult time, her only son, newly foaled the previous spring, had died as well. After her time of grieving passed, the mare had sought for and received permission to forgo mating with another in order to join with the young stallions that had gone to war with men.

Timmon's first mount, Duwan, had come up lame the very next year, having received a wound in the Battle of Bloody Stream that rendered the horse unable to bear a man into battle again. Bonhie had offered her services as his mount and the engineer from Aniza was instantly taken with the golden-haired mare. The two became close, the very best of friends. Timmon had joked to her more than once that, "If you were a human woman, old girl, I'd go ahead and marry you."

Florm had approved of the pairing, for Timmon was seldom involved directly in battle and usually made little use of a mount, while Bonhie exhibited a great affection for the clever man.

Now, however, he and Bonhie were both here, right at the front, tasked with holding the most precious piece of ground on the battlefield – the smooth, black-paved road that descended into the valley of Morkendril, and which, if lost, pierced the army at its very heart.

"Don't worry, old girl," Timmon repeated. "If those bastards come up the road, this cannon will make quick, short work of 'em. You just stay off to the side – okay?"

"I will not shun danger while you seek it," the horse stated.

"I am not seeking it, my friend – I am trying to prevent it," Timmon explained. And then, "We'll all be fine," he said again.

With his hand still on her head, Timmon turned to look once more down the road, just in time to see the great horned heads of dozens of lashers appear above the lines of straining men. He froze. The horned heads grew larger by the moment; the awful truth hit him like a hammer. The beasts were charging the line.

They were coming straight up the pavement.

A few yards in front of Timmon, Muray stood in the center of the road. The fierce, stout commander remained stock-still for a moment, watching the onrushing monsters, and then he turned and waved his sword wildly at Timmon.

"*Gun!*" He shouted simply.

Timmon spun and gestured to his crew, in particular singling out a young soldier named Ryan. "Prepare the fuse! *Get up there –* make ready to fire!"

Ryan leapt up and into the cart where he checked that the fuse was properly inserted into the rear chamber of the gun, and then he put flint to steel and lit a sliver of cedar kindling and waited breathlessly for Timmon's next command. Others lifted the ramrod and sacks of nixite in preparation for reloading the gun once it was fired. All stared down the road with widened eyes.

A gap appeared in the center of Lamont's lines.

Through that gap could be seen a forest of horned heads.

Timmon glanced up at Ryan. "Keep that flame away from that wick until we're ready," he roared, and then he spun to look back down the road.

Muray was splitting his troops in the face of the oncoming lashers, hurrying them to each side of the pavement.

"Move, lads!" He shouted, and waved his sword at them, as if he could speed them along by the force of his will. "Off the road – to each side. *Now!*"

As the men of Lamont fell back and retreated from the road, gray men began to pour through the gap and charge up the black pavement toward Timmon and his cart, many of them turning either way in order to flank the Lamontans. Immediately behind them, rushing through the gap created by the flanking maneuvers of the gray men, came the massed horde of lashers.

Muray turned and screamed again. "Gun!"

"*Fire!*" Timmon yelled and then he dove for the side of the road and angled for the back of the cart.

Ryan dropped the flame to the fuse.

There was a burst of sparks and then a small puff of smoke as the fire disappeared into the rounded chamber of the gun.

And then the cannon awoke with a loud roar. The cart recoiled back up the road, yanking its restraining chains taut, making them hum. Smoke and fire – and hundreds of small rounded bits of steel erupted from its barrel and ripped into the charging mass of gray men and lashers. Most of the gray men had moved aside, in an attempt to flank the men of Lamont. The main force of the blast was directed straight down the road, and the lashers bore the brunt of it.

Flesh and bone, along with leather armor, and even bits of shiny black horn, exploded into pieces as the steel shot tore through their ranks. Few of the beasts remained on their feet and those that did so were missing much of their anatomy, some of it vital.

The threat on the road melted away before the force of the blast.

But behind the first group of lashers, sheltered from the effects of the gun by those in the first group, there came another hard-charging company of beasts – and these were less than fifty yards away.

His chest pounding at the sight, Timmon came to his feet and grabbed the ramrod, yelling at his crew to, "Reload! Reload! *Hurry!*"

One man hurriedly forced a bag of nixite into the barrel and Timmon rammed it home, and then two other men of Timmon's gun crew shoved containers of shot into the opening.

As he stood back to let them get the shot into place, Timmon flung a glance down the road. The lashers were through the gap in Lamont's lines and closing fast.

Thirty yards away, maybe less.

Horror erupted in Timmon's soul.

He was going to be too late.

Shoving his men aside, he rammed the rod into the barrel, pushing the shot deep, yelling up at Ryan to – "Light the fuse – *now!*"

"*Commander?*"

"Now!"

As he desperately forced the shot down into the gun, he could hear the grunts of the enemy and the rasping of clawed feet upon the pavement of the road. The sound of their thumping feet and scraping claws was so close that the straining muscles across his back twitched in anticipation of sharp steel. His heart seemed ready to burst from his mouth and he couldn't draw breath.

Then something large and golden roared past him, going down the road, straight toward the horde of charging lashers.

Bonhie.

"No!" Timmon screamed while he desperately worked the ramrod. "Get back, Bonhie – *now!* – get back!"

The shot was almost in.

Behind him, upon the pavement, there came a sudden eruption of terrific commotion, hoarse shouts, grunts, and the angry whinny of a horse that was abruptly cut off.

"Down commander! Get out of the way!" Yelled Ryan from up on the wagon. "The fuse is lit! The gun is going to fire!"

Timmon yanked the ram from the barrel of the gun and dove for the side of the road just as flame and steel spewed forth and smashed into the lashers at point-blank range.

Bonhie, he thought.

Rolling away from the blast of the cannon, he came to his hands and knees and looked toward the road.

The mare had crashed into the company of lashers at an angle, impeding their forward progress as she made impact from right to left across the whole breadth of the road. By doing so, she had given Timmon just enough time to load and fire.

But the beasts, though hindered from reaching the gun, had taken their fury out on the horse, slashing her to pieces with their huge scythe-like weapons. And the blast from the gun had caught her in the hind quarters as she made for the far side of the pavement, horribly wounded, bleeding forth her life.

Her mangled body lay partway on and partway off the black surface of the road. She did not move.

Heartsick, Timmon rose to his feet and made to run toward her, but was immediately stopped by the sight of Muray, standing in the road, waving his sword and screaming, "*Gun!* Here they come again!"

Timmon looked down the slope of the road. About a hundred yards away, there came another massed company of the great beasts, headed straight up the road for the gun and the center of the army.

But even as he started to turn away to find the ramrod, fire engulfed the onrushing horde. Sizzling and crackling, an explosion of lightning, the golden flame mowed them down like wheat before the sickle. Timmon stopped dead in his tracks and stared. When the smoke cleared, Lord Aram and Thaniel stood in the road, a few yards beyond the burned and blasted remains of the final group of lashers. Even as he watched, the king and the great horse pivoted toward the west and went toward the left wing of the army.

Not a lasher stood upright anywhere in sight.

With the threat to the center now fully removed, Muray immediately began driving the surviving gray men back, slaying them in droves as he did so, repositioning his men across the pavement in preparation for a further defense of the roadway.

Timmon turned to his crew. "Reload the gun," he told them, and then he went to see about Bonhie.

The horse was dead. The beasts had assaulted her with their massive flat-bladed weapons when she smashed into their leading elements, very likely doing enough damage to end her life. But even if that were not so, the blast from the gun had nearly disemboweled her, and had shattered her hind quarters.

She had saved Timmon and his gun crew by her reckless deed, and very likely the center of the army – maybe the battle itself.

Kneeling down beside her, Timmon wept.

44.

As the lashers gathered out upon the level shelf, the gray men disengaged from Donnick's center and moved to the sides, acting as reserves for their comrades there. This action left Donnick's center completely unopposed.

There was nothing he could do to exploit this seeming opportunity, of course – it was obvious that the large mass of beasts to his front intended to come right here, into the gap created by the moving aside of their lesser companions.

A volley of deadly missiles from Matibar's Senecan archers descended upon the lashers, dropping dozens more of the beasts. But there were hundreds.

And on the instant of that aerial attack, they charged.

"Hold, boys – *hold*." Donnick repeated over and over. "Lift the tips of your pikes – anchor the butts of your shafts in the ground. *Make a wall of steel.* Even those beasts can't get through if we hold." He looked back over his shoulder toward the rear. His son and his troop of mounted archers, lances to the fore, were almost to them. Further to the east, Nikolus and his cavalry had also seen the danger gathering to Donnick's front. They were coming as well.

And Matibar was raining the last of his aerial weaponry down upon the ranks of the charging lashers.

Donnick looked along the line. "Raise those pikes – keep them steady. Close all gaps. Courage, men – *hold*." He raised his voice so that it carried along the front, but he kept his tone calm. "Help is coming."

As the grim lord's great horned beasts rushed toward them, Donnick found himself repeating that one word in urgent repetition.

"*Hold.*"

Then Wamlak arrived with his mounted bowmen. Quickly lining his troopers up behind Donnick's line, he gave a shouted command. "Take good aim," he told his archers. "Make every arrow count."

As the lashers came on, Wamlak and his men fired volley after volley. Though not as deadly as the missiles of the men from the east, they nonetheless took their toll. Some of the beasts went down, and many more slowed and fell behind as they tried to relieve themselves of offending darts buried in their flesh.

And yet there were still many – too many.

And they were closing fast.

"Hold!" Donnick exhorted his men yet again.

His arrows exhausted, Wamlak gave another command. "Ready lances! Form a line behind the ranks! Prepare to receive the enemy!"

The charging line of lashers smashed into the line of Elamites and Duridians, swinging their vicious halberds. Men went down, screaming in mortal pain. Gaps appeared instantly. Where the men stood fast, with the butts of their pikes in the earth, the line held, but even here the casualties of that first contact were many and hideous. And it was mostly to Donnick's right, among the men of Duridia, that the line maintained a semblance of order.

To his left, where the inexperienced men of Elam lined up, and where the ground was flatter and more advantageous to the charge of the beasts, gaps appeared upon the instant that the lashers made contact. In places, the monsters went completely through the line and into the rear.

Eventually, under horrible pressure, the line to the right of Donnick gave way as well.

Then, except for one small pocket where Donnick stood, the front simply melted away. Scores were killed, many more terribly maimed, and many that tried to flee were slain in mid-stride.

Ruben and his mounted troops arrived just as the initial impact with its horrific attendant carnage occurred. The cavalryman immediately grasped the fact that the fate of the entire battle would very likely be decided right here.

"Straight into them, Varen!" He shouted aloud, then, "Lances to the fore! *Charge!*"

Without hesitation, he and his troopers rode straight into the lashers that had passed through the lines and were reforming in an attempt to turn the line, east and west. As the horses drove down upon them, the troopers hurled their lances and then drew swords. Lashers went down but so did horses and their riders. Many horses and many riders.

Having fully engaged the line, the monsters employed their huge scythe-like blades with hideous fury, swinging them back and forth, killing and maiming with each stroke. Men fought back valiantly, but on their part the struggle rapidly became purely defensive in nature, using their long-handled pikes to keep the enemy at bay. But the lashers, with their greater strength and reach, wrought havoc.

The fighting became so savage that in places it seemed as if it were raining blood.

Confusion spread and panic grew. As men fell in greater numbers, the fighting moved east and west along the battlefront. To Donnick's right among the ranks of Duridia and west among Elam, more gaps appeared in the allied lines. Small groups of men found themselves cut off and assailed on all sides by vicious beasts. Finding their situation utterly untenable, many men dropped their pikes and abandoned the front, running for their lives.

In the middle, where the line had held up to the initial onslaught, Donnick, Kevan, and Durayne, and a small cohort of about twenty men found themselves cut off from the main line and utterly surrounded.

All around was a veritable sea of lashers.

"Form a circle! Thrust and parry!" Donnick shouted to his companions. "Thrust and parry! These bastards can be killed and wounded. Hold!"

Wamlak's mount, Braska, had been slain in the very first moments by a scything thrust from a lasher's halberd, and he was on foot, joined by a company of his troopers, whose horses had also been slain. His lance gone, sunk deep into the chest of the beast that had killed his mount, Wamlak was fighting with his sword when he saw his father and the small company, alone and surrounded.

Gathering up the dismounted troopers near him, he pointed with his sword. "There! With me! Relieve the general!"

But there was a nearly solid line of beasts between him and his father, and many turned to face this new threat.

Wamlak parried a thrust from a giant lasher and then slid between the beast's massive legs, stabbing upward with his sword into the soft flesh of its underside and was rewarded by a howl of anguish. He regained his feet in time to see Donnick and Kevan go down as a massive lasher swung his halberd with his might, shattering their pikes and slashing through their armor.

"*No!*" Wamlak let out a yell of horror and fury and went for the gigantic lasher that had slain his father.

And in his blind fury and lust for vengeance, he did not see the second beast that slipped in behind him and leveled a killing stroke.

45.

After he released an immense amount of stored energy from the Sword into the last company of lashers that were attempting to pierce the center of the army at the road, Aram watched just long enough to see that they were indeed destroyed. Then he peered further up the road until he could ascertain that the gun and Muray's Lamontans were safe. Satisfied that the center was secure, he and Thaniel turned and went again toward the west.

For over there, upon the level shelf of ground in front of Donnick where Duridia and Elam came together, there was a roiling maelstrom of furious struggle. Hundreds of lashers, perhaps every surviving member of the species from this side of the army, had formed up on that gentler piece of earth and driven straight into the ranks of men. To either side of that maelstrom, there were hundreds of gray men that had peeled away and were assaulting Elam and Duridia in force upon their flanks.

For the moment, however, both Boman and Kavnaugh had turned their wings to face the threat and seemed to be holding, or at least were engaged in ordered, gradual retreat.

But between them, upon that level shelf of earth, the enemy had pierced the army to its core. Even from this distance, Aram could see that lashers ran amuck behind the main body of the army.

As Thaniel topped one crest after another, urged on by Aram, the two of them could see that the situation grew more desperate by the moment.

"Hurry, Thaniel!" Aram urged, even as he knew that the great horse was giving everything he could.

Then, finally, the horse scrambled up a ragged slope and out onto the rocky shelf. He spun toward the south, toward the main ridge and the battle.

The seriousness of the situation was obvious. For perhaps a hundred yards below the brow of the crater rim, the line had dissolved. Clusters of men fought separate battles, each of them harassed by clots of lashers. Companies of horsemen darted here and there, trying to retard the lashers' advance. Horses reared as men threw lances or lashed with swords, but for every beast that stumbled or fell, it seemed that more than one horse and rider went down.

In the center of the left wing of his army, disaster ruled the moment. Aram felt sick.

In the middle of the rocky shelf, directly ahead, a large mob of lashers completed the slaughter of a group of men that had stood alone and reformed to push further up toward the crater rim and the small groups of horsemen that still fought there. As Thaniel neared this horde, Aram scattered them with a blast of fire from the Sword, killing several, wounding more.

There was no time to collect more power from the sun. In three strides, Thaniel would be among the enemy, dozens of them, perhaps hundreds, driving the lines of men each way, toward the east and west.

Aram made his decision. "Get in among them and spin, Thaniel," he commanded the horse. "Turn to the left, rotate, but keep your footing."

They entered the area where the line had stood in the first minutes of the battle. Bodies lay everywhere, of men, gray men, and even horses and some lashers. Aram was about to warn the horse to beware of their own, in case some were wounded only and not dead, but then abruptly realized that such admonishment was utterly unnecessary. In order to keep his footing, Thaniel had to avoid the carnage anyway.

As Thaniel weaved this way and that, making for the center of the horde of beasts that were driving an enormous hole in the army, they passed the spot where the lashers had completed the slaughter of the lone group but moments before. Looking down, Aram was stricken to recognize the bodies of both Donnick and Wamlak among them.

Fury erupted within him, driving away the sickness of heart. He spoke aloud, his voice cold with terrible anger.

"Straight into them. *Let us kill them all.*"

Thaniel crashed into the horde of lashers in about the middle of their long, deep formation and then, using his hooves as a fulcrum, spun in a tight circle to his left. Aram leaned out, twisting his boot in the stirrup for support, and held the Sword out at the level with both hands. As Thaniel turned, Aram let the power of the sun flow through the blade as it filtered down from the firmament above.

There was not enough fire that gathered in it at any one moment to cause flame to leap out in the form of lightning, but it was enough to direct a tongue of searing flame from the end of the blade. Lashers flinched and cringed as the tongue of flame licked out and burned their flesh. In moments, as quickly as Thaniel completed his first full turn, Aram had cleared a space in the heart of the lasher mob.

"Wider, Thaniel," he said. "Swing wider."

By this time, those in command of the lasher horde became aware of the new enemy that had come among them. But he and his horse were alone, and they were still very many. As the monstrous beasts saw their advantage, they also saw opportunity.

This man, after all, was the great prize, worth more to their master than all the rest of the army that had gathered before his gates. With second children flanking the army of humans east and west, they could focus their strength once and for all time upon ridding the earth of this troublesome man.

As one, they turned their attention inward, to the center of their amassed company, upon the man and horse. Six and seven deep, they advanced in a rush, closing upon their quarry.

Even with the aid of the searing fire that flowed through the blade, Aram recognized that there were too many of the massive beasts, and most of them appeared to be harbigurs. Thaniel was further disadvantaged by the mounds of bodies that lay all about, making sure footing impossible. As Thaniel turned in a tight circle inside the mob of beasts and Aram slew and maimed many of their number with the Sword, the lasher horde tightened its circle of death around them.

The Guardians saw the danger as well.

Suddenly, blazing white fire joined with the golden flame of the Sword of Heaven.

Lashers went down in heaps, dying amidst bursts of argent lightning.

But there were still very many.

Out on the edge of this terrible yet astonishing scene, Nikolus and Jared had joined Ruben and Varen, and much of their troop were still alive and able to fight. As the lashers turned away from the men and horses, thinking them vanquished, and crowded in eagerly toward the prize, the horses and their riders took advantage of the beasts' inattention.

Earlier in the battle, when Nikolus and Jared and their company had arrived upon the scene, Ruben and Varen and their half of the cavalry were already heavily engaged. When Donnick's line broke before the lasher onslaught, Ruben and Varen had led their troop into the breach, trying to stem the rising tide of disaster. But because of the fractured nature of the collapse of the line, the horsemen had found it impossible to maintain order as they drove in with their lances.

The lashers, impelled forward by the success and impetus of their charge, had succeeded in isolating the cavalry into small companies; in some places they had encircled even smaller groups. Men and horses were fighting for their lives – and losing. Though, here and there, they succeeded in wounding and even killing a beast, more men and horses went down than lashers. The situation rapidly became grave.

Nikolus took all of this in as he and his troop came up.

Quickly dividing his four hundred horses and riders into four long lines under their captains, he sent them through the melee from east to west. He recognized instantly that it was utterly impossible to save Donnick's formation – it had vanished, killed and scattered. Not a single infantryman stood erect across a hundred yards of front.

There was only to save what they could of the cavalry.

"Gather up our people as you go through!" Nikolus shouted. "Tell them to follow us out – we will reform on the other side and come at them from there!"

Jared sent the same instruction into the minds of the horses. Men and horses were lost as they drove through the maelstrom of battle, but enough disorder was created in the lasher formations by the horses' passage that most of Ruben's men and horses that had survived were able to disentangle themselves and escape the carnage.

As they charged through the breach, using their lances to good effect, though causing few deaths among the great beasts, they found Findaen, Andaran, and a small cohort of horsemen, fighting for their lives against a company of encircling lashers that slashed and swung with their deadly halberds. Findaen's group grew smaller with each deadly moment that passed.

"Swing away, Findaen!" Nikolus shouted, as he and Jared drove past. Jared smashed into two lashers that had focused upon Findaen and Andaran, catching them off-guard. One beast went down, roaring with rage and pain. "Hold on!" Jared told Nikolus and the big brown horse reared and drove his front hooves hard into the face of the second. He was rewarded by the sight of flesh and bone giving way before the force of his hooves. The lasher's features crumpled inward and he went down, never to rise again.

Grasping the opportunity, Andaran leapt away and followed Jared out, along with the rest of the group around him and Findaen.

On the other side of where the lashers had punched through the army, Kavnaugh Berezan had turned his right flank to face the gray men that had massed there, and was desperately trying to rally the men that had survived the breach.

Marcus was there as well, mounted on Phagan, exhorting the men of Elam to, "Stand firm!" When he saw the cavalry sweeping toward him and discerned their intent, the High Prince glanced around and spied an abandoned pike that was still sound.

"Quick!" He yelled to Kavnaugh. "Hand me that weapon, general!"

Kavnaugh retrieved the pike and looked up into Marcus' face. What he saw there gave him pause.

"Your Highness – are you certain –?"

"I will not be left out of this fight, general," Marcus told him, and his tone brooked no refusal.

Berezan yet resisted, holding the pike. "We cannot have you die, Your Highness," he insisted.

Marcus' eyes narrowed into thin bands of steely blue as he reached for the weapon. "This is an hour when one man's life does not matter," he told the general. "Naught but victory counts today. *Give me the pike.*"

The general hesitated but a moment longer. "Take care, my friend, *please*," he replied then, and obediently handed the weapon into Marcus' hand.

Marcus spoke to Phagan. "We are going in with Nikolus and Jared," he told the horse. "Find an opening and join the column."

"As you will," Phagan replied, and finding a gap in the column of horses, swung into the line.

Nikolus and Jared pounded past, swung up the slope and turned back toward the east. "Tell the others of your people, Jared," Nikolus said, "that we are going to attack in one long line – staying clear of the main body of lashers – we will harass them along the edges, kill as we can, but no direct engagement. Tell the horses to explain this to their riders; for there is no time to halt and form up. We must attack now if we are to have any chance to contain this breach."

After a moment, as Jared wheeled and charged back down the slope toward the expanding breach and Nikolus readied his lance to strike, the horse replied, "They understand."

"Alright. Stay clear of those beasts' weapons," Nikolus said. "No more heroics. I don't want you injured – but get me close enough to do what damage I can."

"These foul creatures will not hinder me," the horse replied.

The cavalry made several of these passes. With nearly seven hundred horses still at his disposal, Nikolus was able to configure the nature of the attack so that when the last rider made his pass, he and Jared, as the first in line, came at the enemy again.

The men and horses managed to injure many of the beasts, some seriously, and even slew several. Even so, the cavalry's losses quickly became unsustainable. The great horned monsters swung their deadly, scythe-like halberds with hideous precision. These were Manon's crack troops; they were now deployed in a deadly crescent with no more enemies behind them, and they were taking no prisoners. As gaps appeared in Nikolus' long line, and the lashers continued their methodical advance toward the crest of the ridge, order began to dissolve.

Despair once again made its presence known across the length of that bloody hundred yards.

Then Lord Aram arrived upon the rocky shelf.

282

He and Thaniel charged straight into the midst of the lasher horde and abruptly the nature of the struggle changed.

As knowledge spread among the beasts that the man their master despised, the man that they had all sought for so long, had suddenly inserted himself into their midst, all interest in widening the breach or continuing the fight with the mounted riders left them.

Almost as one, they turned with eager maliciousness toward the man on the great black horse.

Nikolus was quick to recognize opportunity.

"Reform the line!"

From his vantage on Jared's back, it looked to Nikolus almost like a reprise of the Battle of Bloody Stream, with the king isolated and surrounded. But there was a difference this time. Lord Aram was still mounted upon his mighty steed. Thaniel was turning in tight rotation inside the massed lashers, and with each of the horse's turns, more bodies of Manon's beasts mounded up, laid low by Aram's magical sword and by the power of those strange and unseen companions that went with him everywhere.

Perhaps the greatest difference was that, as the monsters bent their focus away from the mounted riders and toward the one man at the center of their troop, the cavalry, all of whom by now were seasoned warriors, and every one of whom was eager for revenge upon the loathsome beasts, already knew the tactic that was called for at this time and in this place.

And they put that tactic into immediate employment.

With swords, lances, or abandoned pikes, Jared and Nikolus, Ruben and Varen, Marcus and Phagan, and the rest of the cavalry once again deployed into a long line and drove back and forth at the rear of the mob of lashers, slashing and stabbing. With renewed vigor and confidence, they assaulted the lashers without pause, causing so much disarray that many of the beasts were forced to reluctantly turn their attention away from Aram and Thaniel at the center of the swirling fight and fend off this new assault from those they had thought finished.

Seeing the change in circumstances that occurred with Lord Aram's arrival, men from Duridia that had fled the terrible lasher assault took heart. Having taken refuge behind the lines of men that still contested with the flanking attacks of gray men, these soldiers had not fled the field, but nonetheless had remained out of the fight.

As Boman moved back and forth along the line of his troops where it angled to face the flanking gray men, he spoke kindly to these frightened men, encouraging them to stand up and lend aid to their comrades that still fought on.

And slowly, under that benevolent persuasion, courage was reborn. One by one, and then in small groups, picking up weapons that others had discarded or dead men had dropped, they formed up and re-joined the fight. Gradually, the Duridians began to push the gray men back.

To the west, finding his own front holding well against gray men only, as their lasher overlords had all gone east toward the fight in front of Donnick, Kavnaugh Berezan also rallied the remains of the regiment that had fled from the enemy's flanking attack at the right end of his line.

Using these traumatized troops as reserves to buttress those that he had turned to face the assault of the gray men the lashers had relieved from in front of Donnick, Kavnaugh created a line that not only held but began to move the gray men back. On the extreme right end of his angled line, the cavalry aided his cause by chipping away at the numbers of gray soldiers with every pass they made as they swung around to go again at the lashers.

The gray men in front of Berezan's Elamites began to break.

Then, as they were pushed back against the melee of lashers surrounding Aram, they broke completely, abandoning the flanking attack and retreating around the mass of lasher overlords to safety. These gray soldiers did not rejoin the main line but went out upon the level area of the rocky shelf where they milled about in uncertainty.

Seizing the opportunity presented by the sudden easing of pressure upon his flank, Kavnaugh left one company angled toward the lasher horde in case the monsters decided to take up where their lesser companions had failed, and looked to his front.

The gray line of the enemy was beginning to falter there as well. It was time to push.

Despite the limited number of reserves at his disposal – most of them battered survivors of the disaster in front of Donnick – Kavnaugh nonetheless chose a place in his line where the strength of the enemy had grown thin and put them in.

"Vengeance, boys!" He told them. "It is time for vengeance for our fallen friends! Now – *drive them!*"

Their courage renewed, these men pushed into the line and broke through, opening up an ever-widening gap.

Minutes later, in front of Kavnaugh Berezan's green troops, the enemy line began to give way.

Over on the east of the breach, throughout the day, Boman had managed his Duridians with his usual pragmatic calmness, and by judicious use of his reserves. As a result of his battlefield acumen and the stout courage of the men of the southern plains, his lines had held throughout the battle. Now, with the tide of conflict turning in his favor, Boman had one last weapon in his arsenal.

When the gray men had first rushed upon his lines and come within range of his crossbows, Boman had instructed his men to fire in conjunction with the release of the spikes. But there had been no time to reload for another volley. There was only to pick up the pikes and receive the enemy. Now, however, with the enemy able to exert but minimal pressure upon him, the time had come to put his remaining missiles to use.

"Third rank!" He shouted. "Drop pikes – load bows!"

Then, when his commanders along the line returned with, "Ready!" –

Boman shouted the command. "Front ranks down! Fire!"

This tricky and dangerous tactic was repeated in the face of the foe, with the ranks rotating back and forth, until each Duridian had exhausted his supply of arrows. Duridia took some casualties but the enemy was reduced even further.

Then the Duridians re-formed their ranks, pikes at the ready, and advanced. The ranks of the gray men to the front began to break in places and stream away down the slope toward the valley floor, even as the flanking attempt of the enemy upon Boman's extreme left continued.

Rather than give chase, Boman thinned his line, extending it westward toward Elam and turning the regiment at the end of his line to face the gray men there and guard against the possibility of a flanking threat from the lashers. Then he gathered up those remaining men from the fractured units that had been with Donnick, rallied them and put them back in as reserves. Before him, too, everywhere, the line of gray men faltered and appeared ready to break completely, even upon his flank.

46.

It was at this moment that the battle turned in favor of the allies. As Aram and Thaniel with the Sword of Heaven, aided by the white fire from the glittering swords of the Astra, fought on, everywhere else along the front of the army Manon's minions were at last beginning to break.

At the extreme eastern end of the battle, Mallet had regained his hill and then some. Gray men that broke and attempted to run back to the valley floor were caught and slaughtered by wolves. The hooked aspect of Mallet's line had gone, to be replaced by a solid front of sharp pikes and Senecan swords.

Olyeg Kraine's troops, after the passage of Lord Aram and his great black horse had slain or wounded most of the lasher commanders; found their footing and began to push the ranks of the enemy back. Both sides still sustained casualties, but most of those now were of the enemy.

Kraine consequently discovered that, in places where the gray men were disadvantaged by terrain and gave way, he could now draw reserves straight from the third ranks of frontline troops in those areas and move them as they were needed elsewhere.

After the sad discovery of Kitchell in the gap that the worthy gentleman had created by his death, Kraine had his body moved back up the slope and away from the conflict. Now, with things to his front in hand for the moment, he decided to go there and accomplish two things – first to pay his respects to his childhood friend, and then to survey the battlefield from the vantage of higher ground.

As he knelt over the body of his friend, Kraine gained the attention of a surgeon working on the wounded nearby. "Did we find the Governor-general's arm?" He asked.

The surgeon, his hands and face caked and streaked with the blood of his patients, looked up with a frown of confusion. "Sir?"

Kraine indicated the stump below Kitchell's left shoulder. The pain and sorrow of looking down upon the remains of his friend injected a measure of frustration into his tone. "His arm – *did we find it?*"

The surgeon raised up to look at the spot indicated and then let out a breath of fatigue and shook his head. "No, sir. We've been very busy for the last hour or so. I will go and look when there is an opportunity."

Immediately, Kraine felt a pang of remorse. "No, lad, sorry for that. I will go and look when all this is done. You just keep at what you're doing."

With that, he stood and looked down over the ongoing battle. In front of his lines, the ranks of gray men were showing strain and signs of impending fracture.

From his part of the field anyway, the battle was starting to look like imminent victory.

To Kraine's left, Thom Sota and his mixed regiment of Elam and Lamont had flanked the enemy and were driving them east and west. As the enemy soldiers encountered the occasional rough ravines in the slope, groups of them would peel away and retreat downhill. With few, if any, lasher commanders to hinder them, more and more of them began to think about remaining alive rather than any further attempt at executing their master's wishes.

As more and more of the enemy ranks broke away, Thom would leave one solitary yet solid line of men in place and rotate all the others either left or right in order to widen the breach and increase the pressure upon his weakening foe. The necessity of command, however, robbed him of the opportunity to engage in any further personal action.

Despite that frustration, Thom Sota was busily justifying Lord Aram's faith in him as a man of war.

To his left, along Edwar's front, things were also improving, moment by moment. Most of the lashers to Edwar's front had long since moved west, toward the road. And over there, for a while, to the front of Timmon's cannon where Muray commanded, things had been in serious doubt. But now the road was secure once more and Muray was once again standing in the front ranks of his troops, guiding the destruction of the enemy that yet remained in front of him.

From his vantage point behind the lines, Edwar had watched with mounting agitation as Muray had been assaulted by masses of the horned monsters. But Timmon's cannon and Lord Aram's fiery sword had caught those beasts in a deadly vise, and now, over there in the center of the army, things were moving in favor of the allies.

In that center, standing upon the road with his front ranks, Muray instinctively knew that the enemy would break if pressed. Already heavily disadvantaged, demoralized by having to fight among the mounds of body parts which were all that remained of their overlords, the gray men faltered. Despite their earlier displays of toughness and resolve, Manon's minions were now also taking casualties that they could not replace.

"Lean into it, boys!" Muray shouted hoarsely as he drew back and thrust his pike to the fore, once again reducing the number of the enemy by one. Ripping his pike free, he advanced, drawing his men with him by the sheer force of his will. "*Drive them* – and the day is ours!"

Scrambling over the prone body of his latest kill, Muray found the torso of a lasher and climbed atop it for a moment, standing in full view of both the enemy and his men.

"Now, boys!" He yelled, and leaping to the front, he sank the business end of his pike deep into yet another foe.

His men went with him.

The enemy broke.

They did not run, but nonetheless began to fall back in full retreat. For a time, because Muray and his men were also obliged to climb over and around mounded lasher bodies in order to give chase, the retreat was a fairly orderly thing. As the enemy retreated further down the road, however, and encountered yet more piles of lasher remains that hindered orderly progress, their lines became fragmented.

Muray now had the luxury of being able to stop and reform his own lines at need, while determinedly pushing the enemy into defeat. Presently, however, his forward movement created a bulge in his lines that was unsustainable, for there were yet thousands of enemy troops stretched away toward the east and the west.

Though to the west, in front of Boman and Duridia, the enemy was in partial retreat, to his right, before Lamont, many were still fully engaged.

"Hold!" He commanded. "Hold the line!"

After a few minutes of stalemate, when the enemy, who had halted perhaps thirty yards from his front rank, showed no interest in continuing the struggle, Muray once again told his officers to hold and he went in search of his father, somewhere over to the right.

Because of Muray's newfound success upon the road after the failure of the lasher charge, the enemy was growing soft all along Lamont's front. He didn't go more than fifty yards before he spied a familiar stout bulk buttressing a now well-formed line. At the moment, no enemy was within striking distance of the old farmer.

And, much to Muray's relief, his ken appeared unharmed.

Eoarl looked around in response to his son's hail.

He grinned. "Hello, my boy – it's good to see you well and standing upright!"

Muray grinned back. "I say the same to you, ken." Then he nodded toward the ranks of the enemy. "They're not pushing us so hard now, are they?"

Eoarl glanced that way, too, and shook his head. "No, they've gone soft in the last few minutes. They don't seem to want to leave, but they don't seem so anxious to test us again, either."

Muray moved up and placed a hand on his father's shoulder. He did not speak but just looked toward the front.

Eoarl shot his son a curious glance. "What now? If they retreat – what do we do? Do we give chase?"

Muray nodded. "I imagine so, although Lord Aram will have the last word on that."

"Where is he?"

But Muray was not obliged to make a reply. Both men looked toward the west where Lord Aram had gone after incinerating the last of the lashers on the road.

Way over there, beyond Boman and Duridia, flashes of white fire, like lightning, told of the king's position and of the battle still raging on that part of the field.

West of Muray's position, Boman was also driving the gray men back. The lines of enemy to his front were even more ragged and thin now than they had been when he had unleashed his earlier

290

volleys from crossbows. Having secured his front, where his men had faced and fought only gray men since the lashers had gone left to the shelf in front of Donnick, Boman had spent the last few minutes reforming the extreme left of his line to face the enemy soldiers that turned it when the lashers struck.

Now, those men that had fled in the face of that attack had discovered new reservoirs of courage under the encouraging eyes and words of their calm commander and were helping to push the gray men back toward the roiling melee around Lord Aram. Boman was anxious to turn the enemy and force them back downhill so that he might find a way to come to the aid of the king.

There were now no arrows left in any of their quivers, but the men of Duridia were perfectly willing to face gray men and even lashers with pikes and swords.

Boman was in the angle of his line where it curved back toward the left away from the tangent of his main line when shouts and the sound of low thunder alerted him to action on his left. Pivoting he saw dust and the bobbing heads of horsemen coming toward his lines. He ran in that direction.

"Make way!" He shouted. "Let the horses pass!"

As his line curved yet again, folding in upon itself, Nikolus, Jared and a company of riders pounded through, covered with sweat and dust – and blood; theirs and that of their enemies. Oddly, even in the din of battle, Boman heard the leather of the saddles creak, the plates of the horses' armor scrape together, and the shards of gravel chime and skitter over the rocky slope as they were dislodged by the violent passage of the horses' hooves.

As the cavalry passed along the southern flank of the enemy that faced Boman's men, they used their lances to deadly effect on those gray soldiers unfortunate enough to stand in their way. Then the horsemen wheeled up the hill in a long line and went back the other way, toward the struggle surrounding Aram.

And as they went, they left Boman with fewer enemies to face upon his flank, and an opportunity to extend his line into the breach that had occurred to his left. Physically grabbing those men that had moved out of the horses' path, he began herding them back around the now-exposed end of the gray men's formation.

"Drive them!" He shouted. "Push them down the slope!"

Then, drawing his own sword, he joined his men in executing the order he had just given.

The enemy broke under the increased pressure. They did not fold their line back into the breach, or pivot away in an orderly manner, but instead they retreated en masse. Sending fearful glances toward the swirling mass of their overlords, and the white fire that flared and blazed in the center of that violent storm, they filed away from the clot of lashers surrounding Aram and moved back and to the right, into a reserve position behind their own thin and faltering lines.

Boman watched the retreating enemy long enough to determine that this behavior was not a ruse, but that they were, in fact, quitting the fight. Then he lengthened his line toward the lashers that assaulted Lord Aram. The cavalry made another pass just then; more lashers were caught off guard and eliminated from the fight, falling among the bodies already strewn about, or stumbling away toward the rear.

The Duridian Governor realized that the ground to his left, stretching into the breach, had become an uneven, unmanageable jumble, with the bodies of countless men, horses and lashers scattered and piled everywhere. This area was so filled with the terrible detritus of struggle as to render the maintenance of martial formation impossible. Climbing a bit of high ground, he looked back toward the east, along his lines. The pressure from Manon's gray-faced soldiers was perceptibly lessening, everywhere along the front.

The crossbows of his men were devoid of arrows; his weaponry was reduced to pikes and swords, both of which required sound order to be effective. Realizing, then, that he could do little to aid Aram without hindering that which the horses were already accomplishing, he instead assigned details of men to remove the dead, both of the enemy and of allies, from the horses' path. At least he might be able to aid the horsemen in their deadly business.

A hundred yards away to the west, beyond the breach, Kavnaugh Berezan, though less experienced than the Governor, had reached the same conclusion. In places along his front, especially at the west end of his lines, where the gray men had been badly disadvantaged by terrain, the fighting had ceased entirely.

His captains had put their rearward ranks to work removing the dead and the wounded up and over the ridge, while the front ranks stood guard, watching the enemy that were, a little at time, easing away from the battle. With less and less happening to his front to concern him, Berezan had also turned his attention to aiding the horses in any way he could.

In the middle of the straining mass of lashers, Aram was making little headway against the mob of giant assailants. Because of the flame that leapt and burned from the tip of his blade, the beasts shrank away from every pass as Thaniel wheeled in a circle, abandoning frontal assault in favor of an attempt to get at him from the rear. Occasionally, the horse would catch one of the beasts off-guard and lunge close, giving Aram an opportunity to add another body to the growing heap.

Still, Aram felt stymied, stalemated at his lack of kills.

But it wasn't a stalemate.

Because Aram leaned to one side of the horse as Thaniel turned in a tight circle, the Astra, while avoiding the Sword, were nonetheless able to rotate with Thaniel, staying to the other side, away from Aram and the dangerous blade, and work their will. With each turning, they slew dozens.

The clot of lashers grew ever more compact, and ever less numerous – though never less determined, it seemed, to try and get at the man on the horse.

And out upon the southern edge of the fight, Nikolus, Jared, and the others were busily reducing their numbers there as well.

Aram couldn't see it from his position in the midst of the conflict, but the outcome was less in doubt with every moment that passed. The army of the allies, even though it couldn't be discerned here in the middle of this violent throng, was winning.

And then, abruptly, it was over.

Suddenly, from the great gleaming black tower rising from the center of Morkendril, two short, booming, low notes sounded, reverberating across the valley floor and echoing among the distant mountains.

47.

All across the battle front, the enemy broke off and began to retreat down the slope.

Here and there, groups of men, their blood still hot, and their battle fury undiminished, gave chase. In places the gray men turned and resisted these small cadres of soldiers, but more often than not Manon's minions simply picked up the pace, until they were fairly running down the slope toward the valley floor.

Around Aram, the conflict abruptly ceased. Thaniel spun one last time to find every enemy falling back and moving away. The lashers did not run, but their rearward pace was not slow either, as they retreated back out the shelf of level ground and began to tumble out of sight onto the steeper earth beyond.

Thaniel stopped turning, breathing heavily, and he and Aram watched them go.

"Do you want to pursue them?" The horse asked.

Aram drew in a deep, shuddering breath and shook his head. "No," he said, and then he looked east and west along the lines. "Let's see to our people, first."

He looked back toward the tower, gazing at it with narrowed eyes for a long moment, and then lowered his gaze to watch the enemy's army recede down the slope. Over to the right, in front of Duridia and Lamont, and further east, where Thom was in command of Elam's left flank, soldiers gave energetic chase to the fleeing enemy. Aram watched this violent chase with only slight concern for a moment, and then, suddenly, another sense became involved.

The hair on the back of his neck stiffened.

He jerked his head around and stared at the tower. His own words sounded in his inner ear.

Manon no doubt has many tricks he will employ.

He looked around desperately for a trumpeter. There were none in sight, but Boman was but forty or fifty yards away.

"Sound *fall back!*" Aram shouted in the Governor's direction. "Quickly – the men must fall back! *Now!*"

Boman stared back for a moment and then spun on his heel, shouting the command further along the line. An instant later, the clear call of a bugle rose into the air. Boman went running, shouting the command to be disseminated further along the front.

Aram looked to his left. In front of Kavnaugh, there was one small cohort of men, no doubt seeking an extra measure of vengeance for the day's blood, giving chase to Manon's troops.

"Tell the general to have those men fall back!" Aram yelled, and then, once he was certain his command was comprehended and would be directed on, he spoke to Thaniel and they rode madly toward the east to spread the word.

In that moment, he could not have said what it was that made his gut coil into loops of anxiety.

But there was *something*. Of that fact, he was certain. The god that resided in the great black tower a few miles across the valley floor would not simply take defeat and admit it. He intended malice of some kind, of that Aram was sure, and if his men were too close when that malice was made manifest, they were doomed.

Thaniel tore toward the east with Aram calling every few minutes.

"Fall back! Sound *fall back!*"

As the bugles sounded along the line and word was spread, most of those giving chase to the fleeing enemy reluctantly gave up the pursuit and returned to their units below the brow of the crater rim. Some few, however, did not.

As the line re-formed in its original position, Aram realized that he was not satisfied. "Fall back further!" He commanded. "Fall back to the top of the ridge!"

And once more the bugles sounded.

Mystified by their supreme commander's strange behavior and attitude, the men nonetheless complied. Within a few minutes, the army was once again on line, standing atop the very rim of the crater. Down the slope, a few groups of men still gave chase. The gray men, and even the lashers, seemed not to notice or care that they were pursued.

On they went, down across the rocky, ragged slope.

Because they were moving downward, and in a hurry, most of Manon's army was on the level floor of the valley in less than half an hour. Once there, they slowed, affected a semblance of order, and began to march toward Morkendril. Watching them, Aram was astonished at how their number had been reduced, how many they had killed, and yet *how many remained.*

There were still tens of thousands of Manon's soldiers that remained capable of continuing the struggle.

A terrible thought made its way into Aram's mind and found uneasy lodging there.

Would they be required to do all this again tomorrow?

No sooner had this thought made him shiver than there came a deep, distant, yet horribly thunderous and deafening *thump!* from the direction of Morkendril.

The whole valley shook, the very bedrock of the ridge trembled, and the tower itself seemed to shimmer like water for one small moment.

Then, spreading out from the base of the tower like a storm wave upon the sea, *something* that could be sensed but not really *seen*, rushed outward with incomprehensible speed. Dust billowed up in its wake.

It caught Manon's thousands and scythed through them like grass before a prairie fire.

Then the something – evil spirit, wave of power, perhaps the shock from a terrible detonation – whatever it was, it struck the slope and began to climb toward the army with awful speed.

"Retreat!" Aram shouted. "*Sound retreat!*"

But there was no time.

The terrible force that could be seen only by the burst of dust it raised as it passed along the ground overtook those men that had pursued the enemy toward the valley floor, knocking them flat. Most did not move again. Those that did move, did not rise, but flailed feebly at the earth around them, obviously dying.

As one man, the army turned and tried to flee over the top of the ridge. Thaniel turned his back to the onrushing, unknown power, but he and Aram stayed, with Aram standing high in the stirrups, desperately waving the men to the rear.

The invisible wave caught them.

It was like being struck by an unseen hammer.

Thaniel went down upon his haunches. An instant later, his front legs buckled beneath him. Aram was knocked forward, prone upon the horse's neck armor and nearly unseated. Men went down all across the front, knocked forward onto their faces, helpless against the force of the shock wave. The cannon was shoved backward, up the road; its anchor chains rattled as they went taut.

The breath was driven from Aram's body. For a very long moment, as he tried to sit upright in the saddle, he found that his thoughts were muddled, unclear. His lungs burned and his mouth gaped as he tried to replenish his body with air. Finally, after several terrible and painful moments, his lungs expanded again. Thaniel struggled back up onto his hooves.

"What was that?" The horse asked, as he shakily established his legs under him and also regained his breath.

Sitting upright once more, Aram looked around. All along the crater rim, just below the brow, the army got haltingly back to its feet and gazed with wide eyes out toward the valley, from whence the *thing* had come. Many men seemed troubled with minor injuries, but from Aram's vantage, he could not discern any fatalities, though here and there some were slow to regain their feet.

"Are you alright, Thaniel?" He asked.

"I am," the horse replied.

"Turn, then, and let's see what is happening in the valley."

Down on the valley floor Manon's army lay unmoving, tens of thousands of gray men and hundreds of lashers, apparently slain by the power that had come forth, blown across the valley, and surged up the slope.

Aram looked closer. Down upon the slopes, those men that had pursued their foe almost to the valley floor also lay unmoving, sprawled upon the slope. Nearer at hand, those that had responded to the bugle's command and had been climbing back toward their lines also lay upon the incline. Some moved not at all, but some had struggled up onto their hands and knees. Others lay writhing, calling in pitiable tones for aid to come to them.

The force that emanated from the tower had slain Manon's army, slaughtered those lower upon the slope, maimed those a bit higher, and then had spared the army, though it bruised it sore.

Evidently, the wave of energy had lost some of its impetus and consequently its killing power as it came up the slope.

Aram looked over and found Boman tending to his men, and checking among them for serious injury. Gaining the Governor's attention, Aram pointed down the slope. "We need to send aid to those men that are injured down there," he told him.

Boman looked down the incline and nodded, but then he lifted his gaze to the tower and hesitated. "Will that *thing* come again, do you think?"

Aram studied the tower as well for a moment and then shook his head.

"It will not," he answered, for suddenly he understood.

The Governor was watching him and saw the expression of understanding spread across the king's face.

"What was that thing, my lord?" Boman repeated Thaniel's question of a few moments earlier.

"It was the grim lord opening his door," Aram replied.

Boman frowned. "Opening his door? – to what end?"

"For me," Aram said. "To the end that I might go in to him."

Boman continued to frown at him, but said nothing further.

"Do not send a detail down to aid those men upon the slope, Governor," Aram told him, changing his mind. "I will have Nikolus send horses to their aid. It will be faster, and we may move them more easily out of danger."

Nikolus and his troopers were behind him, tending to their dead and wounded. Aram glanced out toward where the bodies of Donnick and Wamlak lay, but found that he could not bear to deal with such sadness at the moment. Besides, there was much that needed to be done for those that yet lived.

Speaking to Thaniel, Aram moved away toward Nikolus. As he went, he said to Boman, "Leave a large enough detail to aid the surgeons in seeing to your wounded and your dead, Governor – and then begin moving your troops back over the ridge and down into the little valley into camp. I will have Lamont go ahead of you, and Elam will follow."

He looked up at the sun. It had slipped barely two hours past mid-day. *Had the battle really only lasted less than two hours?*

After commissioning Nikolus to send aid to the wounded that lay down the slope, Aram went along the line, speaking to each commander, giving the same instruction that he'd given to Boman, to organize details to aid the surgeons and then to begin moving in order back across the ridge and down into their camps of the night before.

At the road, he found Timmon kneeling by the body of his dead mount, weeping, trying to move the shattered pieces of her into a less vulgar version of the wreckage that violent death had made of her.

Aram sat quietly and watched him at his terrible labor for a time and then he spoke kindly. "When you can – we need to clear the road, my friend, and get the cannon back over the ridge and down into the valley beyond."

Timmon nodded without looking up. "I'll move it out of the way now – I just didn't want to leave her like this."

"I understand," Aram told him. "I will send a cart this way to bring her out with the rest of our dead."

"Thank you, my lord."

After the various commanders, upon consulting with the surgeons, organized sufficient details for seeing to the delicate task of removing the wounded, and the more sorrowful work of removing the dead, the rest of the army formed into columns and filed back through the cut and down the road into the small valley where they made their camp. Timmon, with one cart bearing the gun and another bearing the remains of Bonhie, went in front.

Nikolus sent men and horses down the slope to retrieve the wounded men that had given chase to the enemy and the bodies of their companions.

Aram knew that he had to see to the sad removal of Donnick and Wamlak, but first he went toward the east, to see Mallet.

The big man was drenched in blood, some of it reddish-brown, but much of it brackish, a testament to the many lashers he had slain that day.

Aram dismounted and grabbed the big man's hand. "I am very glad to see you alive, my friend," he said. He embraced Mallet and then glanced behind around the slope.

"Where is Jonwood?"

Mallet waved one hand down toward the small canyon to the east. "He and some others are seeing to the wounded from among the wolf people, my lord."

Aram nodded. "Thank you for that."

Mallet was watching him closely, a look of unease, almost of fear, evident on his broad face. "My lord – is it true? What I hear of Wamlak, I mean."

Aram met his gaze and then inclined his head in solemn acknowledgement. "The lashers broke through the line by Donnick. Wamlak went to the aid of his father." He sighed deeply as his eyes abruptly stung. "I went that way, too, but I was too late. They both of them died. I am sorry, my friend."

Mallet convulsed, sucked in a great gulp of air, and began sobbing, burying his face in his hands. After some time, in which Aram stood helplessly by with one hand on the big man's arm, Mallet drew in a deep, shuddering breath, choking off his sorrow, and wiped at his eyes with blood-encrusted hands. "I loved that man, Lord Aram. He was as good a friend as any man ever had."

Aram nodded, gulping down his own grief. "I know this, my friend. I am sorry."

The big man turned and glared out across the valley, at the distant black tower. Lifting one hand, he pointed it accusingly. "No one has the right to cause as much sorrow as he has brought us all."

"No – he does not have such a right," Aram agreed. "He never had such a right as that." He reached out and again laid one hand upon Mallet's arm. "Help me remove the army from the field," he said. "And then I will go and visit justice upon him for all of us."

Mallet jerked his head around and looked down at him. He frowned deeply. "You are going in there, my lord? Alone?"

"Yes." Aram spread his hands, indicating the body-strewn battlefield. "That was the purpose of all of this – so that I might go in unto him and evict him from the world, now and forever."

Mallet stared for a long moment, and then lowered his gaze to the ground and nodded. "I guess I knew that," he admitted.

Aram looked around. "Leave the bodies of the enemy," he told him. "See to your wounded and your dead, and send the rest of your men back across the ridge and into the valley."

"I will, my lord. What about Wamlak?"

"I'm going to see about him and Donnick now," Aram said. "And I have heard nothing of Findaen since all this started. I must find him and know that he is well. Don't worry – I will make certain that you know where Wamlak may be found once he and his father are removed."

Aram turned away then to mount up on Thaniel, but Mallet reached out one large hand and prevented him. Aram looked back curiously at the big man.

With his free hand, Mallet indicated the tower. "Are you going in there now, my lord? After you see to Findaen and Wamlak?"

Aram smiled and shook his head. "No. We must get the army safely away before I go in to him. The army must be nowhere near this valley when justice is done upon Manon."

Aram turned again, but once more Mallet stopped him.

"My lord – remember? You told me to be alive when the battle was over."

Aram nodded slowly, watching him. "Yes, I did want that of you; I wanted it very much."

"Then I say the same to you now, my lord."

Aram frowned but gave no answer.

Mallet lifted his hand toward the north once again. "When you have done with him, and the world is free – be alive, my lord, I beg of you."

Aram looked in his eyes for a moment and then looked away, toward the tower of his enemy. "I will do my best, my friend," he said quietly. Then he turned and once more met Mallet's gaze. "But just as you did not abandon your post, here, upon this hill, even though it might have easily cost your life – so then, too, I cannot abandon my destiny, whatever the cost."

He nodded solemnly. "But hear me, my friend – I do not intend to die." He smiled in an attempt to break the somberness of the moment and then looked around. "Now – let us get this army safely off this ridge."

"I will, my lord." Mallet agreed. "And you will tell me where I may find Wamlak later?"

"I will send word," Aram promised as he mounted up, and then Thaniel cantered away toward the west, to see about the dark-haired archer that Aram had once considered the cleverest man of his acquaintance. And lying near him was Donnick, who had been the calmest and most capable of men. These two men, father and son, would be sorely missed whatever the future wrought.

When Aram and Thaniel made their way back across what had been the front, now devoid of living men other than surgeons and those toiling at removing the allied dead, Aram studied the long columns of men up near the crest that were moving toward the west and the road that would take them back toward camp, looking for Findaen. Finally, they passed the road and Aram searched the lines of those men beyond the gleaming black pavement that were slowly filing eastward. At last, they came to where the lashers had punched through Donnick's line.

Nowhere had he found Findaen. No one had seen him since the battle and Thaniel, though he had tried unceasingly, had been unable to contact Andaran with mindspeak. Aram's heart grew heavy with every failure at discovering his wife's brother.

Bodies were strewn all across the space, thousands of them, lashers, gray men, human men, and horses. Aram directed Thaniel out onto the broad shelf where the line had been before the lashers drove it back and destroyed it, looking for Donnick and Wamlak. He spied a trooper kneeling by a horse. Both were covered with dust and dried blood, the grime of battle.

The trooper was attempting to move the body of a lasher so that he might get at whatever lay beneath.

Aram dismounted and moved up behind the cavalryman. "I beg forgiveness for disturbing you," he said. "But have you seen Findaen?"

Startled, the trooper turned and looked back, getting to his feet as he did so. It was Findaen. The horse that stood nearby was Andaran. Neither had been recognizable, caked as they were with the filth of the awful fighting that had occurred in this place. Overjoyed, Aram went to his brother-in-law and embraced him, even as Thaniel reproved Andaran.

"Why did you not answer me?" Thaniel demanded, but he received only a curious look in reply.

"He was hit pretty hard on his headgear – by one of those big bastards," Findaen explained to Thaniel. "I haven't been able to get a word out of him."

"It's good to see you, Fin," Aram said.

Fin squeezed his eyes tight for a moment, and nodded. "It's good to see you, too." Then he knelt down once more. "Help me get this monster off Wamlak, will you?" He asked.

302

Aram knelt down to help him. "I'm sorry, Fin," he stated.

Findaen looked over. "Ka'en is right about that, you know."

Aram frowned at him. "About what?"

"That you have to stop apologizing." Findaen looked around. "None of these deaths is your doing, Aram," he said, and then he looked out toward the distant tower. "They are his – each one of them – *they are his.*"

Though the unhurt and the walking wounded were settled back into camp by the end of that day, it required two more days to gather the more severely wounded into wagons, and to determine which of those that were injured would survive and should be moved, and which of them should simply be nursed into as a painless a death as was possible.

Then came the long, sorrowful, and painful process of burying the dead, and marking their graves. Summer had come to even this far northern part of the world, and the dead simply could not endure the transport across hundreds of miles southward into even warmer climes.

They would stay here; their graves would be the monument to their triumph.

Finally, on the fifth day since the battle, the awful toil was finished; the army broke camp, and accompanied by an unbearably long train of oxcarts carrying the wounded, began winding its way southward through Bracken and toward home.

48.

On the evening of that fifth day, after the army had begun its long journey into the south, and the last of the troops had left the small valley and wound up through the hills and descended toward Bracken, Aram motioned to Findaen to follow and then turned away and went back up to the top of the crater rim. A while later he stood on the ridge with Thaniel, Findaen, and Findaen's mount, Andaran, who had at last regained his inner hearing after the blow he'd received in action. There were no humans or horses or wolves, dead or alive, that remained upon the ridge now except for the four of them.

They stood in silence for some time, each of them gazing out across the shadowed valley at the gleaming tower.

There had been no further sign from the grim lord since he had sent the wave of power out from his tower, across the valley, and up the slope, killing every one of his servants upon the valley floor, and bruising and terrifying the army on the high ground above.

After a time, Findaen looked over. "What now, my friend?"

When Aram turned and looked at him, Findaen sucked in a startled breath. Since the day of the battle, Aram had been subdued, thoughtful, as the wounded were carefully removed from the field, and the bodies of the dead discovered, identified, and placed into the womb of the earth in the small valley behind them.

Now, as he returned Findaen's gaze, Lord Aram's green eyes once more held that deep layer of cold, hard ice.

"Now," Aram said bluntly, "I end it."

Findaen let his breath out slowly. "How may I lend you assistance, my lord?"

Aram smiled a small smile that vanished as quickly as it came. In reply, he went around to Thaniel's other side and opened a pack that was tied to the back of the saddle. The horse's armor had been removed and stored in one of the wagons that was even now wending its way south. All that Thaniel wore was the saddle and this one small pack.

The thing that Aram removed was circular and gleamed in the dim orange light of the hazy evening sun.

Coming back near Findaen, Aram handed him the object. "This is the crown of the kings of Regamun Mediar," he said.

Findaen looked at him with widened eyes filled with concern and suspicion. "What do you want that I should do with it?" He asked.

"Keep it safe, Fin," Aram replied.

"Why do not you keep it, my friend?"

Aram shook his head. "It should not go where I am going."

"Why?"

Aram looked at him. "I would not want it to fall into the wrong hands," he admitted truthfully.

"How?" Findaen asked him harshly, suspicion coloring his tone. "*How* would it fall into the wrong hands?"

Aram ignored that. "Just keep it safe. The day will come when I will ask for it to be returned to me."

Findaen watched him with narrowed eyes. "Will it, my lord? Will such a day come?"

Aram shrugged slightly at this, but he was no longer looking at Findaen. He stared toward the distant tower as if his mind had already shifted from that conversation and had become fixed upon something more urgent or compelling.

"I hope it will, Fin." He replied to the question, but he did not look over. His hard green eyes were fastened upon the dwelling place of his enemy.

Findaen watched him and waited, but Aram did not speak further. Several minutes passed. No sound troubled the air upon the ridge, except the soughing of the cool breeze as it sought the heights.

"Lord Aram?"

Aram looked at him. The king's eyes were hard and distant, as if that which occupied his thoughts lay somewhere else, far away, and his features were without expression. But then, after a moment, he smiled a wry smile. "Keep it safe, Fin – and keep the army safe.

Make certain that every man is far south of this place – and stays far from this place."

Findaen narrowed his eyes. "What about you?"

Aram was quiet again for a long moment. Then, he gave his brother-in-law the same answer he had once given Thaniel.

"The Sword will get me in – and the Sword will bring me out."

"Are you certain of this, Aram?"

Another silence, and then Aram was forced to acknowledge the truth. "I don't know," he admitted. "But I must go in to him; for justice is demanded. Vengeance is demanded. Besides, it is why we came, why so many died here – to open the way to Manon."

He waved his hand toward the thousands of dead bodies of Manon's army that littered the slope and the floor of the valley. "The way is open."

Findaen turned and looked northward, but he was not gazing at the tower; his eyes were fixed on something much further away. Something that could not be seen from this desolate ridge.

"What will I tell Ka'en?" He asked. "If you do not return."

"You will tell her that I loved her and thought of her until my last breath," Aram replied, and then he reached out and gripped Findaen by the shoulder. "But I will return to her, Fin; fear not. How? – I do not know; but I will return to her."

He waited until Findaen looked his way once more and then he smiled, though his eyes remained hard and full of ice. "Now, my friend – get to the south; catch up to the army. Make certain that it continues to move south until nightfall. I will see you when I am able."

Findaen met his gaze for a long moment in silence and then, still silently, he reached out and took Aram's hand, gripped it firmly, nodded, mounted up, spoke to Andaran, and he and the horse rode through the gap and went out of sight to the south.

306

49.

Aram and Thaniel stood in the road for a time after Findaen and Andaran rode away, staring ahead at the tower of the enemy of the world. To the west, the sun sank lower until it rested on the tops of the mountains. Its slanted light cast the tower and the city around it into dusky shades of red, like dried blood.

"What now?" Asked Thaniel.

"Now I must go in to him," Aram replied. "I will ask of you, my friend, that you bear me to the edge of the city, if you will."

The horse made a deep low sound in his throat. "I will bear you further than that, my lord. If it pleases you, I will bear you all the way into his vile presence."

"No – just to the edge of the city," Aram responded. He glanced westward, where the jagged teeth of the dark and distant mountains were starting to consume the blood-red sun, and then he turned to mount up. "Let us go," he said.

Down the road they went, with Thaniel weaving this way and that around the mounded bodies of the lashers that Timmon's gun had blasted into brackish rubble. Some way further and Thaniel once again had to work his way around the burned bodies of those that Aram's Sword had slain. Further yet and they came to an area where there were many lasher bodies, these perhaps less violently slain but nonetheless made dead by Seneca's lethal aerial assault.

By the time they reached the valley floor, only a sliver of the crimson sun showed above the horizon.

A half-mile from the base of the slope, they encountered the remains of Manon's army, these slain by their master. As Thaniel carefully wended his way through the mounded carnage, Aram gazed in astonishment at the bodies. Though seemingly intact in every detail of their swollen bodies, nevertheless congealing pools of blood surrounded them and fouled the air, having apparently leaked from every orifice. The shock wave, by all evidence, had churned their insides to mush.

The breeze that had blown from the north for days had failed; the air was still, and the stench of death permeated the air, causing both man and horse to choke and gag. When Thaniel made his way clear of the ranks of slain gray men and lashers, he picked up his pace, in order to get out of the region of foul, unwholesome atmosphere.

The sun had gone and twilight was stealing into the valley from the east by the time they neared the environs of the city.

"Halt here," Aram told Thaniel.

The tower rose up, up, before them, like a polished black thorn, narrowing to a fine sharp point where it pierced the dark gray firmament far above.

Aram dismounted, looked down the black road toward the bottom of the immense tower, and then turned to face the horse.

"This is as far as you go, my friend."

Thaniel stared at him for a long moment. "Do not do this to me, Aram. Do not leave me behind. Let me go in with you," the horse pleaded.

Aram shook his head firmly. "I cannot," he said. "This is a task for one man, and I must do it alone. Even the Guardians must remain behind, now." He raised his voice. "Is not that true, my lords?"

Thaniel started in shock and moved involuntarily back a step as to either side of Aram the Guardians became visible. Moving at a speed that defied perception, they melded to one side, to reappear on Thaniel's right. Their bodies seemed to glow in the gloom of the twilight. Here and there, tiny points of light glowed even brighter, as if the images of distant stars were embedded in their flesh.

Aram bowed to them. "Even you cannot accompany me here – is this not so?"

Their voices came, like soft, echoed thunder. "We cannot. You must do this alone."

"And my friend – the horse?"

There was a moment of silence before the Astra made reply to this. "We cannot forbid him from entering," the echoed voices stated. "But what would be the purpose? He cannot bear the Sword,

308

nor wield it. And there are passages inside which, due to his size, he will not be able to manage. If you fail, Aram, the horse will surely die as well. What would be the purpose?" The voices asked again.

Aram inclined his head to them in acknowledgement of the truth of this response, and then bowed his head yet again. "You have saved my life more than once, my lords, and for this I am grateful." Going silent for a moment, he peered at them closely. "My lords – do you have any wisdom that you might give me in this moment that will aid me in the hours ahead?"

The answer was returned immediately. "You have been to the mountain of Kelven and have heard his words, and you have spoken with Ferros. Everything that you need to know, you have already heard from them. Remember that which you have heard of those two gods, for in their words you will find the knowledge you need when you face the enemy."

Aram frowned at this vague instruction, even as his mind responded and searched among the memories of his conversations with Kelven and Ferros. After a long moment, he shook his head. "Forgive me, my lords, but I can think of nothing that might –"

"*Forshetha,* Aram." The Astra cut him off in terse manner. "It is not given to us to guide you either in word or in deed to the end of your quest. That work was given to others. To us it was given only to see you to this hour and to this place. Our task is done."

Aram went silent, and then he nodded grimly and reached up and slipped the Call off his neck. He held it out. "I return this into the safety of your keeping. Take it, my lords, in the event that I do not return."

The Astra made no move to accept the slim silver cylinder, nor did they incline their heads to regard the object that was held out to them. The echoed voices came again. "We were not sent to guard that device, Aram – it is nothing to us. We came only to assure that you lived unto this day – to protect you, as best we could, from accidental death."

Aram gazed at them, frowning in his lack of comprehension of this. "But I was told by Florm that –" He stopped himself from rendering what was obviously a foolish response. Of course these two creatures would have access to knowledge that the ancient horse had been denied. He indicated the hilt of the weapon rising above his shoulder. "And the Sword?"

"The dwelling place of Manon is the final destination for the weapon as well," the Astra replied. "Our task is now completed with the Sword of Humber."

At this statement, Thaniel moved forward in agitation and dared to speak. "Is that all the concern that the gods have for this man – that he live to do the bidding and work of those higher? Why cannot you go with him, and assure that he returns?"

Aram raised his hand toward Thaniel in protest but then decided that in fact he would like to hear the Astra respond to this question. He lowered his hand and turned to look at the unearthly creatures. There fell a long silence. Then Ligurian and Tiberion spoke once more. "We have seen the regard that you have for Aram," they told the horse, "and can understand that which you feel in this moment. But we are under command of Him who governs all, and it is His desire that Aram accomplish that with which he has been charged. It is his task and not ours."

The Astra turned back to Aram then, and it seemed to him that they made a subtle motion with their hands. "The grace of the Maker go with you, Aram. Farewell. Be strong and remember all you have heard." And they faded into the night.

Frustrated and angry, Thaniel swung his head back from staring into the now empty darkness where the Guardians had stood and looked at Aram. "Let me go with you," he pleaded.

In response, Aram leaned forward and placed his forehead against that of the horse. "I cannot, my brother," he insisted. "There is no purpose in risking both our lives."

Thaniel was quivering with emotion. "Do not die, Aram, my friend, my brother. I did not bear you across all these years and all these miles to bring you to your death."

Aram leaned back and looked at him. "No – you bore me here that evil might be removed from the world and its people set free."

Leaning around and reaching past the horse's head and neck, he looped the Call around the horn of the saddle and secured it there.

Thaniel's suspicion flared again at this act. He moved back and gazed full into Aram's face. "You behave like a man who doubts his return."

"Of course I doubt my return," Aram replied quietly as he met the horse's scrutiny. "I don't mean to die, Thaniel – I hope not to die. I hope to live and return to my family. But I've been to Kelven's mountain, and I've seen what happens when a god dies. It is calamity. *And I mean to slay one here today.*"

He spread his hands. "How will I survive such an event? I do not know. But if there is a way, I will discover it."

"The world needs for you to live," the horse insisted.

Aram shook his head. "More than anything, the world needs for Manon to die."

Thaniel shifted his massive weight and stamped one hoof upon the smooth black pavement. "If you die," he said, and his voice was low and filled with the anguish of doubt, "the world will be desolate for me. I told you this once, and I meant it. I cannot live in a world where you do not."

Aram reached out with both hands and took hold of Thaniel's head. "Listen to me, my brother. Whatever happens to me – you have to live. *I need you to live.* If I do not return from this doom that is before me – then who will guide the world into the task of rebuilding? I trust no one more than I trust you. The world will need you in the years ahead, more so if I am absent."

Thaniel shifted again and made to speak but Aram shook his head, cutting him off. He sighed deeply. "And what of Mae? Ka'en will tell her of me, but her words will be colored by loss and sadness. I do not care how I will be remembered by the people of the earth. But I want my daughter to know who I was and *how I was.* Who will tell her? Who knows me better than you? – no one."

He let silence fall while he and the great horse stood face-to-face. The muscles across Thaniel's broad chest shook and jumped with the potency of the horse's emotion.

Once more, Aram spoke, "I ask one thing of you, my brother – if I die, tell my daughter about me when she is old enough to hear it."

Then he stepped back and drew himself up to his full height. "But hear this, my friend – *I do not mean to die.*" He moved his hand and indicated the Call. "I will return for that, I promise you."

Thaniel gazed back and did not respond but the suspicion of inevitable pain and loss clouded the depths of his large eyes.

Aram glanced westward toward the jagged ring of dim and distant hills. If the sun was yet in the sky, it could not be seen through the smoky overcast, and the gathering gloom indicated that it either sat upon the unseen horizon beyond those heights or perhaps had even dropped below the far edge of the world.

He turned back to Thaniel. "You have to go now, my brother. And so must I."

Thaniel didn't move.

Aram pulled at his gauntlets and adjusted the Sword on his back. "Go now, my friend. Go and make certain that every element of the army is far to the south of this place. I will be more able to act with clarity of thought if I am sure that no life but my own is in jeopardy." He reached out and touched the side of Thaniel's head. "Please, my brother – go."

Thaniel shifted his immense weight in agitation and blew a great blast from his nostrils. "Come back to us, Aram."

Aram nodded firmly. "I will if I am able." He dropped his hand and stepped back, and then pointed back along the road toward the rim of the crater. "*Please – go.*"

Thaniel stood for a long moment, and then without speaking, he wheeled around and galloped back up the road, dodging this way and that around the heaped bodies of Manon's dead army. Aram watched him go until the horse climbed the distant slope and reached the rim. At the horizon line, already growing indistinct in the deepening twilight, the great horse stopped and looked back, a small dim black shadow against the gathering night.

Aram raised one hand and held it for a moment and then let it drop. "Farewell, my friend," he said quietly.

Thaniel stood silhouetted against the darkening sky for so long that Aram began to suspect that he meant to return, but then the great horse wheeled away, drove through the cut, down the road beyond, and was gone.

Aram drew in a deep breath, and pivoted to look toward the massive tower, gleaming in the dimness. Cocking his head, he listened into the falling night, but there was no sound save that of the chill wind that had picked up once more, to sweep restlessly out of the cold peaks to the north of the valley. He glanced up, into the darkness of the eastern sky, but no stars shone. The firmament was as opaque as flint.

Mustering his courage, he began to move deliberately toward the tower that soared high into the ash-laden sky above him. He was past the heaviest carnage done by whatever power Manon had unleashed upon his own troops; still, surprisingly, individual bodies occasionally lay about on both sides of the road. Several times, he stopped to investigate an imagined sound, perhaps one of Manon's minions that was only injured and not dead. But each time it was confirmed that, in fact, nothing moved in all the valley of Morkendril.

The base of the tower rose less than a mile from his position as the night thickened around him. He quickened his steps and glanced involuntarily once more toward the east. The Glittering Sword of God should be in the sky this time of year, just above the horizon, but he could see nothing of that strange array of red and blue stars. The darkening sky was thick and heavy with the exhalations of the smoking mountains.

The floor of the valley was composed of the detritus from past eruptions from those mountains. Gravel, pounded smooth by the passage of countless booted feet and clawed lasher appendages, extended to either side of the road for as far as he could see in the thickening gloom.

By the time he entered the outskirts of Morkendril, night had fully fallen. The cold wind concentrated its chill strength upon the main avenue as it blew straight into his face. He was still a long way from the base of the tower. The stone huts, separated by narrow bystreets, angled endlessly away from him into the blackness. Often, he stopped to listen into the night, but there was ever only the sound of the ceaseless wind.

Ahead and above, the fang-tooth tower gleamed in the night as if the material of the tower itself were illuminated with a faint greenish light. Off to either side, mounding up into the night, other towers arose, connected to the main structure by crenelated turrets and walls. No one manned them now.

The city was utterly devoid of life.

Feeling his courage flagging, Aram slowed his pace, reached back and unsheathed the Sword. He drew it forth and held it in front of him, at the ready, resisting the stout westward tug it exerted upon his arm.

Silence lay thick, dark, and heavy all about him.

Far overhead, the thin, sharp tip of the tower was lost in the blackness of the sky.

On he went, walking slowly, deliberately, his ears seeming to tingle from the utter absence of living sounds. Eventually, even the wind grew quiet, and seemed content to lie down and die among the dingy streets and avenues.

Ahead of him, darker than the surrounding night, the tower grew closer and loomed ever higher, gleaming blackly.

After what felt like hours of creeping along the smooth black pavement, between the dark streets and empty huts, the road began to descend between two walls of stone. Darkness gathered even more thickly here. Except for the strange gleaming of the vast wall of the tower, his eyes could discern nothing in the gloom.

Down he went, along the slope of the pavement. The huts of Morkendril disappeared into the night above him.

Down, down, he went as if the road would lead him eventually to the realm of the underearth. Then his boots sloshed through an unseen, slowly running stream of shallow, rancid water that gave off the fetid odor of filth when his feet disturbed it. Beyond that liquid rottenness, the road rose gently upward again.

Then, dead ahead, a large rectangle of black abruptly loomed in the gleaming blackness of the tower wall. He'd reached the stronghold of Manon the Grim.

And the door was open.

He stopped, cocked his head, and listened into the heavy stillness.

No sound came to his ear. Not the cry of a night-bird or the chirp of a nocturnal insect. Not even the soughing of the slightest breeze. All was absolutely still.

He stood stock-still, gazing ahead into the night, and drew in several deep breaths. As his eyes adjusted, he found that the black rectangle to his front was not completely dark. A faint, greenish glow emanated from it, and he could make out the smooth surface of a facing wall beyond the opening, several feet inside the entrance.

Keeping the Sword in front of him and at the level, he moved toward the entrance. The green glow strengthened as he came nearer and he could make out the far wall of the interior passageway as well as the vast door that stood ajar from the structure.

Cautiously, he moved to stand against the open door, on the right side of the enormous entrance. Easing along it toward the opening, he peered to his left for as far along the interior passageway as he could. The passage sloped away from him in that direction and there was no one in sight upon it. Stepping back away from the doorway, he eased to the left side, moved up next to the smooth wall of the tower and looked the other way. In that direction, to his right, the passage rose away from him as it wound into the heights. There was no one in sight there, either.

Drawing in a deep breath, letting the Sword lead the way, he stepped through the opening. It was as he'd seen from outside. The passageway was made of a slick black substance. If it was not stone, it was similar in composition, but utterly smooth. To the left the hallway wound downward and out of sight to the right. The other way, it wound upward toward the higher regions of the tower and went away to the left.

Holding his breath, he tried to listen between the deep bass notes of his pounding heart but no other sound came to him. After considering it for a long moment, and feeling uncomfortable with climbing upward if Manon was somewhere below, he went to his left, toward the lower regions, walking slowly and as noiselessly as he could manage.

The ceiling of the hall, which was lit by green stones that shimmered like jewels and were imbedded into its glossy black surface, was high above him, perhaps fifteen feet or more above his head. The passageway itself was wide enough that two or even three lashers could have passed each other with ease. But if any of those beasts had survived the carnage that Manon had inflicted upon his own army, they were not in sight at the moment. And judging by the absolute silence of the place, Aram now believed that in fact none had survived.

He was alone in the tower except for his enemy, the enemy of the world, who lurked somewhere in the shadows of this structure, the stronghold of evil.

There was a faint, oddly metallic odor, pungent and sour, that wafted up from below, from wherever the passage led. Occasionally glancing backward over his shoulder, he moved, step by deliberate step down and around the gentle slope of the passage.

He had gone far enough around the slow curve of the corridor that the tower's entrance had passed out of view beyond the intervening wall when he came to a doorway leading to his right, into the structure. The door was closed and there was no handle; he could discern no means of opening it. With no other idea readily at hand, Aram simply pushed on it and was surprised when it swung easily inward, exposing a large, dimly lit, open area beyond.

Holding the Sword pointed toward the opening as he moved around to where he could more clearly see inside the space beyond the door, Aram glanced each way along the passage, making sure that it was still abandoned, before turning his attention back to the interior space. The room was evidently very large, for it extended away from him beyond the ability of his eye to resolve detail. It was lit by the same method as the hallway, with green, glowing jewels or stones imbedded into the ceiling, which, like that of the passage, was quite high.

All his nerves twitched and the hair on the back of his neck tingled as if it stood on edge. Despite the fact that there was no movement anywhere in sight and no sounds other than those that his boots made upon the smooth black floor, he could not shake the feeling that he was being watched.

Time after time, he turned his head quickly to the left or the right in an attempt to catch anyone or anything stalking him from either direction along the corridor, but never was there another soul in sight.

Summoning his courage, he eased into the room beyond the door and slid to his left to stand with his back against the wall while he surveyed the interior. The room was immense and round, apparently encompassing the breadth of the main structure of the tower. Except for the exterior walls he could discern no supports for the ceiling anywhere. It appeared to him as if the tower had at one time been solid and this room had simply been hollowed out of it.

There were weapons stacked at intervals along both walls as they curved away from him, halberds, lances, even swords, but they were not numerous enough to signify an armory. It appeared, rather, as if each stack of weaponry was the cache of some individual lasher.

There were hundreds of large woven mats scattered here and there, many more than there were caches of weapons. And there were scattered piles of bones, mostly of animals, but there were also some that were fearfully humanlike.

The atmosphere of the room was heavy with a foul pungency, as of decay, rotted meat. Probably, this odor arose from the refuse of past meals of the beasts that had lived there.

Aram's eyes had by this time grown accustomed to the faint green light, but though he peered deep into the depths of the room and turned his head to either side to listen, it became obvious that the vast space was devoid of living beings. He could see no reason to expend time on further exploration of an empty room.

Still, the feeling of malignant observation persisted.

He eased back to his right, peered around the edges of the opening, and examined the outer passage in both directions.

But it, too, was empty.

Easing out into the corridor, still holding the Sword to his front, Aram descended further, going down and around the passage to the right.

How far he went, he could not be certain, but after what seemed like a complete revolution of the vast structure, he came again to a doorway that led into the interior of the structure. This room was already open to him, the door having swung inward.

Abruptly, his senses were assaulted by a strong, metallic odor, as of blood, that emanated from the space beyond the open door. This room, then, was the origin of the scent he'd noticed earlier.

It smelled of blood.

And of other, fouler execrations.

He eased closer to the opening and then looked down at the floor, startled, as his boots encountered a thin layer of a sticky substance that gave off fresh waves of foul aroma when disturbed by the soles of his boots. It was gore, mostly congealed, though whether it was of human origin or lasher, he could not tell.

Apparently, Manon's device for the destruction of his armies out in the valley had also destroyed anything that lived within the tower itself.

The air became suffocating with the pungent odor of death as he stepped gingerly across the swath of blackened gore and peered inside the room. Horror and revulsion rocked him as he gazed upon the furnishings of this vast open space.

Humans had lived here.

But that which had been living creatures was now reduced to mounds of devastated flesh, bone, hair, and cloth scattered all across the floor of the room, from wall to wall. In horror, Aram held his free hand to his nose and examined what he could see of the room from the opening. The other objects in the room told its use. Beds, hundreds of them, were aligned in rows, stretching away to the far distant wall.

Over to the right, sweeping around the room out of sight, between the beds and the wall, there was a broad space filled with tables, barrels, and tall cabinets. Some distance away, incorporated into this space, there was what looked to be an area for the preparation of food. It struck Aram suddenly that he was looking at the place – or at least one of the places – where the young women transported from the south were housed while their wombs were put to use. This suspicion was confirmed by the presence of smaller husks of what had once been living things scattered here and there among the larger corpses that lay everywhere across the room.

His heart abruptly constricted, sadness overwhelmed him, and the gorge rose in his throat, even as hot anger poured into his soul.

This very room, this terrible, loathsome dank space, was very likely the last dwelling place of his sister, lost to him so many years ago.

Pivoting abruptly on his heel, he turned and left the room. Gaining the passageway once more, and breathing hard, as if the horror he'd just witnessed was something that could expunged by the mere act of exhalation, Aram turned to his right. He did not hesitate or slink but strode quickly down and around the passage. Two more time-consuming circuits of the tower proved that there were two more rooms like the one above. After but a cursory look into each, in what he knew to be a futile attempt to determine if anything yet lived, he went on.

The circumnavigations took less time now, as the deeper rooms grew smaller rather than larger. Still, in the passage and in each room he passed, the air reeked with the foul stench of death. Immediately below the third – and the last – of the slave quarters, there was another room, smaller, but with thick walls and a heavier door. The door was shut but opened easily enough when Aram leaned his shoulder against it.

He eased cautiously into the gloom of the narrow room and let his eyes adjust as he surveyed the dim interior. Immediately, he recognized the remains of the three massive beasts which lay dead within, still shackled to the wall with heavy lengths of chain.

The wolves had named their kind *deathmakers*.

Aram had slain their brother far away to the south, on that terrible, dark, overcast day in The Lost.

These monsters, then, had been the sires of the grim lord's vile armies of lashers, cultivated in the innocent young wombs of the daughters of men. Aram made to move toward them and make sure of their demise. Before he took three steps the overwhelming stench and vast thickening pools of gore made it clear that these beasts would terrorize and horrify no more.

There was nothing – and no one – else, in that room. Backing out of its foulness, he gained the passage once more and went again downward, around to the right.

The passage wound down for a significant distance and then straightened out and led straight toward another doorway, which was sealed. Like the room below the tower in the befouled city of Panax far away to the south on the borders of Wallensia, this door was set tightly into its enclosure. He could find no means of ingress. It appeared that if Manon was inside the space beyond, Aram would be obliged to wait for him to choose the moment of revelation.

As he studied this apparently impassable door, however, anger abruptly surged within him. He had not come all this way just to let the enemy decide when and where he should be confronted. Stepping up close to the smooth blackness, he thrust the Sword into the barely discernable seam on the left-hand side.

Acrid smoke boiled up on the instant and the material of the door began to melt and sag away from the opening. He moved the blade away from the jam which was also beginning to disintegrate and then removed it from the door itself. By now the whole door had become fluid and was melting onto the floor of the passage.

Aram stepped back from the blazing hot mess of the melting door and retreated out of the acrid choking smoke which dissipated gradually as it curled up along the corridor. After giving the melted door a few minutes to cool and coalesce into its new shape, he eased forward until he could see into the room beyond.

It was small and dark and as well as he could see from where he stood just beyond the still-heated pile of black goo, also very oddly-shaped. That dark space was ovoid, as if a large egg or geode had once occupied that spot and then burst or evaporated, leaving a chamber behind.

The only furnishing in that egg-shaped space was a chair that appeared as if it had once been part of the surrounding stone and had grown up out of the floor. Directly before this chair, between it and the entrance, there was a basin, formed in similar manner to the chair, and filled with a dark fluid of unknown composition.

Manon was not there, anywhere inside that small, restricted space.

Aram backed away and then retraced his steps up, up, and around the curving passageway, not pausing to re-examine any of the rooms he'd passed earlier. There was no point in spending more time below the level of the earth. The grim lord, apparently, waited for him somewhere above.

When he came to the main entrance, he halted and gazed out for a few moments into the deep night. Though he peered carefully out into the darkness, he saw nothing moving on the roadway that dipped down and then ascended away from him toward the dark plain above. He turned away and kept going, angling up and to the left now. Around and around he went as the tower seemed to grow no smaller. Either the interior part of the tower was solid along this large section or the doors into unseen rooms were invisible. He wasted no time in examining the walls to see if in fact there were any of these unseen entrances, for something told him now, with a certainty that he could not have explained, that his quarry was above him, somewhere in the heights of the structure.

It was only after three or four more circuits that Aram came upon another opening leading to his left, into the interior of the tower. There was no door at the entrance to this chamber and Aram slowed as he approached it. The feeling of being observed had grown as he ascended and grew stronger as he approached the door. Now, perhaps, at last, he would face the destiny that had fallen to him.

With the Sword extended out to his front, he came to the opening and peered inside, moving first one way and then the other as he examined the large room beyond. He could see no one. Still holding the Sword before him, he cautiously entered the chamber. It was vast and utterly without furnishings, and lit, like all the others, by the strange stones overhead. In the very center of the room, there was a glowing green jewel imbedded in the ceiling, much larger than all the rest that surrounded it. This one large jewel-like stone served to illuminate an area immediately below it.

Aram stood still and stared toward the center of the room at this pool of much brighter light, wondering if perhaps Manon might materialize upon that spot.

But many minutes passed in silence and the grim lord did not appear.

Aram carefully scanned the depths and the far sweeping reaches of the vast room, but discerned nothing. The immense chamber was, apparently, quite empty. If Manon indeed occupied that broad space, the god had discovered the secrets of invisibility. But no – no, the god was not here. He swept his piercing gaze back across the room one last time and then turned away, back into the passageway.

As if summoned, he felt compelled toward the heights.

Manon was not in the room behind him, nor anywhere else below; he was more certain of it than ever.

The grim lord waited for him somewhere above.

Glancing back to his right, down the long curving hallway, he turned left and climbed up once more along the dark corridor.

Up and around he climbed, and gradually the circuits around the tower took less time. The structure grew perceptibly smaller. And now there were no more rooms or doorways leading into the interior of the structure. There was only the seemingly endless passageway, climbing up and up. Once, he passed a door in the exterior wall, but like the room far below, he could find no means of getting it open and he was loathe to use the Sword here.

He moved on.

Abruptly, the hallway ended and the entire interior opened up. The floor in front of him fell away, into hideous depths. Beyond the interior wall of the corridor, the tower had apparently been nothing but a shell for many circuits. But, wait, there *was* something in that broad, dark space.

Aram stared into the dimness, willing his eyes to adjust and expose to him what it was that was there. And gradually, it was resolved.

In the center of the emptiness, rising up out of the depths of the tower far below to pierce the void like a spike, a column of smooth black stone soared into the blackness overhead and out of sight.

Where the floor ended at a precipice, a narrow walkway of the smooth black stone arched across to the column or pillar that arose from below. Beginning where the walkway touched the pillar, steps had been cut into the shining black stone column. These steps wound upward and around it until they passed from view, and then reappeared to encircle it yet again in the gloom further above.

Aram hesitated for but a moment and then stepped out onto the suspended walkway.

He had encountered him whom he sought nowhere below.

Manon must be above.

Reaching the encircling steps, he went cautiously upward, into the night, round and around, and around again, and yet again. The column gradually narrowed, grew smaller, and still he climbed.

Then the stairs ended and he rose up and stepped out onto a smooth gleaming platform in the very heart – and the heights – of the tower.

A figure stood in the exact center of the platform, regal, tall, and slender, bareheaded, clothed in silvery robes.

Manon.

50.

The Lord of the World's eyes glowed deeply blue in the dimness.

"Hello, my son," the god said quietly, and the words seemed to slide from his tongue like oil or liquefied honey. He held out one hand in invitation. "You have come to me at last."

Aram made no reply. His heart was racing, making the blood pound inside his head like the ringing of a hammer, not so much from the exertion of the climb but rather from the fact that in that moment he stood face-to-face with the greatest and most powerful evil that had ever troubled the world and its people.

His doom.

His destiny.

The destiny he had not sought but had found anyway and now faced.

The long and dangerous path that his feet had trod for so long ended here, upon this polished black surface, high above the plane of the earth inside a hollow black spike that yet extended far into the darkness above him.

Making no reply to the god, holding the Sword at the ready, Aram gauged the distance to his enemy.

It was about twenty-five feet.

He bunched his muscles and lunged forward.

Manon lifted his hand, turning it so that invitation became a shield.

Aram crashed into an unseen, yet unyielding wall of power and went to his knees, gasping with pain.

"Is this why you have come to me after all this time?" Manon asked in apparent surprise. "To try and slay me?"

Aram could not find breath to return an answer. His lungs were empty; his mouth gaped open in an attempt to pull air back into his body. Pressure surged over and against him, grinding him down onto the smooth floor of the platform.

Then the god dropped his hand. The pressure eased.

Aram sucked in a desperate lungful.

"Do you know what it is that you bear in your hand, Aram?" Manon inquired gently. "I will tell you. It is the key to all things. It is the key to the door of the universe itself."

With his muscles still quivering from the blast of unseen power, Aram nonetheless managed to force himself up onto his knees, holding the Sword defensively in front of him. His lungs yet burned but he felt compelled to give an answer.

"If this is the key to such a great door," he gasped out, "it is a very small one."

Manon smiled. "Very small keys may open very great doors," he said. He stretched forth his hand and beckoned. "Come – give it to me. Be the son to me that I know you can be. Give me the key and I will open the door; then, let us walk through that door together and together *we will astound the universe.*"

Aram looked up and met his gaze but gave no reply. He was unmoved by Manon's offer, of course; still, he did not know what to do. He had not counted on the god's ability to extend the reach of his terrible power beyond his physical person. As his lungs quieted and his muscles calmed, he focused his brain and attempted to assess the problem.

How could he reach Manon and employ the weapon?

He had to somehow penetrate the god's powerful shield. He had counted on the Sword's ability to strike down any barrier, but this had not proved true. Slowly, carefully, Aram came to his feet. He had no desire to engage his enemy in polite conversation, but he had to get closer.

He lowered the Sword. It pulled against his hand, down and to the rear. Based on the weapon's behavior, Aram realized that the sun must even now be climbing the firmament on the far side of the world.

He looked into Manon's night-sky eyes as he took a half-step forward. "If I give you this 'key', my lord, you will slay me, will you not – as you slew my fathers?"

Manon spread his hands wide in a gesture of regret. "Your 'fathers', as you call them, would not listen to reason. I am your god, Aram, and you are my son. Why would I harm one of my own children?"

Aram thought of the murdered thousands lying dead upon the dark plains before Morkendril. He took another small step. "What about those that lie outside your door, my lord – were they not also your children? Yet you slew them."

The smooth features of Manon's gray face attempted to form an expression of sadness. "There is always sacrifice in the building of a new and better world." Then the god abandoned the poorly executed expression of sorrow for a look of concern. "I regret death and the sacrifice of any living thing, especially those of my own making," he replied. "Even when sacrifice is expedient."

His thin eyebrows raised in mild rebuke. "But, Aram – are you not aware that they died for you?"

At this, Aram stared back at him in genuine surprise, even as he eased closer. "For me?"

"Of course," Manon stated. "You are of more value than the full extent of my children – and the whole of that army you brought against the very walls of my home." He leaned toward Aram slightly. "Did you not know this?"

The god was now but a few yards away.

Manon's sapphire gaze dropped momentarily toward Aram's boots and his careful forward progress.

Aram halted.

As he raised his attention once more, Manon let go a quiet laugh. "Would you like to know the truth of things?" He asked softly. "Would you care to know the reason why my brethren gave you that Sword?"

"I know the reason the Sword came to me," Aram replied. He looked down at the floor for a moment, returned his gaze to the god's face, and slid one foot a bit closer. "They wanted me to destroy you."

Manon smiled even as he shook his head. "*Not so*. I was never the object of their thoughts on this matter, whatever you were told. It was you who made me part of this equation."

The god leaned forward once more, seeming to study the darkness behind Aram and to either side, as Aram moved his trailing foot up next to the other. Manon was now less than fifteen feet from him. Still, he kept the Sword down, by his side, letting the distant sun's pull render its position non-threatening.

"They were testing *you*, Aram," Manon said then. As he spoke he continued to study Aram closely. His eyes moved slightly from left to right, as if he sought the darkness that surrounded Aram for something that was as yet invisible to him.

Aram frowned and brought his careful forward movement to a halt. "Testing me?"

Manon straightened up and adopted a conciliatory posture though his eyes still searched back and forth, back and forth. They never appeared to look directly at Aram but seemed always to be seeking something that lay past him or perhaps to either side.

The god deliberately reached around and clasped his hands behind his back. "They – and I – *we all* wanted to know if you could come to a full understanding of the true nature of things before you were given even more authority over the peoples of this world."

Aram had no reply to this arcane statement, so he remained silent. After a moment, Manon shook his head and bent toward Aram once more with his searching gaze examining the darkness and went on. "I do not desire that which is known as the Sword of Humber, Aram. Once you give it into my hand, it will be returned to whence it came and destroyed. You will be made a king, and I will be your councilor should you desire it. This is the way that the world was ever meant to be governed, and is the true consideration of the Brethren."

He held out his hand even as his dark eyes, lit with roiling blue flame, seemed to pierce the space surrounding Aram, searching, searching. "Will you give it now?"

Aram slowly closed to within ten or twelve feet of the god, wondering at the odd turn the conversation had taken. Did Manon really think he could persuade the man before him that all the death and destruction across all the years and all the miles had been nothing more than a test of his worthiness as a monarch?

Aram dismissed that thought. No, something else was at work, something just beyond his grasp. Something that was lost in the sapphire luminescence of the god's searching gaze. At best, Manon was attempting to distract him from the moment. Why? – Aram could not guess.

Nor did he care to plumb the mystery.

326

He did not care about the nature of the grim lord's game; he had come to slay him, meant to slay him, and he was nearly within reach of the god with the weapon that would accomplish the deed.

One more step, Aram thought, and he could make his final move.

He slid one boot forward.

At that moment, Manon straightened up, and smiled a thin, cold smile. The god's obsidian gaze hardened, and his conciliatory demeanor abruptly dissipated.

"*I see that you are alone*," the grim lord said. "The creatures have abandoned you, have they not?"

He thrust forth one hand, palm outward.

Unseen power smashed into Aram, crushing him to his knees, and continued to force him downward, driving him nearly prone upon the floor. Aram quickly closed both gauntleted hands around the hilt of the Sword and raised it up, straining to keep it aimed at the god.

"And now I will take what is rightfully mine," Manon said harshly, and he held forth his other hand, with his palm open and the fingers outstretched toward the blade.

Instantly, the Sword leapt toward the outstretched hand of the god. Aram desperately tightened his grip on the hilt even as it tried to slip his grasp.

"You are so like your foolish forebears, Aram," Manon stated contemptuously. "Forgetting your place in the vain attempt to rise above your station."

Aram could make no reply. The muscles in his arms and his hands strained to retain possession of the blade, even as the awful weight of the god's power – as of a massive mountain – bore down upon him.

"*Release the object*," Manon commanded. "Do it now and I may let you live. I have little desire to squash a worm such as yourself. You must know that the weapon was never meant for the hand of a man as lowly as you. *It is mine.*"

Aram clung desperately onto the hilt and concentrated on maintaining control. The blade was aimed directly at the god. If only he could rise and make one final lunge, there was little doubt that his last effort, combined with the pull that was being exerted upon the

Sword by Manon himself, would catch the god by surprise, and it would pierce him.

But if he were to make such an attempt, he had to get off the floor, onto his knees, and then off his knees and onto his feet.

His muscles twanged against his bones and burned as if his flesh had been set aflame. His lungs ached from the strain of drawing breath after shuddering, painful breath, and his heart fluttered between every hesitant beat.

The pressure seemed to grow by the moment.

Manon's pull upon the weapon was unrelenting.

The unearthly blade began to glow and sing softly, as if with eagerness to go to the hand of the god.

He closed his eyes tightly and thought of Ka'en, and Mae, of Durlrang, Florm and Ashal, Donnick, Wamlak, Kitchell, Braska, and Timmon's mount, Bonhie. He focused his thoughts upon the forms and faces of his friends that yet lived, and on all those that had died.

And in that moment, he determined that he would not fail.

With a mighty straining heave, he forced his body upright, onto his knees, even as his flesh, bones, and sinew stretched and cracked. Using Manon's hold upon the Sword as a lever, he rose, slowly, inch by inch, with his muscles twanging and popping, and his sinew pulling loose from bone.

It was as if he strained to rise under the awful weight of the full mass of a vast and mighty mountain.

Still, he rose up.

Inch by hideously painful inch.

As he forced his damaged bone and shredded muscle to push his body erect, he kept his eyes closed in concentration against the terrible pain, so he did not see Manon's thin eyebrows curve upward in astonishment, and those night-shade eyes widen ever so slightly.

But then those eyes narrowed again and in their depths sapphire flame leaped and churned as the god unleashed the full measure of his power and sent it crashing into the man.

Aram went down, prone upon the floor.

And now the Sword was a lifeline, the only thing keeping him connected to the moment.

"You think to challenge me?" Manon whispered with fierce dismissal. *"I will crush you to dust."*

And in that terrible instant, Aram knew that he had failed.

328

His bones were mush, his musculature tattered. But even had he retained the fullness of his former strength, there was no opposing a power like that which held him now in utter, pitiless thrall.

With every shredded ounce of strength and courage that remained to him, he desperately gripped the hilt of the Sword of Heaven, and knew that it was futile.

He was beaten.

It had all been for nothing.

Then the Sword began to slip his grip, bit by bit, as the last of his strength ebbed away.

He had borne it all the way across the years and the miles, with the hopes of the free peoples of the world on his shoulders, only to fail utterly.

It had come from the heart of the star that burned in the vast firmament above the mountain of Kelven just to end up in the hand of his enemy.

As he thought of Kelven, his mind abruptly lurched and found a moment of clarity.

Understanding, denied him for all this time, finally came.

Kelven.

Ferros.

What was it they had told him?

In the words of those gods, the Astra had said.

And then, with piercing clearness, Aram knew that he was the most offensive and most dimwitted of fools.

How could he have ever thought that the Sword was meant for him, that he was man enough even to touch this blade, let alone wield it with any authority?

Or use it to slay a god.

He could not.

His intent had been an idiot's errand, impossible to execute.

He had been hopelessly blind and stupid, a hapless, witless worm – or worse, when compared to the awesome presence before whom he lay prostrate.

There was but one recourse left to him.

"Forgive me, my lord," he gasped out. "I beg of you."

The pressure eased ever so slightly though the pull upon the Sword lessened not at all.

"Say it again," Manon commanded.

Aram drew in a raspy, shuddering breath. "I beg my lord's forgiveness," he managed to croak out, in barely audible tones.

The pressure eased further.

"So at last – here at the utmost extremity – you have gained understanding?" The god suggested.

"I am ... and have been ... a fool," Aram admitted.

The pressure upon him lessened substantially, though not the pull upon the weapon.

"*Give it,*" Manon demanded.

There was nothing else to be done. "As you will, my lord," Aram replied hoarsely. Opening his hands, he released his hold upon the Sword of Heaven.

Then he looked up as all the pressure upon him left with the release of the Sword. He watched, transfixed, as the shining blade performed a delicate flip as it arced through the air, turning end-for-end so that the hilt came to rest in Manon's hand.

Relieved of the terrible force that the god had exerted upon him, Aram rose painfully and haltingly up onto his knees and gazed upward, open-mouthed and gasping for air, at the god.

Manon's attention was centered full upon the prize. Slowly, with his blue eyes glowing brightly now, he lifted it in exultation.

Slowly up, and then up, the gleaming blade seemed to have captured the god's full attention. Aram was forgotten in the triumph of the moment.

The tip of the blade continued to rise, angling ever so slowly up toward the unseen heights of the tower as the grim lord lifted it in admiration.

The blade rose further.

And further yet.

A slight frown spoiled the smoothness of Manon's brow.

As the blade rose higher, the wide sleeves of the god's silvery robe slid down his uplifting arms, exposing knotted gray muscle.

Manon's mouth tightened and he glanced over toward Aram, hatred darkening the blue flame in his eyes.

But his attention was jerked immediately back to the Sword.

The grim lord's mouth sagged open; he seemed to gasp or perhaps to scream though no sound issued forth as he struggled with the Sword.

Abruptly, Aram understood.

The Sword was rising on its own.

It was pulling the arms of the god upward.

At first, it was apparent that Manon was attempting to bring the weapon under control; then, as bright golden flame erupted and began twirling along its length, it became obvious that he had turned instead to trying with all his might to wrest his hands loose from it.

But it was to no avail.

The Sword of Heaven had him.

The golden flame began twirling faster and faster along the length of the weapon, and then it expanded down over his hands and along his arms. It slowly engulfed the god from the tips of his fingers and spread all the way down to his feet. Once it reached the floor, the fire suddenly lost its golden glow and flamed green.

Manon's mouth flew completely open, and his head tipped back. He appeared to be howling in absolute torment but Aram heard nothing. This platform, high in the darkness of Manon's tower, remained eerily silent. Even the Sword's quiet song had ceased. The only sound that reached Aram's ears came from inside him, from the distressed pounding of his own battered heart.

Manon could now barely be seen inside the whirling column of bright green flame. Faster and faster it whirled. And then tiny bright lights, lightning-white sparks, began to fly from his body. Visible for only the tiniest moment, these sparks flew outward and then vanished upward, in one moment ascending out of view toward the heights of the tower.

At first hundreds, and then many thousands of these sparks appeared and shot upward to disappear into the darkness above.

Manon's head was cocked back at an impossible angle, his mouth open to emit soundless screams of anguish. The green flame engendered a sudden bulge of emerald fire that shot up into the heights of the structure, trailing behind it a thin ribbon of flame that connected it to Manon. Aram leaned his head back in awe to watch it as it struck like green lightning against the very top of the tower.

The top of the tower, far overhead, was blasted away with the force of that lightning strike. As the fire shot up and into the firmament, the smoky clouds of dust and ash were blown away.

Way up there, the night sky appeared.

The Glittering Sword of God became visible, almost directly overhead.

It seemed to Aram that the thin stream of green flame turned a bit as it shot out into the depths of the black sky, angling toward the black hole in the hilt of that constellation of red and blue stars.

Aram put his hands upon the polished surface and struggled to get his enfeebled legs beneath him so that he might stand upright. With great and pain-filled effort, he managed to lift himself up and to stand, weak, trembling, and shaking, trying to marshal his strength and regain his breath. As he stood, he dropped his gaze to Manon once more.

It was obvious that the end of the grim lord was near.

There were no more of the white sparks, and the rapidly twirling green flame nearly obscured the form of the god.

Manon was being shredded.

His end was upon him.

The destruction of Manon, the grim "Lord of the World" was imminent and inescapable.

And when the god's end came, calamity would come with it. Aram turned, stumbling upon ruined legs and knees, and attempted a plunge for the stairs at the edge of the platform, in order to put something solid between him and impending catastrophe.

Because of his tattered bone and sinew, he failed.

It would not have mattered, anyway.

The detonation behind him was of an explosion so very near and yet so immense that it seemed to have occurred at a terrible, incomprehensible distance. He felt as if he were thrown off the face of the earth and out into dark, bitterly cold outer regions. There was a momentary flash of hideous, unbearable pain as Aram's spirit was stripped of its moorings and his body was blown to dust.

The pain flared beyond the limits of endurance and abruptly ended.

And with the cessation of pain came the cessation of life.

Death, the relentless hunter that had sought him for so long, found him.

The last image registered by his living eyes was of countless tiny points of light scattered far and wide across a black and limitless void, beacons of hope in the vastness of cosmic night.

Then there was only darkness.

332

And silence.

Deep silence, like that which inhabits the darkest hour in the heart of winter's longest night.

Utter.

Cold.

Complete.

51.

Several miles to the south of the scene of the battle, Findaen was jarred nearly upright out of fitful sleep by a severe convulsion of the earth. Rolling out from beneath the wagon where he'd made his bed, he instinctively looked north and gasped in shock.

Rising above the northern horizon was an enormous fireball, pocked with flaming shades of gold, orange, red, and – strangely – green. Expanding with terrible rapidity, as if it meant to engulf the entire world, the awful flaming sphere seemed to churn and enfold upon itself.

He stared in awe at the astonishing, terrifying sight.

It appeared as if the whole northern part of the world was being consumed by hellfire.

And then abruptly, his heart sank within him.

Aram.

Aram was there, beneath that fire, and no one could have survived such conflagration. For it looked as if the entire valley of Morkendril, beyond the line of hills, had gone up in that horrific flame.

For one tiny instant Findaen tried to raise a hope against that which his eyes told him, but it was useless. His spirit plunged downward to join his heart in the depth of despair.

Nothing could live anywhere near that boiling inferno.

Aram, no doubt, was caught in the very heart of it; for he had unquestionably caused it by the employment his unearthly, magical sword.

Findaen felt sick as he stared, stricken, into the north.

Then his eye caught something else.

Outlined against the base of the still-rising fireball, a dark mass moved and appeared to sweep toward him.

He watched this phenomenon wide-eyed for a long moment and then he knew – whatever it was, *it was coming*. And it appeared similar in nature to that which had slain the enemy army in the valley of Morkendril.

Had the grim lord possessed one last weapon to loose against his enemies upon the moment of his defeat?

"Everyone find cover! Now!" He yelled even as he dove for the underside of the wagon.

Moments later, the earth heaved and buckled as if it had suddenly become liquid and a storm wave passed through the abrupt fluidity of it. The ground jumped beneath Findaen and a thick cloud of dust rushed through the army's encampment and tore past them.

Findaen kept his head and eyes covered with his hands until the shock wave and its attendant dust cloud had passed beyond him. Then, finding himself shaken but uninjured, he rolled out from under the wagon and once again looked into the north.

The fireball, though still rising high into the night sky, was fading, growing less distinct by the moment.

And then he knew – the shock wave was the result of the calamitous destruction of Manon. Lord Aram, then, had succeeded in his quest. The grim lord was dead. The world was free.

But Aram was gone.

Something large and massive charged past him, going up the road toward the north.

Thaniel.

The great horse was driving back toward the battlefield to discover what had become of his beloved friend and lord.

Findaen started to call out to him but thought better of it.

He turned instead and ran across the road, past the massed tents from which men erupted in confusion, and out onto the open prairie where they'd left the horses, calling for Andaran. Moments later, he'd mounted up, bareback, and he and Andaran were chasing after Thaniel. Hearing other hooves pounding upon the pavement behind him, Findaen looked back. Others had found their mounts and were following. He could see little in the gloom of night, but one of the riders was a huge man.

Mallet.

For the next hour they hurtled northward through the night, across the flatlands of Bracken, through the small valley, and up into the hills beyond.

The sky lightened in the east before they came to the bridge that spanned the stream between the low hills that tumbled up toward the edge of the battlefield.

The fireball had long since passed away, but the earth – even on the leeward side of the ridge – was charred and scorched, and here and there patches of dry grass still burned along the ridge tops; a testament to its enormous size and intense heat.

The road as it neared the cut through the crest of the crater rim was viscous, and smoking, having been melted by the blast. Avoiding that heated pavement that was still congealing into strange new shapes, Andaran lunged off the road to his right, and up the side of the cut, coming out onto the rocky ridge top to the east.

The horse slid to a stop at the crest of the ridge where, five days before such great issues had been decided, and stamped his hooves in response to the uncomfortable heat in the earth beneath his hooves. The entire slope had been blasted and burned. Little could be seen of the valley in the early morning gloom, but one thing was certain.

The tower was no longer there.

The eastern sky brightened further, losing its pinkish hue in favor of pale blue, gradually resolving details of the valley floor.

"Can you abide the heat?" Findaen asked his mount, noting Andaran's discomfiture at the ground's residual warmth.

"I can abide it," Andaran replied. "I will abide it."

As the light grew, Findaen gazed to his front, down over the valley, and was aghast at what had occurred in the intervening hours between the army's departure and his return.

Nothing was left.

Out in the center of the valley, where hours before had stood the mightiest tower on earth, surrounded by the huts and streets of Morkendril, nothing remained, not even rubble. And the ground was very hot out there, glowing red in the pre-dawn twilight.

As the eastern sky lightened further, casting the first glow of the coming dawn down into the valley, it revealed that there were concentric blackish circles of varying widths coloring the valley floor, spreading out from what had obviously been the epicenter of the blast – Manon's tower. With a shock, Findaen realized that these scattered dark bands of pulverized material were the debris from the destruction of that great tower, evidence of the stupendous force that had blown the massive structure to bits.

Thaniel stood several yards off to his left, beyond the cut on the far side of the melted road, with his head low and his eyes gazing out upon the ruin of the valley. The horse was obviously stunned by what he beheld.

Someone moved up on Findaen's right.

He looked over.

Mallet sat there on Markris, staring out over the valley with tears streaming down his broad face.

Findaen nodded at the big man's sadness as he felt his own eyes well up. He turned his gaze back to the blasted valley and nodded again.

"Truly," he said somberly, "a god died here."

But Mallet shook his head. "No, Fin," he insisted. "It's as I always said about Lord Aram, and I was right – he was a god. He was ever a god. *Two gods died here.*"

Findaen did not argue the point, for the scene before him made him doubt everything he had ever thought of as true where it concerned Aram. After a moment, he shook his head in sorrow.

"Whatever will I tell my sister?" He queried softly.

Others arrived, Edwar, Andar, Thom, Kavnaugh, Jonwood, Boman, Matibar, Olyeg, Marcus, and their mounts, and Nikolus, with Timmon behind him on Jared. They pulled up and halted, to form a line of muted astonishment, gazing out over the evidence of the end of the age of gods on earth, wrought by the man who had led them to this place.

Over on the left, without speaking to or acknowledging the others, Thaniel suddenly wheeled and drove southward, away from the scene of utter devastation. Mallet turned his head and watched him go.

"Poor beast," he said. "What will he do now?"

There was nothing to be done, and nothing more to be seen. It was over. Manon was defeated, destroyed, gone from the earth for all time.

But Aram was gone as well.

One by one, men and horses turned away in sorrow and went back toward the south, toward home and freedom, away from the place that, because of Mallet's words, forever came to be known as The Valley Where Two Gods Died.

52.

It took the army two months to trudge southward across the vastness of the plains, where now the fields that surrounded the scattered villages lay green and full beneath the summer sun. Every man among them knew what had occurred in that valley below the ridge where they all had fought and so many had died.

Each of them knew what had been gained by their struggle and sacrifice, and what had been lost.

The grim lord was gone.

But Lord Aram, the monarch that most of them had known and followed for less than a year, was gone as well.

The world would enter a new age of peace and freedom. But the king, the man who by his leadership and by the final act of his life had wrought this new era of liberty, would not be there to guide the world forward.

Despite the ultimate and total triumph of the Great Campaign there was a taint of bitterness.

The age of gods on earth had ended.

But so had the new age of kings.

It had lasted only as long as the tragically shortened life of one man.

By the end of summer, the army regained the green rolling hills of Cumberland, where Elam would march through their gates and into the south. It would require another two weeks for Duridia, Lamont, and Seneca to traverse the valley of the dry lake, skirt the southern slopes of Burning Mountain, cross over the Broad and come to the fortress.

After reaching the plains of Wallensia, Duridia, Lamont, and Seneca would then file away toward the south and east to disperse to their various homelands. While Duridia would go southward across the rolling prairie, and Lamont would prepare to march eastward; Seneca would make ready to descend toward Durck, to find help in gathering the ships that would take them home.

The army rested for a day upon Cumberland's green while the various leaders discussed the future. After agreeing with the leaders of the newly freed lands of the earth about the need to gather again before winter and decide the future of the world, Findaen saddled up and he and Eoarl went ahead, up the valley, around Burning Mountain, across the plains, and through the green hills to break the terrible news to Ka'en.

Riding north along the valley road, having crossed the twin rivers, Findaen found himself hoping that someone else – one of the hawks, perhaps – had gotten there before him and done the wrenching task of informing his sister that her beloved husband had died in the fulfillment of his destiny. Findaen was greatly ashamed of these cowardly thoughts but nonetheless hoped they were true.

But they reached the city to find his hopes would be dashed. No one else had reached her before him – or had found the courage to tell her.

Cree, if she knew of Aram's death, was nowhere to be found, having left the sad task of relating it to another.

Dunna stood at the top of the stairway as they rode up and dismounted below the wall. The stout little woman flew down the steps to rush into the arms of her husband. She buried her face gladly in Eoarl's ample chest and then kissed him fervently.

"Welcome back, my beloved husband," she cried happily as she leaned back to look up into his face.

Immediately her attitude changed as she saw the expression upon the old farmer's features.

"Our boy?" She asked in alarm.

Eoarl shook his head. "Muray is fine – alive and well."

Dunna studied his face for a moment longer and then turned to Findaen. In that moment, it struck her who it was that was absent. With her voice shaking, she tendered the question. *"Where is Lord Aram?"*

Eoarl glanced at Findaen and then gently enfolded his wife once again into his arms. "I'm afraid he is not coming back, Dunnie girl."

Dunna began sobbing, her round little body convulsing with the strength of her sudden sorrow. "Oh, *Ka'en*," she cried. "That poor lass – what will she do now?" With tears streaming down her cheeks she leaned away and looked beseechingly from Eoarl to Findaen and back again.

Eoarl looked over at Findaen. "Go ahead, my lad – go and do what must be done."

Findaen stared down at the ground and then glanced over at Dunna. "Where is she?"

Choking on her words, Dunna replied, "In the house, just putting the wee one down for her nap. We knew that horses were in the valley and she thought –" Unable to finish, she buried her face once more in Eoarl's chest and wept.

Findaen lowered his eyes once more and stared at the earth beneath his boots. After a moment, he lifted his stricken gaze back to Eoarl. Then he sighed deeply, nodded, and without speaking, turned to climb up the long stairway.

He found Ka'en in the bedroom of the house she had shared with Aram. Hearing a step behind her, Ka'en turned gladly. "Aram?" She raised her eyebrows in surprise but then smiled happily at her brother. "*Fin!* Why –?" She stopped cold as she saw his face. "Fin – what has happened?"

Findaen watched her for a long moment, searching his mind for the right words, then, "Aram is gone, Ka'en," he blurted out.

Her eyes flew wide; she went white. "Gone – where?"

"He died, Sis. He died killing Manon. He succeeded – he killed him, but he died as well."

Her eyes impossibly wide, her face white as ice, she lifted her chin and watched him for a long moment in silence. Then, turning her head away, she went to sit in the chair by the window that looked out over the valley.

She did not look at him as she asked, "Did you see his body?"

Findaen shook his head slowly, then, "No," he admitted, "everything was destroyed in the cataclysm."

She turned fierce eyes upon him. Her face was very pale and her voice shook as she challenged him.

"Then how can you declare him slain?"

She turned away and looked back out over the valley as she drew in several deep shuddering breaths.

341

"Before he went away," she said, "my husband said to me that if anyone told me he had died, that person would be a liar. Yet here you are, my own brother, standing there telling me the most terrible of lies as if it were true."

She looked back, her eyes filled with fierce accusation. They stared at each other as the minutes ticked away. Ka'en's breast rose and fell with the rapidity of her breathing. Findaen felt his own eyes overflow to send rivulets cascading down his face. Finally, he spread his hands wide.

"I would give my life to be a liar," he said.

That ruined her.

Her breath caught and she tightened her grip on the arms of the chair until her knuckles went as white as her face.

Findaen started to go to her but she stood and indicated the door. "You ... should go now. Mae will need her rest."

She turned away from him and stalked, trembling, into the back bedroom of her house.

For a long time, Findaen stood there gazing after her, at the open door through which she had disappeared, wondering if he should go to her.

No sound came to him from that room.

Dunna, he thought then, might be the best person to be with her now. He went to the door, looked back once more, and went out.

When he made his way out into the bright sunshine of the great porch, Alvern and Cree, with Kipwing and two pairs of unknown hawks were sitting close together upon the crenellated turrets of the defensive wall. Alvern spoke quietly to Cree, and then to the hawks and to Kipwing. Kipwing and the hawks then mounted up and flew quickly away, the hawks into the east and south, and Kipwing into the west.

A moment later, Cree also rose and flew past Findaen toward the city's interior.

Alvern remained on the wall, gazing stolidly at Findaen.

"Findaen watched the hawk sail over his head. "Where are you going?" He asked.

"I am going in to the Lady Ka'en," she replied.

Yes, he thought angrily, *now you go to her.*

342

53.

Aram was surprised at the pristine quality of his thoughts.

Not that he could see or even feel anything; there was no awareness of anything physical; the terrible, pervasive cold was sensed rather than felt. Yet his thoughts were clear, precise. Even his memory – wherever it was stored and maintained, for he certainly no longer possessed a brain – of the events of the last few moments of his life was crystal clear.

He remembered Manon's dissolution, and his own; he recalled the pain, and the immediate cessation of his being which followed it.

There was no doubt but that he had died.

Nonetheless, the memory vault of his life, going all the way back to his earliest years as a child upon the western plains, was full and clear, without gaps or missing pieces.

But where was he now?

And how was it that he could be aware of being anywhere?

All was dark. Absolute, utter darkness surrounded him. He could see nothing, hear nothing, and without hands or fingers or feet, feel nothing.

Yet there was an unmistakable sensation of *being.*

After a while yet another sensation began to impinge upon his thoughts – or his consciousness – whatever it was that he had become. This new sensation grew until it was everything.

It was the sensation of speed.

He was flying – no, *shooting* – through the cosmic night with a swiftness that defied comprehension.

With absolutely no point of reference in the vast blackness, still he knew that he was being impelled forward at a rate that defied comprehension and strained credulity.

And then, all at once, light began to grow, not from any particular quarter but from all around him. It strengthened without a specific source. It occurred to him then, rather suddenly, that whatever else he possessed – or lacked – he now had eyes, for he could see.

He could see the light.

With the growing of the light and his ability to comprehend it, the sensation of speed slowed.

The light grew exponentially.

And then all sensation of speed abruptly dissipated.

He now had feet, for he was walking. Arms hung at his side and moved rhythmically as he walked. Wonderingly, he lifted his arms, and his hands appeared before his face. Looking down over himself, he discovered that his body was, in fact, whole and intact.

And he was clothed in a robe of purple.

Looking up once more, he found that the light had grown to the fullness of day, though there was still no sky above him and no sun overhead. He was actually inside an enormous hall, walking along a corridor that was lined with columns that soared far overhead. And way up there, there was a ceiling. Immediately ahead of him, set into a facing wall of cream colored stone or marble, there was a door. It was fully light now; he could see about him plainly. The corridor was wide, but no passages or doorways led off from it to either side.

He turned and looked back.

Far away, back from where he'd come, the corridor grew dim, faded, its features growing ever less distinct as it went away from him, and then darkened to featureless night.

He pivoted back to the front, to face the door towards which he had been walking.

The door was wide and tall, intricately carved with symbols whose meaning eluded him, and was composed of two halves. He reached the door to discover that there was no handle or any other discernable means of opening it. But then, as he reached out to feel of its surface, to run his hand along the loops and whorls carved into its facade, the two halves swung away, as if he was expected in whatever chamber lay beyond.

Aram stepped through the door.

And out into a grand hall.

344

Halting in amazement, he looked around to examine these unexpected new environs. To his right, beyond the massive chamber of the hall, out through yet another row of impressive columns, there stretched a vista of rolling hills and meadows, verged by tall, deep forests of immense hardwoods and conifers mixed together that gradually rose toward the heights of great mountains.

He looked the other way, to his left.

More columns, and a courtyard or veranda, edged by carven stone railings that looked out over a wide, forested valley through the middle of which a lake with many inlets and bays glistened in the light of a sun which he could not see because of the ceiling of the hall arching far overhead.

A voice hailed him, yanking his focus back to his front.

"Lord Aram! Sir! You are most welcome in the House of Humber."

The person that tendered this greeting appeared to be a man, except for the fact that his well-formed, handsome face was a bit too long and his eyes perhaps slightly too large. His hair was the shade of burnished copper, his skin bronze, and he bowed with a grace that belied the presence – and ungainliness – of human limbs.

"We have been expecting you," this person continued. "Lord Humber would have welcomed you himself to his house but – thanks to your efforts – he is quite busy at the moment, in the great hall."

A myriad of questions jostled up to the front of Aram's mind, each urgently begging for resolution. The one that found precedence and subsequent enunciation was,

"You are not Lord Humber?"

The being chuckled at this and bowed once more. "Alas – no. I am Samel, but his humble servant. As I stated, he would have met you himself, except for the many that arrived just before you." Samel swept one hand out to his right, toward Aram's left and the vast veranda overlooking the lake. "If you will, my lord, as we await Lord Humber; there is another that desires an audience with you."

Aram looked in the indicated direction and sucked in a sharp breath. Standing beyond the columns, in the light of the unseen sun, next to the carven railing of the veranda, was Joktan. The king was accompanied by a tall, beautiful woman, beneath a tree in full bloom adorned with countless pinkish blossoms.

Joktan and the woman smiled their welcome to him.

Astonished, Aram began to move that way. "I will gladly see Lord Joktan," he stated; then he realized that he might be giving offense, so he halted and bowed to Samel. "By your leave, sir," he said.

Samel held up his hands in genuine distress. "Please! – Lord Aram – you are not to address me thus. You must not bow to me." As he made this statement, he himself bowed deeply. "I am your humble servant. Employ me to resolve any need that you may have."

Aram gazed at him in surprise and chagrin. "I am not fond of being bowed to myself, sir."

Samel smiled at this and stifled another chuckle. "As is well-known, my lord. As is well-known. Now go, sir." He waved his hand again toward the outside. "I will be here should you find that you require anything."

Aram nodded and turned toward Joktan and the woman. As he passed through the high columns and began to descend the steps, he came out into the sunlight. Sensing something odd about the light, he hesitated and looked up to examine the sky.

To his right, low above the wooded hills that rose above the lake, a huge orange disc was far down in the sky, either about to set or in the act of rising. With no knowledge of his environs, Aram wasn't sure which.

But that great orb wasn't the only source of light in the sky. Almost directly above him was another sun. This one was smaller and gave off brilliant blue light. And there was yet another "sun" in these strange skies. To his left, suspended in the firmament about halfway up the sky there shone a bright yellow sun, much like that to which he was used. This star was also much smaller than the massive orange disc to his right and was similar in size to the blue sun that was shining overhead.

The three very differently colored stars that lit the world of Lord Humber's house were on a line, from east to west, or perhaps it was west to east. The result of this alignment was that no shadows were cast upon the ground, except perhaps beneath very large spreading trees or those trees that were clustered together.

"You will grow used to it," Joktan said, and he laughed as he came toward Aram. The ancient king, looking very hale and hearty – even the gray was gone from his thick black locks and his beard – came to Aram and embraced him.

"Welcome home, my son," he said. "Come – meet my queen."

Holding Aram's arm, he steered him toward the tall, slim woman standing at the railing.

She was fair, with skin like pearl, similar to Ka'en's, and her hair was of a deep chestnut, also like Ka'en's. When these unbidden, comparative thoughts of his wife struck him, Aram flinched and hesitated, causing Joktan to slow and look over.

"Are you alright, my son?"

Aram nodded, but did not speak.

After watching him for a long moment during which Aram tried to swallow his distress, Joktan took his arm once more and continued on toward the woman. "This is my queen, Kressia," he said. Pride saturated his words, but it was also accompanied by something akin to regretful longing.

In response to this introduction, Lady Kressia smiled at her husband and then turned that smile upon Aram.

She seemed genteel, and was extremely beautiful in much the same manner as Ka'en. *My ancestor and I prefer similar women*, Aram thought, and another pang rocked him.

Gulping down yet another portion of unbidden sorrow, Aram inclined his head respectfully. "My lady."

As Joktan went to stand beside her, she took the ancient king's hand in one of hers and extended the other to Aram. "Come," she said, "there is no need for such formality, Aram. You are mine, after all."

Aram stared. "Yours, my lady?"

She smiled. "The child that Florm carried away from Rigar Pyrannis all those many years ago was my grandson, and you are descended from him."

Understanding came, then. She was his direct ancestor, as much as was Joktan. Aram and his own parents – and theirs – had all come from this lovely woman, down through the many years and centuries. He took her hand and bent his lips upon it. As he did so, he felt the welling of strong emotion, and his eyes grew moist.

Lady Kressia evidently felt something similar. When Aram looked up, her smile had gone and her eyes had filled as well. "I am sorry for you, my son," she said then, "and I wish..." She trailed off, unable to finish the sentence.

Aram stared at her. "My lady?"

She squeezed his hand. "You are so like my husband, Aram, in so many ways. You and he both sacrificed much to see justice done upon the earth." She moved closer to Joktan but kept Aram's hand in hers. "You both left the one you loved most dearly to see that thing done that was necessary to do. Such acts require great courage and conviction, but also engender much sorrow – both for yourself and for others. I am sorry for you," she repeated.

Aram met her gaze even as another pang seized at his heart. "I knew the cost," he replied simply.

"I know this about you. And yet you went on, unto the very end." She looked away, down over the splendid valley. "She is alone now. And I am sorry for her, too," her voice caught, "for I know what such loneliness is like."

At this, Joktan let go of her hand and placed his arm around her waist, pulling her even closer.

Aram turned his gaze away also, down over the sparkling waters of the lake and then he lifted his eyes to look beyond, toward the horizon of this new world. Though his thoughts in that moment were somber, full of sadness, still his eyes caught a *strangeness* about the horizon line.

Needing something – anything – to distract from his thoughts of Ka'en, he studied the distant horizon, trying to discern what it was that troubled his eye. Then he knew. Those far away mountains that rose beyond the intervening landscape, silhouetted against the glow from the orange sun, were *too far away*. Either those mighty peaks were massive beyond comprehension, jutting above the curve of the world or – there was no curve to this world at all.

And then he understood. The world upon which he stood, lit by three suns – if not more – the place of residence of Humber, him who was Chief among The Brethren, was enormous, huge beyond imagining. Instead of going from view over the curve of the world, those vast peaks fading into the haze went from view due solely to the effect of distance. Because of its immense size, the curve of this planet was extraordinarily gentle.

Samel came down the steps behind them. Aram turned as Humber's servant bowed and spoke.

"Lord Humber will receive you now, if you will, Lord Aram."

Aram looked at Joktan and Kressia and then nodded. "I will come at once."

As Samel turned away, the three of them followed. Aram looked over at Joktan and frowned. "I did not expect to be addressed as 'lord' in this place," he groused.

At that, Joktan threw back his head and laughed and Kressia seemed amused, even as she blotted the moisture from her eyes. As his laughter trailed away, Joktan grinned over at Aram.

"You must get used to it," he replied. "Other than Humber himself, you are the most important personage to ever come into this house."

Aram stopped and stared and his frown deepened. "That cannot be," he insisted.

Joktan's grin faded as he nodded his head. "And yet it is. None here have ever accomplished anything like that which you have done." He waved his arm about the beautiful, expansive grounds and towering buildings. "All here have been set free from the threat represented by the enormity of unbridled ambition coupled with monstrous evil – by your defeat of Manon."

Aram held up his hand in disagreement. "I did not defeat him," he argued. "I did nothing close to defeating him. I simply gave into his hand that which was the instrument of his destruction." He shrugged. "In the end, I was nothing more than a courier."

Joktan had made to move on, but at this he halted near the top step, looking over at him. His expression was somber. Aram stopped as well, gazing back at his ancestor.

"None else could have done – or would have done – that which you did, Aram," Joktan stated with quiet certainty. "And how did you know that the Sword would destroy him? No one knew this, not even Kelven."

Aram shook his head. "I didn't know – until the end. Then I remembered that which Lord Kelven said – that the Sword was not meant to defeat him but to destroy him. And then I realized that it was meant for his hand all along. My sole accomplishment was in bringing it to him."

Joktan nodded. "Yes," he agreed. "And therein we see the immense majesty of the Maker's thoughts and his plans, for He alone knew that only a man would be allowed by the enemy to approach him so closely." His brow furrowed. "I had come to believe that the reason the Maker intended a man for this task was just for this reason – that a man might get close enough to plunge the weapon into him – without arousing suspicion of a trick. Had any of the Brethren borne the weapon to his tower, Manon would have recognized it as arising from deviousness."

He shook his head. "I should have known that Manon would not allow you to pierce him." The frown went away to be replaced a look of amazement. "And that is why the Maker insisted that it be a man – only then would Manon let the bearer of the weapon into his presence, for he knew that his power would prevent an assault and he could wrest it from him and gain possession of that thing which he had come to lust after."

Joktan looked at Aram with blunt admiration. "And all the deeds that you performed with that blade only made him want it the more – indeed, at the end he lusted after it almost blindly, and accepted it willingly from your hand, believing you to be a fool, little more than a pawn of the gods."

"A pawn." Aram smiled a rueful smile. "That is what I was indeed – a pawn."

Upon hearing this, Joktan's eyes grew severe. "No, not so. The Maker planned this from ancient times. He knew the mind of Manon better than the enemy knew himself. He understood that if a weapon appeared upon the earth, apparently imbued with supernatural power, Manon would come to believe that possession of it would at last render him invincible. And this was the Maker's plan."

He had looked away but now turned once more to face Aram. "All that was needed was a man strong enough and courageous enough to bear the weapon into the presence of evil – most powerful evil. That is what you did, Aram. Do not make light of it, for no one here will do so."

Aram stared back at him for a moment and then he nodded slightly.

Samel, who had stood quietly at the top of the steps, listening to this discussion, now regained their attention. "Come," he said once more. "I beg of you. Lord Humber awaits."

They went back into the vast hall where Samel turned to his left and went deeper into the magnificent, cavernous structure that was the House of Humber. On all sides, as they walked, massive columns of pale golden marble rose up to the height of the ceiling. To the right side of the hall through which they passed, vistas of lush rolling meadows with copses of trees, thickly forested uplands, and distant mountains could be seen.

The other way, stairs swept down from the veranda toward the lake, beyond which the horizon faded from view into the haze of sheer distance.

Then the views out into the surrounding landscapes were cut off as they passed through a large archway and into another vast hall, enclosed on all sides. Far above, multi-hued sunlight streamed in through colored panes.

Here, there were many people.

Dressed in fine robes, they were all of a kind, slender, tall, well-formed, and beautiful. They were not human; this much Aram's keen eye observed; they were creatures of a higher order. The males were clean-shaven, though most had long flowing hair of varying shades; most of the females wore their hair, also of different hues and lengths, in braids.

Every one of them turned toward Aram, Joktan, and Kressia as they entered the room.

Samel immediately moved to one side. Bowing, he swept his hand in a grand gesture toward the newcomers.

"Lord Aram has arrived," he stated sonorously.

Aram felt chagrin and irritation rise in him at this flourishing introduction. Already uncomfortable at finding himself in such grand company, and in such a grand place, he had hoped to confer with Humber – who apparently wished to meet with him – in relative privacy.

But such was not to be.

The first of the gathered Brethren to separate himself from the company and come forward, Aram knew instantly.

He inclined his head as the god drew near. "Lord Kelven."

Kelven halted some few paces away and studied him closely for a long moment. "I doubted you, you know," he said.

Aram smiled wryly. "I doubted myself, many times."

Kelven did not return the smile.

"I was wrong," the god admitted freely. "And I have never been happier to be proved so." He cocked his head. "You knew what was meant by Lord Humber's instruction even when I did not."

Aram frowned at him. "My lord?"

"That the sword would destroy the enemy simply by being delivered into his hand," Kelven explained. "You understood this – while I did not."

Aram shrugged and shook his head. "I did not understand it myself until the very end – when I remembered your words, my lord. Until that moment, I was striving with all my strength to pierce him."

Kelven came forward then, and to Aram's immense surprise, embraced him. "Welcome home," he said. "I thank you."

"It was nothing, my lord," Aram replied, taken aback. "It was simply that which I had to do."

Releasing him, Kelven stepped back. "Yes, we have come to expect such sentiment from you, myself but lately." He studied Aram once more for a long moment. "You paid a great price to free the world – indeed the universe – of the enemy's malice."

Aram glanced over at Kressia before answering. "I knew the cost," he stated quietly.

Kelven did not reply to this but simply moved to one side and motioned with his hand. "Come, Aram – meet Lord Humber."

As they went forward toward the gathered company of gods, Aram had little trouble knowing which of them was master of the fine house. They had aligned themselves in a wide semi-circle and Lord Humber stood in the center of this crescent.

The First among the gods was tall, with pale, almost golden skin, auburn hair, and eyes that were the color of polished bronze. He was clad in purple and his robes were lined with white. Next to him stood a female who was nearly as tall as he, also dressed in purple and white. Her skin was fair and her hair was reddish-gold and very long, done up in two long braids that hung down her front.

Aram approached until Kelven, walking next to him, halted, and then he halted as well and inclined his head in respect. "Lord Humber."

Humber stepped back and to the side, holding out his hand. "Walk with me," he said.

The company parted to allow Aram to walk through, and he and Humber went further into the palace. Humber was silent as they traversed along an opulently furnished hallway. Then they came into a circular room that opened to the right out onto a broad area paved with marble from which there led away in several directions, wide, paved roadways or pathways.

Facing this area, just inside the parameters of the structure itself, there was a raised dais. Humber turned toward this wide, paved area that stretched out beneath the sky and halted upon the dais. Folding his hands behind him, he seemed to examine the many pathways that radiated out from that broad area like the spokes of a wheel.

It was then that Aram noticed the travelers. Far out along each of those pathways, there were many people, thousands. Walking singly, in pairs, and even in small groups, they were making their way from the House of Humber and toward the various horizons of this vast world.

"They owe you much," Humber stated, without explanation. His voice was deeply modulated, musical in its baritone aspect.

Aram looked at him curiously. "Who, my lord? Who would owe me anything?"

Humber inclined his head slightly, indicating the multitudes, some of whom were just now passing from view along the various thoroughfares. "They."

Aram frowned out across the lush landscape, puzzling over why strangers passing along those distant paths would be in any way beholden to him. "Who are they?"

"They were the prisoners of Manon. Their souls were his captives. He swallowed the essence of each of them upon death and held them in thrall, drawing upon their life force to increase his own power." His voice changed abruptly and grew harsh as he hesitated for a moment and then spat out a single word. "*Despicable.*"

Aram studied Humber in silence and then dared to enquire. "They were set free upon his death?"

"His dissolution, yes," Humber said. The god looked at Aram. "You set them free."

After a moment, Aram cautiously shook his head. "The sword released them, my lord; I did nothing but bear it there."

Humber continued to gaze at him. "I have come to know you, I think, through the many reports that came to me. I see now what the Maker saw in you when He chose you for this task." Without looking away, he swept his hand out over the countryside. "And that is why I released them – after I told them of him to whom they owe so much – without causing you to face those who benefitted from your actions."

Aram stared after the multitude. "Is my sister among them?"

"She is."

Aram looked at him. "I would like to see her," he said.

Humber nodded. "And you will, in a short while. Your earthly parents live here, upon El-ilysia, in a village on the shores of the western sea. She is being taken there to join them. I need you to remain here with me for a time." The god hesitated and looked away, studying the multitudes gradually disappearing into the distance. "I also thought, perhaps, that it might be wiser to let them have some time together before you visit them. Besides, there was difficulty in presenting you to her without the others knowing who you are as well."

Aram thought about that and then nodded. "I appreciate your consideration, my lord."

Humber turned and watched him for a moment longer and then indicated the interior of his house. "You cannot escape this, however. My brothers and sisters will want to know you, and speak with you, the Lady Elana – my consort – first and foremost of all." A slight smile played around the corners of the god's mouth. "We will dine, and then I will rescue you at a time appropriate, for there are others here that you will wish to see."

Without offering an explanation of this statement, he turned and went back through the house toward the great hall. After taking one last look out over the landscape, Aram followed.

The dining hall of Humber's grand house was situated on the side of the palace opposite the rolling grasslands, and looked out over the valley of the lake through high, floor-to-ceiling windows.

Aram was seated on Humber's right, next to Kressia and Joktan, and opposite Elana, the consort of Humber, who plied him in her gentle voice with many questions. To Aram's surprise, this elegant goddess managed to draw him out, compelling him – unwilling though he was – to speak at length and without inhibition of Ka'en and his daughter, and of his life on earth.

When they had supped on fruits and nuts, and delicately-flavored vegetables – there was no meat – and drank of something that Aram was fairly certain was wine, but of a much finer quality than he had ever known, the company abandoned the table for the veranda that looked down upon the lake.

Humber stayed near Aram as one after another, the members of the company engaged him in conversation, though the Chief of the Brethren said little himself. Finally, he gained everyone's attention and stated firmly, "Lord Aram has other friends here, in my house, with whom he will wish to commune. There will be ample time ahead of us to learn him better as he settles into his long home."

Thus speaking, Humber took Aram's arm and guided him back up and through the house to the place where they'd stood earlier and watched the former prisoners of Manon stream away to the horizons. Reaching the dais, Humber then turned off to the right and made his way, followed by Aram, along a broad veranda that fronted that side of the structure. Eventually, they came to where steps led down from it and directly onto the grassy meadows that stretched away toward darkly forested hills and the vast high mountains beyond.

Humber halted and pointed, stretching out his arm.

"There," he said simply.

Aram looked in the direction that was indicated and immediately sucked in a sharp breath of gladness and amazement. Silhouetted upon a rise, perhaps a half-mile from where they stood, two horses gazed back at them.

Florm and Ashal.

"Go," said Humber. "Greet your friends, but return here soon, if you will."

"Thank you, my lord," Aram answered, and he immediately went down the steps and began to sprint toward the horses.

Florm and Ashal sped toward him, pounding through the tall grasses. He stopped upon the crest of a small rise as they came up. Aram wordlessly threw his arms around their necks, holding back tears as great emotion rose within him. Finally, unable to contain it longer, he sobbed.

After a while, he stepped back and wiped at his eyes.

"I am sorry, my friends," he said.

Florm arched his neck. "This is how you greet an old friend?" He demanded. "With an apology?"

"Yes," Aram replied. "Because I was not there for you when I was needed."

"Oh – I think I see." Florm stared at him. "When the dragons came, you mean? You blame yourself for that?"

"I wasted time examining the use of a new weapon at the fortress," Aram explained. "Had I been there sooner, I could have slain them before they found you and Lady Ashal."

Florm snorted. "Even you, Aram, cannot be in all places at all times." He lowered his head and spoke more gently. "You cannot be blamed, my great friend, for our deaths upon the earth. My spouse and I are together, never to be parted again. And I, for one, was ready to come to my long home. It is right and fitting that we are here now."

The great horse gazed at Aram and then shook his head in wonder. "As for you – Lord Humber has informed us of your deeds, of how you slew the dragons and then destroyed the enemy of the world. We are all amazed, as is everyone in that grand house." He went silent for a moment, watching Aram.

"It is you, my friend, that has given the most," he went on. "As has your mate. Is Lady Ka'en alright?"

Aram shook his head. "I cannot know the answer to that," he said. "I left her in the care of her brother and your fine son."

Ashal's large eyes went soft. "I am sorry for you, Lord Aram – and for her. It is a great sacrifice."

"I knew the cost," Aram repeated for the third time.

"Yes," Ashal agreed, "I believe that you did. But she is paying that cost as well as you."

At this, another pang struck Aram's heart and he closed his eyes in sorrow. "At least she is safe and free," was all he could think to say.

Silence fell between them for a while and then Florm, feeling the need to move the conversation elsewhere, lifted his head and looked toward the grand palace that dominated the skyline. After a moment, he chuckled softly. "Those in that great house do not know what to do with you," he stated.

Aram frowned at him. "Do with me? What do you mean?"

"Your people – and ours – have been coming through the long doorway since time began," Florm explained. "Most that come here settle among the towns and villages of this world into a life of peace and productivity. Others, after a time, go on to other worlds, where there are new and different, and perhaps more difficult, things to do. And some seek assignment into whatever tasks suit them – here, or on one of those other worlds."

He chuckled again quietly as he continued. "No one of your stature has ever come here, my friend, and they are at a loss as to protocol. They cannot simply assign you to this place, or that, or offer you any task worthy of your attention. Even Lord Humber is perplexed. It is said that they have sent a delegation to find the Maker and seek his counsel."

Aram turned around to look at the House. "The long doorway? That is what I came through?"

"It is the passageway from life to life, through death's shadow, when one leaves the world of his birth to enter into eternity," Florm told him. "It is said the Maker constructed it with His own hand."

"Would that I could return along it," Aram said softly.

Florm was silent for a moment, then, "I understand, my friend, but it is a journey that is taken in but one direction, and that is from there to here," the horse stated gently. "I am sorry, Aram."

Aram shrugged and repeated the words yet again, "I knew the cost."

"How is Thaniel?" Ashal asked him. "How was our son when last you saw him?"

Aram turned and smiled at her as his eyes filled again. "Willing, as always, to bear me where I would, even if it meant that he would die with me," he replied. "He wanted to go with me to face Manon, but there was no reason for him to do so. Besides, he is too large to go to the place where I met the grim lord, high up in his tower." Aram lifted his gaze toward the distant mountains as his thoughts turned to his friend. "The world will need him in the years to come. I am glad he is there still."

Florm abruptly turned his head as a movement caught his attention. He looked to his right, to Aram's left, at the forests that rose tall, deep, and dark at the verge of the grasslands. "Over there is someone who will be overjoyed to see your face, and to hear your voice."

"Who?" Aram pivoted that way also, curious as to who it was that had gained the horse's attention.

"As faithful a servant as you ever commanded, my friend," Florm replied.

Two wolves stood at the edge of the trees, a large black male and a smaller, gray female.

"Durlrang," Aram stated in wonder.

"Go to him," Florm suggested. "Lady Ashal and I will await you here."

The old wolf fairly quivered with joy when Aram drew near. After nodding to the female, Aram knelt and threw his arms around Durlrang's neck.

"It is good to see you, my friend," he said, and his voice was choked with emotion.

"And you, master," the wolf replied.

Aram leaned back and looked into his eyes. He shook his head. "I am not your master, Lord Durlrang – I am your friend. I was ever your friend." He looked at the female. "Is this your mate?"

"This is Reuning," Durlrang answered.

Aram nodded solemnly. "I am pleased to meet you, my lady," he stated. "Your mate is one of my oldest and dearest friends. He saved my life upon the earth – and that of my lady – by the giving of his."

Reuning bowed her head over. "It is a great honor to meet you, Lord Aram. The winds of this world and the voices of its forests are alive with the tales of your deeds."

Durlrang laughed quietly. "Even the gods stand in awe of you, master."

Aram turned a severe look upon him. "*Friend*," he said again. "I am not your master – I am your friend. And I have seldom been prouder of any other thing."

At this firm statement of Aram's, Reuning turned a look of amazement upon her spouse. Aram saw it and nodded. "Oh, yes, my lady, Lord Durlrang had as much to do with bringing down the grim lord as any of us."

He turned back to Durlrang. "But enough of that which lies behind us. Are you content, my friend?"

"I am, mast – *Lord Aram*. The woods here are dark and deep, and much to my liking," Durlrang replied. "Lord Humber has given us permission to remain here if we wish."

"And will you?"

Durlrang looked at Reuning and then turned his head to gaze into the lush darkness behind him. "We will," he said.

They talked for a while longer, and then Aram remembered his promise to return to the house. He embraced Durlrang once more as he took his leave. "I will return as soon as I may," he promised.

Florm and Ashal walked with him as he turned his steps toward the grand house of the king of the gods.

54.

Humber stood with his hands folded behind him, and pondered the problem before him, as he watched the man, Aram, renew his acquaintance with the horses and the wolf.

For so long, the universe had stood upon the edge of civil war. Manon had made no secret of his desire to unseat Humber and challenge the Maker Himself, in order that he might be exalted as undisputed ruler of everything.

Humber had grown wary of Manon's power, which expanded to unimaginable proportions with every delving of the Grim Brother into forbidden arts. And the Maker – other than designing and issuing the command for the construction of the weapon – had seemed aloof, distant, as if He did not truly see the threat posed by His wayward child.

And when the Maker insisted that the weapon He had designed be placed into the hands of a mere man, Humber's doubts and unease grew. Besides, at the time, there was no man chosen to wield the weapon. Nor did one come along, though ever so diligently he was looked for. Upon the earth, centuries passed away. The power of the enemy expanded to the point where it was but a matter of time before he subdued all the earth and turned his attention to the stars.

And still no man came that met the Maker's criteria.

Humber's unease – as he found himself, century after century, reduced to a mere spectator – expanded beyond bearing. And as Manon grew in strength, without challenge, doubts about the Maker's designs began to surface among the ranks of the Brethren. There were even a few that expressed the opinion that it had now become necessary to treat with their Grim Brother.

Humber harshly put down all such suggestions even as his own doubts multiplied.

And then – this man came.

When Aram appeared upon the earth, the Maker sent word that a man had been chosen and it was time to make the attempt at ending the threat posed by Manon. Humber gave the instruction, and the Maker's servants, the Astra, took Aram into the place of the weapon's making, that he might seek to wield the blade.

Even though Aram proved himself strong enough to wrest the weapon from the bosom of the star, Humber had worried. Loathe as he was to question the instructions of the Maker, he had nonetheless believed it to be a foolhardy plan. Unlike the rest of the Brethren, the king of the gods had suspected – though without certain knowledge – the real reason for the making of the weapon and what it would do if given into Manon's hand.

But Humber was prevented from passing along exact instructions for the weapon, limited to informing the man – through Kelven – that it was "meant to destroy the enemy, not to defeat him".

Then the man was abandoned to the tenuous wisdom of his own instincts.

The weapon in hand, he was left utterly without guidance.

To Humber's great surprise, the man's instincts had proved unerring.

Forced to simply observe without interference, Humber had watched as Aram moved forward with the weapon in hand, always seeming to find the right thing to do, and doing it. He persevered even when doing that right thing endangered his chances of keeping his own dreams of a life of peace and quiet safe and viable.

At the last, the man had faced his doom with courage and tenacity, astonishing the Eldest of the Brethren with his willingness to suffer ultimate loss in the destruction of evil.

Humber had watched in awe as the final moments of the Maker's plan played out – awe not only for the sublime intricacy of the Maker's design, but also for the courage and determination of the man who wrought its success.

And now the man had come to him. What would he do with him?

The universe was immense, with many worlds, and it was the Maker's oft-expressed desire that all of them eventually fill up with vibrant life. Normally, then, when the inhabitants of Ayden that lived worthy lives upon that world came to the House of Humber, he made them welcome, and gave them to understand their options as free people. They stayed or moved on, as they would.

But where would he put this man?

No one of this man's stature had ever arrived upon the shores of eternity.

It was not that Aram possessed the strength or mental power of any of the Older Children – he was, after all, a member of the youngest race of the Maker's creatures. It was that he had simply persisted in doing what was right despite knowing the enormity of the cost to himself.

And in doing so, he had brought down the greatest evil to ever threaten the peace of the universe.

Humber looked over as his consort, Elana, moved up beside him. The goddess met his gaze for a moment and then she also looked out at the reunion taking place upon the prairie before her home.

"There is no purpose in fretting over this good man, my lord," she said quietly. "His sorrow is too deep, and there is nothing we can do or say to assuage it."

Humber turned a frown upon her. "My house has no room in it for sorrow," he stated in severe tones. "It is the destination that all people from Ayden seek to find, for here, in this place, is the end of sorrow."

Elana nodded. "In almost every case; this is true," she agreed. "But it was not so with Kressia. Long she waited – *in sorrow* – for Joktan. It is the same with this man. His sorrow came with him through the long doorway, and it will not abandon him until *she* comes as well."

Humber's frown deepened. "She?"

"His consort – Ka'en, the woman." Elana looked at him reprovingly. "Did you not hear him when he spoke of her, my lord? His words were filled with love – love that is as yet unfulfilled and will remain so until he is reunited with her. His life is there, with her, unfinished, upon the shores of Ayden. He will never be content here without her."

His brow furrowed more deeply yet, and his tone hardened. "What would you have me do? I cannot send him back – you know this." He went silent for a moment and then, "The lives of humans are not long these days," he suggested. "She will be along soon enough, and then his sorrow will vanish."

Elana was quiet for a time, watching the distant reunion of friends. Then she slipped her arm through his and spoke.

"You are wise and powerful," she said to him, "but I think you understand little of the younger children. And I know that you cannot return him to Ayden, but what seems a short time to you, my lord, will seem very long to him – and to her. Kressia suffered centuries of sorrow and loneliness as she waited for Joktan. Despite being here, in your house; in the end, her sadness seemed to her to be without end, as eternal as the shores of this world."

Humber emitted an exhalation of frustration. "It is perhaps undeniably true that I do not understand the Maker's younger children, nor was I given governance over them, even though my House is their destination once mortal life ends," he admitted and shook his head. "So, then – what do I do with this man?"

When she did not reply, he looked at her and frowned. "As for Joktan remaining upon Ayden after his death, leaving his consort to wait and wonder – that was his choice, and his alone."

She nodded. "Yes, for Joktan knew that once he journeyed here through the doorway, any chance of affecting events upon Ayden was lost. It is the reason Kelven also made the same choice." She lifted one hand and indicated Aram, who was walking slowly toward them over the rolling prairie, accompanied by the horses. "And their choices led directly to that man's choice – which led to the removal of the threat of war that has hung over us for millennia. We owe these men, and perhaps even Kelven, something for such great and willing sacrifice – of which we are the beneficiaries – do we not, my lord?"

Humber shook his head again. "Lord Kelven's reward is the satisfaction that at long last judgment has been rendered upon his enemy. It is the same for Joktan; besides that – *he* is now home." He looked back toward Aram. "As for that man? I would deny him nothing that is in my power to give. But if that what you claim as his greatest desire be true, then it is a thing not in my power to confer. It seems then that I can offer him nothing."

He turned his gaze upon her. "Or would you have me meddle in affairs that are beyond my authority, and bring his woman through the doorway before her time?"

"No, my lord, of course I would not have you do so." She slid her hand down his arm, taking his hand, and sighed. "He has done so much for us; I would that we could repay him in kind."

"I have done what I could," Humber replied. "I have sent word to the Maker to seek His instruction."

"May His wisdom suffice to ease this man's sorrow," she said.

Humber did not respond to this but fell silent.

Out at the edge of the pavement, Aram bade farewell to the horses and turned toward the house. At that moment, the air crackled with energy to Humber's left, causing the god to look that way.

Four Astra appeared.

"Greetings, Lord Humber," the echoed voices of Terro and Firezza thundered softly.

"Greetings, my lords," Humber replied. "Do you come from the Maker?"

"We do."

Humber gazed at them narrowly. "He has heard my request for instruction concerning the man, Aram?"

"He has." The Astra turned as one to watch Aram as he came toward them. "This man is to be returned to Ayden. The Maker desires that the inhabitants of that world benefit from his strength and knowledge in the years that lie before them."

Humber stiffened at this and stared. "I do not know how to accomplish such a thing," he protested. "No one has ever returned along the doorway."

"The Maker designed the long doorway, and built it with His own hands," the Astra reminded him. "He knows what must be done to return the man along the doorway and has instructed us. We will return him if he chooses, but the Maker has given to you the task of convincing him to go."

"According to Elana, there is little doubt as to that which he will decide." Humber watched them for a moment and then looked at his consort and smiled. "It seems as if you will get your wish – the man will be returned to his woman and to his earthly home."

"He must return to the place of his death," the Astra stated.

Humber pivoted to face them and looked at them in dismay. "But that place is far across the surface of that world from his home. Why must he return to that place? Why not return him to his home?"

"He cannot use the body he now inhabits when he returns to Ayden," the echoed voices insisted. "The scattered essences of his former existence remain in the place where he was slain; it is only there that he may be renewed as a human."

Elana moved up beside Humber. "Cannot you – or perhaps Ligurian and Tiberion – transport him from thence to his home once he is made whole again?" She inquired.

"The instruction from the Maker is clear," the Astra replied. "We are to return him to that place and leave him. We are then to inform two persons of his return and our task is ended. The Maker desires that there be no further interference in the affairs of that world."

"Will you at least provide him with a cloak, food and water, perhaps a weapon?"

"He may have only what can be reconstituted from that which he contained on his person at the time of his death," the Astra replied. "We cannot do more."

The Astra glanced once more at Aram and began to fade. "We will prepare to make the journey, should he so desire, Lord Humber. The Maker desires that it proceed at once. We leave him in your care."

Humber nodded and turned to Elana. "If you will, let me speak to him alone."

"As you wish, my lord."

55.

Aram bade Florm and Ashal farewell where the grass ended and the stonework began. "I will return when Lord Humber has finished with me," he told the horses.

As he walked toward the house, he thought he saw the Guardians appear for just a moment and then fade away, but it might have been a trick of the light; his eyes were still not adjusted to a sky with three suns. Besides, no doubt those creatures often came here.

He looked around. Despite the hollow emptiness of his heart he found himself curious about the configurations of the shores upon which death and destiny had cast him.

Whether it was because of the blended light of triple suns or another reason, the landscape that stretched away from him on all sides, though similar to earth in that there were forests and hills and the even greater heights of mountains as it went away to mysterious, haze-shrouded distances, it glowed with richness, both of color and of vibrancy, that seemed beyond his ability to fathom.

With no clear horizon line upon which the eye could fasten, he found it difficult to comprehend or even *sense* the vastness of the world upon whose surface he walked. It was as if the proud house of Humber – which was itself magnificent beyond comprehension – rested on a magical palette of such splendor that its true nature, and attendant reality, defied the powers of observation.

He knew that he ought to be grateful that, after all the travail, he had arrived in such a beautiful place, but the searing pang of loss in his heart would not subside.

The worst of it was that, by now, Ka'en would know that he had lied when he gave her his promise to return to her. That thought tore his gaze from the mysterious far reaches of Humber's world and cast it to the ground, making his stride falter and slow. What would she think of him now? Would a sense of abandonment mar her grief and taint her memories of him?

And what would her life be like in the years left to her, raising their child alone?

He looked up again. Lord Humber stood alone on the broad veranda that surrounded his magnificent house, obviously awaiting him. Craving distraction, he quickened his pace and tried to put the thoughts of his former life aside for the moment.

He climbed the steps and inclined his head to the chief of the gods.

Humber waved one hand as he turned and moved along the veranda, away from the dais, repeating his words of earlier. "Walk with me."

Humber was silent for several moments as they walked along together, and then he said without preamble, "The Maker desires that you return to Ayden – to the earth," he stated quietly.

Aram froze.

Humber went on for a step and then stopped and turned to look at him. "Does this thought trouble you?" He asked.

Aram stared at him, violent hope surging in his breast. "My lord – you stated – if I heard you properly –"

Humber nodded solemnly. "The Maker desires that you return to your life upon the world of your birth."

"Is that – *possible*, my lord?" Aram just managed to ask it, blurting it out; terrified of speaking the question, afraid that the response would belie that which he had heard. And he was equally terrified of giving in to believing the unbelievable promise that his greatest desire might be granted, in case it was all for naught. He did not want to state the contradiction but knew that he must. "I was told that the 'long doorway' as it is named, was a journey that could be taken in one direction only."

"And so has it always been," the god agreed. Then Humber smiled a slight smile. "The Maker, of course, may do as He likes – and He constructed the doorway by His own hand."

The smile faded and the god lifted one hand and pointed back along the way they'd come. "His servants are here, now, preparing for your return along the passageway. All that is required is your consent to make the journey."

Aram felt his knees buckle. "My lord … *yes* – I wish to return to earth if I may."

Humber's smile returned, wry and cool. "You do not approve of my house, Aram?"

Realizing, despite the shock of the previous few moments, that the statement was delivered in jest, Aram managed to smile in return. "It is beautiful, my lord, and you and your lady are most gracious. I hope to return here someday, but …," He swallowed and looked away, out toward where he'd left Florm and Ashal. The horses had moved away and had gone from view.

He looked back at the god, who was studying him closely. Aram inclined his head in gratitude. "My life is there, and I am grateful for the opportunity to finish it."

"You may offer your thanks to the Maker," Humber replied. "For it is His doing." He looked back out across the rolling prairie. "You should perhaps bid your friends farewell, but be quick, I beg you; the Astra are anxious to complete the process. Time moves differently upon Ayden than here; it will be the changing of the seasons by the time you return to that land."

Aram immediately swung to his left, down off the veranda. He was running by the time he descended the steps and reached the paved area that led out toward the surrounding grasslands. "I will return shortly, my lord."

Though astonished at the unlikely turn of events, Florm, Ashal, Durlrang, and Reuning all expressed their gladness at Aram's altered fortune and bade him farewell until that time in the future when they would all once again be together.

"Give our love to our son – and your lady," Ashal requested.

"I will, my lady. Farewell," Aram told them all. He met every pair of eyes, and then embraced each neck as opposing emotions of elation and the sorrow of parting surged within him.

Stepping back, he gazed at them all for a long moment with moisture-laden eyes. "Until we meet again, my friends," he said.

Then he turned away toward Humber's house – and home.

The Guardians, along with Humber, Elana, Kelven, Joktan, and Kressia awaited him near the door that led back along the strange pathway through which he would fly from the heavens and back to the earth – and the bosom of the woman he loved.

Kressia embraced him. "I am happy for you – and her," she said tearfully. "You are my son and so she is my daughter. Give her my love."

"I will, my lady," Aram promised.

Joktan gazed at him with serious eyes. "You will return to earth as more than a legend, my son; you will return as a cause for astonishment. What is most important is that you will be king." He bowed slightly. "Rule well and wisely. I have nothing of wisdom to offer you – you have proven yourself without need of either counsel or guidance." He smiled, though the expression contained a hint of sadness. "I will miss you, my son. I told you once that you were the best of us. Go now, and prove my words."

He stepped forward and embraced Aram tightly. "The grace of the Maker go with you," he said, and then he stepped back and smiled again. "I will miss our talks," he admitted.

Aram gazed into his ancestor's eyes and returned the smile. "It is a loss, my lord, which I will feel more keenly than you."

Kelven reached out then and touched him on the arm. "I will visit your parents, Aram, and tell them of you."

Aram looked at him in grateful surprise. "Thank you, my lord."

The Astra moved toward the door, prompting Humber to say, "It is time to go." The Eldest of the Brethren smiled. "When next you come to my house, perhaps you will stay longer."

Aram inclined his head. "I will. Thank you, Lord Humber, for everything."

He turned toward Ligurian and Tiberion, awaiting him by the door with Terro and Firezza. "Once again, my lords, you have come to my rescue. I am most grateful."

Ligurian and Tiberion nodded silently and then Terro and Firezza spoke. "It will be very cold and there will be pain as you make this journey. At the journey's end, when you again find yourself upon Ayden, you may suffer confusion. Like the pain, however, it will last but for a short time. As you have been told by Lord Humber, no provision can be made for you; we may restore only those things which you wore and bore with you when you entered the tower. We cannot restore that which you name the Sword of Heaven, nor the armor that accompanied its possession –

both were destroyed in the accomplishment of their purpose. Do you understand?"

Aram nodded. "I understand."

"And you wish to return to the earth?"

"I do."

The Astra separated into pairs, Ligurian and Tiberion to one side of the door, and Terro and Firezza to the other.

The door opened.

The Astra spread their wings and enfolded him.

"Then let us go."

Aram stepped through the door.

56.

There was an immediate sensation of tremendous, rapidly accelerating speed. The light faded quickly and the darkness grew until it overwhelmed his senses.

Sight failed, as did all perception of being.

Still, though, he could feel.

Cold.

And pain.

Both sensations increased to unbearable levels, as did the sensation of speed. And still he flew onward, faster, and faster.

On and on, until the cold and the pain overwhelmed him and the sensation of incomprehensible speed coiled his thoughts into tangled ribbons of confusion.

Then, abruptly, there was nothing.

Only a stillness.

The awful pain faded slowly away as his thoughts gradually untangled themselves and found cohesion. The pervasive cold, however, became something more than a sensation then. It was tangible, real, and he felt it with his being, in his fingers especially, and his toes inside his boots.

With his body.

He was corporeal once more.

Light found his senses and strengthened.

He opened his eyes.

And saw the dawning of a familiar yellow sun.

Its strengthening light seemed to be filtered through a haze.

He was lying on his back, upon a hard, rocky surface. Rolling over, he got stiffly to his hands and knees and gazed about him. He was near the middle of a vast wide valley that was surrounded on three sides by mountains and on the other side – which the position of the rising sun told him was south – by a ring of low hills, like the rim of a crater.

Understanding came, not gradually, but in a flash.

This was Manon's valley, the seat of his power upon the earth. But where were the grim lord's tower, and the city that had surrounded it? Though he gazed about him in all directions, there was nothing to be seen upon the valley floor. Everything that Manon had built was gone, apparently demolished in the cataclysmic event of his disembodiment.

Carefully, painfully, feeling every nerve of his reconstituted body, Aram got to his feet, stretched his limbs, and faced south. His boots stood upon slick, glassy rock, blasted to the appearance and consistency of lava by the heat of Manon's dissolution. He looked around in all directions. The valley was empty and void. All that had once existed here was gone.

He pulled his cloak close against the coolness of the morning as understanding reached its fullness. To verify that understanding, he looked once more at the position of the rising sun, which his familiarity with this region told him was well off to the south of due east.

Humber had told him truly. Time moved differently upon the earth than upon the shores of eternity. He had been in Humber's house for what seemed but a day. Much more time had passed here. Summer was gone; it was autumn now. Soon, winter would feel its way out of the mountains behind him with icy fingers and grip this land with a frozen fist.

His army was gone. By now, it had gone far into the south, maybe even had made its way home.

He looked around the desolate valley one last time, pulled up his collar and turned to face the southeast.

Ka'en was there, far beyond that horizon.

A thousand miles or more away.

It mattered not. Aram had made many arduous journeys in his life, and it occurred to him that each of those journeys had led to her, even when he hadn't known it to be so, even those made before he knew her.

This was just one more such journey, and he would make it more gladly than any other.

He began to move, and as his muscles remembered forgotten abilities, his stride quickened and lengthened. He had far to go; he wasn't sure how much of the autumn had passed, and he needed to stay ahead of the winter if possible.

He had no food or water, only the clothing he'd worn when he'd come north with the army. But there was one thing more. Something pushed at his waist as he walked, causing intermittent pressure. As he reached inside his cloak, his fingers closed upon the dagger that had been in his belt. At least there was that.

He wasn't overly concerned about finding water, the hills and hollows to the south would undoubtedly provide. But he would need food and fire, neither of which would come to him easily – a dagger was little use in catching game, and he had not borne the means of making fire upon his person at the time of his death.

Still, despite these difficulties, his heart soared within him.

He was walking toward Ka'en.

He was going home.

The sun had slid past mid-day and was angling westward by the time he climbed the crater walls and came out of the valley. Standing atop the ridge where, some weeks or perhaps months ago, his army had faced Manon's minions, Aram looked toward the southeast, at the many miles of country through which he would journey on his way to Ka'en.

Hills tumbled up on his left. Just beyond them was the valley through which flowed the Secesh River on its way into and through Bracken. To his right, along the tangent of the road his army had travelled on its way here, beyond another low rise, he could see a broad swath of the land of Bracken itself.

He hesitated only a moment before choosing the hills to his left over the flatter, more-easily travelled plains. That way led more directly home.

He glanced up at the sun and then made his way along the ridge top and up into the higher ground beyond. Very little grew here. There were scattered, very scraggly junipers in some of the draws, but by and large, except for grass, the hills to the south of Manon's valley were barren and appeared to have been burned.

By evening, as the sun sank toward the western horizon, he was still among the hills, trudging toward the southeast. The farther he progressed from the valley, the more vegetation, grasses, bushes, and even trees, thickened upon the hills, though the trees, mostly juniper, were clustered mainly in the hollows.

He crossed the heights of a ridge, noted the proximity of the sun to the horizon and decided to descend into a hollow, in order to find a reasonable spot to pass the night. He was tired and hungry – and unwary; even as he smelled the smoke, he did not ascribe any meaning to it.

Finding the bottom of the hollow, he turned left, toward the smell of smoke. Perhaps it was the joy of knowing that he was returning home, or maybe his thoughts were still jumbled from the trauma of disembodiment and subsequent reanimation. But he was unwary, distracted, tired, and hungry.

Rounding an outcropping of rock, he looked up and froze.

Immediately in front of him, in plain view no more than fifty feet away, gathered around a blazing campfire, there were three lashers.

The largest of the three, obviously a harbigur, who had been squatted on the ground facing his way, saw him as soon as he stepped into sight.

Aram backed up against the rock and out of habit reached back for the hilt of the Sword of Heaven before he remembered that it was no longer there. Gritting his teeth in chagrin, he drew his dagger even as the lasher alerted his companions. The three of them rose and turned to face him. Aram felt sick. How could he have been so careless? True, he'd thought that all of Manon's beasts had died in the battle; still, he was a fool to blunder through these darkening hills as if no danger existed.

The big lasher stared at him for some time and then reached down and picked up a sword off the ground. Aram knew that he could not outrun them, especially in his current condition. Nor, realistically, could he put up much of a fight, certainly not against three of the massive beasts.

His heart lurched. To come so near to Ka'en, to be back upon the earth when he thought himself banished from it – how could he have been careless enough to stumble into one more battle that he had little or no chance of winning? Fury rose in him, but it was directed more against himself than against the three huge monsters approaching him.

And they approached.

374

He backed up against the outcropping and tried to organize and calm his thoughts and face the challenge. Two of the lashers, flanking the larger beast on either side, were apparently unarmed. Only the largest carried a weapon – the sword that it held in its right hand. Noting this fact, Aram felt a glimmer of hope arise.

Also, one of the smaller lashers, the beast on the harbigur's right, had apparently suffered an injury, perhaps in the battle. Aram could see no obvious wound, but as it came toward Aram, it limped on one leg, turning the clawed foot at an odd angle as it picked it up and put it down.

If he could manage somehow to avoid serious injury while wresting the sword away from the largest lasher, he would have a chance at evening the odds, if only a bit. Maybe it would be enough.

The lashers stopped several paces from him, forming a semicircle as they faced him. The big lasher, the harbigur, a massive beast, held the sword at his side, dangling next to his massive thigh. He stared at Aram for a long moment and the large, flat-disc eyes blinked.

"Lord Aram?" He inquired.

Aram started and stared.

The lasher's tone surprised him, caught him off-guard, for it bore an undertone of respect, and something else.

Aram let his gaze rove among them, seeking for subterfuge, or the signs of a feint; the tell-tale deviousness that would suggest a trick and a trap. He saw nothing. The creatures watched him openly, awaiting his reply.

"I am Aram," he replied after a moment.

The big lasher stared back at him and then glanced up the hillside behind Aram.

"How are you here?" He asked. "I thought you dead."

Aram nodded, warily, still holding his dagger at the ready. "I was dead," he affirmed. "The Maker sent me back."

Once again, the lasher looked up the hillside. A subtle hint of emotion, perhaps fear, colored his attitude as he gazed up into the darkening hills. "Has the Great Father returned as well?" He asked.

The question surprised Aram, both in its tenor and in the hesitant nature of its delivery.

He frowned. "No," he told the lasher, "your master has not returned. He is gone for all time."

The flat, black eyes blinked again. "You killed him."

"I did," Aram agreed.

Yet again, the big beast looked up the slope. "And he will not return?"

"Never," Aram assured him.

"Never?" The creature persisted.

"*Never.*"

The lasher lifted the sword.

Aram tensed.

The lasher swung the sword up and let the flat side of the blade land with a smack in the palm of his clawed hand. Holding it out before him, as if presenting a gift, the big lasher knelt down in front of Aram.

"I beg of you, my lord," he said, and his tone was pleading, "spare the lives of me and my companions. In return, we will give you our service, our loyalty –" He glanced around, as if searching for anything else he might offer. A plume of smoke from the campfire drifted their way. "– and our food," he finished.

Aram gazed back at him in shock.

Then his eyes narrowed.

"How did you survive the battle?" He asked.

The lasher continued holding the sword in front of him. "I was in command of the left side of the Great Father's forces," he replied. "I had been commanded to turn your flank. When the horn sounded from the tower, I was on the extreme left – upon your right, my lord. I knew that we were beaten." He hesitated and looked down at the ground for a long moment. Then he looked up again.

"I did not trust the Great Father," he stated. The big eyes sharpened with strong emotion. "He made me, and you may think it evil of me to doubt him – yet I doubted him."

Aram stared, unable to conjure a proper response to such astonishing assertions. Finally, after a long moment, he indicated the sword. "So – you do not seek confrontation with me?"

The lasher shook his head vigorously. "No, my lord; I seek – we three seek – your benevolence." He lifted the sword. "Please, Lord Aram, take this as a pledge of my faith."

Aram glanced over toward the fire, noting the absence of other weapons. "Is this the only weapon between the three of you?" He asked.

"Yes, my lord."

Aram shook his head. "Then keep it. You may have need of it." He raised a cautionary hand. "But never use it upon a man unless you are threatened."

The lasher stared. "I may keep it?"

Aram nodded. "As I said – you may have need of it."

"And you will spare us?" The lasher insisted.

"I will," Aram replied. "Please – stand. What is your name?"

The enormous lasher got to his feet. "I am named Hargur," he answered. "I was the Second of the Great Father's – *Manon's* – first children." He indicated the other lashers. "Bildur," he said of the lasher on his right that walked with a limp, "and this is Pentar."

Aram eyed them warily. "And they agree with your doubts about Manon?"

"They do, my lord."

Aram studied the three of them as he tried to master his amazement at the turn of events. "What will you do now?" He asked.

"Serve you," Hargur replied with a surprising response. "If you will have us. We will do whatever you ask of us, my lord."

Aram stared at them for a moment, letting his gaze search the three large faces, but even though he was unsure if he could know for certain whether they were lying, his instincts told him that they were not. He studied the sets of flat black eyes closely, but saw no guile. Slowly, he nodded.

"You need pledge no fealty to me," he told them. "The death of Manon made all the people of the earth free – the three of you perhaps more than any others. You may go – and do – as you like. You are free."

Hargur glanced at his companions and then looked again at Aram. "I cannot say with certainty, my lord," he replied, "but we three are likely the last of our kind upon the earth, and the humans know us only as enemies – or as servants of their enslaver. Unless we are known to them as your servants, they will never accept our presence upon the earth. We will ever be outcasts."

Aram nodded in frank admittance of this surprisingly clear enunciation of the beasts' plight.

"Alright," he said then. "I accept your service. You may travel into the south with me –" He stopped and looked at them closely. "Unless you would rather remain here, in a familiar place."

Hargur shook his head immediately. "No, my lord." He looked around and up at the nearly barren slopes that surrounded the hollow. "There is little to eat here, and –" The big lasher dropped his head almost in shame as he continued on, "– and there are no trees."

Aram frowned at Hargur upon hearing this enigmatic declaration but could make nothing of it. Besides, he was suddenly very tired. With the threat of conflict apparently removed, cold and fatigue found their way into his bones. He put away the dagger, tugged up the collar of his cloak, and looked toward the fire. "I am weary," he told Hargur. "I have journeyed far this day. I would rest by your fire this night."

Hargur stepped aside. "Of course, master, and we have some food as well. You are welcome to it."

It was at that moment that Aram noticed for the first time the general condition of the lashers. Their leather clothes hung from them in rags, and their bellies seemed sunken in comparison to his memories of how lashers appeared in the past.

He glanced around the campsite. The ground within several yards of the fire was packed hard, all around, from the impact of their feet passing over it for some time. There were few animal bones, and those that were there had been broken and gnawed, and the marrow had been sucked from them.

"How long have you encamped here?" He asked.

Since the summer," Hargur replied. "Since the battle."

Aram looked at him narrowly. "And you have not eaten well," he stated.

Hargur shrugged. "There is not much to eat in these hills, never was. But Pentar caught a rabbit today." He indicated the half-eaten carcass, lying on the ground near the fire. "If we had known you were coming, master, we would have left more for you."

Aram cleared away a small pile of old bones and sat down near the flames. "I thank you, but I am not hungry," he lied. "Only weary, and this fire feels good to me."

"Then we will make it hotter." Hargur motioned to the other lashers and they moved away toward a stand of juniper to fetch more fuel.

Aram looked up at Hargur and indicated the ground on the other side of the flames. "Please," he said, "sit."

After the lasher had complied, Aram looked over at him. "Do you not eat grain?" He asked. "Or do you only consume the flesh of animals?"

"We will eat grain gladly, master," Hargur replied. "But there is none about, now. The storehouses were all destroyed in the – when you slew the Great Father."

"There is grain in the villages to the south," Aram replied, watching the eyes of the big lasher. "You did not think to ask for a portion?"

Hargur lowered his head and stared downward, at the fire. "The Great Father commanded me to take all that the slaves had before the battle," he admitted, and there was shame and regret in his tone. "I took much, though not all, but I left them very little. I could not take more from them."

Aram was astounded. "You disobeyed Manon?"

The big lasher met Aram's gaze cautiously. "I did not think it right to cause the slaves to starve."

"They are slaves no longer," he corrected Hargur and he watched the lasher for a long moment. "And I had more grain brought to them when I discovered their lack. Did Manon know that you disobeyed his instructions?"

Hargur shook his massive, horned head. "I alone knew the extent of his commandments concerning the slaves, so there were none to tell him that I had done anything other than as I had been instructed."

Listening to him, Aram was reminded of Florm's assertion that no society, whether it was predominately good or evil, displayed a monolithic acceptance of either attribute. Apparently that rule also applied to the race of lashers.

The warmth from the fire began finding its way through his clothing and into his flesh, especially after Bildur and Pentar replenished its fuel. He looked over the flames at Hargur once again.

"When I asked what you would do, just now, you stated that you would do whatever I asked of you," he reminded him.

"I swear it," Hargur replied. "Whatever you ask of me, my lord, I will do."

Aram nodded. "Good – but *what would you like to do?*" He glanced around at the decrepit campsite set amidst the rocky and nearly barren hills. "Surely, you do not wish to remain here, in this place?"

Hargur also looked around, and then he brought his gaze back to Aram. "We would not," he agreed.

"Where would you like to go?" Aram asked again.

Hargur looked away and let his gaze settle upon a stand of scraggly, half-dead junipers. Once more the odd expression of shame or perhaps of a longing he feared to be unworthy and likely to be denied him, spread across the lasher's features. "Far to the south," he said, "beyond the flat lands, there are forests of great trees." He dared to look back at Aram, who was stunned to see that there was, in fact, an undeniable look of longing in the lasher's eyes. And now, as he looked at his new master, a tiny gleam of hope appeared there as well. "I would like to live among trees," Hargur admitted in quiet tones.

Aram stared, astonished. It had never occurred to him that the great beasts could possess a preference for one particular type of geography over another. But when he thought about it, he realized that, though they had been created in this barren, cold part of the world, many – like Hargur – had travelled far and wide. Like any other intelligent creature, Hargur had discovered that he preferred a different landscape than that which had surrounded him for the bulk of his life.

That thought engendered another. "How old are you, Hargur?" He asked.

"The winter has come and gone more than five hundred times since memory began," the lasher responded.

Aram turned his gaze downward, into the flames. It occurred to him that Hargur had been in slavery for much longer than any of the slaves over whom his "Great Father" once held sway.

After a time, he looked up again. "And you would like to live among trees?"

"I would, master," the lasher answered and he held out his clawed hands and gazed at them for a long moment before returning his gaze to Aram's face. "I think that I could make things from them."

Once again, Aram felt his features set in lines of amazement. "You would like to make things from wood?"

Hargur nodded wordlessly, watching Aram warily, as if he feared rebuke.

380

Aram studied him for a long moment, and then he nodded. "Tomorrow we will go south together," he declared. "I will ask for grain from the villages – from those whose harvest gave them enough to spare – and then we will journey on into the south."

He looked at all three of the lashers narrowly. "Do you understand that Manon will never return?"

They exchanged glances, and then Hargur met his gaze once more. "You slew him?"

"I did."

"And he is gone from the earth for all time?" The lasher persisted.

Aram nodded. "He will never return."

Once again, they looked at each other, and then Hargur returned Aram's nod. "We understand."

Aram leaned forward. "Then you do not fear his artifacts?"

"Artifacts?" Hargur gazed back at him in confusion. "What is a ... artifact?"

"Far to the south," Aram replied, "upon the eastern borders of Elam, there is a great city set among a forest of mighty trees. There is an abandoned city there as well, whose buildings you could use for shelter." He fixed the lashers with a stern gaze. "But there is a tower there that was built long ago by him who was once your "great father". Will it trouble you to dwell near such a thing?"

A strange eagerness seeped into Hargur's flat black eyes. "Do not the humans want this forest – or the city?"

Aram shook his head. "No man will ever dwell there."

"And there are many great trees?" The eagerness in Hargur's eyes and in his voice was obvious and unrestrained.

"Mighty trees," Aram answered, "and many of them. A great forest filled with some of the largest trees I have ever seen."

"And the humans don't want them?"

"They do not – because of the tower that exists in that place," Aram told him. He leaned forward once more. "And you would not fear this tower?"

Hargur shrugged even as the gleam of excitement in his eyes grew. "It is only stone, and the Great Father will not return to dwell in it." He watched Aram for a long moment in silence. "You would let us live among these trees, master?"

"Forever, if you wish it," Aram replied.

Hargur blew a great breath from his nostrils. "I will go," he declared.

"And I," said Bildur.

"And I," Pentar repeated.

Aram nodded in decision. "We will go south tomorrow, into Bracken. There, I will acquire food for our journey." He held up a cautionary hand. "I am going toward the southeast," he stated, "and the forest with the city and the tower lies nearly due south of this place. I cannot go with you." He looked closely at Hargur. "Can you find your way to the forest if I give you directions?"

It was Bildur that responded. "The Second is very good with directions – it is why the Great Father placed him in command of the slave wagons."

At this, Hargur shot his companion a fierce, angry glance. Then, abashed, he stared at the ground for a long time before looking up once more at Aram. "I am sorry for that, master. I never hated humans as some of our kind has done. I despised my work. I swear that I will never harm a human again."

Aram met his apologetic gaze solemnly. "I am sorry for that, too – but it was Manon who is responsible for the great evil that was done. It was for that reason I destroyed him." He looked around at each of them. "We will let it be in the past, but you will each swear to me as Hargur has now done – that there will be no harm brought to any human ever again."

The lashers responded quickly, in near unison. "I swear it, master."

"Alright." Aram looked around and noticed that gloom was thickening in the ravine. The sun had gone and night was falling quickly. "We will take turns tending the fire, and go south at dawn."

"We will tend the fire, master, that you may rest," Hargur offered.

Aram looked at him and noticed that in the light from the fire, the big lasher's emaciated condition was even more apparent. He shook his head. "You need rest as well. We will all take our turn."

Hargur gazed at him in surprise. "As you say, master."

As he lay down on his side near the fire, the thought crossed Aram's mind that he could easily be slain during the night by these beasts who – until mere weeks ago – had been his sworn enemies, but he put it from him. He was almost too tired to care.

382

Besides, had they wanted to kill him, they could have done it at any time since he blundered into their camp.

And the look of longing on each massive face when he made them the offer of a home in the southern part of the world had been unmistakable and real.

He closed his eyes and slept.

By the time the rising sun showed above the eastern horizon, they had abandoned the camp and were moving up through the ravine toward the south. As soon as possible, Aram moved the company up onto the ridge top so that they might walk in the warmth of the sun as they made for the crest of the hills.

At mid-day, they could look southward and see, beyond the edge of the hills, the wide land of Bracken. It was a green land in spring and summer, but now, browns, tans, and yellows pervaded the landscape. The only swath of green in sight meandered through the middle of the land, several miles off – apparently there were evergreen trees that grew along the banks of the Secesh as if snaked through Bracken on its way to the Great Western Marsh.

Villages dotted the wide floor of the valley. The nearest village in sight lay very near the verge of the hills. Aram pointed. "We'll go there," he said, and the four of them turned down off the ridge top to the right and began descending along the bottom of a dry watercourse that fell toward the south.

The valley was yet several miles off and the sun seemed to fall down the sky as they made their way along the winding ravine that slowly dropped toward the valley. Afternoon had faded and evening had taken possession of the earth when they at last stood at the edge of the hills and looked out from a stand of juniper at the village, less than a half-mile off.

Aram glanced over the sun and then looked around. "There is ample wood for a fire," he said. "We can camp here if we must."

He looked up at Hargur. "You and the others must stay here," he told the lasher. "These people know you only as overlords and I do not wish them to be frightened. I will go out and see if I can manage us some grain."

He turned and looked back up the draw. Then he lifted his arm and pointed. "Set up camp behind that corner, out of sight."

"As you say, master," Hargur agreed.

Aram looked back out at the village. Evening had fallen, the shadows were long. There were few people in sight, though smoke rose from nearly every chimney. "I will return as soon as I may."

He approached the village cautiously as evening deepened across the prairie. There was stubble in the fields surrounding the huts. Apparently, they had been able to make a crop, and with no overlords stealing it away, there should be surplus.

When he was less than a hundred yards away, a man walking near the edge of the nearest field to the village looked up and saw him, and immediately ran out of sight among the huts. Moments later, a small crowd gathered, standing warily between two huts on the side where he approached.

Aram stopped and held up his hands, palms outward, showing that he bore no weapons.

"I mean no one any harm," he stated in a voice that carried to the people gathered together watching him.

There was a long discussion among the small clot of villagers, and then one man separated himself and came cautiously toward him. The man seemed to be stooping, peering at Aram as he came.

About thirty feet away, the man stopped, gazing at Aram with widened eyes and staring up into the hills. The man was of medium height, very thin, dressed in torn, ragged clothing despite the chill of the evening, and he had dark hair and dark eyes.

"You – you have come from the north?" The man inquired in halting, astonished tones.

"I have," Aram affirmed.

The man hunched lower, twitching nervously, like a rabbit preparing to scurry away to any available shelter. "Are you a spirit?"

"I am not." Aram lowered his hands to his side. "I am a man like you, and I am hungry. And there are three others with me. Do you have any spare food?"

The man rubbed his hands nervously over one another. "How did you escape from the fire?" He asked with frank suspicion. Holding up one finger, he indicated the hills. "It went high into the sky and burned along the hilltops, when it was yet summer here. You came out of the fire?"

The question puzzled Aram. He frowned and made to inquire as to what the man meant, but then he recalled the devastation in the valley of Morkendril and realized that Manon's dissolution would have been a frightening and cataclysmic event for people dwelling so near to the tower.

After pondering it for a moment, he decided that a carefully couched honest statement was the right response. "I was rescued from the fire by servants of the Maker."

The man straightened up a bit though he still leaned forward and peered at Aram closely. Then, abruptly, he jerked erect in amazement. "You came from the south with the army!"

"I did," Aram agreed.

"*And you are yet alive.*"

"I am."

The man stared up the slope of the hills behind Aram for a long moment. The muscles along his jawline worked with furious agitation. "And the grim lord?" He finally asked.

"He is slain," Aram stated firmly.

"He will not return?"

"He will not."

The man hesitated, darting fearful glances up into the high ground to the north. "How can you be certain of this?" He asked.

"Because I slew him."

The man stood for a moment longer, watching Aram and sending quick glances up into the hills. Then his gaze jerked back to Aram's face and focused there. His eyes flew wide and he knelt down so quickly he seemed to tumble to earth whereupon he bent forward and bowed his head to the ground. "You are the one they name Aram," he stated with abrupt and breathless realization. "You are he they name as king."

"I am he," Aram affirmed.

The man immediately made himself small upon the ground, pushing his forehead into the earth, trembling. "My name is Metch, master," he said. "I am your servant."

"Don't bow to me, Metch – get up," Aram told him, and then, when Metch remained on the ground, he repeated the command more firmly. "*Get up.* Stand up and face me. You are not my servant, and I am not your master. Nor is the grim lord your master any longer. You are free."

Warily, Metch looked up at him, though he remained upon the ground. "You may have our food," he said.

Aram held out his hand. "Get up on your feet."

385

Metch flinched away from the proffered hand even as he rose carefully to his feet.

"I only want whatever portion of your food that may safely be spared to aid me on my journey into the south," Aram replied.

Though Metch had risen up onto his feet upon Aram's stern command, he nonetheless stood unsteadily, as if he might drop again at any time. He peered at Aram. "You slew the grim lord?"

Rather than delve into the attributes of the Sword or attempt to describe the events inside the tower, Aram simply nodded. "I did. He is gone from the earth for all time. He will not return to trouble you again. As I told you – you and your people are free."

Metch blinked at him, and was silent for a moment; then, "We have set the harvest aside, my lord," he said. "It is stored in the granary."

"You have set it aside?"

Metch bowed his head. "For the gathering," he answered.

Aram shook his head. "There will be no 'gathering'," he told the villager. "The harvest is yours and will ever be from this time forth."

As Aram had noticed so long ago, upon the slopes of Burning Mountain, it would take time for those enslaved for generations to comprehend the concept of freedom. The passage of much time was required to heal wounds as deep as those that had been inflicted upon these people.

Slowly, as the sun sank beyond the horizon, he began to move toward Metch, who still appeared as if he was ready to bolt. "Do not fear me," Aram said gently. "I mean you no harm. I only need a bit of your food – whatever portion may be spared."

The villager seemed confused, unable to grasp the meaning of the conversation and the words contained within it like "free" and "the harvest is yours" that he'd just had with the strange man who'd come over the hills, "out of the fire". Lowering his head once more, he pointed behind him. "The granary is at the center of the village, my lord," he said.

"Show me."

Aram followed Metch into the village as the light failed from the west. Metch took him to the center of the collection of huts where one larger building stood alone. Moving to one side of the door of this building, Metch indicated the interior with a cautious hand. "It was only a fair harvest, my lord," he explained sheepishly. "It was planted too late."

Aram paused and looked at him. "Is there enough for your people to survive the winter and still be able to plant in the spring?" He asked.

Metch nodded cautiously even as a frown took possession of his face. "Yes, my lord – more than enough for that," he replied. "But the gathering –"

"I told you," Aram repeated, a bit too harshly. "There will be no gathering – ever again." The he softened his tone and spoke more kindly. "You will learn, Metch. It will take time, but you will learn the meaning of freedom."

Aram moved to the door and looked over a short retaining wall into the interior of the granary. Small windows set high into the outside walls let in just enough of the twilight for him to see that the granary was piled to a depth of perhaps no more than three feet with two different kinds of crops. Still, the entire granary was covered to this depth and it was a reasonably extensive structure.

One crop, by far the larger amount, was grain. The other was a crop Aram didn't recognize. It was similar to grain, in that it was comprised of something which was obvious a seed of some plant, but the individual seeds were larger, fuller, like tiny eggs.

Aram looked back at Metch. "There is another crop besides grain in here. What is it?"

Metch nodded. "Those are banzo seeds, my lord."

"How is it prepared as a food?"

Again, Metch flinched at Aram's gruff questioning. Still, he answered warily. "They are soaked in water for several hours to soften, and then they may be warmed and eaten as they are, or placed in water with wheat and heated to make a broth."

Aram turned back to examine the strange crop with interest. "Do – did – the overlords eat of this crop?"

"Yes, my lord," Metch replied. "In fact, they seemed to prefer it. We are only allowed to keep banzo seed in years when the crop is full, and even then sometimes they take it all."

At this, Aram turned and frowned at him and once more spoke too harshly. "They will never take your crop again, Metch – *I told you this*. There are only three of their kind left upon the earth, and they answer to me." He turned back toward the granary's interior. "Can you spare some of those banzo seeds and a bit of grain for my journey into the south?"

Metch had lowered his head at Aram's fierce tone. "You may take it all, if it pleases you, my lord."

Aram spun toward him in irritation at this response, annoyed by the man's meekness, but then checked himself in time. He must ever remember, he realized, that these people had lived in proximity to great evil for the whole of their lives, generation upon generation. He drew in a deep breath and spoke more gently. "You will get used to freedom, I promise you," he told Metch. "You will – in time. Now, if you will spare me some of your food, I will take only what I and my companions require."

He glanced around in the gathering dark. "Do you have something in which I might carry it?"

Metch nodded, staring at Aram with an odd light in his eyes. "We have bags made of animal skins, my lord – you may have any you desire."

Aram forced a smile. "May I have four of these bags?"

"You may have them all –" Metch caught himself as he saw the hardness come back into Aram's eyes, and he turned quickly away into the gloom. "Four, my lord. I will bring them at once."

Aram stopped him. "May I borrow a pot as well – something to prepare it in?" Then, considering, he amended, "Best make it two."

"Yes, my lord." The villager went into one of the huts near him, re-appearing after but a few moments with the desired items.

When Aram had filled the leather bags with grain and banzo seeds, he secured the tops with leather thongs that Metch provided and then he laid a careful hand on Metch's shoulder. "I thank you for this," he said. "And I will return to repay you, I promise."

He looked around. No other villagers stood nearby that he could see. He looked back at Metch. "Are you the elder?" He asked.

"My lord?"

"Are you the village elder?"

"No, my lord – we have no such thing."

Aram frowned at him. "Then why did you come out to me?"

"The others were too frightened."

Aram nodded. "Then you are now the elder," he told him. Turning away from the look of astonishment in the former slave's eyes, he went back northward toward the hills.

388

57.

That night, over an open fire of dead juniper, Aram warmed a measure of grain in the larger of the two pots, and he and the lashers ate their first decent meal. Hargur and his companions recognized the banzo seeds immediately, prompting Aram to disperse most of that foodstuff to the lashers, keeping but a small portion for himself.

Hargur hefted the bag Aram gave him and looked doubtfully at Aram's. "You did not keep much for yourself, master." And he held his bag out as an offering.

Aram shook his head. "No – you will require more than me, even after you get far enough south where there is more game." He secured the top of his bag and set it aside as he pushed Hargur's away. "You have farther to go than I do and I want you to make the journey well and arrive safely."

Hargur stared at him for a long moment with a strange light flickering in his large flat eyes, and then he also set his bag aside and gazed down into the flames of the fire. "I see why the world follows you, my lord."

Aram glanced at him but didn't reply as he stirred the grain in the pot. That night he slept more easily than the night before.

The four of them were up before the sun the next morning and Aram led them to the edge of the valley of the Secesh.

He pointed to his right, toward a broad area of open fields, now lying fallow in the early light. A slight smile touched his face as he looked up at Hargur.

"I don't want to frighten these people unduly," he said. "They will find it difficult enough to adjust to freedom in the days and weeks ahead, and it will not do for them to get a glimpse of you and the others. I don't want them to encounter those that once ruled over them, if at all possible."

Nodding his understanding, Hargur looked in the direction indicated. "The valley is not overly wide, master. If my companions and I move quickly, we may cross it in a day."

Aram shook his head at this. "There are more villages between us and the far hills," he said. "And they do not know the truth of the altered condition of the world. No," he said again, and he pointed out the willows that lined the irrigation ditches. "I prefer that we cross it stealthily than with speed. If possible, I wish to be unseen."

He looked up once more at Hargur. "Will you and the others bear wood for a fire? It may be that we must pass the night upon the open prairie."

"As you wish, master," Hargur agreed and he looked back up the ravine toward a stand of juniper. "We will return soon."

"Hurry," Aram instructed him. "I wish to gain those willows before full daylight."

All that day, they moved carefully along through the limited cover of the willows that lined the ditches, making speed where they could, crawling when necessary, and even lying prone to remain hidden whenever the denizens of these cold northern villages came within eyeshot.

They crossed the river just after mid-day, slogging through the shallower current near where it fell gently across a gravel bar. By sunset, they were yet two or three miles from the hills to the south. Aram led them into the tenuous shelter beneath a wooden bridge.

As he started a fire, he looked around at them. "We'll be on the move before dawn," he said, "and try to get into the hills quickly where we can make better time."

The sun was less than two hours in the sky the next morning when they at last left the open ground of the valley and moved up into the hills through the shelter of a ravine where the juniper and brush grew thickly, and a clear stream tumbled through the bottom.

Five days later, after climbing up the northern slope of those hills, they found the summit and began descending toward the south. Two days more and they stood on the crest of the lowest group of knolls and looked down over the long valley through which Aram had been transported all those years ago. By narrowing his eyes against flat light of the low-hanging sun, Aram could just make out the indication of the road that ran along the far side of the valley. He pointed directly south.

"Beyond those hills, there is another valley," he said, and he looked at Hargur. "You passed through it many times as you moved along the road by the edge of the plains."

Hargur nodded. "I know this country well, my lord."

"When the road leaves that valley behind, and passes from the plains, it runs through a gap into the land of Cumberland." He looked at Hargur once again. "As you know well."

Hargur nodded.

"Do not travel upon the road," Aram instructed him firmly, "but move upon the east of it, through the cover of the hills until you reach the high ground above the valley of the dry lake."

He looked at Hargur once more until the lasher once again nodded his understanding.

"There," Aram continued, "another road turns away from Cumberland toward the east and goes up the valley of the dry lake. Not far beyond, perhaps a mile or more, there is a place where it turns away to the south and goes up over the hills and down into the land of Wallensia. Have you ever gone there?" He asked Hargur.

The big lasher shook his head. "I know that road, but I have never gone into Wallensia," he replied.

"You will follow it now," Aram informed him. "Cautiously. I do not think anyone travels that road, but you will exercise every caution. Beyond those far southern hills, the road bends eastward alongside the River Stell as it goes into Wallensia." He shook his head emphatically. "There are farmers there – former slaves – and I do not wish to have them see you and your companions. Do you understand?"

"Yes, master."

Aram nodded. "Good. Where the road turns eastward along the Stell, you will abandon it, cross the river, and go toward the south, into the thick forests which you will see before you, next to the wooded hills that separate Wallensia from Elam. The city you seek is no more than two or three days journey to the south of that river, perhaps even less for you. It is there, next to those hills."

He turned and looked at each of the lashers in turn, meeting each set of eyes. "Is it still your wish to go there?"

Hargur nodded at once, without consulting his companions, his gaze fixed eagerly upon the south. "If you will allow it, my lord."

Aram watched him until the lasher looked his way. "I give you that city," he stated plainly, "for as long as you and your companions live. None will disturb you there."

Hargur hesitated and then tendered a softly-spoken question. "Are you leaving us then, master?"

Aram nodded and pointed toward the southeast. "My home is in Regamun Mediar – far away toward the rising of the sun. From this point, you will go south, and I will turn southeast. Thus far, I have slowed you down; you will make better time without me."

Hargur's gaze was fixed upon him. There was a hesitant sort of melancholy evident in the depths of his large flat eyes. "Will we see you again, master?"

"You will," Aram assured him. "When I have once again seen my family, I will come to you and make certain that you are safe and well and unmolested."

Hargur continued to watch him for a long moment, and then the big harbigur knelt down and kissed his boots, almost knocking Aram backward with his great horns as he executed the act.

"Get up," Aram commanded him, taken aback by the action. "There is no need for that."

Hargur rose and met his gaze. "There was need for me to do it, master," he argued carefully and he bowed his massive head. "We will obey you always, master. Command us, and we will obey."

Behind him, the other two nodded solemnly.

Aram reached out and touched Hargur on his thickly muscled arm. "Go carefully," he said in a kind tone. "Get safely to your new home. I will come and see you as soon as I am able."

"Thank you, master." The big lasher gazed at him for another long moment, and then, followed by the others, he turned and loped away into the south, going from sight down along the bottom of a thickly wooded draw.

Aram watched the three lashers as they wound down that ravine toward the south and out of sight, and then he turned toward the southeast and began resolutely to put the many long miles that separated him from Ka'en behind him.

All that day he journeyed up and over the hills that fell away toward the long valley, always heading as directly as possible toward the black mountain –the very top of which he could barely espy far off to the southeast – and home.

When the sun fell down to sit upon the western horizon, he went to the bottom of a draw that wound more directly toward the valley. As darkness gathered in the bottom of the hollow, he found a stand of juniper, started a fire, ate, and curled up on the ground to sleep.

It was a restless night, cold, and he was obliged several times to get up and replenish the fire. Toward morning, as the sky began to lighten in the east, he tried to stir but found himself weary and cold, so he placed a bit more fuel upon the flames and curled up once more, waiting for the warmth of daylight.

As he napped in the morning chill, he dreamed that a wind came and blew upon him, whistling through the air like the wings of a great bird.

The light grew and he eventually rose up to sit by the remains of the fire. As he held out his hands to the heat of the diminishing coals, a voice spoke to him from the top of the stand of junipers, startling him, making him reach instinctively for his dagger.

"Why is it," the voice asked, "that I find the king of all the earth sleeping upon the ground like a vagabond?"

It was Alvern.

Blinking his eyes against the first rays of the sun that were breaking above the slopes, Aram spied the eagle sitting on a dead branch high in the nearest tree.

He grinned in glad recognition.

"And why is it," he replied, still grinning "that you refer to a mere vagabond as 'king of all the earth'?"

Alvern bent a stern look upon him. "It is not within my bounds to reprimand someone of your stature, my lord, but I thought that we agreed that there would be no more of that," he stated.

Aram waved his hands in deprecation. "I know what it is that I must do with the years that remain of my life," he answered. "And I will do it with solemn willingness." He looked up again. "Does that satisfy you?"

"It does," Alvern replied.

The great eagle cocked his head. "How have you returned, my lord? All the world thought you dead."

Aram frowned and ignored that question for the moment in favor of one of his own. "How did you know that I had returned?" He asked. "Or were you traversing these skies for another cause?"

"No," the eagle admitted. "I came to find you. Five days ago, I was upon the high plains of the horses, conferring with Thaniel when two beings the like of which I had never seen appeared before us. They identified themselves as servants of the Maker and told us that you had returned to the earth and that we were to find you and bring you home."

"So Thaniel knows?"

"He is on his way to you," the eagle assured him. "He is no more than four or five days behind me, perhaps less. That horse is big and fast, and he is eager to see you."

"And Ka'en?" Aram looked away for a moment and then looked back up at him. "Does she know of my return?"

"I sent Cree the Ancient in unto her – your lady will believe her more readily than any other," the eagle replied.

"Believe –?" Aram's heart sank upon hearing this. "Did she also think me dead?"

"I am sorry, my lord, but I arrived at the city after Findaen had informed her of the events at the tower. I sent Cree in to her immediately."

Aram stood and looked toward the southeast in silence for a long moment. "And Thaniel is coming to me?"

"He is, my lord," Alvern replied.

"How will he find me – will you guide him?"

"I have already informed the hawks of this region of your location," the eagle assured him. "They will guide him to you."

"Thank you," Aram answered and he looked up at the great bird. "Will you accompany me then, as I journey?"

"I must beg the king's forgiveness," the eagle replied, "but I am under commandment of those even greater than you. The world must be told of your return, including the princes of all lands and your commanders – and I must confirm that the High Prince of Elam was found and prevented before he passed too far south into his own land." The eagle looked down and studied Aram closely. "And then, my lord," he said, "I am to bring something to you."

Ignoring this last statement, Aram asked of the eagle, "Whose commandment are you under?"

"The creatures that told me of your return. I must, at their instruction, inform the world that you have come back to us."

Aram frowned. "But why must the world know? I only wish to see Ka'en now. The world may learn of this in due time."

"I understand this, my lord," Alvern replied. "I understand the wishes of your heart. But your life is not your own – nor does it belong even to the Lady Ka'en. You belong to the world, now."

Aram's frown deepened. "Will you be at the city when I arrive?"

"I would not miss it for my life," the eagle stated, and he mounted up and turned toward the southwest. "Until then, my lord."

Aram, still frowning, raised his hand in salute. "Until then, my friend," he replied.

Three days later, as the sun slid toward the edge of the world, Aram crossed the ancient valley road. A short time later, he stood upon the bank of the wide river, whose name he had never learned, that arose beneath the heights of Camber Pass far away to the northeast and flowed through the long valley. Though it ran low and slow, as did all streams at this late time of the year, it was nonetheless wide, deep, and formidable.

He looked upstream and then down, but could discern no place where the current shallowed as it crossed a gravel bar or other impediment in its inevitable progress toward the distant confines of the Great Western Marsh. Somewhere to his left, upstream, memory told him that there was a bridge, but did not inform him of how far away that ancient construct lay from his current position.

He had no desire to waste more time searching for an easy path across. Besides, this day had been fairly warm, and the evening had not yet cooled, whatever chill the water would impart.

He would swim.

As he stood in the tall grass above the muddy bank, trying to decide whether to disrobe and place his clothes inside the food bag to keep them somewhat dry as he crossed over the wide current, he abruptly felt a thrumming in the ground, as something heavy moving at speed.

Had the lashers returned?

He turned to look behind him, away from the river, and then downstream, toward the west, but saw nothing. He pivoted the other way and looked across the river, southward, even though he

395

was certain that whatever approached would likely not make its movement felt through the broad slow waters.

He was wrong.

A large form appeared, out upon the open prairie beyond the stream, and it was coming toward him rapidly.

It was a shape he recognized at once.

Thaniel.

Forgetting his dilemma on how to get across the wide river, he stood still and watched the horse approach.

Thaniel reached the other side and drove down the bank and into the water without hesitation, plunging toward the near bank with great strides of his long legs. Aram stepped away from the bank as the horse surged through the slow-moving current.

Thaniel reached the shore, climbed to the top of the bank, came near, and lowered his head to peer into Aram's face.

"Aram, my friend," the horse said gladly. "*It is you.*"

Powerful emotion surged upward through Aram's chest and into his throat, rendering speech impossible. He threw his arms around the horse's head and leaned his forehead against him. Tears flowed unchecked down his cheeks.

After a while, he managed to choke out hoarsely, "I am very glad to see you, my brother."

For a time then, neither of them said more.

When finally Aram released him and stepped back, the horse continued to stare at him, looking him up and down with frank and open amazement. "How are you here, my lord, *my friend?* I thought – nay, *I knew* – that you had died."

"I did die," Aram agreed, wiping at his eyes. "But the Maker sent me back."

"Back? – from where have you returned, my lord?"

"From the long home of all our people," Aram told him.

"You went to – *you have seen the long home?*" Astonishment saturated Thaniel's voice as he tendered the question.

"I have. And I have returned from there."

The horse went very still, and his breathing quickened, even more than that brought on by the labor of his long journey across the mountains and the intervening hills. He gazed at Aram in silence for a long moment, then,

"Did you meet with the Lord of All Horses while you were there?" He asked. "And his mate – my mother?"

"I saw your father and mother," Aram replied. "And they send you their regard and wish you well." He reached out and placed a hand on the side of the horse's head. "But, Thaniel, my old friend – they are there, not here." He paused, and then spoke with deliberate solemnity. "I am standing in the presence of the Lord of All Horses. In your father's absence, my friend, that burden falls to you."

The horse stared back at him for some time longer, blinking his large, dark eyes. Then, he said simply, "I am overjoyed to see you, Lord Aram – I cannot adequately express my gladness."

"No more than I am to see you, my brother." Aram replied.

Thaniel swung around until he faced back across the stream. "Come, my lord," he said. "Let me bear you home. Forgive me for arriving without the saddle. I lost it on my journey southward after your – after the battle. I cannot say where it might be now. The Call is gone as well. I am sorry."

Aram mounted up. "There is no war before us now," he said, "only a journey. I will not require the saddle." He thought a moment. "But I do regret the loss of the Call."

"I am sorry, my lord."

"It is alright, my friend," Aram assured him in quiet tones. "We will survive its loss."

He grabbed a fistful of Thaniel's mane and he and the great horse went back across the river, through the valley and then turned up along the edge of the hills toward where they would gain the road that climbed up and over that higher ground on its way to Aram's valley, still many miles away.

Three days afterward, late in the evening, they swung down along the old road and gained the junction where it connected with the great north-south highway. Aram looked up at the western sky. The sun had gone, night came quickly on.

And they were yet two hours or more from Regamun Mediar. For reasons, he could not understand, he was reluctant – despite his need to see her – to startle Ka'en by arriving in darkness.

"Let us camp here, beside the road," he told Thaniel, as he dismounted, "and go on in the morning. There is good water in this stream and grass for you along its banks."

"We cannot go on to the city, anyway," the horse responded, "until Lord Alvern comes."

Aram looked at him sharply. "Why?"

"I am not to bring you unto the city until all is ready," Thaniel answered.

Aram frowned with rising irritation. "What is it that is to be made ready?" He demanded.

Thaniel lowered his head and looked into Aram's eyes. "You cannot avoid it, my lord. I am sorry, Aram, but your life is no longer entirely your own."

58.

"Yes, I heard this from Alvern already," Aram replied as his irritation threatened to become anger. With an effort, he suppressed his frustration and continued on in a calmer tone. "What is it that I cannot avoid?"

"Do not be angry with me, my friend," Thaniel replied. He lifted his head and gazed into the deep black-blue sky of the eastern horizon, beyond which lay the high plains of his youth. "That which you cannot avoid," he said, "was commissioned to occur by those that are higher, even, than you – by the creatures that told of your return to earth." He lowered his head to look again at Aram. "That is why we must wait upon Lord Alvern."

Aram gazed back at him and then acquiesced in silence, nodding shortly and then turning away to go among the trees and gather fuel for a fire. When he had managed, with his dagger and a chunk of flint he found in the rocks along the stream, to set flame to kindling, he warmed some banzo seeds in the pot he'd been given by Metch. After he'd eaten and was seated on a log enjoying the heat from the fire, he was surprised to look up and find Thaniel standing near him in the twilight, watching him closely.

"Have you supped already?" He asked the horse in surprise.

The horse ignored that. "What happened, Lord Aram?"

Aram gazed back at him, frowning, until comprehension came. "In the tower?"

"Did you pierce the grim lord with the Sword?" Thaniel lifted his head to peer at the empty space above Aram's shoulder. "Where is the Sword of Heaven?" He asked.

"The Sword is gone." Aram shook his head as he gave his answer. "No, I did not pierce him with it. He was too powerful. I could not get close enough to thrust it into him. So, I gave it to him."

The horse started. "You *gave* it to him? Then how –?"

Aram smiled ruefully. "That was its purpose all along." He paused and glanced up at the stars overhead, just now beginning to flare and brighten, like candles newly lit in the blackness of the firmament. "Everything that I accomplished with that blade in the years after I received it was intended to make the grim lord desire it, nothing more."

The smile faded. "And he did desire it – he desired it greatly, so greatly that he was blinded to the danger."

Thaniel shifted his massive bulk in astonishment. "You gave it to him?" He repeated.

Aram nodded. "That was the purpose for which it was made. Once in his hand, the Sword awoke to its true meaning. It consumed him, dissolved him, and destroyed him utterly."

The horse stared. "Then you were meant to give it into his hand all along."

"Yes."

Thaniel arched his neck in sudden anger. "Then why were you – and so many others – made to suffer, and die? Why was not the weapon given to him long ago, by them?"

"Consider, my friend," Aram suggested gently. "Had one of the Brethren – the gods – simply tried to give the Sword into his hand, he would have suspected treachery and refused it outright. The grim lord is – *was* – no fool, and he would have guessed at the weapon's purpose. So they gave the weapon to me instead, and I, foolishly thinking that piercing him was the reason for its creation, began a campaign of trying to get close enough to him to put it to the purpose I supposed for it."

He smiled slightly as he met the horse's gaze. "All of which made Manon believe that the gods had given into my hand a weapon containing their combined power – placing the engine of their own destruction within his reach." He shrugged. "It was an intricate deception, and he fell for it."

"And the gods knew this all along? Kelven knew?" The horse inquired and though his anger had subsided somewhat, his voice yet rumbled with disapproval. "Then the deception was practiced upon you as well, and it cost – or nearly cost – your life."

Aram shook his head, though the smile faded. "They did not know, my friend. Even Lord Kelven did not know the truth of it. I

400

think that Humber and Ferros both suspected the Maker's intentions, but even they did not know for certain." He looked up. "If any of them had known, then the enemy, as clever as any of them, would have discovered the truth and the plan would have failed. It had to be – everything had to be – as it was."

He lowered his eyes and stared down into the fire. A look of acute sadness came over his face. "Even all the blood, all the lives that were lost," he said softly. "It all had to be."

When the horse did not reply, he looked up. "It was the Maker's plan, Thaniel, and it worked. Manon took the Sword from my hand willingly. He lusted for it; I gave it, and it destroyed him. He is gone and the world is free."

The horse watched him for a while, then, "How long have you known that such was its purpose?"

Aram shook his head once more. "Not until the very end. At the last, as he crushed the life from me, in the midst of terrible pain, I remembered that which Kelven had said to me – that the Sword was meant *to destroy Manon, not to defeat him*. All at once, I understood what was meant by those words."

The horse went silent, gazing out into the gathering dusk. Then, after a while, he looked back at Aram. "It is right that the gods sent you back," he stated quietly.

"It was not the doing of the gods," Aram corrected him. "Humber did not know how to accomplish my return. Only the Maker has such knowledge. The Guardians returned me to earth on instruction from the Him. It was His doing – it was all His doing. As Joktan said – in all this we are made aware of the immense majesty of the Maker's thoughts."

Silence fell again and then Thaniel said, "I told you once that I could not live in a world where you were absent. I am glad, my brother, that I will not have to endure the truth of those words."

Aram nodded as he added more fuel to the fire. He looked up. "As am I," he agreed quietly.

The next morning, Aram arose early, while the eastern sky was yet pale and pink. He was anxious to get home to Ka'en and his child. As soon as Thaniel came back from the stream where he'd been drinking, Aram swung up onto the horse's back.

"Let's go home," he said.

Thaniel didn't move.

Swinging his head around, he reminded Aram, "We must wait upon Lord Alvern. Please, my lord; it is what must be."

In acknowledgement of this, Aram groaned and then sat still, in silence, breathing deeply, tamping down his frustration and his eagerness to go to Ka'en and his daughter.

After a time, he said, "Cannot we go on for a space, and shorten the distance we will have to travel when Alvern comes?"

Thaniel thought. "We can, my lord," he agreed.

Before they had gone a mile, the eastern horizon brightened. Another mile and the sun rose, warm and bright, in a clear morning sky. Ahead, they could see into the valley, and the pyramids by the junction. Thaniel halted.

They waited in impatient silence, broken only by the sound of birds chirping in the thickets and Thaniel's occasional, "just a bit longer, Aram." Irritation at the lengthening delay began to gather and pool in Aram's heart.

Then, barely two hours after sunrise, Alvern came down and hovered upon the wind. In the great bird's beak, something gleamed.

"You must wait, Lord Aram," the eagle stated. "You must give them a few hours more to gather."

Aram frowned up at the eagle as Thaniel shifted his great weight, stamping his hooves upon the ancient stone.

"Who?" Aram demanded. "Who is gathering – and why must I wait for them?"

"Forgive me, my lord," Alvern insisted. "But all of this is needful. It is necessary that they see you return to them."

"Who are these people that must look upon me even before I may go to my wife?" Aram demanded of the bird once more, and his irritation began to rise and harden into anger. Suddenly, giving in to frustration, he urged Thaniel forward. *I am going to my family.*"

At this fiercely insistent statement, and despite his own reluctance to disobey the instructions of the Astra, Thaniel moved forward, albeit hesitantly.

Alvern tilted his wings and dropped down to stand upon the pavement in front of the horse, spreading his wings wide until they blocked the entire width of the roadway. "Please, Lord Aram, you must accede to this. I understand your impatience, and I regret the delay, but I have been instructed by those that serve Him who is Highest that this must be so."

The horse came to a halt. Aram gazed at the eagle angrily.

Keeping his great wings spread wide, blocking the pavement, Alvern spoke quietly, answering Aram's earlier question, "Those that must look upon you, Lord Aram, and witness your return to them, are your own people." After another long moment, in which he and Aram stared at one another, the eagle continued. "This is the express wish of the Maker, my lord – and is the doing of none other."

"I want to see my wife and child," Aram stated in a hard tone.

"And you will, my lord." The eagle leaned his head down and deposited the gleaming thing upon the road. It was the crown of Joktan. Alvern looked up at him. "You know me well enough, my lord, to know that I would never challenge you. But you told me not a week ago that you knew what you ought to do with the remaining years of your life upon earth – and that you will expend them in that task and the acceptance of that obligation. This gathering of your people is a necessary part of it."

Aram and the eagle continued to gaze at each other as silence came and lay between them, and the morning lengthened with the ascending of the sun.

Then, as he remembered that his returning to earth – which made reunion with his wife and child possible – was the result of great and astonishing kindness on the part of Him who desired that thing which Alvern now related, his anger faded. Aram sighed deeply and nodded his acceptance. "Alright; so be it. How long must I wait?"

"But a few hours, my lord," the eagle assured him, lowering his wings. "Until perhaps about mid-day. I will go now and tell them that you will arrive before the city at mid-day; that will hurry them."

Aram grimaced and looked up at the new day's rising sun. It lacked three hours of finding the apex of the sky. "Mid-day – that long?"

"Please, my lord; I beg of you."

Aram swung down and stood by Thaniel. "Mid-day," he said, "and then I will come and see my family."

"Thank you, my lord." Alvern looked down at the crown. "Lord Joktan – and the Maker – both desire greatly that you wear this crown. It is a symbol of that which you have become."

Aram gazed at him narrowly, smiling a wry smile. "They told you this themselves?"

"No my lord – as you well know," the eagle reproved him. "The beings that imparted to me the knowledge of your arrival on earth told me of this desire on the part of the king and the Maker."

Slowly, Aram nodded and moved forward to retrieve the crown. "I promised Lord Joktan that I would do so," he stated, and he picked it up and placed it upon his head.

Alvern looked at him with approval for some time, and then the eagle folded his wings and bowed his head to him. "May it remain there for many years, my king," he said.

Spreading his mighty wings once more, catching the breeze, the great bird lifted up and flew back toward the city.

Aram and Thaniel spent the rest of the morning walking along the river and reminiscing over shared adventures, though Aram cast many an eager glance toward the slopes of the black mountain. Because of the intervening wooded hills, the city could not be seen, but his gaze was irrevocably drawn to it nonetheless. As if hindered by some greater power, the morning passed away with excruciating timidity. Between myriad anxious glances toward the southeast and the unseen ramparts of Regamun Mediar, Aram kept an anxious eye upon the sun that seemed to hang in one portion of the sky for centuries before climbing higher.

59.

And then, at last, when for Aram the delay had become unendurable, it was time to go. The sun had finally found its way to the very height of the sky. He swung up onto Thaniel's back. "Let's go home," he said, "I can wait no longer." And they headed south into the valley toward the junction with the avenue that led up to the city.

As they came out of the trees and the black mountain and the city at its base came into view, with the long avenue that led toward it, Aram drew in a sharp breath. Hundreds of wolves, hundreds of horses, and more than a few hundred people lined the avenue from the junction all the way to the city.

The wolves were first, closest to the junction with the north-south road, and they bowed their heads over to the ground as Aram and Thaniel swung past them and turned onto the avenue. Oddly, they made no sound. Despite the massed hundreds, the atmosphere along the avenue was so quiet that Aram was able to hear the gentle susurration of the breeze as it passed through the limbs of the trees in the orchard off to the side.

The horses were next, and neither did the ranks of those magnificent people make any sound as Aram and Thaniel passed. Rank by rank, they shifted their front legs and lowered their heads to him.

Then they came to where the humans, both men and women, and surprisingly, even a few children, lined the avenue for the rest of the way to the defensive wall.

Before Aram and Thaniel had turned onto the avenue, those gathered there had believed that they would cheer when the man that would be their king and his mount came into view.

Instead, the crowd gathered before the walls of Regamun Mediar found themselves awed into utter silence by the sight of the tall, gaunt man on the horse – for with their first sight of him there came an abrupt comprehension of what his presence there on that day meant to them and to all the world.

His cloak was stained with the dust of many miles. He bore no weapon, and his brow was encircled by a simple band of gold with three triangular extrusions above its front portion, the middle extrusion slightly taller than the rest. Stamped upon the very front of this circlet of gold, in the middle, there was a symbol, as of the sun in the fullness of its glory.

Watching him come up the avenue, it suddenly occurred to all of them what it was that they beheld. This man had gone into the stronghold of the evil that had threatened to enslave and destroy them and their world, and had slain the god who was the source of that evil. He was then rumored to be dead – *nay, known to be so* – and yet now had returned alive.

No one fortunate to witness this moment on this day would ever forget what his or her eyes beheld beneath the bright light of that noonday sun.

Borlus and Hilla were there, in the foremost rank, between the horses and the people. The bear's small eyes shone with pride though he gave no verbal response as Aram recognized him with a nod of his head.

The sky above was filled with hawks and eagles, but no sound came from those denizens of the skies, either.

Even Thaniel must have realized the majestic import of that thing of which he was a part, for he formed his great, muscular neck into a proud arch as he cantered along the avenue. Only Aram seemed unimpressed by it all, intent as he was upon reaching his wife and child. Still, he deliberately met many of the pairs of eyes that gazed upon him and nodded his head now and again.

Other than the ringing of Thaniel's great hooves upon the ancient stonework, utter silence reigned –

– except for one small voice.

Far back, in amongst the throng, a young boy sat upon his father's shoulders.

"Is that him, Papa?" The boy asked. "Is that him?"

"Be quiet, child," came the father's hushed reply. "Do not speak. *Yes* – that is the great king."

406

At the wall, Aram dismounted, and glanced around at the crowd. Every eye was fixed on him. He let his gaze rove among the throng for a moment, nodded silently once more, and then he went into the passageway beyond where he ascended the stairway up to the porch.

There, he found Findaen, Boman, Matibar, Edwar, Andar, and High Prince Marcus, along with Generals Thom Sota, Olyeg Kraine, and Kavnaugh Berezan. Mallet, Jonwood, Nikolus, Timmon, Ruben, Muray, and many others stood there waiting for him, in a line that stretched from his left to his right before the city.

As he rose above the stairs and stepped out onto the great porch of his city, every man of them went to one knee.

"Please," Aram responded to this action, "stand up." His eye found Findaen. "Where is she?"

"At home, my lord, with your daughter," Findaen replied, but then he indicated the walkway that led out to the dais upon the defensive wall. "But will you not speak to them first, my lord?"

Aram hesitated and then agreed to this necessity. He turned to go, but looked back as he did so. "How will we feed all these people?" He asked. "Has provision been made for them?"

Findaen smiled. "You are as thoughtful and pragmatic as ever, my lord," he answered, and then he nodded. "Yes, Dane and Arthrus have managed to wrestle enough oxcarts filled with food stores across the hills and into the valley to provide for them all."

Aram nodded his approval and then went across the stone bridge, out to the dais, and looked down the long avenue, lined with representatives of the noble peoples of the world. Realization of the truth of an ancient mystery dawned upon him and he looked down, at the metal tubes that passed through the stonework. For the first time, he understood their purpose.

He looked up again.

"Manon the Grim has fallen," he said, "and will not rise again."

And then, as his words resounded through the metal pipes and out along the avenue, the people cheered.

The roar of approval redounded against the ancient stone of the wall like the thunderous wave of a mighty ocean. There were deeper notes that sounded inside Aram's skull; these emanated from the minds of hundreds of horses and wolves. Among those, one voice stood out.

The voice of a bear.

"*All hail Aram the Mighty,*" Borlus repeated, again and again.

Aram waited until the joyous sound finally slackened and then faded enough that he could be heard.

"Over the next few weeks and months, we will order the world for the peace and freedom of all its inhabitants," he declared. "The gifts of the Maker, the gifts of liberty and justice, will guide us in all our deliberations as we build a new world fit for a new age."

Once more, he found it necessary to wait until the roar of approval died down, then, "Your princes and I, the representatives of every nation on earth pledge to you a new age in which every person may live out a life of peace and productivity, without fear of war or any evil brought upon them by those who are stronger. *And this we will do.*"

Once again, a great chorus of approval crashed against the wall. He waited for it to recede and then lifted his hand. "For now, let those among you with the proper skills go into the storehouse of Regamun Mediar, take what is there and prepare a feast for all."

The shouts rose up and rang out again as he turned away.

As he came back onto the porch and to the leaders gathered there, he looked over at Findaen. "It is true? – there is enough in the storehouse to do as I told them?"

"Fear not, my lord," Findaen responded with a smile. "We brought ample provisions with us when we came into your valley. The storehouse of Regamun Mediar is filled to overflowing."

"Thank you, Fin," Aram said gratefully, and then he started to move on toward the city but halted, turned, and looked at them all.

"*Our* valley," he said.

Eoarl and Dunna were inside the main room of his home when he entered. The old farmer embraced him with joy, and Dunna hugged him and kissed his hand, making it wet with her tears. Then, releasing his hand and moving back, she pointed.

"Your lady is just in there," she said.

Aram went to the door of their bedroom, stepped inside and pulled it shut behind him.

Ka'en stood very still next to Mae's small bed, watching him with her eyes wide and soft, like pools of golden amber. Her breath came quick as she stared at him.

"Findaen told me –"

Aram shook his head and held up his hands.

His heart swelled as he gazed back at her.

"Not now, my love," he told her, his voice breaking. "I will explain it all to you – that of it which I understand, anyway – another time." He took a step toward her.

She did not move.

"My husband?" Whether this was a question or a statement, Aram could not discern, for it was delivered softly, almost inaudibly.

He halted, as the abrupt realization of all that she must have heard – and endured – over the last few weeks washed over him.

"I am Aram," he assured her, "your husband."

Her eyes filled and overflowed. Still, she did not move.

Aram blinked at the sudden moisture that seeped into the corners of his own eyes. "I told you, Ka'en," he said softly but firmly, "that when all of this was over and Manon defeated, I would come home to you and I would never leave you again."

He spread his arms wide, longing for the feel of her. "It is over – *I am home.*"

She ran to him then and he strode forward and enfolded her in his arms, pushing his face down into her hair, filling his senses with the wildflower scent of her.

As he held her tight, his heart full, he sent a thought up, up into the distant realms far above and beyond the earth. "Thank you, Maker in the heavens," he prayed, "for my life."

And the Maker looked down and smiled upon the satisfactory conclusion of that which had troubled Him for so long. For one moment, one heartbeat of the universe, He pondered that which had been done by one of His lesser children, accomplished by virtue of a stout heart, a determined will, and an unwavering commitment to do what was right because it was right – and found Himself amazed. Then, content, He lifted His gaze, and turned and walked into the far reaches of His domain, to see what new thing He might find to do there.

End Book Five

Kelven's Riddle Book Six

AND RETURN PEACE

1. The Reign of Aram

When Aram the Magnificent, as he came to be known, ascended the ancient throne at Regamun Mediar, there was no ceremony. For when he returned from the north – and from even more distant, darkly mysterious regions – and rode up the avenue to the city, the crown of his fathers, the symbol of his authority, was already upon his brow.

He had become king in a manner that transcended ritual.

As the celebrations that attended his ascension came to an end the people, many of them soldiers, veterans of The Battle Before the Tower, reluctantly filed out of the valley and away over the green hills to the south toward their distant homes. Aram and Ka'en stood together upon the grand avenue and bade them all farewell.

Nikolus and Timmon, however, he asked to either remain or to return to him ere the winter set in, to receive instruction on all that which the king hoped to accomplish over the next months and years. For despite wanting a period of peace with his family, Aram knew that many things in his new kingdom begged the attention of clever, capable hands.

Nikolus replied only that he wished to go to Derosa and recover Jena, whom he asked leave to marry before the year was out. Upon granting this, Aram told him to, "Choose any home, either in the city or out upon the verge of the avenue, and make it your own."

Timmon, who like Nikolus elected to stay in the east rather than return west to Aniza as was the expressed desire of many of his compatriots when the death of Manon released them from servitude, was extended the same offer. The clever man did not hesitate but immediately sought permission to secure a house near the base of the tower at the upper level of the city.

For three days after the people began filing away to their various homelands, Aram and the princes of the earth spent a good part of each of those days discussing the future. It became apparent during these talks that the relationship between Aram and the others had been altered yet again. Already readily recognized by all of them as their monarch; his stature among them had become something not only apart, but inarguably *above*.

He had always been, for all of them, a personage of enigma; now there was the added depth of mystery imparted to him by his absence from the earth for the space of nearly two months – time undoubtedly spent in that dark and strange land beyond the border regions of death.

Then, of course, there was his astonishing return from those regions.

The deference paid him was not demanded by him, nor was it evident in his attitude that it was even expected, yet it was given to him because of that which he had always been and because of that which he had become.

From the beginning of his reign, many titles were bestowed upon him, used easily and naturally by those that were now his subjects – among these were the *great*, the *mighty*, the *magnificent*, the *dragonslayer*, even *godslayer*.

He would tolerate the use of none of them in his presence, only accepting simply that he was, at least for the moment, king.

This remarkable and often-demonstrated attitude of humility and self-deprecation on his part, of course, did nothing but add to the legitimacy of those titles in the minds of others. As a consequence of that legitimacy, they found ever wider usage with all people, in all corners of the earth.

Except for one lone man.

Mallet, as he had always done, still insisted that Aram was a god, believing it to the end of his days, ever resistant to all argument or persuasion in opposition to that belief.

After the necessary conferences were completed, the princes of the earth went off to their respective homelands, most still mounted, for many of the horses, including Thaniel and Jared, opted to remain with the men they had borne into battle, rather than return to the high plains for the winter. Some even elected, with Thaniel's permission – that worthy person now being universally recognized as the Lord of All Horses – to make the journey across the passes to the east in order to gather their mates and families to them and bring them out into the greater world.

Aram and Ka'en spent the last weeks of that autumn, as the leaves turned gold and red and then brown, and fell to their final resting place upon the rich soil of the valley, in the peace and quietude that Aram had always desired.

Eoarl and Dunna remained with them. Muray, grousing that he "would be ever a soldier, never a farmer", nonetheless returned to Lamont to see to the holdings of his family there.

The ensuing winter was quiet across all the earth. There was sorrow in every land that had sent soldiers to the Great Battle, as the men returned from war, and the cost was counted by the absence of those that did not return, and were now buried in that small valley below the ridge where they had offered up the ultimate sacrifice.

But there was also pride.

Yes, Aram the Great had finished the grand campaign when he had gone in alone to face the grim lord, but it was the effusion of their blood that had opened the way. As time passed, mothers found their bereavement and grief being slowly replaced by the dignified compensation of that singular sort of honor that is afforded only to those who have given birth to heroes.

Some widows went on to live out their lives alone, convinced that no other man could ever measure up to him that had given his all for his homeland, his prince, his woman, and his children. Others found men to help them rear the offspring of the fallen hero. Many of those surrogate fathers were men that had stood beside those that fell on that grim mid-day so far off to the north.

Fathers of the honored dead, upon finding the pain of grief being dulled by time, would tell tales of the bravery and the mighty deeds that their sons had committed during the Great Battle. And, as whiskey flowed, and the tales were repeated; the heroes of the Great Campaign grew in stature, and grew again.

In the southwest of Lamont, near the ancient holdings of an ancient family, Muray, Captain of Excellence, told similar stories of his own ken, a man of sixty-two that had stood in the line, facing the grim host of Manon with the best of them.

In the Valley of the Kings, Aram spent many a day by the fire, watching his daughter grow slowly but delightfully from an infant to a child as winter tightened its grip and the snow deepened out upon the great porch.

Thaniel stayed in the valley, even occasionally coming up the stairway from the snow-covered rolling swales of the valley to stand before the fire in the great hall, communing with Aram and Eoarl and Timmon as those three indulged in cups of hot kolfa, and now and then tapped one of Eoarl's kegs.

Nikolus had married Jena in the late fall and he and his new bride had temporarily moved into the great house in Derosa with Findaen, pending the preparation of one of the homes in the city of the king as a permanent dwelling place. Ka'en's brother, who by law could not be addressed as Prince, which title would remain with Aram until such time in the future when Ka'en's daughter, Maelee, would become a woman and choose a spouse, nonetheless was made ruler of Wallensia pending that time by decree from Aram.

Many of the discussions around that fire in the great hall concerned the various projects that Aram remanded to Timmon and Nikolus, those worthy gentlemen being named respectively Chief Engineer and Chief Architect of the realm. A few of those projects could be completed over the course of the next year or two, but many were of such immense size that they would necessarily consume decades.

These projects included the restoration of the bridges across the River Broad at Stell, the repair and rebuilding of all the roads throughout the kingdom, and the refurbishing of the façade of the city itself damaged by the dragon, as well as the restoration of every structure along the avenue and downstream at River's Bend.

First, though, as most of those projects would require vast amounts of labor, material, and consequently money; Aram needed another thing to be accomplished. In the spring, he intended to take Timmon and Nikolus over the passes and onto the high plains to see what could be done about spanning the deeply quarried gorge where lived that anachronistic beast, the Choalung.

There were two reasons for this. Firstly, and before all, Aram wished to recover the remains of Joktan from the barren ridge top where they lay and remove them inside the pyramid where they would be interred with those of his queen, Kressia. Secondly, he intended that the great wealth that had been bequeathed to him by his ancestry be brought west and stored at Regamun Mediar, where it could be more easily accessed and put to use restoring all regions of the earth to a semblance of the glory they had once known.

Upon being informed of all that his monarch desired of him and Nikolus, including the order in which Aram wished them to be accomplished, Timmon's mind turned instinctively to still another project. The engineer had planned to remain in Regamun Mediar for the whole of the winter, but now found his thoughts turned away from that prospect. Going outside one unseasonably warm day near the turning of the year, he pivoted and gazed into the south for several minutes.

When Aram came out to join him, Timmon turned to him and begged the use of Huram for the remainder of the winter.

"Why?" Aram asked him.

"I have often been troubled – as I know you have as well, my lord, by the fact that Wallensia is separated in two halves all along the length of the Broad," Timmon told him. "By your leave, I would like to go south to Stell and see to constructing a ferry there, using one of the bridges as a support structure. It would be temporary, for use only until we can see to the restoration of the bridges, but I promise to make it sound and serviceable."

Aram gazed back at him with surprise and sudden gladness. "Go," he said, "and do so with my gratitude."

Another incident that had occurred in the late fall, just before the winter came and shut them in the valley, particular gladdened Aram's heart. This event also relieved the fierce anxiety Thaniel had endured since his mad rush into the south and away from the battlefield in the north after the fall of Manon.

Two months after the battle, as the armies of Duridia and Lamont passed by the southern flank of Burning Mountain, a saddle was discovered, lying in a ravine just to the south of the roadway. A small silver cylinder suspended from a chain looped around the horn of the saddle told of its owner. Stored in Arthrus' shop in Derosa when it was yet believed that Aram was gone for all time, it had at last been remembered, retrieved, and brought north to the city.

The Call came once more into Aram's possession.

Spring arrived rather earlier than usual the following year; almost as if the earth itself understood that a new age had dawned

416

upon it. Intending to give Mae another few months to grow before taking her on an extended visit of all his subject principalities, Aram collected Nikolus from Derosa. Then, along with Timmon, who now was once again mounted on Duwan – the horse having finally and fully recovered from his wounds – rode up over the eastern pass, through the gray and rotten snow that yet clung to the shadowed places in the pass, and down onto the high plains.

The next day, just after mid-day, leaving the horses at the southern edge of the jungled forest that surrounded the ruins of Rigar Pyrannis, they worked their way inward until they came at last to the rim of the chasm. Aram pointed out the obvious obstacles, informed them of his need to find a serviceable way across, and then sat on a mound of ancient piled stone and watched the two of them. His Chief Engineer, along with his newest brother-in-law, also now his Chief Architect, wandered back and forth along the edge of the gorge, gesturing to one another, indicating *this* – and then *that* – for the consideration of the other. And by turns simply gazing across at the enormity of the problem.

Then, as the day wore away, while Aram still sat and waited in the thickening shade, the two clever men sat down, and ignoring the gaping chasm to their front, began to design a solution to their king's need.

The next day, after camping upon the low hill to the south of the forest where the spring arose and gurgled southward, they went in again and for hours, measured first this, and then that, and then discussed – and argued over – how to solve the difficulties presented by *this*, and by *that*.

But the problem remained enormous and so far, unsolved.

On the early morning of the third day, while Nikolus and Timmon once more entered the dark jungle to see whether or not they might examine the problem from yet another, previously undiscovered angle, Aram and Thaniel rode off to the east. Aram told the two men that he meant to journey all the way to the shores of the Inland Sea, promising to return the next day to hear that which had been decided by them, if anything.

Reaching the sea late in the day, Aram dismounted and the two of them walked the shores as the sun declined to the west, and the breeze freshened off the water. The curiously long-legged waterfowl rose up in great flocks, squawking their disapproval at having been disturbed.

Coming up onto a low ridge, where the northern mountains rose up before them in grand display, they halted, and Aram gazed northward. Another low, thickly wooded ridge could be seen a few miles off in the distance, at the base of those mighty mounds of rock. Aram stood still for a moment and then pointed.

"There, my friend," he said to the horse. "That farthest ridge, there, the one just visible in the mist. That is where I spent the remains of that winter when I returned from Kelven's mountain." He turned and looked at Thaniel. "I would ask your permission to build a home on that ridge – something small, where my family and I might spend a part of each summer, away from.....everything else."

Thaniel gazed in the direction indicated for a brief moment and then looked over at Aram. Deep, rumbling laughter abruptly redounded and burst out from him as if it were as tangible as his head or his hooves and not simply a product of his thoughts.

Confused, and somewhat irritated by this response, Aram stared back at him.

Thaniel shook his great head.

"*Aram*," he said. "My king, my brother, my friend."

Surrendering once more to mirth for which Aram could discern no cause, the great horse shook his head and mane yet again.

Then, gaining control, he looked at Aram with his enormous eyes gleaming from the effects of high good humor. "You would *seek permission* from me, my lord? Why?"

He looked around him, at the great body of water to his east, and then back toward the immense grass-covered hills that rolled away to the west. "All of this is yours, my friend," he told Aram. "You are king of *all* the earth, remember? You seek permission from no one for any action that you may wish to take. Certainly, you should seek nothing from me, for even if such a thing were within my ability to grant or deny, I would deny you nothing."

Aram narrowed his eyes and looked at him sharply. "Despite my promise to act as monarch," he stated, with a hint of irritation coloring his words, "I will never infringe upon that which rightly belongs to others." He swept his hand behind him, indicating the broad land, greening up with the advent of spring. "This is yours, my friend, every mile of it, from north to south, and east to west, and ever will be, just as it was your father's before you." He bent his sharp gaze closer. "If you truly insist upon granting my words and wishes the power of decree, my friend – then, hear this."

He rose up to his height and spoke with solemn gravity. "I hereby decree that no man may ever dwell, certainly may never build a house or other permanent structure, upon that region of the earth known as The High Plains of the Horses, without the express permission of the Lord of All Horse, Thaniel the Brave."

With only the hint of a smile tugging at the edge of his mouth, he looked over at Thaniel. "Does that satisfy?"

The horse gave himself over to mirth once more, but as his laughter died away, he looked at Aram curiously. "Are you serious in this, my lord?"

"Unquestionably," Aram replied.

Thaniel turned his bulk until he faced Aram squarely. "Then, my king, if it pleases you to do so – I pray thee, construct a house upon that ridge so that you may come here every summer and spend many a pleasant afternoon and evening with him who counts you as his greatest friend and only brother."

The suggestion of the smile upon Aram's face went away, and he inclined his head soberly. "Thank you, Lord Thaniel," he said.

They camped that night upon a low ridge a hundred yards west of the sea and rose before dawn and went down to the shore. While Thaniel dipped his nose into the water, Aram watched the sky brighten behind the jagged, raw horizon of the eastern mountains beyond the sea, and sighed.

Turning away and looking into the west, where the shadows of twilight wrestled for supremacy with the growing power of the dawn, he said, "I suppose we should get back and see what those two clever men have decided. Then," he sighed once more, "there is much to do elsewhere – and I must see it done."

Backing away from the shore, Thaniel looked at him and then gazed into the gloom of the northern reaches of the high plains. "When will you commission them to build the home we discussed yesterday, my lord?"

Aram shook his head. "Not soon, I fear. There is much to do elsewhere that is more pressing," he answered. "Much."

They reached the edge of the forest south of Rigar Pyrannis while the sun was yet two hours in the sky. Nikolus and Timmon sat on a log upon the brow of the low hill where they'd made their camp, heads bowed over a piece of parchment on which, from time to time, one or the other of them would scribble a correction or suggestion.

Timmon looked up as Aram dismounted. His eyes were grave. "It will take the better part of this year, my lord – certainly all of this summer season – to accomplish a crossing of the chasm. Maybe, in fact, longer than that." He indicated the monstrous tangle of growth before him. "It will be constructed necessarily of wood, and none of these trees are usable. We need good straight trees, of rather extensive height from which we can construct girders and supports for the main frame of the bridge."

He lifted his hand once more to the jungle before him. "These – impressive in size – are far too twisted and bent for our needs."

Aram nodded and lifted his eyes to the west. "There are stands of great firs upon the eastern slopes of those mountains, some of enormous size," he suggested.

Nikolus stood and inclined his head in agreement. "Yes," he affirmed, "and we will have to cut them there, trim them, and bring them here. But that is not the greatest challenge," he stated, and then waited for Aram to question this statement.

Aram looked from one to the other. "What is the worst of it?"

Nikolus glanced at Thaniel before responding. "In order to span the chasm," he said, "we must do so in two sections, and we estimate that it measures more than one hundred feet across. It will be necessary to construct the near side first, rendering it stable, and then creating a temporary bridge over the remainder in order to move men and material to the other side to build the opposing half of the bridge."

He paused again, casting another sharp glance at Thaniel.

"Go on," Aram told him. "Explain the difficulty."

"As I stated, my lord," Nikolus continued, "the chasm extends for more than a hundred feet. The trees we will require must be quite long – and consequently will be very heavy. Then – there is that thick growth that covers the street which allows access from the open plains to the chasm. It must be cut down and removed, and the way made clear, if we are to be able to move the necessary materials to the site."

"We will have to construct towers upon which to anchor the near side of the bridgework," he continued, "and to lower the braces down upon the wall of the chasm which will stabilize the southern half of the bridge, once it is constructed, while we move men and material across a temporary walkway to the chasm's northern side." He spread his hands wide. "All of this work will require vast amounts of brute strength – strength which, I fear, cannot be provided by men and oxen alone."

Once more, he hesitated, glancing yet again at Thaniel. When the pause lengthened and a frown came and deepened upon Aram's face, Jared, who had stood to the side, abruptly snorted and moved forward. He did not address Aram but spoke to his cousin.

"They will need the aid of our people," he told Thaniel. "This is that which my friend hesitates to say. Oxen will not suffice to move such large timbers from the western mountains, nor will they supply the necessary strength to remove the ancient growth from the way that leads into the city. They will require the aid of many strong horses."

As the nature of the obstacle to his engineers' task became clear to Aram, he also turned to look at Thaniel. "I would not ask this of you, my friend," he said quietly, "unless my need was great."

Thaniel swung his head and looked back at him. The low rumble of his good humor resounded inside Aram's mind. "You need not look so serious, my lord. My people have ever stood with yours since the forging of the great alliance between Ram and Boram. Do you not remember that which my father told you in the abandoned town far off to the south?"

Aram nodded. "He stated that your people had aided Joktan in building the road from Lamont into Seneca. He said this in the abandoned town where we came upon the image of the great horse at the eastern edge of the Lost."

"Just so," Thaniel replied. Swinging his head the other way, he looked at Nikolus and Timmon. "When will you need the aid of our people?"

Nikolus looked at Timmon who gave the reply. "Soon," he said. "It will take a matter of some weeks to gather men to do the work of cutting and preparing the trees, and to clear the road into the city, but we hope to complete the construction of Lord Aram's bridge by the end of summer. Soon," he repeated. "Very soon."

Thaniel swung his head further, to focus upon Jared. "I leave it with you, cousin," he said, "for you will accompany Nikolus in that which he does while I must go with the king. Find those that are willing from among our people and tell them what is needed."

Aram inclined his head to the horses. "Thank you, my friends." Then he looked at Nikolus and Timmon. "As Thaniel stated – we will leave it with you."

2. The Journeying Forth of the King

Wallensia, the Lashers, and Duridia

Though Mae was barely more than a year old, the child was strong and healthy. Aram was anxious to go forth and see to the governance of his kingdom, and he wished not to be separated from his wife and child. Besides, Ka'en was now queen as much as he was king, and the people would wish to see her and come to know her.

Several regions of his newly-formed realm, such as Duridia, Lamont, and Seneca had for some time been well-governed. Elam, the greatest and richest principality of them all, was now in capable, sure hands in the person of young Marcus. Wallensia, though much of it was still shattered by the many years spent under the boot of the grim lord, would, under Findaen's strong guidance, undoubtedly rise again. Other regions, however, such as Aniza and the great plains in the west, and Bracken in the north, lay in ruins, and he intended to begin the restoration of those parts of his kingdom as soon as was possible.

He meant to visit the more established parts of his realm to find leaders willing to go and aid those regions in climbing up out of the mire of centuries of servitude and ruin. To that end, he meant to journey almost constantly from these, the first weeks of spring, until the end of autumn. And he intended to take his family with him. Journeys of such length and breadth would require that they move quickly across the face of the earth, so there would necessarily be no oxcarts employed in the movements of him and his family; they must travel on horseback.

He had spoken of this difficulty to Arthrus in the previous autumn. Once again, the highly-skilled iron monger had come up with a solution, though it actually made no use of iron or steel at all, but rather was constructed of wood and cloth.

As Huram was now the official mount of the queen, Arthrus had measured the horse, especially about his front quarters, in particular determining the length of his neck, and the width of his back. Then he had constructed an ingenious device, a sort of basket that was fitted to the front of Huram's saddle. The basket, comprised of cloth and just the right size to hold a child, was suspended from two opposing x-braces by stout leather thongs.

The result of this clever construct was that Mae, rocked back and forth in gentle fashion by Huram's movement along the road, could sleep while the horse went forward at whatever speed suited Ka'en. Upon seeing this device demonstrated by his wife and child, as Huram cantered along the avenue, Aram was confident that he could now go forth and visit the larger part of his realm before winter prevented travel once more.

Yvan had gone into the east with Matibar and Yerba had died along with his rider during the cavalry's action in the Great Battle, but Thaniel found two young horses, named Keth and Caulyer, which he recruited to bear the temporary housing and supplies for Aram and his family.

They headed southward across the green hills, where spring was busily pushing new life up through the leaf-carpeted earth and out the ends of the sap-swollen limbs of the trees. Coming down onto the plains, they went first to the east and into Derosa, where Aram found the tailor, Suven, and requested the construction of a large replica of the king's horsehead standard. Then he sent a thought skyward, summoning Alvern.

"Have Palus find Captain Keegan, wherever he may be upon the ocean," he instructed the eagle, "and bring him to Durck within the next two weeks, if possible."

Then, while waiting for Suven's work to be completed and comprehending Ka'en's desire to visit with friends she had not seen since the previous summer and to show her daughter to the many admirers, Aram stayed for three days and spent his time discussing practical matters of governance and restoration with Findaen.

424

After promising him that the full restoration of the bridges across the Broad at Stell would be next on Nikolus and Timmon's agenda upon the completion of their work on the high plains, Aram listened to Findaen describe how many of the farmers had given up their assigned plots in the valley of the Weser. With the advent of a sure and permanent peace, they had gone back out onto the plains to rebuild old farmsteads and to plow large portions of the prairie into fertile fields once more.

Rober had come east of the Broad as he had told Aram he would do, but upon hearing that the grim lord had been destroyed, had changed his mind and gone back over the wide current to more familiar ground.

All up and down the Broad, on both banks of that mighty stream, the earth prepared to offer up her bounty even as the idea of freedom took root, grew, and blossomed in the hearts of the men and women that labored over her.

On the morning of the fourth day, anxious to take advantage of the continuing fine weather, Aram informed Ka'en that it was time to move on into the south.

He then went to look for Findaen, to bid him farewell.

Findaen was nowhere to be found.

An hour later, as Aram and Arthrus were loading the two young horses with supplies at the ironmonger's workshop, hooves sounded upon the road. Aram turned to look down the track that led toward town.

Findaen came up the dirt track on Andaran. Behind him, Hilgarn and four other men, all dressed in uniforms of crimson and gold, like the colors of the horse-head standard that Hilgarn bore at the end of a staff suspended above his head, approached. Behind them there were four more horses lacking riders.

As Andaran slid to a stop, Findaen grinned down at Aram.

"Your wife – the queen – has been busy yet again, my lord."

Aram frowned. "What is the meaning of this?"

"Lady Ka'en," Findaen said, "believes that the king should not travel the length and breadth of his kingdom unescorted – and I concur with that judgment." He indicated the mounted men behind him. "Hilgarn, you know, of course. These men are Brandan, Rayn, Finn, and Paual, and their mounts are Garsia, Silich, Kritap, and Fasr. All rode with the cavalry and were heavily engaged in the fighting

425

when the lashers broke through Donnick's lines. They are all of them trustworthy and anxious to serve you in this capacity, my lord."

Aram inclined his head to the five men and horses. "I thank all of you for your service to your people and your homelands," he stated solemnly. Then he turned back to Findaen. "I understand that this is Lady Ka'en's wish," he told him, "but I have no time to gather more supplies and make provision for lodging these men while we are upon the road."

Findaen grinned and glanced at Arthrus, who smiled broadly. Then he indicated the four riderless horses. "My lord, meet Lenad, Divad, Wetham, and Surcam. They are young and without riders, and have gladly volunteered to bear whatever is required on your journey."

"I thank you," Aram acknowledged the horses, and then once more he turned to Findaen as his frown deepened. "There is still the matter of supplies."

In response, Findaen looked over at Arthrus, whose smile broadened further.

Turning toward his shop, Arthrus threw wide the door. There, lying upon the floor in neatly bound heaps were four double-slung packs, sized to fit upon a horse's back. "Your Lady left nothing undone, my lord," Arthrus stated, looking back at Aram. "There remains only to secure these to the horses, and you will be ready."

Aram shook his head, but the frown left his features to be replaced by a smile. He looked at Arthrus, and then at Findaen, and then at the others. "We will leave within the hour," he told them.

Not wishing to brave the ferry and current of the Broad so early in the year, when it ran high and rough around the low islands, especially with Mae in her basket at the front of Huram's saddle, Aram led the troop instead along the edge of the green hills. Angling up through the forested slopes above the headwaters of the mighty stream, he led them around the massive spring where the main source of that great river welled up from the earth, and thence down the western bank.

Moving as quickly as he dared, by early afternoon he had passed through Rober's village, pausing for a few minutes to speak with the young village elder, and then had moved beyond the next village to the south.

As his company was larger than he had anticipated, and no routine had yet been established for setting up camp at eventime, he halted while the sun was yet more than an hour in the sky, bringing the company to a halt where a clear stream flowed out of the hills toward the river. But the chore of preparing the camp went better than he had hoped, for the men that accompanied him had gone into the north with the army and were all veteran campaigners.

The next day, they made Stell just before mid-day. After an hour spent looking through the abandoned city, in an effort to judge the extent of the ancient capital's destruction and what might best be done to start it on its way to restoration, Aram went back westward, crossed northward over the Stell and moved upstream along it. As they went, he stopped briefly at each village to monitor the progress of people newly set free from slavery and to inquire as to any needs they might have. Then he went west as the day waned, looking for a shallow place where he could affect a crossing to the south bank.

That evening found them camped on the southern side of the Stell, in a small copse of trees a few miles across the prairie from that stream.

Aram had his sights fixed next upon Panax. He meant to keep his promise made to Hargur to come and check on him and his companions, and to discover whether in fact the three lashers had managed to find their way to the ancient abandoned city.

The next morning they went due south, toward the dark green band on the horizon that grew and expanded and gradually resolved itself into a mighty forest. Swinging further east in order to avoid the marshes that bordered the streams that came out of the hills to the west and flowed slowly northward toward the Stell, Aram entered this great forest before mid-day and found the remains of the old road, where he turned westward.

Soon, and rather abruptly, the forest failed. The mighty trees thinned and refused to go further as the company exited their dark environs and entered the confines of the ancient city of Panax.

Ka'en looked around in amazement. "No one lives here? But – why?" She asked incredulously. "It is beautiful – not burned or crumbled or ruined at all."

"It was abandoned because of the great evil perpetrated here," Aram told her. "An evil committed long ago, by Manon and its compliant, decadent citizenry. No humans will ever live here. It now belongs to the last remnants of another race. At least that is my hope." Speaking to Thaniel to slow, he ordered the column to a halt.

Cocking his head, he listened carefully into the empty streets and vacant avenues. No sound came to his ear. Had Hargur and his companions turned aside somewhere? Or had they been slain by men along the way as they journeyed out of the north? No – that latter thought could not be, for if it were so, word of it would have come to him. Raising his voice then, he shouted into the stillness. "Hello!"

No answer was returned to this greeting, but Hilgarn, a few yards behind, abruptly asked him. "What is this curious thing, my lord?"

Aram turned to look at him. The young standard-bearer was gazing to his left, down one of the avenues that led toward the center of the city.

"It appears to be some kind of cart," Hilgarn said.

Thaniel moved back next to Hilgarn and Aram looked down the street. Upon the pavement, almost to the avenue's intersection with the next lateral street, there was parked a very oddly-shaped wooden conveyance.

"Let's go look," he told Thaniel.

The cart was apparently newly made, for the wood bore no patina of age. There were but two wheels beneath a large square basket-like bed. Attached to the underside of the vehicle and extending in front of the cart were two long poles that were set wide enough apart and were long enough to accommodate an ox, yet were lacking in any obvious means of attaching traces.

Aram dismounted and examined the thing more closely. He readily determined that it was indeed of relatively new construction, and then he straightened up and looked around. No one was in sight. The cart was parked before a large, low building comprised of a single story that was set back from the street a ways and fronted by a square, flat area of grass. The walkway that reached back to the entrance to this building, unlike the stonework near the buildings to either side, had apparently been swept clean of debris, or perhaps it was rendered so by use.

Moving closer to the structure along the walkway, Aram examined the building. A new wooden door was set into the frame at

428

the front, and new shutters framed the windows to either side; these were open at the moment, exposing a dark interior.

"Hello!" He called once more.

Again, no answer came, but an instant later, his ear caught the echoing of a sharp yet distant sound, arising from the gloomy woodland beyond the east side of the city. Going south to the next intersection, he looked eastward, toward the forest.

The edge of the city was less than a quarter of a mile away. Leading into the woods from that point there was a well-travelled path which had been recently cleared of brush and debris. Two or three of the larger trees had been cut down and removed. The tracks of a wheeled vehicle showed in the soil beyond the pavement where they had rutted the soft earth. These tracks led into the dimness beneath the great trees.

As he stared, wondering, the short, sharp sound came to his ear once more. Turning back to Hilgarn, he motioned for him to go back and join the others. "Stay with the queen," he said. "I will return shortly."

Drawing his sword, he went to where the track entered the forest and followed it into the gloom. As his eyes adjusted, he looked around in astonishment. A great deal of labor had been expended here. Tucked back into a side track, there was yet another of the odd, double-wheeled carts.

The sound came again, closer now, and it sounded very much like the striking of metal or stone on wood. Then there was a sharp, cracking sound that rose in volume and intensified, broken by the guttural voice of a lasher.

There followed a terrific Crash! This sounded to his front and off to the right, and was followed by silence.

He hurried forward.

A short way further on, the forest opened up into a clearing dotted with the stumps of great trees. On the far side of the clearing, three lashers were at work, clearing the limbs from a fallen giant. Nearby were two more carts.

"Hello!" Aram called once more.

Hargur, Bildur, and Pentar jerked erect and looked across the clearing at him. Upon the instant, all three came sprinting toward him.

Aram sheathed the sword.

429

"Master! You have come!"

"I have come," Aram agreed, grinning.

He pointed back toward the city. "The queen and a company of men are with me. Allow me to fetch them and I will return."

Aram and his company spent two hours with the great beasts, lunching in the clearing, admiring their workmanship, and deflecting repeated declarations of gratitude for allowing them to settle in the ancient abandoned city.

"And the presence of the tower doesn't trouble you?" Aram asked at one point.

"No, master," Hargur assured him. "To us, it is a reminder of your great kindness."

"How did you acquire the tools for working in wood?" Aram wondered then.

In response, Hargur went over to the tree they had felled and returned with what was obviously an axe. The handle was made of wood. Attached to the smaller end, bound with loops of some kind of rough, woven twine, was a large piece of shiny black rock, sharpened to a fine edge on either of its sides which extended from the point where it was attached to the handle.

Aram ran his thumb along the edge, flinching as he drew a line of blood.

"What is this?" He inquired. "It looks of flint, but I have never seen a piece this large."

"It came from the ancient tower," Hargur said.

Aram looked up in surprise. "You took this from Manon's tower in the city?"

Hargur shrugged. "It did not come easily."

At this, Aram smiled soberly. "I am happy to hear that structure has some value beyond its intended purpose."

Sitting there upon a stump in the coolness of the forest, gazing down at the sharp black edge of the axe, Aram abruptly thought of Timmon and Nikolus, up in the ruined city of the high plains, struggling to construct their bridge.

He looked up at Hargur. "Are you happy here?"

"Yes, master, very happy."

Aram watched him. "I have something to ask of you," he said.

"You may command anything of us," the lasher replied.

430

Aram looked around, at the carts, at the fallen trees, and the abundant evidence of extensive labor. Then he met Hargur's eyes.

"Will you leave this place – for a short while only – to lend aid to my friends? You can return immediately afterward," he promised. He leaned toward the immense lasher. "By doing so, you will help the world to accept your presence, and let them come to see your being here as a good thing." He indicated the cart standing nearby. "Workmanship like that would be prized by anyone, anywhere."

He looked from one to another of the great creatures. "When the world comes to know of your ability to work in wood; perhaps you will have found your purpose."

"We will ever do as you command, master," Hargur replied quietly, as he lowered his head.

"Look at me, Hargur." When the lasher had complied, Aram shook his head. "It is not a command, it is a request. Nay – not even that; it is a suggestion only." He leaned forward once more. "You must live in this world with the rest of us, and I do not wish for you to be isolated, set apart, hiding in this great forest. Come; join with the world, my friend; be a part of us."

Hargur blinked his flat, expressionless eyes. "But will the humans accept us, master?"

Aram considered for a moment. "Not all," he admitted. "At least, not at first. But the world will do as I require. In time, you will become as natural a part of the affairs of the earth as the rising of the sun and the ending of the day."

Hargur kept his gaze fixed upon Aram's face as he tendered a cautious question. "May I ask, master – what is this thing that your friends need of us?"

Aram lifted a hand and indicated the northeast. "They are building a great bridge across a deep chasm upon the high plains to the east of my valley." He dropped his hand and looked at each of the lashers. "Your great strength – and your skill in shaping wood – will be greatly appreciated, and will be a great help in completing that project."

He met each set of flat black eyes once more and then said, "I need this project completed by the end of the year. Without your help, that outcome is doubtful."

Hargur glanced to his left, at Pintar, and then back to his right, at Bildur. "We will go," he said.

Aram nodded. "Thank you. We will leave at dawn. Gather your tools, and food for a long journey."

The next day they retraced their route back northward along the banks of the Stell, with the lashers loping easily along with them. As they passed the scattered villages, Aram made no effort to hide the fact that, trailing at the rear of his company, jogging behind the horses, there were three of those creatures that had once been overlords.

It was obvious to all that they were his servants now, a fact that would undoubtedly cause a measure of consternation and even some suspicion. In time, Aram knew, those great beasts would cease to be something feared, or even remarked upon. Eventually, he hoped, their presence upon the earth would be considered as mundane and as natural as rain falling from heavy gray clouds, or the blue of the clear skies that came after the storm.

Leaving Ka'en at Derosa, Aram took the lashers up through the valley, across the pass to the east, and over the grasslands to the encampment of men and horses south of the jungle surrounding Rigar Pyrannis.

He stayed long enough to get Nikolus and Timmon to accept the presence of the mighty beasts, to learn that they would harm no one, and come to an appreciation of their strength and skill.

Then he went back to Derosa, collected Ka'en and Mae and went southward into Duridia.

Boman and Lenci gladly opened their spacious house to Aram, Ka'en and all their company. For four days, they ate well, drank fine wine, laughed often and easily, and talked. No mention was made of the events of that far-off valley in the northern reaches of the world.

On the morning of their intended departure, Aram and Boman went out to find the street in front of the governor's house filled in both directions with the citizens of Duridia, all of them anxious to get a glimpse of their king and queen. Among that throng were many veterans of the Great Campaign. It became immediately apparent to Aram that there would be no departure from Duridia that day.

For hours, Aram and Ka'en, accompanied by the Governor and his wife, moved among the gathered citizens, communing with many of them on whatever subject they desired.

At mid-day, Boman ordered the storehouses to be opened and an impromptu feast followed, prepared and devoured upon the main streets of Mandin. Later, casks were opened, and kegs were unplugged. The revelry lasted deep into the night. It was not until late the following morning that Aram and his company once again prepared to go to the east into Lamont.

While he waited for Ka'en to say her farewells to Lenci, Aram looked over at Boman. "Where was the border between Duridia and Wallensia in ancient times – do you know, Governor?"

Boman nodded. "There is a region of high ground," he said, "now thickly wooded, several miles north of the wall."

"I know this high ground," Aram agreed.

Boman turned and looked that way. "It is said that in ancient times, there was a road that came down across the prairie with a way-station at the border. The road, if indeed it ever existed, is gone now, apparently swallowed up by the eternal grasses."

He lifted his hand and extended his thumb over his shoulder. "Another road went westward through the mountain passes to Stell. The boundary was at the top of the pass. That road, though no longer paved with stone, is still in reasonably good condition along much of its length, as is the one that goes east out of Duridia, toward Lamont." He looked at Aram. "You have travelled upon the road into Lamont, of course, so you will know it well."

"Shall I rebuild those roads?" Asked Aram.

"My lord?"

"I mean to restore all of the ancient thoroughfares, so that commerce may travel easily throughout the land," Aram replied. "Shall I rebuild your roads, Governor?"

"Why ask this of me, Lord Aram?" Boman looked at him through narrowed eyes. "You are king of all the earth, my lord. Duridia is yours as well, more than it is mine. You may do as you like, here, as in any other of your lands."

Aram shook his head. "Not so, my friend. None are 'my lands'. I do not intend to do as I 'like' in any nation of the earth, nor do I mean to meddle in the lives of people. The fall of Manon made us all free. My task, more than any other thing, is to ensure and safeguard that freedom – for all people."

He looked up at the sun, shot a glance toward the house, and then looked back at Boman and asked once more. "Shall I rebuild the roads into Duridia, Governor?"

Boman smiled and nodded. "If you will, my lord. Duridia will do what it can to defray the cost."

Again, Aram shook his head. "The kingdom was left a great fortune, for just such purposes as this. Nikolus and Timmon are opening the way to it even now, that it may come to Regamun Mediar."

"Ah," Boman reached into an inner pocket and retrieved a golden coin and held it forth where it gleamed in the morning sun. It was a monarch. "This would be a part of that fortune, my lord? You gave me this – and five others – when first we met, remember?"

"I do," replied Aram, grinning. "You thought perhaps that I meant to try and buy Duridia's friendship."

"I apologize for that, my lord," Boman said and he held the coin out toward him. "Will this – along with the others, which are stored within – pay Duridia's part in the building of the roads?"

"No, I beg of you, Governor; keep it, and the others, here in Duridia," Aram told him. "Keep them as a reminder of a friend's clumsy attempts at diplomacy."

Boman laughed and then looked at his king through shrewd eyes. "Diplomacy," he said, "is perhaps the only thing at which you are clumsy, my lord."

Aram held out his own hand. "Come to Regamun Mediar at any time, my friend. You will always find a welcome there."

Durck, Lamont, and Seneca

The sun was upon the western horizon and the distant sea stretched away like strangely luminous black cloth when they crested the ridge above Durck and descended the road toward the tavern. A stout wind was sweeping down the channel that led to the left toward the open ocean, and the waters of the bay were choppy, covered with frothy white caps. Three ships lay at anchor in the bay, rocking with the tide. The nondescript blue-and-gray striped standard of privateers flew from each mast.

Mullen met them in the yard of the tavern, bowing so low as to risk falling upon his face. "Welcome, my lord and my lady!"

He shot a glance at the horsehead standard flying above Hilgarn before once more bending his stout body toward the ground. "Keegan tells us that a great many changes have occurred upon the earth, my lord, wrought by your magnificent self."

"There is no need to wax poetic, Mullen. Where is Keegan?"

Mullen grinned sheepishly and indicated the interior of the tavern behind him. "Inside, my lord, with Lubchek and both their crews, trying desperately to put the place in order. We did not know you were coming. They have been here for weeks, spending every silver and copper in their purses. My casks are in danger of running dry. If Keegan's last cargo had not been many barrels of Lamontan whiskey, which he was willing to sell to me and is now buying back in prodigious amounts, I would have closed my doors long ago."

He glanced backward, toward the dark interior as something crashed and broke against a table or perhaps the floor. "They are celebrating your great victory, my lord." His sheepish grin widened crookedly. "As you might imagine, the place is a mess." He turned to Ka'en and bowed again, deeply, shaking his head mournfully. "It is certainly no place for a mother and a child, my lady."

"You put us up at your own home once," Aram reminded him.

Mullen brightened. "And it is at your disposal now, my lord." He grinned broadly and gestured up toward the house at the base of the bluff. "The door is open."

Aram smiled as Thaniel turned away. "Tell Keegan that I will return within the hour to speak with him. He should make every attempt to be sober."

"Yes, of course. As you will, my lord."

After settling Ka'en and Mae in Mullen's house and leaving the four young soldiers to guard her, Aram took Hilgarn, along with the flag he had commissioned of Derosa's tailor, and went down to the tavern. This time, Keegan and Lubchek, with a sizeable cohort of wide-eyed sailors, awaited them outside the weather-worn central structure of the town of Durck.

The pungent odor of whiskey permeated the air, competing with the smell of sea and salt for supremacy.

Keegan bowed extravagantly. "It is good to see you, my lord. I hear that the wizard's cannon was a vital – uh, was at least a small aid to you in your great victory."

Aram treated the privateer to a rueful smile. "The gun helped us tremendously, captain," he assured him. "And I thank you for your aid in finding it and bringing it to the army."

"It was nothing, my lord," and now his words held the added weight of sincerity as he straightened up and looked at Aram. "You are my king now, Lord Aram, and I pledge to you my honest and dependable service always. If ever I can do aught for you, my lord, you need but speak."

Aram's attitude sharpened abruptly and his smile vanished as he indicated the interior of the tavern with one hand. "I am counting upon your service, captain, *as always*; and there is, in fact, something I would ask of you."

Keegan's eyes widened at the sharpness in Aram's tone, but he inclined his head. "Whatever it is, my lord, I will do it."

Aram's smile returned; a smaller version of its former self. "You should, perhaps, allow me to ask it of you first – and then we will see."

Once they were seated at a table inside the dingy, dim-lit tavern, Aram sipped at his glass and looked across at Keegan. "There are two things that I would ask of you, captain."

Keegan, from whom the effects of the liquor had begun to dissipate, nodded solemnly. "I am at your service ever, my lord."

"The first thing I would require," Aram went on, "is simple enough. I would ask that you and your ship be at Sunderland, in Lamont, two weeks from today, outfitted and prepared to take me and my company into Seneca."

Keegan nodded again. "I will be there, my lord. Sunderland is known as a free port, and Lamont has ever been more welcoming to my kind than those lands to the west – Elam, in particular."

Aram was watching him with stern eyes. "That, my friend," he said quietly, "is the second thing that I will ask of you."

"My lord?"

"You have profited by your service to me, have you not?" Aram asked him.

Keegan frowned. "I have, my lord, but that is not why –"

Aram waved this away. "Why do you serve me, captain?"

436

The privateer looked down at the table for a long moment. Then he looked up. There was no hint of inebriation in either his tone or his words as he stated, "At the first, my lord – I confess – it was mostly out of fear of your strength and authority. But then, as I witnessed that which your strength and authority wrought in the regions of the world where they are recognized, it became something more." He bowed his head. "I am your servant, my lord, not because of fear, or because of gold, but because of gratitude. Command me – I will do whatever you wish me to do."

"Then you will be a privateer no longer," Aram stated firmly. "I want you to fly my standard upon the mast of your ship, captain."

Keegan stiffened, raised his head and stared. "My lord?"

Aram smiled a solemn smile. "I must have someone that reports to me alone, who knows his way around out there, upon the broad sweep of the ocean, in whose integrity, judgment, and loyalty I may place complete trust."

Keegan continued to stare, his eyes wide. "I will not be a privateer? – "

"Unless you refuse my request, captain – no."

Dismay spread across Keegan's face. He looked down at the table once more as he gave his hesitant reply. "It is my livelihood, my lord.....and.....has been my way of life since my youth."

Aram smiled. "I did not say, captain, that you must abandon the life and occupation of a free trader." He leaned forward and spoke firmly. "From this time forward, all trade that moves upon the waters of the great sea must be free. No one nation may own the ocean, or tax the commerce that moves upon it. Each land may make and enforce whatever law it wishes to govern the ports of its cities, but the sea must answer to my law alone."

He leaned back and looked around at them all. "No one," he said sternly, "will operate outside the boundaries of my law – and that law is that *the sea is free* – free from oppression like that which was until recently practiced by Elam, but also free from lawlessness."

His voice took on the weight of command. "No one may prey upon the ship or the cargo of another," he warned them all. "Even as the ocean must be free; those that trade upon its vast waters must practice honesty and lawfulness."

He brought his hard, stern gaze back to Keegan. "Do you understand me, captain?"

437

Keegan stared at him for a long moment. Slowly, the light of comprehension brightened in the depths of his eyes. "And you want me to enforce your law, my lord?"

"Just so," Aram affirmed. He smiled. "You may continue to trade, Keegan, and the payment that was promised you and Lubchek on the day Burkhed died will continue, for you and your crews. But from this day forth, you will fly my standard and answer to me. And for those that encounter your ships, it will be as if they met me."

He waited for a moment and then asked him, "What say you, captain?"

Keegan continued to gaze at him. "All trade will be free?"

Aram nodded. "Free and honest, captain, or I will take action personally to make it so."

Keeping his gaze fixed on Aram's face, Keegan slowly nodded. "I will fly your standard proudly, my lord, and act as your agent in whatever manner you desire."

Retrieving the rolled-up standard from Hilgarn and handing it to the seaman, Aram said, "Then remove the blue and gray, captain, and fly this in my name."

And so it was that Captain Keegan, reared from his youth in the lawless society of pirates, and who had once served as mate for the fearsome giant Burkhed, went willingly into the service of the king. Before the last days of his life, he came to be known as the Admiral of the Ocean, the one man most trusted by King Aram the Magnificent in the enforcing of the laws of free and open commerce upon the great waters of the southern sea.

By the end of his life he had also become one of the richest men in the world, for Aram made good on his promise to render one gold monarch for every faithful year of service. He never married, but there was a woman in Kolfaria in whose house he often stayed while in port in that land. This woman bore and raised up three children in the apparent absence of a father, all of whom were fair-haired and slightly-built like Keegan, and to whom, upon his death, he left both his ship and his fortune.

After leaving Durck, Aram and his company went through Lamont, stopping to stay for two nights with Muray, whereupon, over many a late-night mug of ale, the captain and his monarch

438

reminisced over the day that they met, when Aram and his Sword set on fire the gates of Lamont.

Leaving western Lamont, Aram and the company crossed the mountains and came down into Sunderland, where Willar welcomed the new king and queen with as much fanfare as his wealth could supply. The elderly chief warder's daughter, whose health had been failing for some time, had passed away during the previous winter. Upon learning this, Ka'en took his hand and mourned with him, and then she placed Mae into his arms.

Willar looked down upon the child whose parents were his monarchs, his supreme lord and lady. As the little girl cooed up at him, and wrapped her tiny fingers around his, his tears dried, to be replaced with a look of wonder.

He looked up at Ka'en, his faded eyes shining. "Thank you for this, my lady. My life is full now, complete; for I have seen the future of the earth, and it is bright indeed."

Late in the next day, as the sun fell close to the ragged, hilly horizon to the west, the mountain of Lamont rose up severe and dark before them and the gates of Condon came into view.

A crowd was gathered at the gates.

Foremost among them stood Jame, Vitorya, and Edwar.

All three bowed low, and then the Hay of Lamont stood erect and spoke graciously. "Welcome, my king and my queen. Kipwing informed us of your imminent arrival. I am most happy to see you once again."

Aram nodded. "And you, my friend," he answered. "Tell me – is there room at the Silver Arms for a group of weary travelers?"

Jame's face fell and he shook his head. "I am sorry, my lord. When Kipwing told of your arrival in the land and that you would come to Condon, the people streamed into the city from all around. There is not a vacant room left in the city." He bowed his head. When next he looked up, it was to reveal a look of high good humor.

"I am afraid, my lord and my lady, that you must be content – if it pleases you – with staying in my own house. The Great Hall of Lamont, after all, is as much yours as it is mine."

"We will be honored," Aram returned.

At this, Jame's good humor abruptly vanished in favor of an expression of deepest sincerity. He shook his head with firm denial.

"Nay, my lord," he stated. "The honor that you do my house this day will hallow its humble halls forever."

He stepped aside and indicated the street that led up through the city beyond the gates. "Come in, my lord and lady, if you will."

The horses were released to graze upon the grassy slopes to the south and west of the city and the soldiers were quartered in the barracks with many of those that had stood beside them upon that barren ridge off to the northwest. Aram and Ka'en walked with their hosts up through the city toward the great house that stood on the highest hill. All along the way, the streets were lined with citizens who stared, wide-eyed and overawed, at the sight of the great king and his queen, accompanied by their own beloved Hay, his mother and her consort, moving on foot through the narrow passageways of their capital city.

There were veterans of the Great Campaign in the crowd, easily recognized by their uniforms, worn with pride in the presence of their king, and in some cases, by the scars of injuries suffered in the Battle Before the Tower. Aram and Ka'en halted and spoke with each and every one of these men.

Hours passed, so many that Ka'en was obliged, now and then, to accept offers of hospitality for her and Mae that were extended to her often along the route. Darkness fell and night overtook the earth long before they reached the house on the hill.

After a late supper, as Aram and Jame once more walked the gentle environs of the Hay's garden, the young man turned to Aram.

"Lord Joktan is gone now, I suppose, my lord?"

Aram nodded. "He has at last gone home."

"My garden will miss him." Jame tilted his head back and looked up at the countless stars shining bright in the clear, black sky. "Your victory over the grim lord set him free, my lord."

Aram did not respond to this but simply looked up as well and stared out across the vastness of the universe. Much of that which had occurred in the past year had by this time dissolved into the deep well of misty memory, and taken on a dream-like quality. It sometimes seemed impossible to him that he had gone out there, somewhere, among those millions of far-away suns, and stood for a brief moment upon the shores of eternity.

But he had.

He had seen Joktan in the state of final contentment, united once again with the woman that he had, for thousands of years, loved from a distance, across the great divide. Kelven was there, too. And Florm was there with Ashal, and faithful Durlrang with his mate. They were there, and he was here, and that was as it should be.

He was happy to let memories fade, and life to proceed.

He dropped his gaze to find Jame's eyes fixed upon him. As he could never be certain what was on the mind of the young ruler of Lamont, he waited in silence. After studying the face of his monarch, Jame looked away, down across the dark town, where, even at this late hour, light yet shone from many windows. Occasionally, from unseen courtyards here and there, raucous laughter floated up.

"I told you once, my lord," Jame said then, "that you had the look of a man who had been touched by the Maker himself. I confess to you that it is more pronounced, now." He looked back at Aram. "I hear from many sources that you left the earth for a time, no doubt to wander mysterious, distant shores."

Immediately upon rendering this statement, Jame held up his hand and shook his head. Either he saw Aram's expression darken, even in the tenuous light of the stars, or, more likely, his natural intuitiveness prevailed.

"I would not presume to ask you to relate that which you have experienced, my lord. No doubt it would be beyond my ability to comprehend, in any event." He turned his gaze away once more, but looked back immediately. "When first I saw you, Lord Aram, you walked into my hall bearing a weapon of unspeakable power, a sword with which you might have reduced this land to ash. Yet you exhibited only deference and politeness. I knew then that you were utterly unique upon the earth."

Jame looked up at the crown that rested on Aram's brow, at the triangular edges gleaming in the starlight. He straightened up, dropped his hands to his sides and bowed deeply.

"May your reign last long, my king," he stated solemnly.

Aram looked back at him in silence, and then he inclined his head. "And may I ever have the benefit of your counsel, my friend," he returned.

Jame looked at him with a peculiar eagerness brightening his eyes, even in the gloom.

"Speaking of that, my lord –"

"What is it, my friend?" Aram asked of him, when the young man hesitated.

Jame glanced briefly away. "It's just that I would dearly love to look upon your marvelous city."

"You are always welcome there," Aram returned.

Jame continued to gaze at him with a sardonic smile upon his young features. "It's just that – well, it is a long way from here to there, my lord."

And then Aram understood. He nodded, smiling. "Thaniel knows you, my friend, and he knows his own people. When we are returned into the west, I will instruct him to choose a suitable companion for Your Grace from among his people and send him here, to you." He chuckled. "Then you may come to visit with me whenever you like."

Jame bowed once more. "I will try very diligently not to be a bother, my lord."

At that, Aram grew serious. "I will always be glad to receive a friend," he said.

The company remained in the great house at Condon for another week, and then Aram reluctantly bade Jame, Edwar, and Vitorya farewell and they went back to Sunderland. Keegan's ship, with the great crimson and gold standard of the king flying from the mast, lay at rest in the harbor.

After one more night with Willar, which second visit raised the elderly gentleman's sprits further; along with his standing in Sunderland – *the king and queen have stayed with him twice* – they boarded ship and prepared to sail for Seneca.

The sailors rowed the ship out through the entrance to the harbor. Once upon the open sea, the ship was turned, and the great sail on the main mast unfurled, caught the wind, and billowed large and full. Keegan's ship hove out onto the dark solemn blue of the deep and tacked eastward toward Seneca.

Ka'en stood at the rail, gazing first toward the land that was slipping away to become a fine line of brown upon the northern horizon; and then she turned and gazed southward out across the heaving swell of the sea that grew a deeper shade of blue with every mile the ship drew away from the shore.

There followed then nine days of novel experience. Ka'en watched in amazement as Keegan and his crew constantly worked

442

the sails and kept the ship moving eastward, often angling slightly to the north and then to the south in order to make headway upon those occasions when the wind blew against them. While generally blowing favorably at their back, from west-to-east, it nonetheless sometimes came at them from ahead of the bow, seeming to do all it could to prevent them from making progress.

As she marveled at the machinations of sailors and sailcloth, Ka'en observed to Keegan. "I don't know how you do it, captain. It is almost like magic – the way you can sail *into* the wind."

Keegan grinned and glanced up at the snapping sails. "Aye, my lady," he replied. "She is a capricious mistress, is the sea – and the wind is her consort. The trick is to dance to her tune as she works her will, and deceive her into helping you even when she thinks to prevent you."

Four days into the voyage, the southwestern horizon lowered and grew dark. A wide, tall, black band of cloud thickened upon that horizon, and the wind picked up and blew harder. The sea rose and fell with increased energy, and the ship heaved and rolled upon the waves.

From the first, the horses had been quartered below decks, but as the weather worsened, Thaniel would have none of it. The great horse came topside where he stood in the middle of the main deck, hooves splayed wide, and his head low, staring glumly ahead.

"This is no place for me or my kind," he complained to Aram.

Fighting his own measure of queasiness, Aram stood with his own feet planted wide apart and gazed the other way, toward the gathering storm on the southern horizon line.

"No – nor for me," he said simply. "Especially if that storm catches up to us." He gained Keegan's attention and pointed. "Will that come here?"

The captain grinned. "Not likely, my lord." He indicated the north, where the line of land along the horizon had increased both in width and height as the pilot moved the craft closer. "We'll hug the shore as close as we dare, just in case," he said. "There are some coves along here where we can ride it out if need be, but –" He pivoted and glanced back toward the southwest. "Big storms usually stay out over the deep water and blow on to the east without coming ashore along here. That's why the Lost is such a dry place, you know."

443

In contrast to Thaniel and Aram, Ka'en seemed to enjoy the excitement provided by the wild, rough seas as she walked the deck eagerly; rather easily negotiating the rocking motion of the ship. She bore Mae bundled up in her arms as she turned her eyes, brightened by the thrill of it all, first this way and then that to gaze about her in exhilaration.

Keegan's prediction about the storm to the south proved true. Though it kept the seas churned up and foam-capped; over the next two days, the area of rough weather passed by them and gradually faded away over the southeastern horizon. Eventually, the ocean grew relatively calm once more, relinquishing its restless, frothy upheaval for the rolling, gentle heaving that was its wont.

They were now sailing close to land which had taken on the green hue of Seneca. The mountains on that land's western borders rose up and showed themselves, tall and greenish-black off to the north.

Three days later, on calm turquoise-colored seas under a hot sun, the ship put in at Tollumi.

As with Lamont, the leaders of Seneca had been notified by Kipwing of the imminent arrival of the king and queen.

Matibar and Andar awaited them on the quayside with their mounts. As Thaniel came down the gangplank, he turned his head and looked at Yvan. "How do you find Seneca?" He asked.

"One gets used to trees, my lord," Yvan replied. "And there is always grass in every season."

Andar and Matibar inclined their heads to Aram and Ka'en.

"Welcome to Seneca, my lord and lady," Andar stated.

They rested in Tollumi and then went on toward the northeast and Mulbar the next day. As they journeyed beneath the towering trees, it was obvious that great changes were occurring in Seneca. The stones of the ancient roadways that had been removed and stacked among the brush of the forested wayside were now being replaced as pavement. Groups of laborers were hard at work resurfacing the road every few miles.

Aram looked over at Andar. "How may I aid you in this endeavor, Your Worthiness?"

Andar smiled and shook his head. "It is our responsibility, my lord. We are simply undoing the foolishness of the past." He turned and pointed westward. "And we are rebuilding the cities as

444

well." His smile widened as he looked back at Aram. "I intend that this land will someday be one of the finest in all your kingdom, Lord Aram."

Aram returned the smile. "It is so, already," he said.

"How is your family, Captain?" Ka'en asked of Matibar.

"You will see for yourself, my lady," Matibar replied. "For they are at Mulbar."

"Indeed they are," Andar interjected. "For Captain Matibar is a counselor, now – and the one I trust most."

Upon reaching Mulbar, Aram and his family were placed once again into the well-appointed accommodations of the common house at the bottom of the main avenue. Aram spent the next several days meeting with Seneca's High Council. Many of the old men that had sat there before were no longer present, though a few remained. The elderly gentlemen that had witnessed Aram's first foray into their land with a measure of reserve and even resentment were now fairly beaming with the honor of meeting their king.

Aram was surprised to see the burned post still standing at the north end of the grove. Andar saw his curious look and told him, "My father had it removed into the forest and replaced after your demonstration with the Sword, my lord." He shrugged. "When I ascended, I brought it back as a sort of monument – and a reminder."

Ka'en and Mae whiled the time away with Matibar's family. The queen was especially taken with Hilri, Matibar's tall, slim, elegant wife, and they talked extensively of motherhood. Hilri, who had given birth to four children, and was experienced in the ancient and honorable arts of both nurturing and discipline, was a fount of knowledge that Ka'en drew from daily. Mae played with Hilri's children, all of whom were older, but very solicitous of their young and precocious playmate who learned to trust her feet and to walk and even run for the first time.

Two weeks later, when the summer was passing its fullness, Aram and Ka'en went back to Tollumi to embark for the west and Elam.

Standing on the quayside, Andar bowed to Aram. "Seneca is ever at your service, my lord," he declared. "Whatever your need."

Aram smiled. "The exotic lumbers produced in this land are highly prized in the west, Your Worthiness," he replied. "May they be all that is ever at need."

He turned to Matibar and his features grew solemn. "The battle would not have been won without the work of your archers, Captain. I thank you."

Matibar appeared taken aback by this unexpected expression of gratitude. He frowned. "Everyone did what had to be done, my lord," he answered.

Aram watched him for a long moment. "Yes," he agreed then. "And may it never be forgotten."

"Will you return, my lord?" Andar asked him. "My house will ever be open to you, and I will wish for you to see – and hopefully approve of – that which we do in years to come."

Aram nodded. "I will return every second or third year, Your Worthiness, for as long as I am able." He held up his hand in salute. "Farewell, my friends."

"Farewell, my lord."

Elam, Cumberland, Aniza, and The Plains

Despite Thaniel's fierce attempts at convincing Aram that his hooves would take him readily and speedily into the west, thereby avoiding another contention with seasickness, Aram agreed with Keegan that the pathways of the sea would be quicker, and bring them to Elam before the end of summer. Glumly, the great horse made his way up and onto the deck, where he stood with his hooves splayed wide, and refused again to go below with the rest of his people.

Once more, they sailed forth upon the deep and Keegan set his sails for the Straits of Kolfaria.

"There is almost always foul weather in the Straits, my lady," he told Ka'en, "but it is yet summer. I suspect we will pass through unmolested."

"I do not mind a bit of rough weather, captain."

Keegan nodded at this, but then looked over at Aram and Thaniel, standing uneasily side-by-side in the center of the main deck. He grinned. "Perhaps you will take my side when the king's temper grows as foul as the weather, my lady?"

446

Ka'en smiled. "His temper is very much like a storm, captain – it rises quickly and often grows very dark before expending itself, but then dissipates and is followed by brightest sunshine."

Keegan's grin broadened. He looked up as a gust of wind caught the mainsail, making the fabric snap and pop, the ropes hum with tautness, and the main mast groan with effort. He moved quickly away. "Look lively there, lads – let's not lose some canvass. We'll likely need every inch of it soon enough."

The weather, as it turned out, was very fine as they passed through the Straits of Kolfaria. Ka'en roamed the deck and gazed southward at the mysterious island, immense and dark against the hazy horizon, from which came one of her favorite beverages.

"Do you put in there often?" She inquired of Keegan.

Keegan's eyes twinkled in response. "Oh, yes, my lady, very often."

Something more than three weeks later the great Elamite port of Eremand came into view. As the Nighthawk cleared the southern end of a rocky, heavily forested headland that jutted into the ocean, a broad expanse of calmer water lay to the north, beyond a region of frothing agitated surf that extended westward from the end of the headland.

"Sunderland Bay," Keegan told them. "Once we swing to the west and get around the end of the reef, we'll enter the protected waters of the bay." He pointed to the sunlit spires rising along the east side of the calmer water, a few miles away. "Eremand."

Once they found the end of the reef and turned back to the northeast into the bay, the sails were furled and the sailors rowed the ship the rest of the way into the harbor of Elam's greatest and most populous city. Aram, who had never looked upon it, along with Ka'en, gazed in wonder at the splendor that rose up a gentle slope away from the edge of the water.

Kipwing had remained behind, in Lamont, after the journey into Seneca, but Alvern had come back west and had seen to it that the winds bore news of Aram's arrival to Elam. Marcus, Amund, Kavnaugh, Olyeg, and Thom awaited them at the docks.

After one night in Eremand, the company went northward, to Farenaire. Two days of travel brought them along the main street and toward the palace late in the afternoon.

Aram looked over at Marcus. "I see that you have repaired the doors, Your Highness."

Marcus smiled. "I did, my lord – after you repaired our land."

Inside the hall, another surprise awaited Aram. Not only did the horse-head, gold and crimson flag of the king fly high above the colors of Elam on the ramparts of the palace outside, but Marcus had caused a throne to be constructed at a higher level than that of the High Prince. The royal standard adorned the wall just above this higher chair.

Aram turned a curious gaze upon Marcus.

In response, the young High Prince indicated the upper throne with one hand. "Your seat, my lord," he told Aram. "It must be that whenever the king is present, the prince is lesser."

Other than Aram and Marcus and their companions, and the palace guards, there was no one else in the hall. Aram took a moment to digest the words of the Prince and then said,

"There will be other kings – and other High Princes – in the coming years, Marcus. What might they think – and make – of this arrangement?"

Marcus shrugged, but his eyes hardened. "I care not, my lord – to be blunt." He turned to face Aram fully. "I have seen what manner of man you are, Lord Aram, and it tells me what sort of monarch you are and will be." He waved one hand, indicating the broad world beyond his doors. "Every action you take and every writ you execute will become precedent for all those that come after you."

He leaned forward earnestly. "And every monarch that follows you, my lord, will be obliged to behave in a manner consistent with those precedents, as will every prince that follows me in Elam." He straightened up and spoke solemnly. "It is my intention, my lord, to expend my life in aiding you in the making of a world that will know peace and freedom for ages to come."

Aram nodded in sober agreement. "Thank you, Marcus."

Then he looked up and contemplated the high throne for a moment. A slight smile spread across his face as he looked over at the High Prince. "You don't expect me to sit there now, do you?"

Marcus laughed. "It is your seat, my lord; you may sit or not as you like." His laughter faded and he grew serious once more.

"When business is conducted in this hall, however, and you are in the land – then it is expedient that your word be weightier than mine."

At this, Aram cast a glance over at Marcus' companions. "If you truly mean this, Your Highness –"

Marcus frowned. "I do, my lord."

Aram glanced over again. This time, his gaze rested for a moment on Olyeg and then upon Thom. He looked back at Marcus. "Then I would like to steal from you, my friend – with your approval, of course."

Marcus' frown deepened. "Steal from me?"

"I want Olyeg and Thom, Marcus," Aram said then. "I have need of them."

Holding up his hand to prevent a response, he continued. "The great northern plains of the world have lain long in the chains of the grim lord and will find it difficult to rise above the legacy of misery that has oppressed them for centuries. That region must be guided by a firm, wise, and trusted hand in the years immediately before us. Do you doubt this?"

Marcus shook his head. "I do not."

Aram watched him closely. "Can you suggest a man more suited to such a task than Olyeg Kraine?"

Marcus looked at Olyeg for a long moment and then met Aram's eyes. Reluctantly, he shook his head. "I cannot think of any man I would trust more," he replied. But then he frowned. "Have you asked General Kraine about this, my lord?"

"I have not," Aram conceded. "To do so is not in my province, but rather in yours, Your Highness."

Marcus nodded slowly and then looked over. "Olyeg?"

Olyeg inclined his head. "I will do whatever is required of me, my lord, but I confess that I doubt my ability."

Aram turned to face him. "This is not a requirement, sir, but a request."

Kraine frowned. "This seems a task for which you yourself are much more suited, my lord – or even Marcus."

Aram held the general's gaze for a moment. "It is necessary to raise the people of the northern plains up out of the mire of servitude in which they have languished for generations. To do so will be exceedingly difficult labor. But it must be done – and it must be done by someone with nothing else to distract them from that task." He waited a moment before going on. "I trust you, Olyeg – and I must place this burden upon someone I trust."

Olyeg met his gaze and then looked for a long moment at Marcus. After another moment of hesitation, he smiled and slowly nodded. "I am old, it is true, but I admit that I am not yet ready for the grave. And I confess to doubts about my ability to accomplish that which you desire. But I must also confess that I find the chance to do something meaningful in this new world extremely gratifying. What are your instructions, my lord?" He asked Aram.

Aram nodded his thanks. "We will go with you into the north in a few days' time. As for instructions? Just this – teach those people to manage their own lands, to care for their families, and to learn to live in freedom. I will see that any need you may discover will be met."

Olyeg inclined his head once more. "Thank you, my lord."

Marcus frowned at Aram and tendered a reluctant question. "You mentioned Thom as well, my lord. May I ask why?"

Aram glanced over at the general. "The men that fought with us before the tower have gone back to their homes – to their towns, villages, and farms. And that is as it should be. Nonetheless, I would like to build and retain a force that is comprised of willing young men from every land throughout the realm. A force that will stand ever ready to defend the kingdom or any of its regions against the encroachment of an enemy. A force that will answer to the throne at Regamun Mediar."

Kavnaugh Berezan's eyes narrowed at this. "But the enemy is defeated, is he not, my lord? Do you expect Manon to return?"

Aram shook his head. "Manon is gone for all time. But the world is large, general, and we occupy but a small part of it. What lies beyond the great Western Marsh – do you know? For I do not. And what about the regions beyond that – or to the south of the Southern Ocean?"

He met the eyes of every man in the room. "It is not that I know of an enemy that may come against us – for I do not. But it is better to prepare for the unknown in times of peace than when the enemy of which we are not aware is upon us and at the gates. Is this not wise?"

He moved one hand and indicated the eastern wall. "To the east of Seneca lies a land that is known as Farlong. The Farlongers

450

are not a part of this kingdom, nor do I wish by force to compel them to become so. In the past, they have been but a sometimes nuisance to Seneca. What if they decide to be more than that?"

He moved his hand slightly. "To the southeast of Farlong, there are great islands, dark and mysterious, adrift upon the ocean. I saw them once, from the – I saw them once, long ago. Who or what dwells there? I know not. It is the duty of the throne at Regamun Mediar to defend all borders of the kingdom, and to do so, I must have an army – and a general to command that army."

Every man present in that room exchanged a sober look of confirmation of the wisdom of Aram's words with his companions.

Marcus turned to Aram and nodded. "Of course you are right, my lord." He grinned ruefully. "So you intend to take Thom from me then?"

Aram looked at Thom. "That is, of course, up to him. And even if he accepts my request, General Sota may live wherever he likes – here in Elam, if he wishes. But I will need him to travel the far reaches of the kingdom regularly and to report back to me."

Marcus looked over. "Thom?"

Thom's eyes gleamed as he inclined his head in reply. "I will be honored, my lord," he said to Aram.

Aram turned back to Marcus. "What of Cumberland? What has been done about the governance of that land in the absence of Kitchell?"

"The High Council of Cumberland has elected a man named Wethurfurd Dalez as successor to Kitchell," Marcus answered. "Wethurfurd was a captain of Cumberland's host and fought at the tower. Also, he was a nephew to Kitchell." He frowned. "Because of the nature of our ancient relationship with that land, I was asked to go north and confirm the selection of Wethurfurd, my lord, but now that you are here –"

"No, Marcus," Aram said, cutting him off. "You will of course confer the confirmation. I will go with you, for I would also like you to accompany me into Aniza, to begin the process of restoration in that land as well." He shook his head. "There is no need to alter relationships that have stood the test of time, especially those between your throne and the lands of Cumberland and Aniza."

Then he lifted his gaze to the high seat that had been placed for him. "For the moment," he told Marcus, smiling, "I think that I would rather sit somewhere more comfortable."

"That can easily be arranged, my lord."

The king and queen rested in Elam for more than a week and then the company, joined now by Marcus, Olyeg, Thom, and many others, went north to Cumberland. Wethurfurd, the soldier who had avenged the death of Kitchell, was installed as Governor-general, and then the party went westward over the hills and into Aniza where Aram officially installed Ruben as Governor of that land and Marcus promised the former cavalryman every aid in bringing about the rebirth of his homeland.

Frost was seen riming the low places in the rolling green of Cumberland and the leaves of the trees upon the northern hills were showing the first vestiges of color when Aram and Ka'en finally wished Marcus, Thom, Kavnaugh, Amund, and Olyeg farewell, leaving them to their respective tasks while they turned eastward toward Wallensia and home.

It was cool and cloudy with a lowering sky on the day that they departed Derosa and went across the hills into the valley. Despite an early start, night had fallen when they crossed the rivers.

Nikolus and Timmon were already at the city, having abandoned the high plains when an early snow threatened to close the pass. The bridge across the gorge at Rigar Pyrannis was nearing completion, they informed Aram, but was not yet ready to bear the weight of heavy traffic.

"I am sorry, my lord," Timmon told him. "Would that we had finished within this year. One month, I assure you, after spring returns, and we will be finished."

"It matters not," Aram said, "for there is plenty to keep you busy afterward. But we need the treasure of my fathers in order to finance all that must be done." He looked closely at his engineers. "The lashers?"

Nikolus laughed. "Had it not been for those great beasts," he told Aram, "we would need much more time than another month to complete the bridge."

"So they were a help to you, then?"

"A very great help," Timmon replied.

"Where are they now?"

"They have gone home to Panax – but promised to return with the spring."

Satisfied with this information, and noting that Ka'en and Mae had already accompanied Dunna to their home in the city's second level, Aram turned to Eoarl. "I am tired, my friend, and thirsty."

Eoarl grinned. "Sit, my lord, and take your ease. I will tap one of my finest kegs."

The lashers, over time, came to be accepted by the peoples of the earth, prized for their ever-willing aid in difficult tasks requiring the application of stout muscle and bone. And the great beasts' work with wood produced myriad useful objects highly sought-after by farmers, merchants, and the like.

There was, however, one curious thing done by them.

In the second year after the Great Battle, a pilgrimage was organized for all those that lost men in that terrible struggle. As the families of the fallen visited the sacred graves and gazed curiously out over The Valley Where Two Gods Died, it was found that others had made the journey to the north as well. The three lashers, Hargur and his companions, were seen gathering something from the floor of the valley itself.

Later, it was discovered that what was gathered were bits of the debris from the destruction of Manon's tower. These bits of black stone were subsequently brought by them back to Aram's valley, where they were piled in an empty field just south of the city, next to the limits of the orchard. The lashers never explained this act, but continued to do it faithfully, year by year, so that the pile of stones grew.

Observing them in the act of doing this one year late in his life, Findaen groused, "If they don't stop this – the day will come when we can rebuild that accursed tower right here!"

Ka'en watched with pensive eyes as Hargur, Bildur, and Pentar added their burdens to the growing pile of stones, and then she laid a hand on her brother's arm.

"Leave them alone, Fin," she said. "It's just something they need to do."

3. The Age of Peace

As the years of Aram's reign lengthened and became more than a decade, the roads throughout all the land were gradually repaired, bringing all parts of the kingdom together. It was learned then that the crossings of the rivers at the lower end of the valley were actually stone culvert bridges that had been submerged by floodwaters over time. Nikolus and Timmon oversaw the dredging of the channels until the bridges once more rose safely above the current. The bones of the dragon, upon the ridge between the rivers just downstream from these culverts, can be seen gleaming strangely in the light of the sun unto this day.

Over time, wide paved roadways linked every part of the kingdom, including Seneca. The road across the Lost was rebuilt and manned way-stations erected once more at intervals where there was a dependable water supply. The wild folk abandoned Lamont and scattered once more throughout that rocky, dry wilderness. It was a group of that wild folk who discovered that the Mountain of the Deep Darkness had been leveled in a horrific blast, caving in upon itself and sealing the entrance to the Pit.

For Aram, when he heard this, the news confirmed what he had suspected – that every bit of Manon was gone from the earth.

There was nothing upon the horizons of his realm, in any direction, that threatened the peace.

Keeping nothing for himself, the king put the treasure of his ancestors, brought out of Rigar Pyrannis, to work throughout the land. Money flowed freely, and commerce flourished.

Peace and freedom prevailed.

Ka'en gave birth to another daughter, named Ania in honor of Ka'en's grandmother, Lancer's mother. This girl, fair-haired like her older sister, grew tall as she grew older. Mae and Ania were both comely and spirited, causing Eoarl to remark to Aram one day, "I don't know what will cause you the most anxiety, my lord – the hordes of young men who will inevitably come around, or the fierceness with which your daughters will greet them."

Aram grimaced in reply and only partly in jest. "They are high-spirited, are they not?"

Eoarl laughed. "You will forgive me, my lord, but they come by it rather naturally."

Aram scowled at his friend. "I assume that you mean from their mother."

"Yes, from their mother, of course," Eoarl responded, as his grin broadened. "What else would I mean?"

When Ania was three years old, Ka'en found that she was once again with child. On the day of the child's delivery, Dunna came out of the birthing room to summon Aram. Seeing the solemn expression on Dunna's features, Aram came to his feet.

"What is the matter – is Ka'en alright?"

"She is fine, my lord."

"Then what is the matter?"

Dunna shook her head. "Go on in – she will tell you."

Aram burst into the room to find his wife smiling up at him.

"You have a son," she informed him, softly. "I have my heir – two, in fact – and now you have yours."

Aram took the child, gazing with wonder down upon the boy, as black-headed as himself. "What is his name?"

"That is up to you, my love. Give him your name, if you like."

Aram shook his head. "Every man should have a name of his own." He looked at her. "What is his name?"

"I would name him Naetan," Ka'en replied.

"Naetan?"

Ka'en nodded. "There is a tale, told to me when I was young, of a monster that came up out of the ocean, swam up the River Broad, and terrorized the people of Stell and the countryside round about. Naetan was the name of the hero who challenged the monster and defeated it, driving it back into the sea."

Aram looked down upon the boy once more. "Hello, Naetan, my son," he said.

Four years later, Ka'en gave birth once more, to what was to be her last child, another girl. And at last, she agreed to employ the name of her mother. The girl was named Margra'eth. She was dark-haired and dark-eyed, like her older brother, and like him, grew up slim and tall.

As Naetan grew to manhood, it became apparent that he was calm and level-headed, much like his grandfather, Lancer. Years passed, peace pervaded the land, and Aram tired of the day-to-day affairs of the realm. He began to delegate more and more of the responsibilities of governance to his son, and Naetan, quietly and with calm efficiency, took quite easily and naturally to holding the reins of authority.

In the twentieth year of her life, Mae married a man from Stell named Daved, who was named Prince of Wallensia. Findaen, older now, and gray-haired, willingly stepped down into the role of Chancellor, a position once held by his father.

Jame, the Hay of Lamont, now in his thirties, took to visiting the capitol more and more as Ania grew to womanhood. One day, when she was eighteen, Jame approached Aram and Ka'en with his head lowered and his manner steeped in diffidence. As the young ruler of Lamont stuttered and muttered in his attempts to express that which was on his heart, Eoarl, now very old, and a widower, shook his head in amiable disgust.

"I am so blind that I can't see the sun on a clear day," the old farmer stated, "but I sure as hell can spot a man hopelessly in love."

And so Ania, who – when asked – was very much disposed to marry Jame, did so, and then went eastward to become Dame of the land of Lamont.

Three years afterward, Margra'eth announced that she was disposed, in her own right, to marry Bertar, the eldest son of Matibar of Seneca.

And so it was that the children of Aram and Ka'en came to be scattered far and wide throughout the kingdom. In due course, as time passed, they were compensated by the arrival of grandchildren who came often to visit them, and the streets of Regamun Mediar, now fully restored and fully populated, reverberated with the shouts and the laughter of a third generation of royalty.

When Naetan was nearly thirty years of age, he took to wife the granddaughter of Olyeg Kraine, a woman by the name of Nathlie.

456

Within four years, Nathlie had given birth to a daughter, Nina, and then a son, Joktan. Aram, who had offered no input on the matter, was nonetheless immensely gratified by the choice of the name for his grandson.

With Naetan now dealing with the majority of the concerns of the kingdom, Aram and Ka'en spent most of their summers at the cottage on the ridge above the river in the north of the high plains, below the mountains.

Thaniel had also taken a mate, named Shael. One summer morning, very early, as Aram left Ka'en asleep and wended his way down to the shores of the sea to watch the rising of the sun, he found Thaniel waiting for him. For a time, the two old warriors watched in silence as the first of the sun's rays flared above the sharp teeth of the mountains beyond the Sea.

Sensing agitation on the part of the horse, Aram looked over at him. "What troubles you, my friend?"

"I would ask something of you, Lord Aram," Thaniel said after a moment.

Aram turned toward him. "Anything that is in my power, I will do," he replied.

Thaniel swung his head around and looked at him. "I have a son."

Aram smiled widely at this news. "Shael has given birth?"

"Last evening, just after sunset," the horse affirmed.

Something in the horse's demeanor gave Aram pause. "Is there a problem?"

"No, my lord – the child is fine, as is his mother," Thaniel responded. He looked away for a moment and then looked back. "I would like to name the child Aram, my lord."

It took a moment for this to register, and then Aram frowned. "Cannot you think of a better name – that of your father, perhaps?"

At this, Thaniel swung his head around to face Aram fully. "No, my lord," he stated. "For there is no better name for my son than that which is borne by my brother."

Aram met the horse's gaze for a long moment and then inclined his head. "I am greatly honored, my friend. More than you can know."

After that, Aram and Thaniel often met upon the shores of the Inland Sea as the sun climbed up over the sharp-edged eastern horizon. Usually, they did not speak. After all that they had shared, there was little to say. Sometimes, however, one or the other of them felt compelled to reminisce.

"Do you remember Wamlak?" Aram asked one morning.

"He was the cleverest of men," Thaniel replied. "And a great warrior."

"I wish he had lived," Aram said. "And his father, Donnick, as well. Would that they had both lived."

"The world will always miss them," Thaniel agreed. "There is a void now that only they could occupy."

Unknown to them, Ka'en and Shael, accompanied by young Aram, were never asleep as their husbands believed, but had slipped down the ridge as was their wont, to stand in the shelter of the trees upon the height and watch the old warriors welcome the new day.

And each of those new days looked down upon a world ever more at peace.

4. The Horses

From the beginning of Aram's reign, many of the horses abandoned the remote and protected range of the high plains to move out into the world and dwell with the men with whom they had gone to war. A few remained in the high country with Thaniel, but most did not. As a consequence, there began to be a division within the ranks of those people.

One summer day, troubled by this apparent and growing division, Jared left Nikolus and traveled alone up and over the pass and onto the high plains. He found Aram and Thaniel communing together near the king's cottage. After greeting Jared and perceiving that the rangy brown horse wished to speak with Thaniel privately, Aram excused himself and went inside.

Jared broached the subject without preamble. "Our people are becoming two people," he told Thaniel. "Some have stayed in the wild, but most have gone to live among men. Many even work with men, aiding them in their daily labors."

"This rumor of horses working with men has come to my ears," Thaniel agreed, "and I realize that some of our people wish to bond with men in this way. But understand, Jared; by doing so, they will become something less."

"Something less?"

"Our fathers' ancient alliance with men was based upon equality," Thaniel told him. "But now I hear that there are those of our people who pull plows in the fields for men – like oxen. Is this true?"

"Some do – yes, my lord," Jared answered hesitantly. "But they do so as friends – comrades – the same as when they went into battle together. Besides, men have always been ascendant in the alliance. Lord Aram, after all, is not just the king of men, but the king of all."

"True," Thaniel agreed, "but we never plowed their fields."

He looked away and gazed at the eastern horizon for a long moment. When that moment grew even longer, and still he did not speak, Jared broke the silence. "You may forbid it, of course, if it displeases you."

At that, Thaniel turned back and looked at him. "No," he replied, "I cannot."

"But you are the Lord of All Horses, now," Jared reminded him. "Our people must obey your writ."

"There is now no need for a Lord of All Horses, Jared. Nor will there be ever again. Thanks to Lord Aram, the world has forever changed. The old ways are gone, and will not return." He swung his head and looked away once more. "The age of gods on earth ended when Aram destroyed Manon, and with the conclusion of that age, many things are irrevocably altered, including the need for a lord for our people."

He hesitated for a moment, still gazing away, and then looked back and continued. "Even the need for a general alliance may be reasonably argued to be unnecessary. In this new age, men and horses may make their own alliances – of a personal nature, if they like – without the need to consult with me."

Jared stared at him. "And this is to be our future?"

"And our present," Thaniel answered. "Hear me, Jared – the world has changed, and we must change with it." His voice grew low and quiet. "Lord Aram would never ask it of me, but what I say is nonetheless true. If his field required plowing, and there were no oxen to accomplish the task, I would willingly step into the traces for him."

Jared's eyes widened. "You – *in front of a plow*? I cannot accept that you would do this – even if it were for the king – for I would not."

"Accept it not, then," Thaniel replied. "It is nonetheless true. As I said – Lord Aram would never ask it. You know him; he would turn the entire field with a shovel before he would ask such a thing. But that fact does alter the reality of this new world in which we live. Horses must make their own way in it now, without a lord to guide them. Each must decide for himself how he will live out his life. As for me, I will remain here – and with Lord Aram."

"Do we truly risk becoming something less?"

"What else is there for us?" Thaniel asked bluntly. "There is only to live here in the wilderness or to live among men. Each of our people must choose which – I will make the choice for no one."

"Then we will undoubtedly become two people," Jared stated glumly.

"You are yet alive, and are very clever," Thaniel told him. "And you know both worlds. You may guide our people that dwell in the world of men – remind them of who they are – and I will guide those that remain here. And you will be a bridge between us."

Jared went silent and looked away. After a time, he said, "I will come often to seek your counsel, my lord."

"You need not seek my counsel, Jared," Thaniel replied. "For you will know better than I what is required of horses dwelling in the world of men. But I will be glad to see you whenever you come."

And so Jared went away, and Thaniel stayed with Aram, and the truth of Thaniel's words is demonstrated by an -

Incident in the Year 1712 of the Age of Peace

Upon the eastern banks of the Broad, less than a mile south of Stell, there lived a young man by the name of Keegan. He was an only child of aged parents, born when his mother was in the change of life. He had been given that name in honor of an ancient mariner who lived centuries earlier in the time of Aram the Magnificent. Captain Keegan had been a rough and rugged seaman whose exploits were expounded in a book of history that was perused often by the young man's father.

Keegan – the young farmer – had lost both of his parents when he was but seventeen. They had gone across the river and beyond Stell to the hamlet of Cottonwood to help his mother's sister and her family when they were ravaged by illness. Both had contracted the same illness and succumbed.

Though prior to tragedy his young life had been consumed by dreams of going south to the ocean and sailing forth upon it like his ancient namesake, Keegan had inherited the farm upon his parents' deaths and for five years after their loss he dutifully worked the ground, making it produce as a sort of monument to them.

He owned no oxen – those that pulled the cart that had taken his parents beyond the Broad were never returned. Nor did he seek to recover them, for there was a large brown horse that had been in his family since before the time of his great-grandfather who sufficed to do the necessary heavy labor. The horse had once had another name, but Keegan simply called him Big Brown. Though Keegan's father insisted that the histories told the truth when they stated that horses had once communed with men; Big Brown had never once responded to the spoken word.

One evening in spring, Keegan led Big Brown along the banks of the river as the sun sank toward the horizon. As they walked toward the house, he reached out and laid his hand on the broad shoulder of the horse.

"Long day – hey, big fella?"

Big Brown, as usual, gave no reply.

Keegan gazed westward, admiring the way the rays of the setting sun spun warm bands of red, yellow, and orange color upon the roiling surface of the Broad.

Then something else caught his eye.

At the bottom of the bank, jutting from the mud at the edge of the water, something gleamed.

Bringing Big Brown to a halt, he dropped the leather traces and walked to the lip of the bank, looking down. "What is that?" He wondered.

It looked like the hilt of a sword.

Dropping over the rim, he crab-crawled down the dirt bank and slid into the mud, wetting his boots in the water at the stream's edge. He seized the object and drew it forth, and immediately whistled in astonishment and admiration.

For it was indeed a sword.

Incredibly light and utterly unblemished, it appeared as if it could have been placed there but moments earlier. Clutching the prize, he scrabbled back to the top of the bank where he wiped it free of mud and muck on his trouser leg.

After admiring it for several moments, turning it back and forth so that it gleamed in the failing light of the sun, he went back to where he'd left Big Brown.

He held it up before the horse.

"Look here, big fella – I found me something!"

Unnoticed by Keegan, who was still admiring his prize, a light flickered into life deep inside the large eyes of the great horse. He was also gazing at the gleaming sword.

"Yes, indeed," Big Brown said then, and his voice sounded deep and sonorous inside Keegan's mind. "You have certainly found something, young man. *Something*, indeed. And I knew him once to whom it belonged."

Keegan nearly dropped the sword in amazement. "Big Brown – you – *talked*!"

"I did," the horse agreed. "And my name is not Big Brown – it is Jared."

Keegan stared, speechless, for several moments. "Why have you never spoken before this?" He asked finally.

"There was no need. I understand you, and what you require of me, and there was no need for me to respond." Jared went silent for a moment, then, "Also – for a time – I forgot how to speak," he admitted, "until I looked upon that sword."

Keegan stared at Jared, wide-eyed, for another minute, and then he looked back at the gleaming weapon. "Whose was it?" He asked.

"Lord Aram lost it in the current one night, when he and Thaniel attempted to cross by the light of the moon and stars," Jared told him.

Keegan's eyes flew wider. "Aram? Aram the ancient king? *Aram* – the Magnificent?"

Jared laughed, a low rumbling sound. "He was none of those things when he lost that sword – he was simply a lone warrior, trying to escape his many enemies."

Keegan lowered the sword and gazed at the horse. "*You knew him?*"

"I did."

"I know that your people are long-lived," Keegan said. "But I did not know you lived as long as that. How old are you, Jared?"

"I have forgotten," the horse admitted. "Eight or nine thousand years, I suppose."

Keegan whistled his astonishment at this, and then asked, "What was he like?"

"Lord Aram?" Jared laughed again. "Have you not read your histories?"

"Yes, and I know what is said of Aram the Magnificent. But *you knew him*, Jared. You can say what he was really like."

"Well, I can tell you this," Jared stated. "Whatever your history books say of him? I can assure you – he was more than that."

The horse turned his gaze upon the sword. "You know, Keegan," he said. "With a weapon like that in his hand, a man might go anywhere."

Keegan also turned his eyes to the sword. Then he grinned and looked back at the horse. "You are right, sir," he agreed. "And I will never be content as a farmer. *Where shall we go?*"

It is said that Jared and Keegan travelled far and wide; that they looked upon distant marvels, and solved great mysteries; that they embarked upon wondrous quests, and saw them faithfully to the end. It is even stated that they met and befriended a dragon.

The truth of this assertion is doubted by most, and fervently believed by others.

But theirs is a story that is told in full elsewhere.

5. The Wolves

After the Battle Before the Tower, most of the wolves, like Goreg and his band, went back into the wild to live out their lives away from the things of man. Some few others, like Leorg and Shingka, followed Gorfang's lead and lived near or even among men, melding their lives with humans in ways both intangible and tangible. Over time, many of that folk, born of a race that required submission to a master, became utterly domesticated, even taking as their names those given to them by the men whom they served.

The wolf people that remained in the wild gradually became separate, and estranged, both from their domesticated kin and from the world of men at large.

Still, they remembered their history and their involvement in the momentous events of the days of Aram the Walking Flame. No one born among those denizens of the wild was ever given either of two names – Aram or Durlrang, for these names were too sacred to be bestowed upon any others that came after them. Durlrang, who was especially revered, and was named by his people as Anduram zhe Conraduam ne Formentius – He Who Ran With the Walking Flame – became known, over time, as the Father of His People. And for several generations after his death, there were those among that people who declared with solemn certainty that the great Lord Durlrang had once helped The Walking Flame to slay a dragon.

6. The Bears

Borlus, the first bear in thousands of years to gain and retain communion with a human – Lord Aram himself – stayed in the hills to the north, near the valley, for the duration of his life, along with his wife, Hilla. The rest of his kin, including his first-born son, who was named after the king, retired into the wild, away from direct contact with humans, and remained so forever.

They kept one legacy of the days of Borlus, however.

A singularly unimaginative race, they adopted and retained two names that were to remain in use among their kind until the end of time.

These names; Aram, meaning *The Mighty* – and Borlus, *The Great Friend*, were bestowed upon generation after generation of males born unto that people. There were times, in fact, when it seemed as if every male bear upon the face of the planet bore either the one name or the other.

As for the first Borlus; he and the king retained their special friendship until the end of their days.

7. The Absence of Alvern

Alvern and Kipwing remained in close communion with both Aram the king and with Jame, the Hay of Lamont. As for Cree; having loved the queen from the beginning, she grew as close as a sister to Ka'en. As for the rest of that people, however, hawks, eagles, and other lords of the air; over time they became distant from the race of humans until eventually, except for those three special relationships, communion was lost.

As for Alvern, he came often to Regamun Mediar, both to report news from throughout the kingdom, and to simply commune with an old friend.

The time came when he did not come.

Days passed and became weeks, and then months.

Concerned, Aram summoned Kipwing.

"I have not heard from your grandfather in many days," the king said to him. "Do you know where he may be found?"

Kipwing looked at him sharply. "Many days, my lord?"

"It has been several weeks since last I spoke with him," Aram affirmed.

"But this is not like him," Kipwing protested. "You are his nearest friend, Lord Aram. He would not stay away from you for so long without reason."

These words intensified the concern in Aram's heart. "Will you find him?"

"I will go and search for him at once, my lord – as will all my kin," Kipwing replied, and spreading his wings, he lifted up and flew away.

Though eagles and hawks searched every known corner of the globe, Alvern was never found, nor was his body discovered. For

Aram, it eventually became obvious that the great eagle had died in a manner and a place that prevented discovery of his remains, and consequently, certainty of his passing. But Alvern the great eagle was unquestionably gone, the last of his generation, and Aram mourned for the loss of an old and dear friend.

With Alvern's kin, however, another legend arose to explain the ancient eagle's absence.

It was said – and widely believed by the lords of the air – that he had flown to Kelven's mountain, that he had climbed the winds up to the very top of that great height, and finding Kelven gone, had continued on, out among the stars, until he caught the very currents of eternity, and thence flew to his long home, having never experienced the darkened halls of death.

.

8. The Death of Ka'en

The winter of Ka'en's seventy-third year of life was long, cold, and harsh. Storm after storm mounded up over the mountains to the north and marched down over the valley, dumping their icy burden. Ka'en was often ill during that winter; on more than one occasion Aram noticed that her face was as pale and white as the snow that piled up so prodigiously out upon the great porch. Worry over her deteriorating condition caused him to ignore all else and stay near her, spending his days and nights maintaining the fire in their bedroom and bringing her meals of which, day by day, she consumed less. Most nights he slept in the chair next to the bed, so that she could rest.

A doctor had been summoned to stay in the house where he could more closely watch over the health of the queen.

One morning Aram awoke to the brash sound of a breeze freshening determinedly out of the south. Upon hearing this welcome indication of a possible improvement in the weather, he rose stiffly, straightened his creaking bones and leaned over to check on Ka'en, who was still sleeping, albeit restlessly. Her breathing was hesitant, short, and shallow.

He went to the window and slid back the shutter just enough to peer outside. Gray clouds, ragged and low, scuttled out of the south, driven northward across the valley by the stiffening wind. Rain squalls spattered against the shutter. He put his hand forth and felt of the air. It was cool, but warmer than it had been in many weeks.

"What are you...doing...my love?"

Aram wheeled away from the window to see Ka'en looking at him; her head turned a bit his way, and the faded topaz centers of her eyes slid all the way into the corners, straining to see him. He went to her, moved the chair closer, sat down, and took her hand in his.

Her fingers were cold, like the crust on the snow beyond the window.

"Spring is coming," he told her. "It's warmer this morning."

She smiled tiredly but did not reply.

"Are you alright?" He asked.

"I...am...fine."

"But your hand is so cold," he said, frowning, as he gently rubbed it between his hands in an attempt to restore warmth. "Do you feel like getting up? I'll make kolfa."

She shook her head, but the movement was so slight as to be nearly imperceptible. "No, my love," she told him in frighteningly soft tones. "I will not...be...getting up today."

Alarmed by those words, and by her paleness, her halting speech, and hesitant breathing, he persisted, *willing* her to be stronger. "Can you eat something?"

She watched him in silence for a long moment.

"Thank you...for my life," she said then.

These words, delivered in quiet, low tones, sounded fearfully like a farewell. His frown deepened as dread abruptly took root in his heart. "What do you mean?"

She closed her eyes and smiled a thin, slight, soft smile. "It has been...a great...adventure."

Holding her hand with his right, he put his left on the side of her face. That skin was terribly cool to the touch as well. He sucked in a fearful breath. "There is more life – more adventure – to be had," he told her desperately.

She tried to shake her head once more, but failed. "Not for me, my love," she replied.

Her eyes opened and looked into his.

"I love you," she said.

Aram felt the cold hand of fear strengthen its hold on him. "Don't leave me," he pleaded. "I will call for the doctor."

"*No*," Ka'en told him, and for just a moment her soft voice was stronger and her lovely eyes shone. "He can do nothing for me now. I am going where you have already been, my love. I will await you there."

"Stay with me, Ka'en, *please*."

But at that moment, though she still looked up at him, her eyes were no longer focused on his face. Her gaze seemed to be fixed upon a point somewhere beyond him. "Look, Aram – do you see?" She said, and there was a weak, faint tremor of excitement in her tone. "There are flowers...blooming above the snowbank, just there. Let's go to them."

Then her eyes closed and she did not speak again. An instant later, her chill hand lost its feeble grip on his.

Taking both her hands in his, he tried desperately to rub warmth back into them, calling sharply for the doctor. Naetan came to the door, took one look, and then shouted down the hall.

"Doctor – come quick!"

In the end, Aram did not allow the surgeon or anyone else to touch her, for she was gone and he knew it. He bent down and laid his head upon her breast. He did not weep, he did not speak; no sound came from him. Unwilling to intrude upon his grief, Naetan and the surgeon stood back.

Quietly, Naetan wept.

The morning seemed to grow suddenly dark as the silence of unbearable loss and sorrow gathered and thickened in the room.

Outside, the world turned inexorably toward the coming of spring, but Ka'en's spirit would not walk abroad beneath the cheerful sun of that gentler season; she would never feel its warmth.

She would remain behind, with the winter.

9. The Death of Aram

Aram spoke very little to anyone in the days that followed Ka'en's passing, nor did he eat much. Other than to give directions that, once her body was prepared for burial, and those that wished to see her had done so; Ka'en was to be placed into the earth of the old orchard near the bodies of Florm and Ashal. Other than that, he refused any and all communication. Room was to be left beside her for Aram himself, whenever his own time would come. After burial, a tomb was to be raised over her.

On the day of her internment, Aram stood at the head of the crowd, but he said nothing while Maelee, Ania, Naetan, Margra-eth and others tearfully extolled the well-known virtues of his absent queen and their mother. When all was over, he continued to stand with his head down and his eyes closed as the crowd slowly dissipated. No one dared disturb his thoughts.

When all had gone, he lifted his head and gazed long at the newly turned mound of earth. Then he went into the city and shut the door to his room.

Later that evening, Naetan went to check on his father. Quietly entering the room, he found Aram standing at the window, gazing down over the valley. A grayish-black bag was suspended from one hand. The king turned toward him and held up the bag.

It contained the remaining monarchs he had brought out of Rigar Pyrannis so long ago. Aram's memory told him that there should have been forty-four of the golden discs, but there were two less than that. Somewhere, sometime back along the course of his life, he must have parted with them, but he could not recall the instance. It mattered not – there were more than enough to meet his current need.

He shook the bag as he met his son's gaze. "These are mine," he stated fiercely.

Naetan shrugged and smiled. "They are all of them yours, my lord," he replied.

Aram stared at him for a moment without returning the smile, and then lowered the bag, shaking his head. "No," he said. "Your mother was right about that. The gold – all of it – belongs to the people." He lifted the bag once more. "Except for these. These are mine."

"What do you mean to do with them, my lord?" Naetan inquired.

Aram answered that with a question of his own. "What do you name men that create likenesses of living people from stone?"

"Men that make likenesses –?" Naetan frowned. "Sculptors?"

The king's features quivered with impatience. "Is that what they are called – those that can create the likeness of a person out of stone? Sculptors?"

"Yes, father."

Aram drew in a deep breath and looked closely at his son. "Can you find one of these men that saw the queen in her life? Someone that knew her, saw her, and can create her likeness in stone?"

Naetan nodded his comprehension of his father's desire. "I will send word throughout the kingdom at once."

Aram shook the bag. "Tell him that I will make him rich."

Naetan hesitated and then nodded. "I will ask him to state a fair price for his labor, my lord." He held up his hands to prevent Aram's retort. "Fear not, my lord – I will find the very best sculptor in all the land, one who knew my mother in her life. And he will be paid handsomely."

Aram shook the bag again. "With my gold," he insisted.

Naetan nodded again and then turned to go and execute his father's desire. "As you will, my lord."

At the door, he hesitated and looked back. "You should come to supper, father. You have eaten nothing of which I am aware. It has been a most difficult time, and you must rebuild your strength."

In reply, Aram's face grew dark with sadness. "Rebuild my strength? To what end?"

Naetan frowned, both at the words and the tone with which they were delivered. "To the end that you might keep your health, my lord. My mother has gone to her long home; I do not wish to lose my father also."

"Why should I not go there as well?" Aram stated angrily. "There is no point in me being here when she is there."

Naetan's frown deepened and he turned away from the door and back into the room to face his father. "But there is a point, my lord," he argued. "More than that – there is a reason. You are our king. You are my father. We need you to be here."

Aram's expression of sadness strengthened upon his gray and grizzled face. "I am not needed here," he insisted, shaking his head. "I am not a king, my son. I was never a king. I am just a man who – once upon a time – was good with a sword." He paused and frowned down at the floor. "No," he admitted, "even that is untrue. It was the Sword that was good – I simply wielded it for a time."

He continued to look down at the floor for another long, quiet moment and then lifted his gaze to his son. Raising one hand, he pointed his finger at Naetan. "You, my son – *you* are a king. You are everything that a king must be. You build, you manage, you *administer.*"

A single tear overflowed and traced a tangent down his right cheek. "*You* – you are king, my son – you are *the king*. Not me." He lowered his hand. "I am just a lonely man that misses his wife."

Naetan shook his head in disagreement, even as his own eyes grew moist. "No, father – I can never be what you are."

At this, Aram's eyes dried and his voice hardened. "Nor should you wish it – for that would make you *less* than what you are. Hear me, my son. Do you not think that I have watched you govern in my name while I walked the gardens of the high plains with your mother and whiled the days away wandering those green fields with Thaniel?" His eyes narrowed and his voice grew harsher yet. "You are more than me. Far more. In the years to come, the world will prosper under the wise influence of your mind and your hand."

He turned away from Naetan and looked once more out the window, down over the city and the valley beyond. His voice, when again he spoke, though drenched with sorrow, was firm. "The world can ask nothing further of me. I have done all I can. I am done here. Without her, I am nothing."

"Father –"

Aram turned back toward his son and raised his hand, palm outward, silencing him. "Will you find me a sculptor?"

Naetan watched him for some time, and then nodded. "I will, my lord."

"And see if you can discover where it is that Gorfang has taken himself," Aram asked him.

Naetan glanced sharply around the room before looking back at his father. "Gorfang is gone?"

"I have not seen him since yesterday," Aram replied.

Naetan frowned in remembrance. "I heard a wolf howling in the night."

Aram nodded. "Undoubtedly, it was he. There is no need for him to be alone now. Send the hawks to discover him."

"At once, my lord."

But Gorfang let himself be found before the hawks could discover him. On the morning after Ka'en was placed into her grave, the workers constructing her tomb found his body lying atop the freshly turned earth.

Beside him lay another lifeless body, that of a hawk. Cree the Ancient, who along with her first spouse, Kota, were the very first of their kind upon the earth, had abandoned mortality and joined her mistress beyond the borders of death.

On orders from Aram, they were both of them buried next to the queen.

Naetan spent the next several weeks seeking a sculptor who had seen his mother in her life, sending word throughout the kingdom that any artist that met the criteria would be made wealthy indeed. At last, acting upon information given him by Marcus, he found the man.

The sculptor's name was Parfin, and he came from Vergon. He had met the queen on several occasions when she and Aram had come to the palace of High Prince Marcus at Farenaire. Naetan traveled to Vergon and looked upon the artist's work and found it surpassing all others. When asked if he could render a likeness of Lady Ka'en, even in her absence, Parfin asserted that he could.

When asked about price, the artist frowned and shook his head. "The honor of rendering the queen's likeness will be payment enough."

Naetan smiled at this. "We shall see what my father thinks of that," he replied.

Informed by Aram himself of that which he wished to see rendered in white stone, Parfin then scoured the land for the finest column of alabaster. Once the raw substance of his vision was in hand, he went into the room off the great hall where Aram had put him, and went to work.

The day came when the artist sent word to the king that the likeness of the queen was ready for his inspection. Aram went into the room and returned an hour later, wiping his eyes. Parfin, he told Naetan, had done "exactly as I wished."

The next day, at mid-day, Parfin moved his creation out across the great porch and over the walkway to the dais that looked down the grand avenue. The statue was covered with a blue cloth.

The artist waited until Aram went down the stairway out through the gates and then onto the avenue to stand by the bench near Ka'en's tomb at the edge of the orchard. The entire population of the city had gathered upon the avenue, including many that had come in from the surrounding farms and villages to witness the unveiling.

When Aram was in position and looking up, Parfin reached up and slipped the covering cloth from the sculpture.

A collective murmur of approval arose from the crowd.

It was the image of their departed queen.

Cast in pure white alabaster, the sculpture represented Ka'en standing at the wall, turned slightly to one side with her hand upon the stone, gazing down the grand avenue, just as Aram had seen her all those years ago when their love was first declared.

After the crowd had finally dissipated, Aram sat down upon the bench in the sun gazing up at the representation of his beloved wife and smiling. Sometime later, he dozed in the warm sunshine, with the smile still upon his face.

It was only when Naetan went out to call his father in to supper that it was discovered that the king had died.

The relentless hunter, Death, had found Aram once again.

And this time Mortality would keep his prey.

The winds – and the eagles and hawks that rode upon them – flashed the news of the king's passing to all parts of the kingdom. Within three days, everyone from Vergon to Seneca knew that he

476

had died. Shocked and stunned, for most, the everyday exigencies of life ceased upon the moment to matter. Workmen laid down their tools, and merchants closed their places of business, wending their way to their homes or to public houses to stare at one another in disbelief. Farmers stood in their fields, the day's necessary labor forgotten and abandoned, openly weeping.

The only king that the world had known in ten thousand years was dead. For many, especially those under a certain age, there had ever been only one man who held their daily peace and security in the palms of his capable hands.

And now he was gone?

It could not be fathomed.

As his body was being prepared, people from all parts of the kingdom, princes and citizens alike, packed parcels for the road and began instinctively to wend their way toward Regamun Mediar. Those that were fortunate enough to be mounted had the only real chance of reaching the capitol ere he was put into the ground. Still, mounted or on foot, they came.

For most of those pilgrims, it was simply that they found that they *needed* to come.

In far-off Seneca, where the distance was much too great, even for a mounted man, to arrive in time for the king's internment, word came to the grove on the hill at Muldar, brought there by Goldtalon, the grandson of Kipwing. Upon hearing this, Andar, who by now had grown gray and lean and could legitimately claim the title of "eldest", turned and looked at the other members of his council, seeking out especially Matibar.

"What now?" He said simply.

Matibar, blinking his eyes against an abrupt surge of moisture, nonetheless answered with his usual pragmatism. "Naetan has been effectively administering the kingdom for some time," he replied. "He will make an able monarch."

Andar, his own eyes wide with disbelief, nodded at the truth of this. "Still," he said, "Lord Aram *gone* – and so soon after the queen. The world is substantially emptier than it was just a moment ago."

He gazed down at the ground between his feet for a long moment and then, without speaking, rose and went toward the hallway leading out. Matibar came to his feet as well.

"Where are you going, Your Worthiness?"

Andar hesitated and looked back. "To get very, very drunk," he replied.

Matibar watched him for a moment and then gathered his robes about him. "I will come with you," he said.

"I am drinking whiskey – not beer," Andar warned him. "I am in need of drink stronger than that to which you are accustomed."

"Yes," Matibar replied testily, "and I mean to join you.'

Andar frowned. "You have never had a taste for whiskey in the whole of your life, my friend."

"True," Matibar agreed. "There was never a reason before."

And those who were now the old men of Seneca, all of them, as one, wended their way down the hill to the common house where Lord Aram had been wont to stay when he came into the east.

On the day of Aram's internment, the valley was filled with men and horses. Wolves and bears gathered on uninhabited hilltops and the sky overhead was fairly black with eagles and hawks.

Naetan spoke, as did Marcus, though neither knew exactly the right thing to say in the face of such loss.

Jame, old now and white-haired, tried to speak but failed. He looked down for a long sorrowful moment when the words would not come to him, shook his head, and then simply stepped back into the crowd.

Findaen, old and bent, the hair upon his head as white as sundrenched snow, refused the attempt to express that which was in his heart.

Nikolus and Timmon spoke, each of them expressing their deep sense of loss at the passing of him who had freed their homeland, and indeed the whole of the world.

Thom Sota stood off to one side, tall and erect, martial in every aspect, even in his old age. He shook his head when Naetan looked over at him with raised and questioning eyebrows.

Of the old companions, only Mallet yet lived, and the big man was inconsolable. His great frame shook uncontrollably, and every so often a loud sob escaped him, despite his making every attempt at maintaining decorum.

In the end, Aram the Magnificent was placed into the tomb with a minimum of fanfare amid immense and unbearable sadness.

After evening came and night drew on, driving the last of the mourners to their homes or to other locales where they might nurse their sorrow, Thaniel remained. The great horse stood all night with his head lowered to the earth. When the sun rose in the east, he lifted his head, and gazed for a long moment at the tomb that housed Aram's remains. Then, without speaking, he turned and went down to the river, climbed the wooded slopes beyond, made his way over the pass, and came back onto the high plains.

Though Thaniel the Warrior lived for almost six hundred years more, he never again left those high plains, nor moved out among the world of men. He never once came back into the valley of the kings; for with the death of this one man, with whom he had shared so much, he felt that something majestic and mysterious had passed forever from the earth, leaving it desolate.

Perhaps a month after his father's death, when the valley was once again serene, Naetan, finding sleep elusive, arose and walked the great porch in the depths of the night. Only a pale sliver of the moon contended weakly with the stars above. Going out onto the dais, he looked down the avenue.

Something below him and to the right arrested his attention.

A figure, barely discernable in the night, stood upon the pavement before his father's tomb. The figure was tall, slender, and dressed in robes of silver. He turned and glanced up at the king standing atop the wall and his eyes glowed bronze in the darkness.

Naetan caught his breath, for though he had never seen him, he knew who it was that stood there.

Ferros, the great god who cared for nothing and no one, had come up out of his deep realm to stand for a few moments by the tomb of the man who had changed the world.

10. The Reigns of Naetan I and Joktan II

Naetan became king on the fortieth day following his father's death, and on this day there was a ceremony. All the princes of the earth were there. Findaen his uncle was chosen to place the crown upon his brow, and thereby declared him monarch.

Naetan was as his father had described him – capable and competent, diligent and driven, always with a sincere concern for the welfare of the people of the world as his guiding principle.

Because he had overseen the general affairs of the kingdom during the last several years of his father's life, there was effectively no transition period. Other than a pervasive sorrow at the loss of Aram and Ka'en that lingered for some time, the people of the world noticed no difference in the administration of the king's business. It was during Naetan's reign that the roads throughout the entirety of the lands under the writ of Regamun Mediar were at last finished.

And because of Naetan the First's sound management of the kingdom's wealth, commerce prospered.

King Naetan's son, Joktan, was more like unto his fierce grandfather than his father in temperament. The young prince was possessed of a fierce disposition and of a quick, hot temper, and seemed daily disappointed that there was no enemy at the gates of the land, no adversary that threatened the kingdom, no insurrection to subdue.

Once, upon hearing that certain elements of the Farlongers had made an incursion into the borders of Seneca, the prince raised a small force and went there to confront the "enemy". As things were, the "invasion" was simply an attempt by a small group of scoundrels to steal a valuable supply of lumber from a Senecan mill near the frontier.

Andar, being placed in difficulty by the fierce presence of the heir to the kingdom, whose blood was up and hot for conflict, appealed to the throne and the aged General-in-chief, Thom Sota, was dispatched to bring calm to the situation and to carefully disentangle the prince and his temper from the region.

As he aged, Joktan grew calmer, married, and upon the death of his father ascended the throne and ruled wisely and well.

Joktan II lived to the age of one hundred and seventeen, and his reign lasted longer than that of his father or of his grandfather before him, or that of anyone that came after.

It was he that caused the statue to be built and placed upon the Grand Avenue in front of the city that stands there unto this day.

It is of a tall man who bears upon his back a Sword of power. He is flanked by an immense black horse and a large wolf. With his wings spread wide, standing upon the back of the horse, is a great eagle.

The inscription reads thus:

ARAM, SON of CLIF, SON of JOKTAN, SON of RAM

THANIEL, SON of FLORM, SON of ARMON, SON of BORAM

DURLRANG, SON of DURANG, SON of URFANG

ALVERN, SON of SILWING THE FIRST

Honor these names always
For these are they that led the great alliance
Of the free and noble peoples of the earth
That destroyed the tyranny of evil
And brought us peace

THE END

Made in United States
North Haven, CT
27 November 2021

11650291R00288